JOURNEYS THROUGH THE RADIANT CITADEL™

CREDITS

Project Leads: Ajit A. George, F. Wesley Schneider

Art Directors: Kate Irwin, Emi Tanji

Writers: Justice Ramin Arman, Dominique Dickey, Ajit A. George, Basheer Ghouse, Alastor Guzman, D. Fox Harrell, T.K. Johnson, Felice Tzehuei Kuan, Surena Marie, Mimi Mondal, Mario Ortegón, Miyuki Jane Pinckard, Pam Punzalan, Erin Roberts, Terry H. Romero, Stephanie Yoon

Rules Developers: Jeremy Crawford, Makenzie De Armas, Ben Petrisor, Taymoor Rehman

Senior Editor: Judy Bauer

Editors: Janica Carter, Dan Dillon, Keith Garrett, Scott Fitzgerald Gray, Laura Hirsbrunner, Kim Mohan, Christopher Perkins, Hannah Rose, Jessica Ross

Senior Graphic Designer: Trish Yochum

Graphic Designer: Matt Cole

Cover Illustrators: Evyn Fong, Sija Hong

Cartographers: Sean Macdonald, Mike Schley

Interior Illustrators: Mia Araujo, Alfven Ato, Tom Babbey, Zoltan Boros, Dmitry Burmak, Ekaterina Burmak, Nikki Dawes, Olga Drebas, Ejiwa "Edge" Ebenebe, Jessica Fong, Merlin G.G, KNIIO, Julian Kok, Ryan Alexander Lee, Adrián Ibarra Lugo, Andrew Mar, Brynn Metheney, Thabiso Mhlaba, Robson Michel, Hinchel Or, Vicki Pangestu, Claudio Pozas, April Prime, Julio Reyna, Domenico Sellaro, Brian Valeza, Jabari Weathers, Shawn Wood, Zuzanna Wuzyk

Concept Illustrator: Shawn Wood

Cultural Consultants: Nivair H. Gabriel, Jaymee Goh, Carmen Maria Marin

Narrative Design Consultant: Whitney "Strix" Beltrán

System and Narrative Design Consultant: John Stavropoulos

Project Engineer: Cynda Callaway

Imaging Technician: Daniel Corona, Kevin Yee

Prepress Specialist: Jefferson Dunlap

D&D STUDIO

Executive Producer: Ray Winninger

Director of Studio Operations: Kyle Brink

Game Architects: Jeremy Crawford, Christopher Perkins

Design Manager: Steve Scott

Design Department: Sydney Adams, Judy Bauer, Makenzie De Armas, Dan Dillon, Amanda Hamon, Ben Petrisor, Taymoor Rehman, F. Wesley Schneider, James Wyatt

Art Department Manager: Richard Whitters

Art Department: Matt Cole, Trystan Falcone, Bree Heiss, Kate Irwin, Bob Jordan, Emi Tanji, Shawn Wood, Trish Yochum

Senior Producers: Lisa Ohanian, Dan Tovar

Producers: Bill Benham, Robert Hawkey, Lea Heleotis

Director of Product Management: Liz Schuh

Product Managers: Natalie Egan, Chris Lindsay, Hilary Ross, Chris Tulach

MARKETING

Director of Global Brand Marketing: Brian Perry

Senior Global Brand Manager: Shelly Mazzanoble

Associate Global Brand Manager: Sara Chan

Senior Marketing Communications Manager: Greg Tito

Community Manager: Brandy Camel

Social Media Marketing Managers: Nicole Olson, Joshua Morris

Special thanks to Farai Chideya, Renee Knipe, Carlos Luna, Mary Anne Mohanraj, Stephanie Nudelman, Jessica Price, Diego Valdez

ON THE COVER

A mischievous wynling soars above the Dyn Singh Night Market, avoiding people from countless lands and illusory shop signage, in this cover by Evyn Fong.

ON THE ALT-COVER

The aura of the Radiant Citadel illuminates the ancestral shapes of the Dawn Incarnates, gemstone manifestations of stories and spirits, in this cover by Sija Hong.

620D0996000001 EN
ISBN: 978-0-7869-6799-5
First Printing: June 2022

9 8 7 6 5 4 3 2 1

CE UKCA

Disclaimer: There is no guarantee that the light of the Radiant Citadel will be visible to the naked eye on your plane of existence, but know that it is there, whether seen or not.

Tell us what you think of *Journeys through the Radiant Citadel*. Take our survey here!

CONTENTS

WELCOME TO THE RADIANT CITADEL

I N THE HEART OF THE ETHEREAL PLANE LIES AN ancient and mysterious city called the Radiant Citadel. Through tradition, cooperation, and ancestral magic, fifteen civilizations are bound to this wondrous site. *Journeys through the Radiant Citadel* is an anthology of exciting adventures that explore the cultures and myths of these realms.

The adventures in *Journeys through the Radiant Citadel* were created by members of the DUNGEONS & DRAGONS community with connections to various real-world cultures and mythologies. Embarking on the adventures of the Radiant Citadel will expand your gaming horizons, can give your characters new perspectives, and might change the way you look at fantasy tropes and traditions. As adventures are the lens through which we explore fantastic worlds, they shape who our characters are and what they believe in. The greater the variety adventures offer, the richer our characters and, by extension, our gaming experiences.

From glittering night markets to undersea cities, from curse-afflicted villages to angel-ruled city-states, these adventures provide a pathway to never-before-seen lands and stories. The gates of the Radiant Citadel stand open, and a rich tapestry of stories is yours to explore.

USING THE ADVENTURES

The Journeys through the Radiant Citadel table summarizes the adventures in this anthology. Each adventure is designed for four to six characters of a particular level, but you can adjust it for larger or smaller groups as well as for characters of higher or lower level by making a few changes, like swapping one monster or trap for another, changing the number of foes in an encounter, or adjusting DCs to make important tasks easier or harder for the characters to accomplish.

Each adventure in this anthology is versatile, and characters might become involved in any of the following ways:

- The characters have ties to the plot as detailed in the "Character Hooks" section in each adventure.
- The characters have journeyed to the Radiant Citadel, and their connections to individuals or organizations there lead them to investigate the plot.
- A character hails from the land where the adventure takes place and has a connection to the plot.

These short adventures work best with players who like exploring new lands and finding clever solutions to complex challenges. That said, each adventure contains opportunities for exploration, roleplaying, and combat to appeal to players of all persuasions.

RUNNING THE ADVENTURES

To run these adventures, you need the fifth edition core rulebooks: *Player's Handbook*, *Dungeon Master's Guide*, and *Monster Manual*.

> Text that appears in a box like this is meant to be read aloud or paraphrased for the players when their characters first arrive at a location or under a specific circumstance, as described in the text.

The *Monster Manual* contains stat blocks for most of the creatures encountered in these adventures. When a creature's name appears in **bold** type, that's a visual cue pointing you to its stat block as a way of saying, "Hey, DM, get this creature's stat block ready. You'll need it." If a stat block is new, the adventure's text tells you where to find it.

Spells and equipment mentioned in the adventures are described in the *Player's Handbook*. Magic items are described in the *Dungeon Master's Guide*.

EXPLORING NEW REACHES

Each adventure in this book introduces a new location—be it a city, a nation, a region, or otherwise. Before running an adventure, review the gazetteer presented at the adventure's end. Aside from providing an overview of the people and plots in that land, each gazetteer provides cultural details useful in describing the setting and making it feel vibrant.

SETTING THE ADVENTURES

The locations in this book can be incorporated into any D&D setting or a world of your own design. Each adventure includes a "Setting the Adventure" section that suggests where you might place the adventure. Weave these locations into your version of your favorite world, adding them where you like—even replacing other lands on your world map. Alternatively, use the Radiant Citadel (see the following pages) or planes-spanning magic to place these locations in entirely new worlds, and use them as the thresholds of realms defined how you please.

Journeys through the Radiant Citadel

Level	Adventure	Description
1–2	"Salted Legacy"	A conflict between rival night market vendors draws characters into a hunt for a mysterious saboteur and a series of whimsical contests.
3	"Written in Blood"	A community is terrorized by a horror lurking in a distant farmhouse.
4	"The Fiend of Hollow Mine"	The cure for a spreading curse leads from an abandoned mine to a city celebrating the departed.
5	"Wages of Vice"	A murderer stalks the streets during a raucous festival.
6	"Sins of the Elders"	A slighted spirit takes vengeance on the community that forgot her by stealing their memories.
7	"Gold for Fools and Princes"	Mysterious creatures cause a gold mine to collapse, precipitating a race between rival princes to save those trapped.
8	"Trail of Destruction"	A legendary creature reawakens and begins a chain reaction of volcanic eruptions that threaten the land.
9	"In the Mists of Manivarsha"	A local champion goes missing after a deadly flood, leading to a search for her along the rivers of a vast swamp.
10	"Between Tangled Roots"	Rageful spirits provoke a dragon to go on a deadly rampage.
11	"Shadow of the Sun"	Rival factions clash in an angel-ruled city on the brink of rebellion.
12	"The Nightsea's Succor"	A quest for ancient lore reveals threats from the past and leads to a mysterious nation beneath the waves.
13	"Buried Dynasty"	Agents of a long-lived emperor seek a timeless secret to keep their ruler in power at any cost.
14	"Orchids of the Invisible Mountain"	Adventurers must travel to the Feywild and the Far Realm to prevent otherworldly forces from tearing a land apart.

New Homes

At your discretion, players can create characters who are from the locations presented in this book. Consider allowing players to review the gazetteers of the lands that appeal to them. Each gazetteer provides questions you can ask players during character creation to help them create characters immersed in their homeland.

Thoughtful Introductions

While exploring the locations introduced through these adventures, be thoughtful about how you role-play and describe groups of people. Consider the guidance here when running adventures.

Broad Descriptions. Describe everyone's features, not just those whose features are different from your own.

Detail, Not Stereotypes. When describing a character's appearance, strive to detail more than just one thing and avoid descriptions based on stereotypes. The more you can say about body type, hair style and texture, skin tone, clothes, accessories, and the like, the more dimension a character has. As some societies strongly associate ethnicity with skin color, take extra care when describing characters' skin colors. Consider a range of literal descriptions, such as copper, umber, onyx, or ebony, with modifiers such as rich, lustrous, warm, or cool.

Gradual Explorations. You don't have to reveal a setting's entire culture at once. Skip details that aren't immediately relevant to characters, and reveal details as they arise. A scene in a tavern presents opportunities to introduce distinct foods, while a market trip is a great time to note varieties of dress.

Highlight What's Familiar. Highlight what's familiar in a culture and how it's like other locations. This can help characters ground their experiences and better understand where they're visiting.

Online and Streamed Games. Just as you don't have to breathe fire in real life to play a dragonborn in D&D, you don't need to be from the cultures that inspired the adventures in this book to play characters from them. However, take care to portray characters as three-dimensional people with relatable desires and fears.

One person's culture isn't another's costume. If you dress up, simple outfits are best. Avoid leaning into stereotypes or clothing with real-world religious significance. Instead, focus on "everyday wear" from the cultures you're exploring. Don't change your skin color, alter your features, or emulate hair styles you wouldn't normally have to appear like a different real-world ethnicity. Similarly, avoid mocking real-world accents in your roleplay.

THE RADIANT CITADEL

GATHERING PLACE OF STRANGERS AND STORIES

AGAINST THE UNENDING MIST AND UNSEEN terrors of the Ethereal Plane, the Radiant Citadel stands bright as a bastion of hope. It's a living relic of the ingenuity and collaboration of twenty-seven great civilizations. Abandoned and lost for ages, the Citadel was resurrected from its slumber and reclaimed by descendants of those societies, though some peoples remain missing. The city serves as a nexus of diplomacy and trade, a repository of histories and secrets, and a thriving sanctuary for those seeking safety or a better life.

The Radiant Citadel is a miracle of architecture, a floating city carved out of a single, massive fossil that snakes around a colossal gemstone shard known as the Auroral Diamond. The luminescence of the Auroral Diamond is mirrored in the constellation of fifteen structure-sized gemstones, the Concord Jewels, which orbit the city and provide transportation to the far-flung homes of the Citadel's founding civilizations. In the haze of the Ethereal Plane, the Auroral Diamond is a scintillating beacon visible from leagues away. The diamond itself seems to have moods, changing colors unpredictably, but it is always visible for wanderers lost and in need. Just beyond the city whirls a massive, ever-threatening, ethereal cyclone known as the Keening Gloom—a looming threat that's a grim reminder of the Citadel's precarious position.

Heroes and paupers meet on equal footing in the Radiant Citadel. By common agreement, power and resources are equitably shared. Dignity is afforded to all, and great need is met with great aid.

FEATURES

Those familiar with the Radiant Citadel know the following details:

Hallmarks. The Radiant Citadel is an extraplanar refuge known for its collaborative society and ecological beauty. Local traditions of oral storytelling preserve ancestral wisdom from many worlds.

People of the Radiant Citadel. The majority of the Radiant Citadel's populace comes from the civilizations that govern the city. This makes the population an ethnically diverse mix of humans, dragonborn, dwarves, elves, gnomes, and halflings, along with a variety of other races.

Languages. Common is widely known, along with dozens of other languages.

NOTEWORTHY SITES

The Radiant Citadel is a testament to a lost age of extraordinary magic and mythical beasts. The city rises from a gargantuan fossil, and every road and building has been carved from it. The Citadel is a place of beauty and wonder, with a vast array of vegetation and a multitude of sites and inhabitants.

AURORAL DIAMOND

The Auroral Diamond is the heart of the Radiant Citadel. A massive gemstone of unfathomable power, its life-giving magic runs through the entire city; the city's vegetation, water, light, and unique artifices depend on the Diamond.

The Auroral Diamond changes color for unknown reasons. Sometimes it holds a color for an entire year, while other times it shifts twice in a single week. Rarely does it ever repeat a color. Some scholars believe each color represents the birth of a new civilization somewhere in the multiverse, and repetition of a color means the death of that civilization. Other scholars hypothesize the changing colors are a countdown to some unknown event.

The Auroral Diamond is indestructible. Whatever magic hollowed out the gemstone's center and created the Preserve of the Ancestors (described later) is unknown.

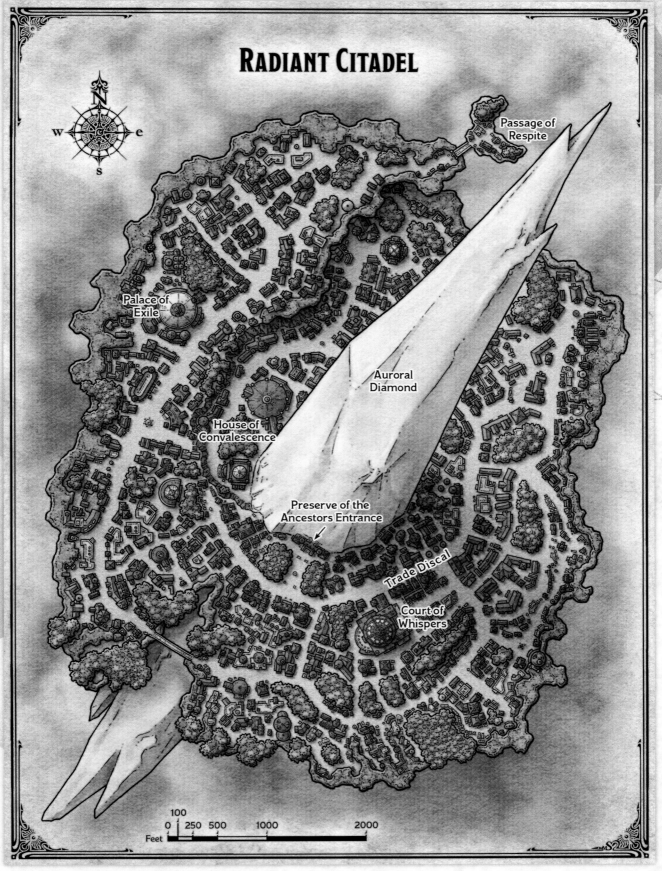

RADIANT CITADEL

Passage of Respite

Palace of Exile

Auroral Diamond

House of Convalescence

Preserve of the Ancestors Entrance

Trade Discal

Court of Whispers

100
0   250 500   1000   2000
Feet

MIKE SCHLEY

MAP 1.1: RADIANT CITADEL

COURT OF WHISPERS

The denizens of the Court of Whispers barter for current knowledge. Heralds, criers, bards, and griots buy and sell information from the fifteen founding civilizations active in the Citadel, as well as other lands. Skilled scouts and spies can also be hired for short-term reconnaissance or long-term infiltration. The Court is a mixed outdoor-indoor space with quiet alcoves and open plazas, and plentiful work is available here for talented adventurers.

The Speakers for the Ancestors—the leaders of the Radiant Citadel—employ freelancers from the Court of Whispers to keep track of major concerns in their people's homelands, as well as potential threats to the Citadel, while the Shieldbearers of the Citadel (see the "Palace of Exile" section) seek information so they can identify crisis points where their operatives are needed. Even common citizens might hire folk from the Court to find missing loved ones, locate lost family treasures, or gather information on rivals.

Powerful organizations and individuals from across the planes send agents to the Court of Whispers to collect information and do business on their behalf. Noteworthy examples include the Harpers of Abeir-Toril, Sigil's Fraternity of Order, and agents of the planes-traveling gnome fixer Vi.

HOUSE OF CONVALESCENCE

The House of Convalescence focuses the life-giving energies of the Auroral Diamond, allowing for incredible feats of healing magic. This makes the House of Convalescence an oasis for the sick, the injured, and the desperate. It also draws clerics and healers of many traditions. Most come to serve those in need, but some seek to understand the magical properties of the place itself.

Magic is affected in the following ways in the House of Convalescence:

Diamond Components. When the spells *raise dead*, *resurrection*, *revivify*, or *true resurrection* are cast in the House of Convalescence, a diamond material component is never required.

Hit Point Maximum. When creatures would normally roll one or more dice to restore hit points with a spell, they instead use the highest number possible for each die. For example, instead of restoring 2d6 hit points to a creature, a spellcaster restores 12.

THE KEENING GLOOM

Just beyond the light of the Radiant Citadel rages the Keening Gloom, a massive ethereal cyclone. Nothing that enters the cyclone is seen again.

When explorers rediscovered the Citadel, the Keening Gloom hungrily circled the city. Its endless howl struck terror in their hearts and engulfed several adventurers. After the heroes entered the Citadel and reawakened its power, the cyclone was driven back. But in times of turmoil within the Citadel, the cyclone ominously draws closer.

Scholars have studied the Keening Gloom for decades but have only theories about its nature, its connection to the Radiant Citadel, and what befalls those caught in its terrible throes. Many fear the cyclone cannot be held at bay forever.

PALACE OF EXILE

The adventurers who discovered and reoccupied the Radiant Citadel were from the civilizations that founded the city long ago. Among them, several had been set on the path of adventure after conflict or disaster drove them from their homes, and the Citadel provided solace. In turn, they established the Palace of Exile to help others in need.

The palace was named in honor of Socorro the Exile, its founding leader. He was a refugee of war in the land of San Citlán, and he selected one of the most beautiful complexes in the Citadel to house the needy as they arrived. He swore that while his homeland was occupied, he would be an exile and would make his home in the Palace, alongside any others with nowhere else to go.

The Palace of Exile has spacious living quarters with adjoining gardens and recovery centers, where refugees are cared for physically, mentally, and emotionally as they make the transition to either living in the Radiant Citadel permanently or relocating to a new land. The Palace's staff coordinate with the House of Convalescence to provide the best possible aid to the sick and wounded.

THE RUBY PANGOLIN, DAWN
INCARNATE OF SIABSUNGKOH

The Shieldbearers, the Radiant Citadel's dedicated search-and-rescue force, are headquartered at the Palace of Exile. Where there is a need, the Shieldbearers help.

PRESERVE OF THE ANCESTORS

The Preserve of the Ancestors is a sprawling, domed wilderness cut into the heart of the Auroral Diamond. Lush vegetation grows directly out of the diamond, and the expanse is dotted with jackalberry trees, whistling thorn, and zebrawood. Insects, small birds, and the occasional hare make their home here. In the center of the Preserve is a circular, in-ground amphitheater that serves as the meeting place of the Citadel's ruling council, the Speakers for the Ancestors.

While the Preserve has little indigenous wildlife—mostly birds and small mammals—a sect of druids frequently brings injured animals here to be healed and rehabilitated. The Preserve is where the druids keep animals that can no longer survive in their native habitats, creating a menagerie of rare creatures from across many worlds.

Drawn by the power of the Auroral Diamond, spirits from countless lands make their home in the Preserve. Spirits from the same lands or of similar origins inhabit tiny jewels and assemble into amalgamations known as Incarnates. Some are small collections of spirits, but the greatest—related to the citadel's founding civilizations—are larger-than-life beings that embody the wisdom of ages (see the "Incarnates" section for details).

TRADE DISCAL

Encircling the Auroral Diamond, the Trade Discal is a massive marketplace designed so that the founding civilizations could trade on equitable terms. It serves the needs of cities and nations or major trading companies, rather than individual sellers or producers, which is enforced by its high taxes and fees. Large quantities of goods, such as entire herds of animals or tons of metal ore, can be transported via the Concord Jewels (described below) to the Trade Discal quickly and safely.

The Trade Discal is a vital outlet; if something were to happen to it, the impact would be severe for both the Radiant Citadel and the civilizations that depend on it. Adventurers are sometimes hired to oversee the transport of commodities to and from the Citadel or to negotiate on behalf of a major trading company or government. Normally this is a smooth process, but when large amounts of gold are involved, trade is never risk free.

Concord Jewels

Beyond the Radiant Citadel drift the Concord Jewels, which connect the city to its founding civilizations. Each Jewel is a building-sized vessel capable of holding hundreds of people and tons of goods. Though the Jewels take a variety of shapes, their interiors are similar. A cylindrical core holds containers for goods, including livestock. Surrounding the core is seating for passengers. The Citadel employs official operators called Clavigers to pilot the Jewels.

Each Concord Jewel is linked to one of the civilizations that founded the Radiant Citadel. A Jewel unerringly travels between the Radiant Citadel and the homeland of the Jewel's linked people. Even if the Jewel's people have migrated to another world on the Material Plane, the Jewel finds its way to their current home.

While not in use, the Concord Jewels orbit the Radiant Citadel in an incandescent constellation. Each Jewel corresponds to one of the founding civilizations and resembles a giant gemstone of the type noted for that civilization on the Concord Jewels table. Missing civilizations and their Jewels are not listed and can be detailed as you please.

Concord Jewels

Civilization	Jewel
Akharin Sangar	Turquoise
Atagua	Yellow Quartz
Dayawlongon	Serpentine
Djaynai	Water Opal
Godsbreath	Jasper
San Citlán	Fire Opal
Sensa	Amber
Shankhabhumi	Moonstone
Siabsungkoh	Ruby
Tayyib	Sard
Tletepec	Obsidian
Umizu	Pearl
Yeonido	Amethyst
Yongjing	White Jade
Zinda	Bastite

Controlling a Concord Jewel

At a Concord Jewel's center are controls for the structure. A creature adjacent to these controls that spends a minute manipulating them can make a DC 14 Intelligence (Arcana) check. On a success, the creature can direct the Concord Jewel to take one of the following actions:

Land. When commanded to land, the Jewel automatically settles into a safe position adjoining the Radiant Citadel or on the surface of a Material Plane world. From this site, creatures can move back and forth between the Jewel and the location. Sections of the exterior walls of the lowest 15 feet of the Jewel then become immaterial and semitransparent, allowing passage into and out of the Jewel.

Embark. A Jewel that has landed moves away from a location. If the Jewel is near the Radiant Citadel, it moves into the open Ethereal Plane and orbits the city. Otherwise, it rises 600 feet off the ground and hovers. A Jewel flies at a rate of 50 feet per round.

Plane Shift. The Jewel and everything on it shifts between planes. When it does so, it teleports either to the Deep Ethereal several thousand feet away from the Radiant Citadel or to a specific site on the Material Plane in the land the Jewel is linked to. When a Jewel teleports to its linked land, it appears 600 feet above a site where it can land and hovers there. The location where a Jewel arrives is noted in the "Setting the Adventure" section of each of this book's adventures.

Clavigers

Clavigers oversee the Concord Jewels. Each Speaker for the Ancestors chooses the Clavigers for the Jewel linked to that Speaker's civilization. A dozen Clavigers are assigned to each Concord Jewel, and at least two keep watch from each Jewel as it orbits the Radiant Citadel and guide it during its travels. Clavigers not only maintain transit and trade to and from the Radiant Citadel but also serve as ambassadors from the city to the founding civilizations. Many Clavigers go on to become Speakers for the Ancestors.

Life in the Citadel

The Radiant Citadel is a city of immigrants. Several of the explorers who reclaimed the Citadel were refugees who escaped hardships that plagued their lands. They chose the Citadel as their home, despite its strangeness and the surreal surroundings of the Deep Ethereal, as it presented an opportunity to start anew. Most of the city's current inhabitants are descendants of the fifteen founding civilizations active in the Citadel, but all are welcome.

Some find living in the Deep Ethereal too disquieting to stay or chafe at the confines of the Citadel. Others depart out of fear that the Keening Gloom will destroy the Citadel. Their numbers are replenished by new arrivals who seek a different life, want to study the city's lore, or find solace in the city's peace and safety. The Citadel's society is shaped by this ebb and flow. Traditions, customs, and values are a mix of old and new; while some adhere to rituals no longer followed in their homeland, others create their own novel practices.

Art and Culture

The Radiant Citadel's diaspora communities constantly learn and borrow from one another, creating a culture unique to the city. This evolution is displayed in the art, the clothing, the music, and—perhaps mostly vividly—the food of the city. While cantinas, tea houses, and eateries serve food and drink from specific communities, the most popular cuisines are fusion dishes like couscous infused with habanero and saffron, panela-coated fried yams, and kimchi tacos.

Diplomacy

Relationships between the Radiant Citadel and the founding civilizations are often shifting. The Citadel sends diplomats abroad and houses embassies from foreign governments, but this goodwill is not always reciprocated. The Citadel's uniqueness makes it a target of foreign actors who seek to exert subtle or overt control over it. At the same time, political activists, dissidents, and revolutionaries seek to exploit the city's neutrality to their advantage, even staging incursions against their home governments from the relative safety of the Citadel.

Governance and Politics

The Radiant Citadel is governed by a council known as the Speakers for the Ancestors. Each Speaker is a descendant of one of the founding civilizations currently known to the Citadel. They are chosen by their community and affirmed into office by the wise and ancient Dawn Incarnates. The Speakers for the Ancestors meet openly in the amphitheater in the center of the Preserve, and Citadel residents often watch their debates. All laws and major decisions of the city are decided by majority vote of the Speakers. Debates can become heated; because each Speaker represents very different constituents, consensus and compromises might take days or even months to reach. Those citizens of mixed ancestry or unconnected to the founding civilizations can choose a Speaker for the Ancestors to represent them. They register with the Speaker's office, and from then on, participate in future elections for that Speaker.

Governance is public, transparent, and participatory. Laws are not static but evolve to meet new challenges and needs. Subcouncils and committees manage the city under the guidance of the Speakers. Complexities persist in governing a highly diverse city with varied customs, beliefs, and social norms, but robust civic engagement helps the city overcome adversity.

The Obsidian Eagle,
Dawn Incarnate of Tletepec

Law Enforcement and Justice

Public safety and peacekeeping are administered through a variety of councils and organizations designed to address specific issues. The House of Convalescence helps those living with mental illness, while inspectors investigate nonviolent crimes and use nonlethal methods of detainment. Theft is uncommon in the city, and rehabilitation and restorative justice are preferred methods of addressing wrongs. Highly trained local guards mobilize to handle the rare incidents of violence, and citizens are expected to proactively intervene if needed. The worst offenders are sentenced to a controversial Djaynaian punishment wherein the criminal is subjected to a ritual that prevents them from repeating their crime and then is banished from the city.

Lifestyle and Society

Denizens of the Radiant Citadel strive to sustain an egalitarian society. Every citizen is entitled to a basic income that affords them the necessities of living and dignity in lifestyle. Food, water, and green spaces are equally accessible throughout the city. The House of Convalescence turns no one away; healing is priced according to one's means, and the poorest are served without charge. All housing is public, distributed, and administered through the city's councils.

Since the city's resources are limited due to the Citadel's relatively small area and its strange nature, foodstuffs and other materials are carefully conserved, and goods are reused or recycled when possible. Similarly, most food is vegetarian and is grown in green spaces throughout the city. Whether served in a home or an eatery, most animal products must be imported and so are subject to high tariffs.

Tariffs and Taxation

Taxes are progressive to help reduce the gap between the most affluent and the poorest. High tariffs on imports keep the public coffers full, but the Speakers lower or remove tariffs for civilizations in trouble. Similarly, visitors to the Radiant Citadel pay a toll to enter. Those who come with nothing except good will pay no fee. Those with big pockets and big hearts give more according to their conscience rather than risk the rebuke of the city's guards. Rich and poor alike can instead offer something unique that might be to the liking of the Incarnates, such as a lost song, a secret tale, or a rare piece of art. Those who choose this option may present their gift to the Dawn Incarnate of their choice. If their toll is accepted, the visitor is allowed to stay in the Citadel.

Groups of the Citadel

Several groups hold influence within the Radiant Citadel, guiding and protecting the city's peoples.

Incarnates

The keepers of vast wisdom from distant lands, the Incarnates are collections of spirits bound within gemstones. Each of an Incarnate's component gemstones holds a spirit from the same land on the Material Plane. These might be nature spirits from a particular place or the spirits of individuals who once dwelled there. Upon forming, an Incarnate manifests a unique personality and identity, a gestalt of its constituents and their shared background. The greater the number of spirits that make up an Incarnate, the broader and deeper both its personality and its knowledge are.

Most Incarnates are small, no more than a handful of gems in the shape of a plant or animal. The least of them originate from spirits lost on the Ethereal Plane and are tiny collections of wayward spirits of similar origins with nowhere else to go. The largest and most influential are those of the fifteen founding civilizations collectively known as the Dawn Incarnates. Spanning more than a dozen feet in height, these Incarnates are composed of thousands of smaller gems of the same type. Each holds court in a portion of the Preserve, such as the Amethyst Tiger's knoll or the Obsidian Eagle's aerie.

The Dawn Incarnates have existed since the creation of the Radiant Citadel. While the Citadel's creators left behind no texts, it's believed that their collective wisdom is held by the Dawn Incarnates.

The Dawn Incarnates know everything that transpires in the Preserve of the Ancestors, which is why they require the Speakers for the Ancestors to meet there. While they do not interfere in the

In the Preserve of the Ancestors, a traveler seeks the wisdom of the Amethyst Tiger, Dawn Incarnate of Yeonido.

THE AMBER SCORPION,
DAWN INCARNATE OF THE
SENSA EMPIRE

AUDIENCES WITH INCARNATES

An Incarnate and its constituent spirits are not malicious or duplicitous, but they do not necessarily answer questions easily or without a price. Some require the completion of a quest, while others might give a puzzle to solve. Some speak plainly; others respond in poem or parable. And some refuse to speak at all.

DAWN INCARNATES OF THE PRESERVE

Each Dawn Incarnate that inhabits the Preserve of the Ancestors is related to a founding civilization active in the Citadel, as detailed on the Dawn Incarnates table.

DAWN INCARNATES

Civilization	Dawn Incarnate
Akharin Sangar	Turquoise Lion
Atagua	Yellow Quartz Kapok Tree
Dayawlongon	Serpentine Banyan Tree
Djaynai	Water Opal Saltwater Salamander
Godsbreath	Jasper Pecan Tree
San Citlán	Fire Opal Xoloitzcuintle
Sensa	Amber Scorpion
Shankhabhumi	Moonstone Water Lily
Siabsungkoh	Ruby Pangolin
Tayyib	Sard Elephant
Tletepec	Obsidian Eagle
Umizu	Pearl Carp
Yeonido	Amethyst Tiger
Yongjing	White Jade Flowering Pear Tree
Zinda	Bastite Caiman

A grim anomaly, a dead Dawn Incarnate known as the Sapphire Wyvern, disturbs the tranquility of the Preserve of the Ancestors. It lies inert, its gemstones blackened and cracked. Scholars believe it was the Dawn Incarnate of one of the Radiant Citadel's twelve lost civilizations, but all efforts to awaken it have failed. What happened to it and the eleven absent Dawn Incarnates of the other founding civilizations, none know.

SPEAKERS FOR THE ANCESTORS

The Speakers for the Ancestors are the ruling body of the Radiant Citadel. Candidates are chosen through an election among the diaspora of the people they represent. Once a candidate has been elected, they must face the fifteen founding Dawn Incarnates and pass their tests. Some Dawn Incarnates question the candidate until they are satisfied, while others send the candidate on a quest. These trials ensure Speakers understand each of the founding civilizations of the Radiant Citadel.

day-to-day administration of the city, they hold the Speakers responsible to the duties of their office. While a Dawn Incarnate has never removed a Speaker for the Ancestors (see "Speakers for the Ancestors" below), it is believed they could do so if displeased.

IDENTITIES OF THE INCARNATES

Each Incarnate has a unique, amalgamated personality. Most who interact with an Incarnate interact with this primary identity. However, an Incarnate's primary personality is not a repository of its constituent spirits' knowledge; these spirits have their own thoughts and personalities. While an Incarnate broadly knows what its spirits know, a wealth of information is locked inside them. A constituent spirit within an Incarnate might be awakened by evoking the spirit's name or presenting something of significance to that spirit. Once a spirit is awakened, it takes over as the dominant personality of the Incarnate for a matter of minutes and might share its specific memories.

A spirit knows only what it has observed. A nature spirit that inhabited a small pond might know a great deal about the fisher who visited its banks every week for fifty years, but might not know that person's name or where they lived. An ancestor spirit might know the intimate details of their family and town, but nothing about their neighbor's great-grandchildren. Each spirit is a single window into the civilization; together, an Incarnate's spirits have a wide but not infallible perspective on the history of their people.

JESSICA FONG

Once a Speaker for the Ancestors is chosen, they hold office for ten years. At the end of their tenure, they can step down; if they don't, they must face the same selection process again. There is no assurance a Speaker will be reelected, or if they are, that the Dawn Incarnates will approve them again.

As founding civilizations are rediscovered and rejoin the Radiant Citadel, the council is expanded, and the new Speakers gain power equal to that of their peers.

A Speaker's Role

The Speakers for the Ancestors face incredible challenges in their role. They must maintain the internal stability of a large and diverse city and ensure its people are treated equally and fairly under the law. Simultaneously, they manage a complex relationship with the founding civilizations. The Speakers' first duty is to the Radiant Citadel, which sometimes puts them at odds with the governments of the founding civilizations, particularly in tariff disputes or major crises. Thus far, the Radiant Citadel's policy is to resolutely remain neutral in all conflicts—whether they involve the founding civilizations or otherwise. However, the Citadel seeks to rescue refugees and send humanitarian aid to the limits of its resources.

While decisions by the Speakers are made by simple majority, each Speaker has a very powerful veto that prevents them from being marginalized by political alliances.

Power of the Speakers

While in the Radiant Citadel, each Speaker rightfully chosen by the Radiant Citadel's people and the Dawn Incarnates can take an action to exert control over the Concord Jewels in the following ways:

- They can deactivate all Concord Jewels that are in orbit around the Radiant Citadel, preventing the Jewels' controls from functioning and rendering the vessels stranded.
- The Speaker who deactivated the Concord Jewels can reactivate the Jewels. (The rightful successor of a Speaker who deactivated the Concord Jewels can also take this action.)

Since every Speaker has the ability to paralyze trade and major transit to the city, they are forced to find diplomatic resolutions to disagreements. Though the use or threat of a veto might prompt furious debates and intense rivalries, eventually the Speakers for the Ancestors find solutions.

Bound to the Citadel

Once a Speaker no longer holds office, they lose the powers related to their position. If a Speaker steps down before the end of their term or dies while in office, all basic necessities in the Radiant Citadel gradually cease to function. Unless a suitable replacement for that Speaker is elected and approved by the Dawn Incarnates within thirty days, plants in the Radiant Citadel stop growing, wells run dry, and lighting ceases to function. Similarly, a Speaker cannot leave the Radiant Citadel for more than thirty days before the city's basic utilities begin to fail.

Speakers for the Ancestors are often celebrated heroes capable of handling most danger that comes their way, yet they are so vital to the integrity of the Radiant Citadel that each is carefully protected, both magically and by contingents of guards.

Sholeh

Sholeh is a legendary figure in the history of the Citadel. Having led the successful effort to rediscover the Radiant Citadel, she was the first Speaker for the Ancestors and is the only originator of that position to still hold the office. This is, at least in part, because she is a famed **ancient brass dragon** of Akharin Sangar. Unlike many of her kind, she is neutral good and a pragmatic, shrewd leader. For two hundred and fifty years, she has been a consummate councilor and has deftly managed the complex

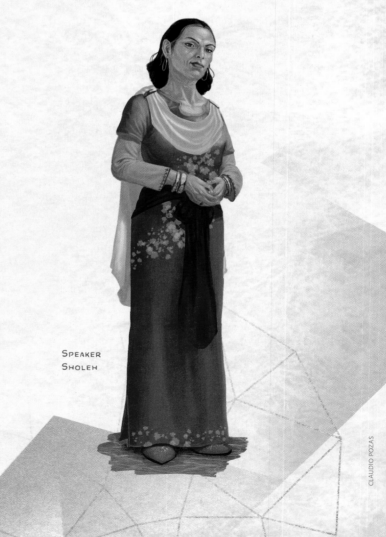

Speaker
Sholeh

CLAUDIO POZAS

politics of the city. She hopes to find the missing twelve founding civilizations and believes the fate of the Citadel depends on it.

Known affectionately (or derisively) as the Old Lady, she often takes the form of an older, brown-skinned human woman. Quick to anger and quicker to love, she has rivals and adversaries aplenty, but friends and suitors in even greater number. She loves a good drink, loves dancing even more, and spends her free time with the common citizens of the city. More frequently, she's legislating in the council or negotiating in a secret corner of the Court of Whispers, trading for information or sending spies on missions.

She has a complex relationship with her homeland. While she loves Akharin Sangar, she refuses to bend to the will of its angelic ruler, Atash. Rather than oppose him directly, she plays a delicate political game even as she worries about the future of her native land.

In recent years, the weight of leadership has taken a toll on Sholeh. She picks her scales in private as she tries to find relief.

Personality Trait. "True leaders must see what others do not, but they must remain connected to those they lead."

Ideal. "I will find the missing twelve and bring back the full glory of the Radiant Citadel."

Bond. "I love the city and all its people. I will do anything for them."

Flaw. "Do I exist only because others need me?"

Shieldbearers

Since their founding, the Shieldbearers have led the Radiant Citadel's rescue and relocation missions. Typically organized in cohorts of four to six members, they are deployed to lands in crisis. Strict rules of engagement prevent them from impacting local conditions or taking sides in a conflict; their mandate allows them only to extract those in danger and defend themselves if attacked. They are among the bravest of the Citadel, and heroes who die in service to the Shieldbearers receive the city's highest honors.

Shieldbearers stand ready to make the ultimate sacrifice to save the vulnerable and the defenseless. Many members adhere to a tradition of getting a ritual scar or tattoo after each successful deployment, designed to represent a pivotal moment in that quest. The most accomplished veterans display such body art with pride.

Many adventurers who come to the Radiant Citadel eventually join the Shieldbearers, particularly those with the folk hero, soldier, or outlander backgrounds.

Arayat

Arayat (neutral, human **assassin**) was born to a family of Dayawlongon freedom fighters who had no more wars to fight. Peace did not bring them prosperity, and the family's glory faded. Arayat grew up on the streets until luck brought him to the Radiant Citadel. He soon joined the Shieldbearers, which gave him meaning and purpose. Defying the odds, Arayat has survived hundreds of deployments to the most dangerous situations across the founding civilizations and beyond. He is a master of the Dayawlongon martial art of eskrima and favors a pair of shortswords in combat.

Now in his forties, he leads the Shieldbearers. He is a canny tactician and a highly competent leader, but he bristles against the rules of engagement imposed on the Shieldbearers by the Speakers for the Ancestors. He has cremated a hundred fallen comrades-in-arms and seen horrors few can comprehend. The toll has pushed him to his limits, and he believes a more aggressive, proactive strategy will save lives. But thus far, he has not defied the council.

In secret, Arayat drinks heavily. It is the only way he can sleep at night.

Personality Trait. "I will do anything and everything to protect the innocent."

Ideal. "I was born to save those who cannot save themselves."

Bond. "The Shieldbearers are my family and the Citadel my home."

Flaw. "I cannot stop seeing the faces of those I've lost."

Citadel Defenses

The Radiant Citadel's location within the Deep Ethereal makes it difficult to assault. It keeps no standing army, but its council for defense has contingency plans it frequently refines based on intelligence from the Court of Whispers.

The city's primary protection is a powerful ward that can be activated by the Speakers for the Ancestors. When all fifteen are assembled in the council room at the center of the Preserve, by unanimous consent they can erect a diamond sphere that envelops the entire city. The diamond sphere resembles the Auroral Diamond in texture and color and deflects all attacks. Nothing can pass or teleport through it.

If the diamond sphere cannot be erected for any reason, the Radiant Citadel is not helpless. Due to its many mysteries and its magical properties, the city attracts an unusually large number of powerful adventurers and spellcasters. If the citadel is attacked, no fewer than a dozen **archmages** and twenty **mages** led by Sholeh rally. If required,

Arayat, commander of the Shieldbearers, also mobilizes his Shieldbearer **veterans**, while the other Speakers for the Ancestors call on the citizenry to bolster the city's defense.

The Auroral Diamond's illumination also provides strong protection. It radiates bright light throughout the city and dim light 1,000 feet beyond the city's borders. This light is akin to sunlight, which many natives of the Ethereal Plane and evil Undead abhor.

ENTERING THE CITADEL

Most visitors come to the city by passage on one of the Concord Jewels. However, it's possible to find the Citadel through exploration of the Deep Ethereal. The Auroral Diamond acts like a beacon for the lost and hopeless, and many who seek the Radiant Citadel within the Deep Ethereal find their way there within a few days of searching.

There is only one official entrance to the Radiant Citadel: the Passage of Respite. The Concord Jewels dock adjacent to it, and people using other means to travel to the city are directed by guards to enter through it.

At any time, six **guards** are stationed at the Passage of Respite. They are led by a **mage** responsible for accepting tolls. These guards often employ magic items, such as *helms of telepathy*, when suspicious of the motives of a visitor. A **priest** from the House of Convalescence also attends the gate, ready to assist the ailing.

It's possible to bypass the Passage of Respite by teleporting or flying into the city, but anyone caught doing so faces massive fines, and repeat offenders risk banishment.

LEGENDS AND LORE

Two hundred and fifty years ago, the great brass dragon Sholeh undertook a quest to find the Radiant Citadel. For millennia, the dragons of her lineage had recounted tales of its glory. As threats loomed on the horizon, Sholeh looked to the legend of the Radiant Citadel as salvation.

Sholeh gathered a mighty expeditionary force of adventurers from the civilizations she believed originally created the Radiant Citadel. Their travels took them across perilous planes and to distant worlds, and many died or gave up in despair. Only a quarter of the heroes who set out completed Sholeh's quest, but the adventurers' sacrifices were rewarded. In the depths of the Ethereal Plane, the Radiant Citadel lay dormant and abandoned by all but the Incarnates of the Preserve of the Ancestors. Yet it was undiminished in its grandeur, waiting for its inheritors to reawaken its power for a new era.

Many believe that the full potential of the Radiant Citadel can be unlocked only when the twelve missing civilizations are found and their representatives join the Speakers for the Ancestors. Some hypothesize the Citadel can unleash an incredible weapon, while others believe the Concord Jewels can be used to travel anywhere in the multiverse, or that the Radiant Citadel can be shifted between planes. The most fervent dream about tapping the power of the Auroral Diamond to resurrect lost civilizations and worlds.

Some scholars studying the Radiant Citadel's origins posit that the Citadel is a relic of the mythical First World and was a vital center of diplomacy between great cultures before a cataclysm shattered that world. Others speculate that it was a fortress, a refuge, or even a weapon in a war that transpired in the last days of the First World. Thus far, the Dawn Incarnates have declined to answer scholars' questions on the subject.

Recently, two founding civilizations were discovered and reconnected to the Citadel: the Tayyib Empire and Umizu (detailed in "Beyond the Radiant Citadel" at the end of this book). This success has prompted new rumors in the Court of Whispers about the twelve civilizations still missing and how they might be found.

CITADEL ADVENTURES

Consider the plots on the Radiant Citadel Adventures table when planning adventures in the Radiant Citadel.

RADIANT CITADEL ADVENTURES

d4	Adventure
1	A revolutionary from San Citlán tries to hire the party in the Court of Whispers to uncover the plot of a corrupt council member in their homeland (see the adventure "The Fiend of Hollow Mine").
2	The committee that oversees the Trade Discal asks the party to negotiate with Atash, the angelic ruler of Akharin Sangar, for increased trade with the Radiant Citadel (see the adventure "Shadow of the Sun").
3	The Dawn Incarnate of Atagua declares it is willing to reveal the location of one of the missing civilizations if the characters prevent an alien evil from encroaching on Atagua (see the adventure "Orchids of the Invisible Mountain").
4	The Keening Gloom edges toward the Radiant Citadel. The Speakers for the Ancestors hire the characters to find out what is causing the cyclone's approach and reverse it.

FLEEING DISASTER, A FAMILY DISCOVERS THE BASE OF A
CONCORD JEWEL—A GATEWAY TO THE RADIANT CITADEL.

USING THE CITADEL

The Radiant Citadel links to a multitude of worlds.
While the fifteen lands presented in this book are
the best known, you can decide where else the Concord Jewels reach and what connections they create
to future adventures.

REACHING THE RADIANT CITADEL

While the Concord Jewels already create paths
between many realms, you can place the missing
Jewels anywhere you decide, linking more lands to
the Radiant Citadel. Characters can learn about and
travel to the Radiant Citadel, or their adventures
might begin in the city. Consider the following ways
to introduce the Radiant Citadel in your campaign:

Citadel Locals. The Radiant Citadel is a hub for
those seeking adventure, but it's also home to
thousands. Either the characters have lived in the
city all their lives, or they're stationed there by a
world-hopping organization.

Founding Residents. The characters are from locations detailed in the gazetteers throughout this
book. They already know about the Radiant Citadel but journey to it seeking to learn more.

Ruin Explorers. A group discovers that the land
they're adventuring in was once the site of one of
the founding civilizations. That civilization is lost,
but the Concord Jewel connecting it to the Citadel remains.

Sanctuary Seekers. A disaster threatens the characters' home, but their timely discovery of a Concord Jewel allows them and their community—a
forgotten founding civilization—to escape.

CONNECTING ADVENTURES

The Radiant Citadel is a useful tool for connecting
D&D adventures. The Citadel doesn't connect to all
places in the multiverse—just the Material Plane locations linked to it by the Concord Jewels.

As you develop your campaign, consider what adventures—or parts of lengthy adventures—you want
to run. Rather than spending time determining how
characters get between remote locales, create links
between adventure sites via the Radiant Citadel.
Perhaps your next adventure is in a land presented
in this book, or maybe it's somewhere else you decide has a Concord Jewel that links it to the Citadel.
Use the Citadel's network of Jewels to create permanent connections between any lands and adventure
sites you please. Groups from the Citadel, like the
Shieldbearers or the spies in the Court of Whispers, can then point the way toward adventure. This
makes the Radiant Citadel a useful bridge between
wherever your characters are and any adventure in
your D&D library.

SALTED LEGACY

AN ADVENTURE FOR 1ST-LEVEL CHARACTERS

A SERIES OF DISTURBANCES PLAGUES THE Dyn Singh Night Market, an endlessly changing maze of stalls filled with incredible wares, enticing smells, and magical lights. Accusations fly as the characters become entangled in a feud between the well-respected Tyenmo and Xungoon merchant families of the Siabsungkoh valley. To prevent the families' conflict from escalating, the characters must earn the trust of the market's vendors and gain their help to unmask who's behind a rash of vandalism and thefts.

BACKGROUND

The Xungoon and Tyenmo families have always had a complicated relationship. While their trades and relationships to the Dyn Singh Night Market differ, their stubbornness and intense family loyalty are the same. Both believe they're paragons of what a night market merchant should be while also believing the other family has been jealously sabotaging them for years. Despite this, the current heads of the two families, Lamai Tyenmo and Kusa Xungoon, have vowed not to continue what is now a multigenerational rivalry. These family heads have even begun to seek each other's counsel and plant the seeds of friendship. But in recent weeks, thefts and vandalism targeting both families' businesses have rekindled old suspicions, and the feud threatens to reignite.

PRONUNCIATIONS

The Siabsungkoh Pronunciations table notes how to pronounce key names in this adventure.

SIABSUNGKOH PRONUNCIATIONS

Name	Pronunciation
Dyn Singh	DIN sing
Gammon Xungoon	GAH-mun zun-GOON
Kasem Aroon	ka-seem ah-ROON
Kusa Xungoon	kus-AH zun-GOON
Lamai Tyenmo	lam-EYE tea-EN-mo
Madam Kulp	MAH-dum kuhlp
Siabsungkoh	SAB-sung-koh
Tut-krogh	tut-KRO-gh
Vi Aroon	vee ah-ROON

SETTING THE ADVENTURE

The Dyn Singh Night Market could be any city's bustling trade district. Use the following suggestions to help contextualize the market and all of Siabsungkoh in a wider world:

Through the Radiant Citadel. Residents of the Radiant Citadel seeking a different selection of goods than those available in the Trade Discal might be referred to the Dyn Singh Night Market. Those who travel to Siabsungkoh arrive a quarter mile from the market, which is impossible to miss.

Eberron. Given its eclectic array of goods, vendors, and colorful magical signs, the Dyn Singh Night Market could be part of Sharn's Tradefair Market, with the overseeing Dyn Singh Merchant Collective being House Cannith, House Ghallanda, or some combination of other dragonmarked houses.

Forgotten Realms. The Siabsungkoh valley might appear amid the Cloud Peaks of Amn or along the Vilhon Reach. The Dyn Singh Night Market can make a distinctive addition to any region known for trade.

VISITING THE NIGHT MARKET

Before starting the adventure, use the following hooks or work with players to determine why the group has come to the Dyn Singh Night Market:

Connoisseur. The group seeks a rare treasure, local delicacy, or expert artisan available only at the night market. Alternatively, they want to sell a possession to or obtain an appraisal from a merchant with an unusual specialty.

Market Regular. A character grew up in the land surrounding the night market, and visiting the market is an important part of their life. Coming to the market and showing it to their friends is an exciting treat.

The rivalry between the Xungoon and Tyenmo families disrupts the peace in the Dyn Singh Night Market.

Trade Expedition. The characters represent their homeland, a group with which they're affiliated, or the Radiant Citadel. They want to establish trade with a vendor at the night market or obtain goods for those in need.

WELCOME TO THE MARKET

Hundreds of temporary stalls, tents, and vendor carts fill the Dyn Singh Night Market with wonders to tempt even the pickiest customers. The shops surround three golden tents in a sunken plaza. Merchants set up during the afternoon, but most don't open until twilight when the evening's cool air attracts customers.

The vendors are a tight-knit community, and many have attended the market for decades. Their wares vary from common goods to rarities. Some merchants price their wares plainly; others haggle, trade, or exchange goods for favors. Notable shops in the market include the following:

Madam Kulp's Silk. This store sells luxurious silk garments for no less than 50 gp apiece.

Spicy Brothers. This stall sells spices, peppers, and spicy dishes like cucumber fire smoothies and honey-glazed hot chips for 5 sp each.

Trusty Leek. This street food cart specializes in bite-sized and skewered seafood dishes. It relocates regularly throughout the evening.

Tyenmo Noodles. This food vendor offers vegetarian noodle bowls made with handmade noodles and fresh green tree beans for 1 gp.

Vada's Otherworldly Goods. This shop sells pastries and desserts for 1 sp each. The signature vanilla bun is made from a secret family recipe and sells for 2 gp.

Va's Lucky Amulets. This shop hocks a mixture of charms and curios, the most popular being monkey's bane charms and owl's wing rings, both of which are said to fend off sickness and animal attacks. The trinkets are nonmagical and cost 2d10 cp each.

Xungoon Family Seafood. This food vendor sells fishcakes, fresh wailing slug, diamond-throated carp, and shimmering vampire fish for 1 gp apiece.

RIVAL VENDORS

Dyn Singh Night Market vendors Lamai Tyenmo and Kusa Xungoon inherited a long-standing rivalry between their families, but they want to move past it. Circumstances and family grudges conspire to exacerbate their enmity. In the course of the adventure, the characters are drawn into their conflict.

VICKI PANGESTU

KUSA XUNGOON

LAMAI TYENMO

Lamai Tyenmo (lawful good, gnome **commoner**) has dark, wild hair and a wide smile. She recently took over as head of the Tyenmo family business, Tyenmo Noodles. The weight of the new responsibility hangs heavy on her, but she is determined to make her family proud.

>**Personality Trait.** "The land sustains us, and we honor her by sharing what she provides."

>**Ideal.** "I will add to my family's legacy by becoming the most successful vendor in the market."

>**Bond.** "My grandfather took care of all of us; now we must take care of him."

>**Flaw.** "I refuse to back down from a fight if the honor of my family is on the line."

KUSA XUNGOON

Kusa Xungoon (lawful good, kobold **noble**) dresses in impeccable purple-and-gold silk gowns and has polished horns. She runs a respected market stand, Xungoon Family Seafood, and seeks to expand her family's business. She cherishes her son, Gammon, whom she's teaching to take over the business.

>**Personality Trait.** "Success for my business and success for my family are one in the same."

>**Ideal.** "My family's legacy will spread across the land."

>**Bond.** "My son is the light of my life."

>**Flaw.** "It's not that I'm paranoid; it's that a lot of people want what I have."

EXPLORING THE MARKET

Read the following text once characters reach the Dyn Singh Night Market:

> As the sun dips below the horizon, the Dyn Singh Night Market twinkles to life, gradually igniting in a dazzling display. The smells of food carts filled with pot stickers, coconut desserts, spiced meats, sticky buns, and more drift amid bright bouquets of glowing flowers and magical lights in the shapes of vendors' wares and whimsical mascots. Crowds of shoppers wander the stalls, drawn by the colors, smells, and music.

Give the party the opportunity to wander the market and visit some of the aforementioned vendors or stalls. Indulge in descriptions of colorful magic lights and glowing vendor signs; tempting street foods; and the array of peoples who make up the crowd, from humans and gnomes to kobolds and orcs.

CAUGHT IN THE MIDDLE

As characters explore the market, read or paraphrase the following:

> Shouting rises over the sounds of haggling shoppers and the sizzle of cooking street food. A shrill voice cries out, "Give it back, you little thief!"
>
> "No, you're the thief!" replies a youngster with a panicked squeak. An instant later, a frantic kobold bursts from the crowd clutching a sizable bunch of green onions. A flustered gnome woman chases him.

Gammon Xungoon (chaotic good, kobold **commoner**) stole a bunch of green onions from Lamai Tyenmo. Gammon believes Lamai first stole these onions from his mother. At the moment, neither is interested in listening to reason.

Gammon clumsily collides with a random character, bounces off them, and falls to the ground. A moment later, Lamai catches up and attempts to yank the green onions from Gammon's hands while railing at him. A character can separate the squabblers by intervening physically and succeeding on a DC 12 Strength (Athletics) check or by engaging diplomatically and succeeding on a DC 12 Charisma (Persuasion) check.

Less than a minute later—whether or not the characters get involved—Gammon's mother, Kusa Xungoon, appears from the surrounding crowd.

FAMILY FEUD

Kusa Xungoon intercedes between Lamai and her son, sternly telling the gnome shopkeeper, "That's enough, Lamai! You're behaving no better than our parents did: stealing from me and attacking my son!"

This kicks off a fresh bout of arguing, with Lamai claiming she saw Gammon steal the onions (which is true). Gammon accuses Lamai of first stealing the onions from their seafood cart and knocking it over (which is speculation). Rapid-fire, increasingly outlandish indictments and assumptions follow. If the characters don't interrupt the argument, Kusa notices one or more of them. Read or paraphrase the following text when she does:

> The arguing kobold woman notices you and turns from her son and the irate gnome shopkeeper. "You! You strangers look like capable sorts. I'm Kusa Xungoon, proprietor of market-famous Xungoon Family Seafood: for a fish typhoon, you'll wish for Xungoon! Help us deal with this scoundrel and I'll make it worth your while!"
>
> "Scoundrel?!" the gnome shouts, turning your way. "You don't look like you're wrapped up in market politics. I'm Lamai Tyenmo. Help me figure out what's going on here, and I'll give you a lifetime supply of delicious noodles from Tyenmo Noodles!"
>
> Both women turn toward each other again, quarreling anew over what they'll offer you to help them.

Kusa and Lamai argue in front of the characters, upping their offers to include as much as 100 gp, as well as increasingly grandiose delicacies and family cooking secrets such as a feast of thrice-fried tarrasque trout or the secret of making bewildering mobius noodles. Both vendors are eager to prove the other is to blame for the vandalism and sabotage both of their market stalls have been suffering. Neither has entertained the notion someone else might be to blame for their ill fortune or that other shops might also be affected.

Kusa and Lamai stop bickering either when the characters interrupt them or when their argument meets an appropriately ludicrous climax. At this point, the party can choose to ally with one or the other for a 100-gp reward and a lifetime supply of free meals at their employer's cart. The request from either vendor is the same: investigate the shopkeepers' stands and the surrounding market and prove their rival is sabotaging them. The shopkeeper will take any evidence the characters find, present it to the Dyn Singh Merchant Collective that oversees the market, and have their rival banned from the market. If the characters don't want to pick sides but agree to investigate, both shopkeepers convince themselves they've successfully hired the party.

If the characters refuse to get involved, one of the shopkeepers approaches them later under calmer circumstances, restating their concerns about their shop's safety while making their offer again.

AROUND THE MARKET

Following the heated exchange, the gawking crowds and shopkeepers disperse. The characters don't get far before another market vendor approaches them. This human man wears a flashy green shirt with a high collar and gold filigree trim designed to look like hot peppers. He smiles while shaking his head as he approaches and introduces himself as Kasem Aroon, one of the owners of the Spice Brothers stall.

KASEM'S PLAN

Kasem Aroon (chaotic neutral, human **noble**) and his twin brother, Vi Aroon, own and operate the Spicy Brothers stall, which features rare peppers and spices. While Vi has a zest for life, Kasem is reserved and calculating. He's also the one behind the sabotage currently afflicting the Tyenmo and Xungoon stalls.

Several weeks ago, Vi told his brother he's getting married and moving to a distant land. Kasem knows he can't continue Spicy Brothers without Vi's charm and concocted a plan to buy out another successful business. But most businesses in the Dyn Singh Night Market are family shops the owners would never consider selling. While on a trip to get more stock for Spicy Brothers, Kasem encountered a trio of rare Fey creatures called wynlings. Kasem befriended them with a few sweet fruits and brought them back to the night market. He now bribes his invisible friends with fruit to cause disruptions around Tyenmo Noodles and Xungoon Family Seafood. He doesn't want to hurt anyone, but he hopes to make life in the market uncomfortable enough that one of the families sells its shop to him for a low price.

KASEM'S TOUR

Upon meeting the characters, Kasem laments that the families can't get along. He encourages the characters not to ruin their night embroiled in politics and offers to show them around the market. If the characters accept, the tour lasts an hour, during which Kasem points out the stalls detailed at the start of the "Welcome to the Market" section. He tells the characters about the Market Games in the central plaza, describing them as a vapid tradition created to provide cheap thrills.

Kasem encourages the characters to enjoy their evening, avoid the Market Games, and stay away from vendors who give the market a bad name. Any character who succeeds on a DC 14 Wisdom (Insight) check realizes Kasem is trying to keep them from getting involved in market politics. If confronted about this, Kasem insists he just wants them to have a delightful time at the market and departs soon after.

MARKET INVESTIGATIONS

Once the characters decide to look into the events at the Tyenmo and Xungoon shops, they're free to start their investigation. A character who visits one of the shops and spends at least 5 minutes inspecting the space can make a DC 14 Intelligence (Investigation) check. On a successful check, the character discovers nothing unusual except for a few persimmon peels (see "Kasem's Plan" for details on the origins of these peels). A character who further investigates these fruit peels learns no stalls in the night market currently sell persimmons.

Kusa and Lamai are at their respective shops, but neither is much help to the characters' investigations. Each is convinced her rival is to blame for a string of thefts and accidents, despite having no proof. If the characters ask about these events at nearby booths, other market vendors initially claim not to have seen anything strange. If a character succeeds on a DC 10 Charisma (Persuasion) check, a vendor says, "Market business isn't for outsiders. We keep our issues to ourselves." During initial investigations, other shop owners refuse to speak about the Tyenmo-Xungoon rivalry or strangeness at their stalls. Characters can learn more once they've made names for themselves in the market (see "Learning More" and "What Vendors Know").

If the characters guard or stake out either Tyenmo Noodle Bowl or Xungoon Family Seafood, no strange events unfold while they're nearby. Investigations using magic also reveal nothing out of the ordinary.

LEARNING MORE

If the characters ask either Kusa or Lamai why their fellow vendors are loath to get involved in their investigations, the shop owner explains other vendors view the characters as outsiders. During the conversation, they mention the following points:

- The vendors probably see the characters as nosy strangers and want to protect their own.
- Reputation and being part of the market mean a lot to local vendors.
- There's an easy way to quickly get a reputation in the market: participate in the Market Games.
- The Market Games are prestigious events held at the market's center. Winners are temporary, minor celebrities throughout the market.

The shop owner speculates other vendors would view the characters as more than just visitors if they win some Market Games. See the "Market Games" section for more details.

GAINING RENOWN

Characters who participate in Market Games increase their renown among the Dyn Singh Night Market's vendors. Renown is a numerical value that starts at 0. Each player tracks their character's renown separately. Every Market Game notes how much renown characters gain by participating in or winning the event. The Dyn Singh Night Market vendors grow more willing to share information with characters as the characters' renown increases, as detailed in the "What Vendors Know" section.

WYNLING MISCHIEF

The characters aren't the only ones roaming the night market. After each Market Game, or whenever the characters are away from the Tyenmo and Xungoon shops, roll on the Market Mischief table to see what trouble the wynlings cause.

MARKET MISCHIEF

d4	Event
1	A fire at Xungoon Family Seafood causes the stall's right leg to collapse. The stall is now crooked.
2	Two dozen vanilla buns are missing from Vada's Otherworldly Goods. A trail of powdered sugar leads to Tyenmo Noodle Bowl.
3	A rain of persimmons pelts either the Tyenmo or the Xungoon shop. The owners are battered but unharmed, and persimmon juice is everywhere.
4	Gammon spots a large wok from Tyenmo Noodle Bowl at Xungoon Family Seafood. A character who examines the wok and succeeds on a DC 14 Intelligence (Investigation) check notices the wooden handle has been gnawed by child-sized teeth.

MARKET GAMES

The Market Games take place inside three golden tents located in the Event Grounds, which are situated in the center of the Dyn Singh Night Market. Vendors sponsor events to advertise their wares and attract visitors to the market. The current sponsor of each tent decides how its interior is arranged. The following three events are now being hosted:

Aroon Family Pepper Challenge. A test of endurance hosted by the Spicy Brothers.

Battle Prawn Challenge. A cooking competition hosted by Sid Squid of the Trusty Leek.

Hide-and-Seek Challenge. A game hosted by Madam Kulp's Silk.

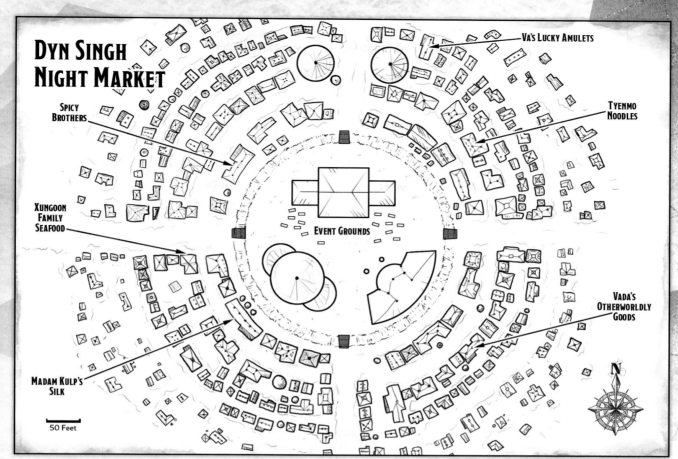

Labels on map:
- VA'S LUCKY AMULETS
- SPICY BROTHERS
- TYENMO NOODLES
- XUNGOON FAMILY SEAFOOD
- EVENT GROUNDS
- VADA'S OTHERWORLDLY GOODS
- MADAM KULP'S SILK
- 50 Feet
- N

MAP 2.1: DYN SINGH NIGHT MARKET

PARTICIPATING IN THE GAMES

Characters who wish to participate in the Market Games need only show up at an event tent and ask to compete. The Market Games run several times throughout the evening. The rules for the three Market Games appear in the sections that follow.

Characters who win a Market Game gain 1 renown with the Dyn Singh Night Market's vendors (see the "Gaining Renown" section). As characters gain renown, the market's vendors share more information with them (see the "What Vendors Know" section). If a character participates in and loses all three Market Games, they still gain 1 renown, as locals respect their tenacity. If a character wins all three challenges, vendors are impressed and call them *reah*, which means "coals of the same fire."

AROON FAMILY PEPPER CHALLENGE

The Spicy Brothers, Kasem and Vi Aroon, are energetic and eccentric lovers of all things spicy. They sponsor the Aroon Family Pepper Challenge in the southwest event tent. This test of fortitude and willpower was created by their father years ago, and it's a tradition they've kept up now that they own the family business.

One of the Spicy Brother's assistants, a human garbed in a garish red-and-green uniform, welcomes characters who seek to participate in the Aroon Family Pepper Challenge. The assistant outlines the rules:

- Participants sit at a table with a basket of mixed peppers and several pitchers of milk.
- During each of the event's three rounds, participants must select one pepper from the basket and eat it.
- Any participant who eats a pepper each round without reaching for milk or leaving the table until the three rounds are over is declared a winner.

Violence and magic are not permitted during the event, but no one checks for magic effects cast prior to the competition.

If the characters agree to the rules, the assistant asks them to wait a few moments for the next event to begin. If four or more characters choose to participate, they are the only contenders in the event. If fewer characters take part, other locals (**commoners**) join the event from the audience, ensuring there are at least four participants.

Greet the Heat

After a short wait, the characters are escorted into the main area of the tent.

A crowd applaud from nearby bleachers as you're led into the broad, open space of the event tent. Before you is a square table bearing a massive basket of colorful peppers and several pitchers of milk.

"Welcome, challengers, to the Aroon Family Pepper Challenge!" shouts a bombastic announcer standing near the table and wearing a red, pepper-themed costume. "I'm your host, Vi Aroon! Is everybody ready to Greet. The. Heat?!"

The characters are directed to sit at the table. As soon as they're seated, Vi (chaotic good, human **noble**) briefly recaps the rules and asks if there are any questions. Once any questions are addressed, the challenge begins.

KASEM
AND VI AROON

Running the Challenge

The challenge unfolds over three rounds, with challengers eating their peppers one at a time, starting with the participant closest to Vi and going clockwise around the table.

On their turn during each round, each participating character must choose a pepper from the basket and eat it. The peppers are from the Spicy Brothers' unique stock, and nothing about them reveals their taste or intensity. The character must roll on the Random Spicy Pepper table to determine what sort of pepper they pull, along with any special effects that pepper has. The character must then make a Constitution saving throw. The DC depends on the pepper they chose. On a successful saving throw, they manage to eat it. On a failed saving throw, they eat the pepper but have disadvantage on the next saving throw they make during the challenge. If a character fails a saving throw by 10 or more, they either reflexively reach for milk or leave the table. Either way, they lose.

Vi offers color commentary during the event, encouraging the crowd to cheer participants and daring competitors to take dramatic bites.

Random Spicy Pepper

d10	Pepper
1	**Dud!** The pepper is not a pepper, but a cherry tomato. You do not need to make a saving throw.
2–5	**Common Pepper (DC 10).** This pepper has no special effects.
6–7	**Sweet Heat Pepper (DC 12).** The pepper is hot but delicious. You do not have disadvantage on this saving throw if you would normally have it as a result of eating another pepper.
8	**Burning Waves Pepper (DC 16).** The heat from this pepper comes in waves. You must make two consecutive Constitution saving throws this round against this pepper.
9	**Flamethrower (DC 18).** If you fail your saving throw against this pepper, you belch or gasp spice into the air. The next challenge participant to eat a pepper has disadvantage on their saving throw.
10	**Skull-Face Pepper (DC 20).** The spice is intense. For an instant, every participant's face looks like a skull to you. This is unsettling but has no other effect.

Ending the Challenge

The challenge ends when every participant is disqualified or has eaten three peppers. Winners and losers alike are rewarded with big bowls of creamy yogurt. Any character who wins the challenge gains 1 renown with the Dyn Singh Night Market's vendors.

ZUZANNA WUZYK

JAGGED KOI PRAWNS ARE JUST ONE UNEXPECTED DANGER OF THE GAMES AT THE DYN SINGH NIGHT MARKET.

After the challenge is completed, characters can ask Vi for information about the thefts (see the "What Vendors Know" section). Soon after the characters start questioning Vi or as they leave the tent, Kasem arrives with news regarding trouble in the market. Roll on the Market Mischief table in the "Wynling Mischief" section to determine what has transpired.

BATTLE PRAWN CHALLENGE

Sid Squid's Trusty Leek sponsors Battle Prawns: The Shrimpening. Sid's shrimp cakes were voted best dish during a festival competition last year. This challenge, held in the northern event tent, tests participants' inventiveness and versatility as they prepare giant versions of his signature dish.

The tent is decorated in a nautical theme, heavy on rope decor and brass fixtures. Sid (chaotic good, human **noble**) and five assistants, all wearing yellow chef's outfits, eagerly invite visitors to participate in Battle Prawns. If characters ask, Sid explains the challenge is simple: assist in making a gigantic shrimp cake in record time. Participants must rapidly prepare prawn meat and chop beans for the sous-chefs. If they perform these preparations fast enough, they might complete the recipe in record time. Unless the characters specifically ask, no one mentions the unusual prawns used in this challenge (see the "Battle Arena" section).

Up to four characters may participate in the event. If fewer characters take part, some of Sid's assistants (**commoners**) join them to create a team of four. No rules forbid magic during this event.

Characters who participate are invited to don yellow aprons that match those of Sid and Sid's assistants. The next challenge begins shortly.

BATTLE ARENA

Sid's assistants lead participating characters into the main part of the tent. The arena is depicted on map 2.2. Read or paraphrase the following description as the characters enter:

> Excited onlookers crowd the bleachers within this vast, open tent. One half of the space is crowded with cooking tools: a pair of oversized woks and two long cutting stations containing bundles of foot-long green beans. The other side holds a pool-sized glass tank filled with water. The water churns as large, shadowy shapes move within.

BATTLE PRAWN CHALLENGE

HIDE-AND-SEEK CHALLENGE

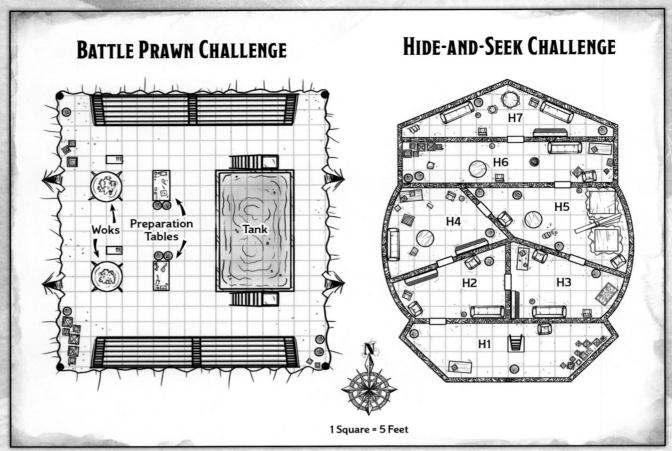

1 Square = 5 Feet

MAP 2.2: MARKET CHALLENGES

The western half of the arena holds the cooking implements and ingredients needed to prepare the shrimp cakes. The eastern half contains a 10-foot-tall tank of water and several gigantic jagged koi prawns. Steps at either end lead to the top of the tank.

Participating characters are directed to take places near the preparation tables at the center of the tent. Sid welcomes the crowd and enthusiastically announces they'll prepare giant shrimp cakes—hopefully, in record time. Sid directs the audience's attention to two special ingredients: delicious green tree beans and giant, jagged koi prawns.

RUNNING THE CHALLENGE

One of Sid's assistants explains what participants need to do in more detail than before: prepare a bundle of green tree beans and slay a jagged koi prawn. If the characters can perform both tasks in 6 rounds or fewer, they win the challenge. While Sid works the crowd, the assistants can answer any questions with details from this section. The assistants direct participants not to move from the preparation tables until Sid gives the signal.

Starting the Challenge. Once any questions are answered, Sid's sous-chefs position themselves around the large woks, ready to transform the ingredients into the final dish. Unless fewer than four characters are participating in the event, these assistants won't help to prepare the beans or the prawns. Sid leads the audience in counting down; "Three ... two ... one ... start!" At this point, the characters and prawns should roll initiative.

Bean Preparation. Massive bundles of green tree beans cover both preparation tables. Participants must chop or mash the beans with the various cooking knives at the table (treat them as daggers), their own tools, or other methods. Each pile is a single Small object with AC 10; hp 15; and immunity to cold, poison, and psychic damage. A pile is rendered unusable if it takes any amount of acid, fire, lightning, necrotic, or radiant damage. Once a pile of beans is reduced to 0 hit points, the sous-chefs add the prepared beans to the woks.

Prawn Preparation. The large tank contains four 8-foot-long jagged koi prawns (use the **giant sea horse** stat block). Participants must slay one of the prawns. Waiting sous-chefs then fish the prawn out and drag it to a wok. The prawns are not initially hostile but defend themselves if they take damage. They have half cover from any creature attacking from outside the water.

If the prawns reduce a character to 0 or fewer hit points, Sid ends the challenge while the sous-chefs get any wounded participants to safety.

ENDING THE CHALLENGE

The challenge ends when participants complete both tasks, give up, or are defeated by the prawns. If the characters fail at either preparation, Sid's assistants complete the preparations and then cook and serve the giant shrimp cakes.

If the participants completed both tasks in 6 rounds or fewer, the shrimp cakes are made in record time. Characters who participated in the challenge gain 1 renown with the Dyn Singh Night Market's vendors. If the challenge took longer than 6 rounds, Sid's crew and the audience remain in high spirits as they eat the delicious shrimp cakes, but the characters gain no renown.

As Sid thanks the characters for participating, trouble befalls the market vendors. Roll on the Market Mischief table earlier in the adventure to determine what happens.

HIDE-AND-SEEK CHALLENGE

The Hide-and-Seek Challenge is sponsored by Madam Kulp, who creates luxurious fashions from silk spun by tut-krogh caterpillars. Her event takes place in the eastern event tent. This challenge doesn't have an audience.

When the characters enter the tent, read or paraphrase the following text:

> Seated at the middle of this sizable empty tent is a wizened gnome at work amid tangles of colorful yarn. Several fuzzy, kitten-sized blue caterpillars drowse on her, nestled in her clothing and hair. The gnome peers up and says, "Welcome! I am Madam Kulp. Are you here to play hide-and-seek with my gentle friends?"

Madam Kulp is an elderly gnome woman (neutral **noble**). If the characters accept her challenge, she hops up and opens a trapdoor at the center of the tent. A ladder descends into a dark, messy room full of boxes and furniture.

Madam Kulp explains that below are a series of rooms where several tut-krogh caterpillars (use the **lizard** stat block) are hiding. Her challenge is simple: descend the ladder and bring back four caterpillars within 1 minute. Any number of characters may participate, and they may use magical assistance as long as the caterpillars aren't harmed—Madam Kulp is adamant about the caterpillars' safety. If the characters agree to these rules, they may descend into the maze when they are ready.

RUNNING THE CHALLENGE

Once the characters have descended the ladder, read or paraphrase the following text:

> The ladder descends into a dimly lit room smelling of dust and sweet spices. Musty furniture and crates are strewn about the space. A door leads north.

The challenge area is depicted on map 2.2 and includes seven rooms. Unlocked doors connect the spaces, all of which are filled with colorful but worthless clutter. The doors are rickety and fit loosely in their frames, allowing tut-krogh caterpillars to move between the rooms unimpeded. Area H1 is lit by a lantern shedding dim light; the other areas are dark.

Starting the Challenge. When the last character reaches the bottom of the ladder, Madam Kulp shouts, "Ready? Go!" At this point, the characters should roll initiative.

Finding Caterpillars. Four tut-krogh caterpillars hide among the cluttered rooms, one each in areas H3, H4, H5, and H7. A character can determine whether there is a caterpillar in a room by spending an action and succeeding on a DC 13 Intelligence (Investigation) or Wisdom (Perception) check.

Collecting Caterpillars. Once a character finds a tut-krogh, they can convince the caterpillar to come with them by succeeding on a DC 10 Wisdom (Animal Handling) check. Alternatively, a character can grab a caterpillar by succeeding on a DC 12 Dexterity (Sleight of Hand) check. A caterpillar flees to an adjoining room if attacked or if a character tries to grab it and misses.

ENDING THE CHALLENGE

The challenge ends either when the characters bring the four caterpillars to area H1 or after 10 rounds pass, whichever occurs first.

If the characters successfully complete the challenge, the shop owner is delighted and declares them winners. Any character who participated in the challenge gains 1 renown with the Dyn Singh Night Market's vendors.

If the characters fail, Madam Kulp invites them into the tent and commiserates that tut-krogh caterpillars are tricky creatures. She invites the characters to try her challenge again later.

Soon after leaving the tent, the characters learn a misfortune has befallen a market vendor. Roll on the Market Mischief table to determine what transpired.

CHARACTER ADVANCEMENT

The characters all gain a level after group members participate in the three Market Games. If they don't complete three Market Games, characters gain a level once they reveal Kasem is the source of the disruptions at Tyenmo Noodles and Xungoon Family Seafood.

What Vendors Know

Vendors in the Dyn Singh Night Market know a great deal about the market's inner workings, their fellow shop owners, and daily gossip. While they're typically polite, they share little information with strangers. If characters gain renown by winning Market Games, the following vendors share the facts for the renown values equal to (and lower than) the renown of the character conversing with them. See the "Gaining Renown" section for additional details.

Vi Aroon

Kasem's twin and co-owner of Spicy Brothers, Vi Aroon, loves what he does. He knows nothing about Kasem's plans but can be convinced to share the gossip on the What Vi Aroon Knows table.

What Vi Aroon Knows

Renown	Gossip
0	Vi shares that he and Kasem had a fight earlier but doesn't reveal why.
1	Vi explains he is getting married and moving to a distant land where his betrothed lives.
2	Vi confides that Kasem is angry about Vi's impending marriage. Kasem told Vi he's making a mistake by leaving the family business.
3	After Vi told Kasem he was getting married, Kasem took several days longer to perform the regular supply run. He returned with extra crates that he keeps in the Spicy Brothers' private tent.

MADAM KULP

Madam Kulp

Madam Kulp is a gnome seamster who works with the silk of tut-krogh caterpillars. She can share the gossip on the What Madam Kulp Knows table.

What Madam Kulp Knows

Renown	Gossip
0	Madam Kulp makes a blunt comment about the characters' demeanor or appearance.
1	Madam Kulp says her tut-krogh caterpillars become nervous whenever she walks them around the Tyenmo or Xungoon stalls.
2	Madam Kulp believes Lamai and Kusa would never intentionally harm one another, due to the damage their families' feud caused their parents.
3	Madam Kulp thinks Kasem has some manner of strange pet. She saw him feeding oranges to a weird, monkey-like creature, but her eyes aren't so good.

Sid Squid

Sid Squid owns the Trusty Leek, a stall near whichever shop hired the characters. They are the head of one of the market's newest families—a band of adventurers turned business owners. Sid can share the gossip on the What Sid Squid Knows table.

What Sid Squid Knows

Renown	Gossip
0	Sid changes the subject to relate a story from their adventuring days.
1	Sid explains that a few vendors like to see the Xungoon and Tyenmo families fight. If the two get along, it could strain other vendors who have ongoing deals with both families.
2	Sid overheard Kasem talking about buying a family business to run, which is against market tradition.
3	Sid saw Kasem stash something orange under the Xungoon family's stall right before a sabotage occurred.

ZUZANNA WUZYK

Other Vendors

Many vendors within the Dyn Singh Night Market have general knowledge about the Tyenmo and Xungoon families as well as recent thefts in the market. These vendors can share the gossip on the What Other Vendors Know table.

What Other Vendors Know

Renown	Gossip
0	The vendor changes the subject, directing characters' attentions toward their goods.
1	The vendor notes disturbances at the Tyenmo and Xungoon businesses cause quite the commotion.
2	The vendor says some people believe the Tyenmo and Xungoon shops are haunted. Passersby claim to have tripped when there was nothing in their way.
3	The vendor describes seeing a blue monkey near the Tyenmo or Xungoon tent.

Revealing the Plot

After the characters complete a few Market Games and make inquires around the market, they likely learn the following facts:

- No one has seen members of either the Tyenmo family or the Xungoon family sabotaging the other family's stand.
- Vi is leaving the market, making Kasem's future uncertain.
- Kasem is behaving strangely and seems fixated on the Tyenmo and Xungoon stands.

If the characters take information pointing toward Kasem to either Lamai or Kusa, the aggrieved vendor listens but remains fixated on her rival. Neither believes someone else is responsible unless the culprit confesses, the characters present accounts from other vendors, or the characters reveal a wynling.

Investigating Kasem

If the characters suspect Kasem of inflaming the Tyenmo-Xungoon rivalry, they might investigate him further. The brothers have a tent for storing supplies and conducting business next to their Spicy Brothers stall. Characters who visit the shop can slip into the tent by succeeding on a DC 12 Dexterity (Stealth) check. The tent contains business records, cots for both brothers, a large crate marked "peppers" that holds three straw-lined bird cages, and a box of persimmons.

Kasem used the cages to smuggle the wynlings into the market, and the creatures use them as tiny homes. Persimmons are rare in the market, but they are one of the wynlings' favorite foods. Kasem uses the fruit to encourage the wynlings to harass his targets, promising them the treats when they do good work or stashing them in other vendors' stalls. While the cages and fruit aren't enough evidence of Kasem's wrongdoing on their own, they might help the characters reveal Kasem's plot.

Revealing the Wynlings

The characters might suspect Kasem is using a creature to harass the Tyenmo and Xungoon market stands—either due to stories from vendors or from what they've witnessed themselves. If a character casts *detect evil and good* near one of the sabotaged stalls, it reveals the presence of a Fey creature nearby, a wynling drowsing on a nearby stall roof. If approached, the wynling turns invisible and flees.

A character can convince a wynling to reveal itself by going to either Tyenmo Noodles or Xungoon Family Seafood and holding out a persimmon. Doing so causes at least one wynling to appear and try to take the fruit. A character can befriend a wynling once it reveals itself by succeeding on a DC 10 Charisma (Persuasion) check. If characters who can speak and understand Sylvan ask the wynling questions, the Fey creature squeaks the following details in reply:

- Kasem found the wynlings in the nearby mountains and brought them to the market recently.
- The wynlings live with their friend Kasem at the Spicy Brothers tent.
- Kasem offers the wynlings persimmons to do errands and to play in certain places (usually the Tyenmo and Xungoon stalls).
- The wynlings aren't malicious; they're just playful and really like persimmons.

The wynlings have no loyalty to Kasem, but they also don't understand why anything they've done is wrong. If the characters show the wynlings to Lamai or Kusa, the vendor is surprised and wants to know why the wynlings are harassing her. The wynlings explain they've only done what Kasem asked them to—thinking it was all good fun. If Kasem is confronted with the wynlings, the creatures are clearly friendly with him. Kasem then confesses he sowed discord between the Tyenmo and Xungoon families to make it easier to buy their stalls.

Confronting Kasem

If characters challenge Kasem with details they learned about him from local vendors, he laughs them off, explaining the market is full of gossip. A character who succeeds on a DC 10 Wisdom (Insight) check realizes Kasem is hiding something. If the characters confront Kasem with multiple accounts or pieces of evidence, they can coax a confession from him (see the following section). If characters take a more hostile approach, Kasem defends himself. Kasem has the statistics of a **noble** and calls out to three **wynlings** (presented at the end of this adventure), who appear and aid him.

CONVINCING KASEM TO CONFESS

The characters can convince Kasem to confess by presenting all three of the following rumors to Kasem—or presenting two and succeeding on a DC 12 Charisma (Intimidation or Persuasion) check; if the characters do so, Kasem then confesses to everything in the "Kasem's Plan" section:

Brother Leaving. If a character asks Kasem about his brother leaving the market, he grows agitated and notes that he's felt betrayed by his brother since Vi decided to abandon their business.

Buying Businesses. If a character presses Kasem about him buying either Tyenmo Noodles or Xungoon Family Seafood, he explains he's looking out for his future. He doesn't care that there's no precedent for buying a family business.

Strange Pets. If asked about the cages and fruit in the Spicy Brothers tent or reports of him having a strange pet, Kasem grows flustered and claims he's thinking about getting a parrot.

RIVALS EXPLODE

If the party fails at the Market Games or reaches dead ends in its investigations, the Tyenmo-Xungoon rivalry comes to a head when Lamai and Kusa get into a public scrap at one of their stands. While the shop vendors fight, any character can make a DC 12 Wisdom (Insight) check to notice Kasem watching with a smile. Not realizing he's being watched, Kasem offers a persimmon to something unseen on his shoulder and the fruit rapidly vanishes. Characters who confront Kasem with what they saw and succeed on a DC 14 Charisma (Intimidation) check convince him to confess to everything in the "Kasem's Plan" section.

CONCLUSION

The adventure ends when Kasem's plot—and potentially the wynlings—are revealed to Lamai or Kusa. If the characters haven't already confronted Kasem, Lamai or Kusa finds him and publicly accuses him of sabotaging her stall. If the vendors are backed up by the characters, witness claims, and evidence, Kasem quickly confesses. Market guards usher Kasem from the market and forbid him from returning unless the characters intercede on his behalf. If the characters advocate for Kasem, another vendor offers to adopt him into their family if he promises no more deceit.

In the aftermath, Kusa and Lamai are quick to apologize to one another and reconcile their differences. They thank the party and award the characters 100 gp and a lifetime of meals from their stalls.

SIABSUNGKOH GAZETTEER

Amid a vivid patchwork of rural farms and dense mountain jungles stands the bustling, unforgettable Dyn Singh Night Market. The heart of the valley of Siabsungkoh, this regional market attracts visitors from distant lands with delicious foods, rare treasures, and all manner of unpredictable fortunes. Tourists nicknamed this ever-changing district the "Dancing Night Market" due to its festive atmosphere and the colorful displays of magical lights that illuminate vendors' wares.

Beyond Siabsungkoh's regional market district, lush jungles are home to rare plants and animals, including the famous bioluminescent lau-pop flower. These flowers bathe the mountains nightly in soft, blue-purple light. Well-kept roads crisscross the region, connecting the populous Dyn Singh Night Market with the scattered communities of the Outer Edges, which border the mountains.

Tradition, trade, and enterprise influence culture in Siabsungkoh. Families spend generations cultivating reputations as experts in varied trades or fields. The inner workings of the markets where families meet and trade are complicated, rife with competition and alliances. Rival families occasionally clash with one another; their conflicts typically take the form of insults and rumor-mongering, but sometimes escalate to violent scuffles. Some traditionalists fear losing their cultural identity and connection to the natural world, and they wish to disrupt the growing impact of mercantilism on local life.

SIABSUNGKOH FEATURES

Those familiar with Siabsungkoh know the following details:

Hallmarks. Siabsungkoh is a land known for its cosmopolitan markets and its people's tight family bonds and ties to nature.

People. Siabsungkoh is a cosmopolitan area inhabited mainly by humans with dark, wavy-to-curly hair, brown eyes, and skin tones varying from medium tan to deep brown. Alongside humans, dragonborn, gnomes, kobolds, and orcs number among the land's most populous residents.

Languages. Maynah, which translates to "river tongue," is the native language of Siabsungkoh. Most locals also speak Common and Draconic.

SIABSUNGKOH

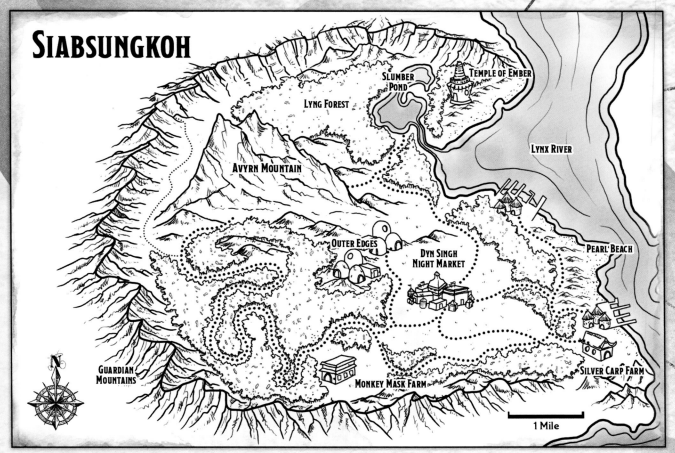

Map 2.3: Siabsungkoh

NOTEWORTHY SITES

Siabsungkoh features lush, tropical jungles surrounded by mountains. The valley is small but buzzes with energy, as both locals and tourists frequent the markets that serve as a hub of community life.

DYN SINGH NIGHT MARKET

Traders from Siabsungkoh's scattered communities flock nightly to the Dyn Singh Night Market, an ever-changing, town-sized market. Food vendors take center stage, selling noodles, seafood, pot stickers, and other delicacies from colorful stalls and carts. Visitors might sample fine desserts, seek the expert works of artisan families, or be entertained by groups like the folklore-sharing Dancers of Smoke.

Becoming a vendor at the Dyn Singh Night Market involves gaining the favor of the five oldest families of Siabsungkoh, then paying a large fee to "prove success." While this approval process was initially created to prevent corruption, many would-be vendors spend years saving for the fee even after earning the families' favor. Many older families have grown greedy and try to stifle competition from new vendors.

OUTER EDGES

The region of Siabsungkoh that borders the wilderness, the Outer Edges are overgrown with lush greenery and lau-pop flowers. Many of the scattered communities here and across the valley reject the bureaucracy and crowds of the market district, braving the dangers of the nearby wilderness to stay self-sufficient. Merchants not accepted in the Dyn Singh Night Market do business here, some trading in doubtful goods and sinister magic. For example, the Nyvrn Candy Cart sells an array of magical and cursed candies, while Hiccup's Generally Nice Goods barters "discounted" Sangarian rugs and "semi-genuine" painted porcelain from the Yongjing.

Some Outer Edges residents chase knowledge of the natural world, such as the scholarly Preed family, whose members believe the land has grown angry and will soon swallow Siabsungkoh whole.

AVYRN MOUNTAIN

Centuries ago, a young sorcerer named Phi Maymoon scaled Avyrn Mountain and pleaded with the nature spirits there to protect Siabsungkoh from invaders. Locals who believe this legend climb the mountain and leave offerings of food and drink on the cliffside to show respect and provide nourishment to the sorcerer. They believe Phi's pact with the spirits protects them still.

Beyond this memorial is the domain of the mountain's spirits. The mountain guardian, Saan, resides within a cave at the mountain's top. It is said the bonds of friendship are tested within Saan's cave. Explorers who prove true to their friends and family are blessed; those who don't find their relationships shattered.

LIFE IN SIABSUNGKOH

The following truths are known to those who live in Siabsungkoh or travel through these lands.

DYN SINGH MERCHANT COLLECTIVE

The finest merchant families in Siabsungkoh make up the Dyn Singh Merchant Collective. These families worked for generations to grow their businesses' reputations and the quality of their wares. The collective sets laws for trade throughout the land, issues licensing for harvesting natural resources, and establishes the rules of business in the night market. However, their success pushes some greedy members of the collective to keep the group exclusive so they can maintain their own power.

THE FIVE FAMILIES

Siabsungkoh is ruled by the heads of the land's five oldest families, three of which are members of the Dyn Singh Merchant Collective. In recent years, the government has expanded the market further to encourage greater trade opportunities. This pushed the market into the center of local life, rankling traditionalists and causing many to believe the nation is sacrificing its ties to the natural world.

FAMILY FIRST

Siabsungkoh is a collectivist society centered on family and deep group loyalties. Families are often blended and can grow through marriage, through adoption, or by simply choosing to accept someone as a family member. Found families are equal to traditional families and often adopt a family name or symbol. The first families that settled Siabsungkoh are said to have been of different blood but the same spirit. Those who operate alone through choice or act in self-serving ways are often called *tuah*, which means "of lonely heart."

VISITORS WELCOME

Siabsungkoh's people have a reputation for being friendly and welcoming; however, trust is reserved for those who earn it. Locals are overly polite and use double-speak when addressing strangers. Newcomers who learn the customs and work within the cultural framework, however, can earn places and renown within the communities.

SPIRITS OF THE LAND

Most Siabsungkoh residents deeply appreciate nature and the spirits that inhabit it. Individuals often leave cut mangoes in streams as offerings for the nature spirits, or spend time at the Lynx River or Slumber Pond to meditate on reflections in the water. Some forgo the duties of family, seeking to attune with nature and work the will of the spirits at the Temple of Ember.

Many animals are believed to be messengers of the spirits. Of particular mystical prominence are tut-krogh caterpillars—which create stunning iridescent silk before they transform into tea-moths—and pangolins, which are said to comfort souls in times of hardship.

NAMES

Names in Siabsungkoh are shaped by family identity, class, and trade. The following names are among the most common in Siabsungkoh:

Feminine. Aom, Pathma, Ratari, Suree, Tunlaya
Masculine. Arthit, Chon, Kiet, Prasong, Somboon, Tai, Teera
Gender-Neutral. Aryn, Detch, Makok, Phi, Rune, Vyndr, Wayo
Surnames. Dunedow, Jollion, Myahkoon, Rhusaang, Suwan

LEGENDS OF SIABSUNGKOH

The oldest legend of Siabsungkoh tells of a young sorcerer, Phi Maymoon, who made a pact with nature spirits to protect Siabsungkoh from invaders that were closing in from the west and south. In an act of desperation, Phi climbed Avyrn Mountain and pleaded with the spirits to protect the land's people. The spirits answered Phi's call. With their combined power, they shifted the earth around Siabsungkoh to form jagged mountains that blocked the invasion. This exchange of power was not without a cost—Phi traded their life to form the barrier that protects Siabsungkoh. Phi's magical power lives on in the mountains and is supposedly the force that gives lau-pop flowers their remarkable glow. To this day, many honor the spirits of Siabsungkoh by tending gardens of lau-pop flowers or climbing Avyrn Mountain to leave offerings to Phi.

ADVENTURES IN SIABSUNGKOH

Consider the plots on the Siabsungkoh Adventures table when planning adventures in Siabsungkoh.

Siabsungkoh Adventures

d4	Adventure
1	A night market vendor uses their business as a front to deal in illegal exports, like tut-krogh caterpillar eggs or wynling wings. The Dyn Singh Merchant Collective hires the characters to pose as buyers.
2	A **revenant** appears at the Temple of Ember, seeking help to avenge its death at the hands of Damen Rak, head of one of the five families that oversee Siabsungkoh.
3	A group of **bandits** with twenty trained pangolins (use the **cat** stat block) pose as merchants, release their pets when the characters pass by, and blame the party for the escape. They demand recompense for the lost animals.
4	**Wynlings** (see below) harass a community's wagons every time they head to market. The locals hire the characters as guards.

Characters from Siabsungkoh

If players want to create characters from Siabsungkoh, consider asking them the following questions during character creation:

What is your family known for? Are you artisans, chefs, outcasts, or something else? What sort of reputation does your family have?

What have you done or refused to do in the name of your family? Did this protect your family or yourself? Did this change your relationship with your family?

What is your connection to the Dyn Singh Night Market? Does your family have the favor of the families that run the market? What do you look forward to buying whenever you visit? Do you oppose the market's expansion or welcome it?

Wynling

Playful and mischievous, wynlings defend mountain heights and alpine vales against trespassers. A wynling rarely engages a threat directly, preferring to deter intruders by harassing them with thefts and pranks. Many travelers return from lands protected by wynlings with stories of vanishing equipment and curious eyes staring from the shadows.

Wynlings typically live on the mountains they protect, but they often venture into nearby settlements, lured by high-spirited music and sweet foods. Away from their open, wild homes, wynlings cause all manner of mysterious accidents.

VICKI PANGESTU

Wynling
Tiny Fey, Typically Chaotic Neutral

Armor Class 15
Hit Points 21 (6d4 + 6)
Speed 30 ft., fly 40 ft.

STR	DEX	CON	INT	WIS	CHA
3 (−4)	20 (+5)	13 (+1)	10 (+0)	14 (+2)	16 (+3)

Skills Sleight of Hand +7, Stealth +7
Senses darkvision 60 ft., passive Perception 12
Languages Sylvan
Challenge 1/2 (100 XP)   **Proficiency Bonus** +2

Actions

Slam. *Melee Weapon Attack:* +7 to hit, reach 5 ft., one target. *Hit:* 7 (1d4 + 5) bludgeoning damage.

Cloak of the Mountain (Recharge 4–6). The wynling magically turns invisible, along with any equipment it is wearing or carrying, for 1 minute or until it makes an attack roll.

Reactions

Trickster's Flight. Immediately after a creature the wynling can see misses the wynling with an attack roll, the wynling can move up to 30 feet. This movement doesn't provoke opportunity attacks.

WRITTEN IN BLOOD

AN ADVENTURE FOR 3RD-LEVEL CHARACTERS

Every year, the Awakening Festival draws folk from across the rich expanse known as Godsbreath, uniting celebrants as they tell their history in song and set the course for the upcoming year. But the mood turns grim when a group of farmers suddenly turns violent, manipulated by an unknown magical malady. In the aftermath, well-known trader Aunt Dellie fears for her goddaughter Kianna—a worker at the farm the attackers came from, deep within the outlying farmlands known as the Rattle. When the characters investigate, they are pitted against a lurking evil that uses a young woman's grief and loneliness to lure new victims.

Background

Life in Godsbreath revolves around community and agriculture, with locals working hard to feed themselves and keep their land strong. But as the crimson-tinged farmland known as the Ribbon becomes less fertile each year, groups of young farmers and adventurers have begun to plant crops along the dangerous borderlands called the Rattle. Despite the constant threat of monstrous predators, new volunteers keep working in the Rattle to help provide for their people. If the bounty of the Ribbon continues to fade, learning to survive in the Rattle will prove vital to supporting Godsbreath's people.

But the Rattle is home to more than feral beasts. A nightmarish Undead known as a soul shaker has risen from these bloody lands, targeting a young worker named Kianna at a remote farm.

Fractured Soul

An evil Undead called a soul shaker (detailed at the end of this adventure) manipulates many of the events in this story. Its origin and objectives are tied to one of the most infamous hauntings in Godsbreath.

Stories tell that Cradlelace Lake was once a thriving but isolated farm, home to a large, happy family. But during a terrible storm, a sinkhole swallowed the farmhouse, then flooded, drowning the house in brackish muck. Tales say the house's residents struggled to escape the pit, but the farm's owner—desperate to keep her family with her—dragged them back into the sinking house. In the aftermath, when neighbors arrived at the sinkhole's edge, they found six pairs of severed, Undead hands struggling to escape the muddy water.

In the years that followed, more tragedies befell those who came near Cradlelace Lake, as if the buried dead sought to add to their number. Among those lost was a young man named Culley, who vanished into the water in front of his friend Kianna.

Unlike most lost to the lake, Culley eventually emerged—at least, part of him did. A single Undead hand escaped the lake, and it eventually found others of its kind known as crawling claws. Gradually, these unthinking Undead combined into a soul shaker. Although the mind of this new horror was a fractured amalgam of thoughts, it remembered the lost soul named Culley, whose memories were the seed of its being. It also remembered the last living person Culley ever saw, his dear friend Kianna.

Driven by instinct, shattered memories, and the discordant urges of dozens of tiny Undead, the soul shaker grew in power, then sought out its old friend.

Pronunciation Guide

The Godsbreath Pronunciations table shows how to pronounce key names in this adventure.

GODSBREATH PRONUNCIATIONS

Name	Pronunciation
Culley	CUH-lee
Dellie	DEH-lee
Dre	DRAY
Kianna	kee-AHN-uh
Polder	POHL-der
Tungsten	TUHNG-sten

ENCHANTED FARMERS ATTACK AUNT
DELLIE ON THE STREETS OF PROMISE.

MIA ARAUJO

SETTING THE ADVENTURE

Use the following suggestions to help contextualize
Godsbreath in a wider world:

Through the Radiant Citadel. Characters traveling
from the Radiant Citadel arrive in Godsbreath
about a mile outside Promise. If you wish to
further detail this land, use the "Promise Gazetteer" section at this adventure's end as a departure point.

Forgotten Realms. Godsbreath could be a region in
Turmish, with Promise replacing Alaghôn or Non-
thal. Godsbreath could also be part of Featherdale
in the Dalelands, adding its distinctive agricultural
bent to this rural dale.

Ravenloft. All of Godsbreath could be a Domain of
Dread. The Darklord of this domain might be a
member of the family lost at Cradlelace Lake or
the vengeful spirit of Culley.

CHARACTER HOOKS

The characters might become involved in the
dangers affecting Godsbreath in any of the following ways:

Awakening Festival. The characters come to Promise, Godsbreath's largest settlement, for the Awakening Festival, either accompanying traders or at
a connection's invitation. This annual celebration
is marked by the multiday *Awakening Song*, a
communal retelling of the land's history and a memorial to those who've passed on.

Friends of Kianna. One or more characters are
childhood friends of Kianna, a good-natured
young woman who goes missing in the course of
the adventure. They've received a strange message from her inviting them to Promise, but when
they arrive, she's nowhere to be found.

Honored Guests. A trader the characters have had
past dealings with—perhaps from the Radiant Citadel or the Dyn Singh Night Market—invites the
characters to Promise to participate in a business
deal with Aunt Dellie.

STARTING THE ADVENTURE

The adventure begins when the characters arrive in the town of Promise or, if they are already there, as they explore the Awakening Festival. Read or paraphrase the following to set the scene:

> In the town of Promise, the annual Awakening Festival is underway, and the streets are alive with vibrant music. As the history of the land is recounted through song, musicians play instruments of many kinds. Their performances meld together as passersby join in during choruses, uniting the entire community in a single collective celebration.

Anyone on the streets of Promise during the Awakening Festival hears what the locals call the *Awakening Song*, a collection of songs recounting local histories. Characters who spend an hour exploring the festival learn much about the history of the land. They also have advantage on Intelligence (History) checks related to the *Awakening Song* made for the rest of the adventure.

During the festival, stalls throughout the community sell local crafts, musical instruments, and street foods. Small straw dolls wearing colorful shirts and dresses are widely available for 5 cp each. A doll can be made to resemble the buyer for 7 cp. The dolls are a popular local craft and nothing more.

EYES OF BLOOD

After the characters have engaged with the local festival as much as they please, the character who has the highest passive Wisdom (Perception) score notices a group of celebrants acting strangely. Read or paraphrase the following:

> As part of the crowd begins another verse of the *Awakening Song*, four people wearing the garb of farm folk wander into their midst. Rather than singing, they stare blankly. Then they surge forward into the celebrants, raising rusty farming implements.

Four farmers attack the festival-goers. They use the **cultist** stat block; their rusty, bladed farming implements have the same statistics as scimitars. Any character who engages the farmers sees their eyes swirl with crimson, resembling bloody, unshed teardrops. Characters have no way of knowing it yet, but this is a mark of the soul shaker's control (see the "Soul Shaker" section at the end of this adventure).

The festival-goers closest to the strange farmers panic and flee. Unless the characters do the same, the attackers target them.

Only one local holds their ground: a surprised woman named Aunt Dellie (**commoner**). She clearly recognizes some of the strange farmers and tries to reason with them to no avail. Aunt Dellie shouts for the characters not to kill the farmers, noting that they're not behaving like themselves.

MEMORIES OF DEATH

When the last farmer is defeated, locals return to tend to the wounded. The farmers are known to many in the crowd, prompting confusion over their strange appearance and what caused them to attack. Talk of curses begins to spread.

Investigating the Farmers. A character who fought the farmers or examines them afterward can make a DC 13 Intelligence (Arcana or Religion) check. On a success, the character can tell the farmers are being magically controlled. Spells like *detect magic* also reveal that the farmers are surrounded by an aura of enchantment magic. While this magic—the effects of the soul shaker's *geas* spell—lingers, the farmers' eyes keep their crimson hue.

If the farmers are healed or roused from unconsciousness, they refuse to speak. They don't attack again, but the locals keep them restrained.

The characters likely don't have the resources to remove the enchantment affecting the farmers yet—only destroying the soul shaker or waiting approximately a month can do this. Even if the characters do remove the effect, the farmers are confused and remember nothing helpful.

Strange Parchment. As the characters investigate the situation, Aunt Dellie notices that one of the farmers was clutching a crumpled sheet of parchment. She opens it, and nearby characters hear her curse in concerned shock. Aunt Dellie hands the crumpled parchment to any character who asks about it. It bears a charcoal sketch of a child struggling to swim in dark water while being grasped at by hands beneath the surface.

AUNT DELLIE

Aunt Delanore "Dellie" Godsen (neutral good, human **commoner**) is a savvy operator with an honest reputation, a soft heart, and a talent for hearing a bit about everyone's business. A trader and skimmer boat pilot, Aunt Dellie has never been afraid to go her own way and knows much about Godsbreath's lands and threats. Although she's a small woman, Aunt Dellie's charm and knack for survival have gotten her through numerous near disasters. Everyone calls her "aunt," a trend started by her beloved goddaughter Kianna.

Personality Trait. "Tell the truth of where you've been, and I'll let you know where you ought to be going."

Ideal. "I'll make trouble for trouble itself if that's what it takes to make someone smile."

Bond. "A place is the people you meet—and the ones you help along the way."

Flaw. "Nothing short of a god is going to take me down."

A GODMOTHER'S FEAR

Aunt Dellie clearly recognizes the sketch on the parchment one of the strange farmers had with them. Her strong voice shakes as she explains its significance:

- The sketch was drawn by Aunt Dellie's goddaughter, Kianna. Aunt Dellie knows her art style, and this is a scene she draws regularly.
- As a child, Kianna saw her friend Culley drown in Cradlelace Lake while they were playing.
- Since Culley's death, Kianna has used art to work through the sadness and guilt she carries to this day.
- Kianna is currently working a farm in the Rattle—a half-day's travel from Promise. She was due to return to town for the Awakening Festival, but Aunt Dellie hasn't seen her yet.

Characters who investigate further and ask those nearby about the attack learn that the strange farmers all worked in the Rattle—a dangerous but fertile farming region haunted by deadly predators.

While the locals speculate about the fates of other farmers in the Rattle, Aunt Dellie has no patience for debates on what to do next. Aunt Dellie implores the characters to go to the Rattle where Kianna was working and make sure her goddaughter is safe, while she stays in Promise to organize a larger investigation. She offers the party 100 gp to undertake this mission, and 100 gp more if the characters return her goddaughter to Promise safely.

Aunt Dellie gives the characters directions to the Rattle, but she doesn't know exactly where Kianna's farm is. The characters must search for it once they reach the Rattle.

AN UNEXPECTED OFFER

After the characters finish their conversation with Aunt Dellie, another local approaches them. Read or paraphrase the following text:

> A broad-shouldered woman wearing a multicolored dress that complements her dark skin approaches boldly, sizing you up from beneath a stylish hat. "I overheard your conversation with Aunt Dellie. You see, nothing important gets past Lady Dre. I hear you're bound for the Rattle? Excellent—I'll accompany you. We should depart at once."

LADY DRE

Lady Dre (chaotic good, human **scout**) is a trader who makes an impression on everyone she meets. Tall and broad with shoulder-length locs, she's known for bright-colored clothing meant to catch the eye of potential business partners. She's a shrewd negotiator, thanks in no small part to her storytelling skill. Personable but focused, Lady Dre is willing to forgo short-term gains in favor of long-term growth.

Personality Trait. "Half of business is showmanship, and I love to take center stage."

Ideal. "Trades are like people—uniquely beautiful if appreciated properly."

Bond. "Every deal is a promise, and I always keep my promises."

Flaw. "It's okay if you lose, as long as I'm winning."

BUSINESS CONCERNS

Lady Dre was horrified by the attack, and she wants to make sure no other folk in the Rattle are in danger. Characters who succeed on a DC 12 Wisdom (Insight) check recognize her motivations are not

LADY DRE

entirely altruistic. If pressed, Lady Dre admits she has made trade investments with several Rattle farms. She wants to ensure that no threats interfere with her getting first pick of the harvest.

If the characters are reluctant to allow Lady Dre to accompany them, she tries to win them over by offering the use of her horses and a comfortable wagon. She remarks that if the characters are going to head into a mystery, they should be prepared to transport anyone who might have been harmed or afflicted.

If the characters choose not to travel with Lady Dre, she accepts their choice and heads out on her own soon after they do.

THE LARGER TRUTH

As the characters prepare for their journey, a human in scholars' garb approaches them. A character who succeeds on a DC 14 Intelligence (Religion) check recognizes the human as a Proclaimer of the Covenant, a servant of the pantheon of local deities who seeks new stories for the *Awakening Song*.

PROCLAIMER TUNGSTEN WARD

Proclaimer Tungsten Ward (lawful good, human **acolyte**) is small of stature and soft of voice, and their worldly appearance belies their young years. Despite Ward's relaxed demeanor, their approachability covers a calculating personality. Thanks to Ward's history of making friends, trading favors, and pulling strings, even rivals find the Proclaimer difficult to directly oppose. Ward seeks evidence of the gods' influence and motives in all things. Ward then adds such evidence to their orders' records and creates new verses of the *Awakening Song*.

Personality Trait. "I listen for the words you dare not say."

Ideal. "I'll know more about the gods than the gods themselves."

Bond. "The Proclaimers of the Covenant know what story needs to be told."

Flaw. "I don't really care if you believe—I care if you obey."

FOR THE RECORD

Proclaimer Ward introduces themself and briefly explains that they research magical manifestations across Godsbreath that they believe are signs of the gods' power—or challenges to it. Having witnessed the attack and spoken with locals in the aftermath, Ward wants to join the characters' expedition. The Proclaimer hopes to investigate what led to the farmers' strange behavior and determine whether it's linked to other misfortunes in the region, like the waning crop yields in the Ribbon. If the results are significant enough to weave into the *Awakening Song*, Ward assures the party that each character's name will feature prominently.

PROCLAIMER
TUNGSTEN WARD

TO THE RATTLE

The farm Kianna works at is 12 miles from Promise. Whether the characters are traveling by foot or using Lady Dre's wagon, at a normal pace it takes half a day to reach the Rattle.

Once the characters are underway, read or paraphrase the following to summarize the journey:

> The journey from Promise leads north through the Ribbon, where clustered farmhouses dot the dark-red ground between stands of scattered woods. Eventually, the road dwindles to a track. The stands of trees grow denser and the farms fewer and farther between as you near the lands called the Rattle.

Any character who succeeds on a DC 14 Intelligence (Nature) check notices that many of the farms in the Ribbon are touched by blight and the animals are thin. Either Lady Dre or Proclaimer Ward can explain that agriculture in the region has been deteriorating for years, forcing locals to farm the Rattle despite its dangers.

If the characters stop at any of the farms they pass in the Ribbon, they see no sign of danger, but no one at the farms knows Kianna.

LAST STOP

As the characters push into the Rattle, they near a weathered farm surrounded by crops that look healthier than those they saw in the Ribbon. Not everything about the farm is hopeful, though:

> Growls and excited yipping resound from the field surrounding a nearby farm. The source isn't clear, but from the motion of the tall crops, something moves swiftly through the fields parallel to the road.

A character who succeeds on a DC 12 Wisdom (Perception) check realizes two groups are moving through the fields, one in pursuit of the other, though the dense crops block their view. Characters who enter the fields find visibility reduced to 10 feet. A character who succeeds on a DC 14 Wisdom (Survival) check finds the trail of whatever just moved through the fields and can easily follow it.

SAVAGE SCAVENGERS

If the characters follow the movement through the field, they come to a clearing and see an old farmer fleeing three horse-sized coyotes. The farmer is about 30 feet ahead of the coyotes. If the characters didn't enter the fields, a moment later, an old man stumbles from amid the crops and falls into the road. Three massive coyotes are soon upon him. In either case, the old man has no hope of defending himself against the creatures.

Massive coyotes are a persistent threat in the Rattle. The three coyotes use the **dire wolf** stat block, while the farmer they pursue is a **commoner**. A coyotes flees if reduced to 10 hit points or fewer.

If they're with the party, Lady Dre and Proclaimer Ward try to pull the farmer out of danger while the characters fend off the coyotes.

When the fighting ends, the farmer is bloodied but angrier at the animals than scared. He thanks the characters and introduces himself as Uncle Polder.

UNCLE POLDER

Uncle Polder (neutral good, human **commoner**) is an old man with a stocky build and an easy smile. He walks at an amble and speaks with a drawl—but his mind is constantly working, developing solutions to any problem he faces. Polder has spent many seasons in the Rattle and is dedicated to helping others thrive—in part to rid himself of the guilt of leaving a friend behind when he escaped a bulette attack during his first season.

Personality Trait. "If I can't get it done, I know someone who can."

Ideal. "Everyone's life is worth saving."

Bond. "I understand what it is to survive the Rattle—and what you can leave behind there."

Flaw. "I'm all about helping the community, as long as I get the credit."

LIFE IN THE RATTLE

Following the battle, Uncle Polder thanks the characters and asks what brings them out this way. He invites them to water their horses and refresh themselves, gesturing to his nearby farm.

Uncle Polder's house is typical of farmhouses in the Ribbon and the Rattle—a wood-frame, single-story building with a large porch, bounded by trees. The other farmhouses in the surrounding part of the Rattle are all part of the same pact—a communal collection of farms whose inhabitants live, work, and share with each other. Uncle Polder's farmhouse is one of the largest in the group, suggesting his importance to the community.

Uncle Polder is glad to answer any questions the characters have about the area. Use the following points to guide the conversation:

- There's always trouble in the Rattle, but Uncle Polder can't recall any unusual problems this season.
- He's met Kianna and knows the farm she works at, though it's part of another pact. It's not far from Uncle Polder's, but people in the Rattle mostly stick close to home. The farmers of the two pacts don't interact often.
- Uncle Polder recalls helping Kianna's pact set up early in the season. He keeps an eye out for people who might not be a good fit for life in the Rattle—and Kianna seemed to have things on her mind other than farming.
- When Kianna and others of her pact came to Uncle Polder's pact a couple weeks ago to trade for tools, she seemed to be embracing life in the Rattle. She spoke of how happy she was that someone named Culley was coming to join her soon. Uncle Polder assumed Culley was another worker coming late to the farm.

From their conversation with Aunt Dellie, the characters remember that Culley was Kianna's friend who drowned many years ago. If Proclaimer Ward is with the group, Ward also recalls the story of the child's death, as the Proclaimer was responsible for adding Culley's drowning to the *Awakening Song*.

If told the truth about Culley, Uncle Polder is surprised; Kianna spoke as if Culley were a close and current friend.

Uncle Polder allows the characters to rest at his home as long as they please. When they're ready to go, he gives them detailed directions to the farm Kianna works at a few miles away.

Fallen Farmhouse

As the characters continue on their journey, they notice the environment changing around them after only another hour of travel. After they've traveled about a mile from Uncle Polder's home, read or paraphrase the following description:

> The open fields have all but vanished behind sparse woods at the far edge of the Rattle. The air smells stagnant and carries the taste of metal. Through the trees, multiple small farmhouses hunch amid a patch of green fields.
>
> Suddenly the ground begins to shake, causing the road ahead to ripple, but just as quickly as it started, the shaking fades away.

A character who succeeds on a DC 14 Intelligence (Nature) check realizes the tremor likely wasn't an earthquake but something local, such as a collapsing cave or something moving underground. Lady Dre and Proclaimer Ward have never heard of earthquakes in the Rattle, but they know that bulettes occasionally trouble local farmers.

Sinister Sinkhole

After another 10 minutes of travel, another tremor shakes the ground. This time, the tremor causes a 10-foot-square, 10-foot-deep sinkhole to open beneath Lady Dre's wagon (or a random character if Lady Dre isn't with the party). Each creature in the area must succeed on a DC 15 Dexterity saving throw or fall 10 feet, taking 3 (1d6) bludgeoning damage. Characters who said they would be mindful of sinkholes or unstable ground after the previous tremor have advantage on this saving throw.

Any creature at the bottom of the hole finds they're not alone. Four **crawling claws** scrabble free from the dirt at the bottom of the pit and attack any creatures within. After the Undead are dispatched, any character who examines the disembodied hands and succeeds on a DC 16 Wisdom (Perception) check can tell that the creatures were digging through the loose earth—though it's not clear to what end.

If Lady Dre is accompanying the characters, her wagon is now trapped within the sinkhole. Lady Dre decides to stay and figure out a way to get the wagon unstuck—she has rope in the back that might prove helpful. She insists the characters go on ahead. Proclaimer Ward stays to help Lady Dre if they're both with the party.

X Marks the Spot

The farming community Kianna is a part of isn't just one farm, but a cooperative of adjacent farms. As the characters reach the location Uncle Polder directed them to, they find seven farmhouses, each about an eighth of a mile apart.

As the characters approach the nearest farm, they find the surrounding fields overgrown and the plants rotting. Crows flit between perches on the fences, but there are no signs of people.

Nearly all the houses have been sloppily painted with a large and muddy red X. The interiors of these farmhouses are utilitarian, featuring only a few rooms for sleeping and a small kitchen. No creatures are within, and the accumulation of dust makes it clear no one's disturbed the rooms for some time. Every farmhouse bears a sign that something's wrong. Roll on the Farmhouse Conditions table for each building to determine what.

Farmhouse Conditions

d4	Condition
1	The windows are shattered, and the shards of glass are spattered with dried blood.
2	Clothing and belongings are strewn everywhere, all covered in crimson mud.
3	Human bones, freshly gnawed by animals, litter the floor of every room.
4	A strange image is painted on the wall in red mud. It depicts either a cluster of arms with no central body or repeating red hand prints.

A character who investigates at least two of the farmhouses can make a DC 14 Wisdom (Perception) check. On a success, they notice one farmhouse doesn't have a red X painted on it. This building is the farmhouse where Kianna resided, and it also serves as the pact's communal meeting house.

Kianna's Farmhouse

A farmhouse near the center of the steading serves as a main kitchen, dining area, and meeting place for the smaller houses around it. This is the farmhouse where Kianna was a resident. As the characters approach, read or paraphrase the following description:

This large farmhouse appears abandoned like the smaller houses around it, but no X marks it. Farming implements lie abandoned in the mud, and wild plants have grown up to the house's faded wooden porch. The crops in the surrounding field appear sickly.

Kianna's Farmhouse Locations

The following locations are keyed to map 3.1.

F1: Overgrown Yard

The house's yard is muddy red clay. Several rusty shovels and rakes lie scattered about.

Farming Implements. A character who looks around the back of the house sees a pitchfork stuck into the earth near the house's northeast corner. On further investigation, they see it's stuck through the severed hand of a young woman. The characters have no way of knowing this, but the hand was once a crawling claw and was dispatched by a farmer.

Sickly Crops. Wheat and corn struggle to grow in the fields surrounding the house. Any character who succeeds on a DC 14 Intelligence (Nature) check can tell the plants around this farm are sickly because something's wrong with the soil. A character who succeeds on a DC 16 Wisdom (Perception) check notices raised paths through the dirt, like mole tunnels, though no creatures are obvious. Although it's not evident, the soul shaker's evil and the excavations of the crawling claws have spoiled the land around the house.

If Proclaimer Ward is with the party, the Proclaimer investigates the crops and grows concerned. Ward stays in the field and documents the strange blight rather than joining the characters inside.

F2: Porch

A large wooden porch wraps around the front and one side of the farmhouse. Its planks creak ominously when stepped on, but there is no danger here. Closed curtains shroud the windows, but the doors to the interior are unlocked and ajar. Both lead to a musty central hallway.

Doors. The doors leading off the hallway are closed but not locked.

F3: Living Room

The furniture in this living room is haphazardly arranged and looks close to falling apart. Beneath, the floor is covered in hundreds of handprints painted using crimson mud.

The art style is similar to that of the picture Aunt Dellie found in Promise. Any character who succeeds on a DC 14 Wisdom (Perception) check notices a break in the pattern under a chair. If the chair is moved, it reveals a muddy depiction of two children—one is reaching for the other, who is being dragged into the water by large hands. Scrapes in the muddy image form the name "Culley."

F4: BEDROOM

The bedroom holds a bed and writing desk for a single occupant. Most of the space is neat and orderly, but the desk is strewn with art supplies and scraps of paper bearing fragmented images.

Paintings. Any character who riffles through the paper on the desk finds repeating images of hands, lakes, and wide eyes looking up through water. The largest work shows a pair of eyes with handprints for pupils. All these images look similar in style to the picture Aunt Dellie found in Promise.

Chest. A small chest against the wall is unlocked and holds work clothes sized for a woman. A character who searches the chest and succeeds on a DC 12 Intelligence (Investigation) check finds a pair of overalls with a pocket containing thirteen rings—plain rings, wedding bands, and formal jewelry sized for men and women—worth 2d10 gp each.

F5: DINING ROOM

> A long plain table, a wooden sideboard, and several chairs lie shattered on the floor. The debris is streaked with crimson stains.

This dining room has been ransacked, and red mud covers the furnishings and floor.

A character who approaches the table hears scratching coming from under it. Nothing is immediately visible beneath the table, but characters who investigate more closely find six **crawling claws** clinging to the underside. Once discovered, the monsters attack.

After the crawling claws are dispatched, any character who searches the room thoroughly can make a DC 16 Intelligence (Investigation) check. On a successful check, the character finds several floorboards that have been pushed up from below, as though the crawling claws dug their way up through the loose soil beneath the house.

F6: KITCHEN

> This kitchen has been torn apart. Pots and pans are scattered everywhere, and rotting food streaks the floorboards.

In the center of the room, four enchanted farmers stand facing each other, their crimson eyes unblinking. Each holds a sharp knife or farming implement. They don't react when the characters enter or if they are touched or spoken to. They react only if harmed, stolen from, or commanded by the soul shaker. Each uses the **cultist** stat block. Although the farmers are initially harmless, their appearance and lack of reaction are unnerving.

Pantry. The foodstuffs and supplies that once filled the pantry have been ransacked, and a large cupboard stands open. A trapdoor in the pantry's floor opens to reveal a 10-foot-tall ladder descending into a darkened cold-storage cellar. The stench of something rotting rises from below.

F7: CELLAR AND TUNNEL

Shelves bearing root vegetables and other foodstuffs line the walls of this unfinished cellar. The south wall has partially collapsed, revealing a dark, narrow tunnel.

The smell the characters noticed above is worse here, issuing from the tunnel. Character who have a passive Wisdom (Perception) score of 15 or higher hear the faint sound of a woman singing farther down the tunnel.

Characters who proceed 40 feet into the tunnel see a faint light emanating from around a bend.

Tunnel Song. As the characters move through the tunnel, the song's volume increases. The characters recognize this as part of the Awakening Song they overheard in Promise. This part of the song tells the story of a young man named Culley. Rather than its usual content, where the boy dies by drowning, the song has been sloppily rewritten to feature Culley being saved by his closest friend.

F8: CAVERN

> The tunnel opens into a lantern-lit, packed-dirt chamber, where the cause of the stench becomes apparent. A dozen bodies lie strewn across the floor, all wearing the clothes of farmers. Many of their limbs have been cleanly removed and set into a sizable pile on the far side of the cavern. In the center of the room, a young woman is singing.

The bodies are the farmers missing from the surrounding farms—save for Kianna. They've been killed and dismembered by the soul shaker.

Kianna. The young woman is Kianna (chaotic neutral, human **commoner**). She looks like she's in a dream state, and she holds a knife loosely, but her eyes aren't crimson like those of the other farmers. Kianna stops singing as soon as she notices the characters and says, "Please go. You shouldn't be here." If the characters speak with Kianna, she drifts between fearfully urging them to leave and coaxing them to stay and meet her friend, Culley, her mood and manner shifting erratically. Use the following points to guide the conversation:

- Kianna confirms she's the person the party seeks. She's saddened at any talk of Aunt Dellie having sent the characters to find her.
- She speaks brightly of how Culley finally came back to her after she lost him in Cradlelace Lake. It was so good to hear his voice again!
- When Kianna heard Culley's voice beyond the cellar, she dug and found this old cavern.
- Something happened to the farmers when they entered the caverns. After that they did whatever Culley said—including hurting one another and marking the houses with X's to note who had visited the cellar.
- If asked about Culley, Kianna sadly says her friend drowned long ago—then cheerfully says he didn't drown because she saved him. He went away for a long while, but he came back.
- If asked where Culley is now, Kianna fearfully says he's sleeping after having fed. She believes her song helps keep him quiet, but she's tired.

As the characters speak with Kianna, a character who succeeds on a DC 12 Wisdom (Insight) check notices Kianna's eyes darting to the pile of limbs whenever she speaks brightly of Culley.

If the characters ask Kianna to leave with them, she seems confused and scared, saying she can't. If she's coerced, or if a character investigates the pile of limbs, the soul shaker awakens.

Soul Shaker. When the characters try to leave the area or disturb the pile of limbs, the heap begins to move, revealing itself as an Undead made entirely of arms and hands. This is a **soul shaker** (detailed at the end of this adventure). This creature has a fraction of the memories of Kianna's friend Culley, but the horror has perverted those thoughts, seeking to control Kianna, manipulate her guilt, and use her to lure other victims into its lair. When it reveals itself, the soul shaker targets a character with its telepathy, whispering things like "Come play with us!", "Are you lonely?", and "Be with us forever!" as it attacks. It might also relate snippets from the "Fractured Soul" section of the adventure's background.

As soon as the soul shaker awakens, if the farmers the soul shaker controls are still in area F6, it summons them to aid it. The four farmers (use the **cultist** stat block) arrive in 2 rounds.

Kianna is confused and terrified, and she stays out of the battle.

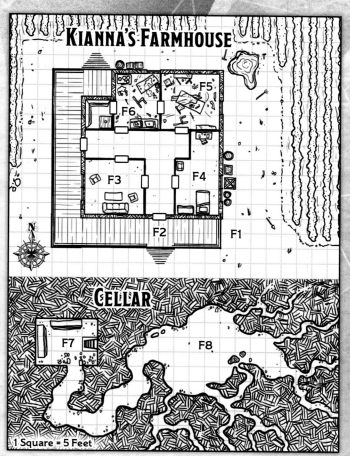

MAP 3.1: KIANNA'S FARMHOUSE

CONCLUSION

Once the soul shaker is defeated, its grip on the farm's residents fades.

KIANNA'S STORY

After the soul shaker is destroyed, Kianna collapses into unconsciousness. A character who examines her and succeeds on a successful DC 14 Wisdom (Medicine) check can tell Kianna is sleep deprived and has been tormented by the strange creature. She wakes after an hour, unable to remember anything that's happened in recent days except for glimpses of strange hands and menacing words spoken in her dead friend Culley's voice. Kianna shares that she blames herself for Culley's death at Cradlelace Lake, and when she heard his voice, she thought the gods might be giving her a chance to make amends. Now she just wants to return to Promise.

If asked about or shown her paintings from areas F3 or F4, she has no memory of creating them, though they're clearly in her art style. A character who succeeds on a DC 18 Wisdom (Insight or Medicine) check recognizes Kianna is no longer suffering any supernatural effects, but the character also suspects her experiences might have affected her more deeply than she realizes.

The Farmers' Story

If any of the farmers survived, the crimson hue vanishes from their eyes after the soul shaker's destruction, and they thank the characters for saving them. Even if the farmers in the house didn't survive, one or two lost in the fields arrive at the farmhouse—perhaps with Proclaimer Ward.

The farmers remember only snippets from the last few days, and the last thing they recall clearly is preparing to return to Promise for the Awakening Festival. They also share that Kianna had been behaving strangely, growing increasingly convinced that her dead friend was speaking to her. The farmers can also relate details from the adventure's background or about Cradlelace Lake if asked.

Although the farmers can't reward the characters with much in the way of wealth, they gift the group a *Heward's handy haversack* they had stashed with tools in a nearby shed. The first character to open it, however, finds that a **crawling claw** has gotten itself trapped within. It tries to escape as soon as it is detected.

KIANNA

If Proclaimer Ward is with the party, the Proclaimer stays with the farmers to help them either get back on their feet or join Uncle Polder's community.

Back to Promise

If Lady Dre came with the characters, she and the horses have extracted her wagon from the sinkhole and are waiting for the characters.

When the characters return to Promise, Aunt Dellie is overjoyed if Kianna is safe and tearful if her goddaughter met a bitter end. Either way, she's grateful to the characters for uncovering the truth and ending the soul shaker's threat. If the characters defeated the soul shaker, she relates that the enchanted farmers in town have regained awareness. Aunt Dellie rewards the characters with her promised payment and offers them free passage on her boat whenever they please.

Godsbreath Gazetteer

Generations ago, a land was plundered by enemies whose names are lost to time. Five gods came together to save as many of the land's beleaguered inhabitants as they could by taking them to a new home. Those the gods saved named their new land Godsbreath, in honor of the deities who brought them across a vast sea to a new life. These inhabitants banded together to build strong communities and protect themselves from danger. From one generation to the next, they share stories of their past, of the distant lands of their ancestors, and of the unfulfilled promise of reunion with ancestors left behind in a lost land.

In Godsbreath, danger and beauty walk hand in hand. Along the southern coast, the murky, monster-stalked Nightwater Islands support tight-knit communities whose colorful houses perch on stilts. On the mainland, rising from the shore of Nightwater Cove, stands Promise, a town of brightly painted buildings and bustling trade. Northward lies a band of crimson soil known as the Ribbon—the source of this land's agricultural prosperity—which weaves through woods and floodplains. Beyond the Ribbon spreads the treacherous land of the Rattle, a territory that might hold the key to Godsbreath's future.

Each year, Promise's streets fill with people celebrating the Awakening Festival, which centers around retelling Godsbreath's past and reckoning with its present. But every year the struggle to survive becomes more dire, as the land sickens and monstrous threats become more numerous. Why the land is turning against its people is a mystery to the people of Godsbreath and a matter the gods remain silent about.

JABARI WEATHERS

GODSBREATH FEATURES

Those familiar with Godsbreath know the following details:

Hallmarks. Godsbreath is a land known for its cooperative agricultural communities and the importance its people place on maintaining their oral history.

People. The people of Godsbreath have skin tones ranging from the medium brown of copper to the near black of ebony, and most have tightly coiled dark-brown hair. Nonhumans and humans of other lands are rarely seen here; most who do live here dwell in Promise.

Languages. The people of Godsbreath speak their own language, known as Godstongue, as well as Common.

NOTEWORTHY SITES

Godsbreath is bounded by the treacherous waters of Nightwater Cove and the dangerous expanse of the Rattle.

THE NIGHTWATER ISLES

The Nightwater Isles rise from the waters of the murky cove from which they take their name. Though islanders mostly keep to themselves, their homes are visible from quite a distance, perched as they are on stilts to protect from floods. Each is painted in bold colors that not only honor the gods, but keep away the many monsters haunting the cove, including giant crocodiles, shambling mounds, and green hags.

Though each island has its own cultural and trade specialties, all the islands are connected to each other via flotillas of skims—flat-bottomed boats that ply the waters of the cove, operated by pilots known as skimmers.

THE RIBBON AND THE RATTLE

The zone of fertile crimson soil known as the Ribbon cuts a wide swath through the gray-brown plains that stretch from the water's edge to the lands of the Rattle. Most inhabitants of the Ribbon live on small family farms joined together in pacts—resource-sharing alliances forged by common interest.

Inexplicably, the Ribbon's soil grows less fertile each year, and no living soul in Godsbreath knows why. Residents of this land have been migrating into the fertile but dangerous lands of the Rattle. But Rattle farmers are threatened by oversized coyotes, bulettes, and other threats. Farmers whisper of strange magic that manifests without warning, causing unusual weather and reshaping the soil. Some believe these effects might be connected to ancient magics affecting the land or the will of the region's primary gods.

PROMISE

Promise is a town situated where the soil of the Ribbon meets the Nightwater Cove coast. Its paved streets and colorful two-story buildings are home to Covenant worship houses, trader storehouses, schooling circles, and more. Promise is also home to the annual Awakening Festival, which brings together folk from across Godsbreath. Participants trade wares, relive their shared history through the call-and-response *Awakening Song*, and settle regional disputes at the communal and annual summit known as the Meet, where canny traders and powerful pacts seek to gain influence.

LIFE IN GODSBREATH

Those who dwell in or travel through Godsbreath understand the truths underlying life in this land.

COMMUNITY AND CONSENSUS

Each community in Godsbreath is self-governing, with intercommunity and regional disputes settled at the annual Meet. Held in Promise during the Awakening Festival, this public forum between community leaders seeks majority consensus on each issue raised. The Meet continues until all items are resolved or half the participants leave.

Crime in Godsbreath is rare, and justice in this land focuses on making the wronged party whole. Decisions on how to make amends come through groups known as sevens—assemblies of the seven people who are closest at hand when an accusation of criminal behavior is made, but who have no direct stake in the outcome. For the most severe wrongs, offenders are banished to uninhabited islands, though they retain the right to travel to the Meet each year to seek reconciliation with the larger community.

THE GODS' TALE

The influence of the deities who founded Godsbreath is captured in the Covenant tales—verses of the *Awakening Song* that tell stories of the gods' past exploits and share signs of their current influence. The bright colors found on homes throughout the region each honor a Covenant god, and many people craft and carry charms to invoke a favorite god's protection.

PROCLAIMERS AND THE COVENANT

The Proclaimers of the Covenant are the acolytes of Godsbreath's deities, tasked with promoting worship of the Covenant and maintaining the *Awakening Song* as a living history of this land. They take turns traveling throughout Godsbreath, listening to deeds of local renown that could be added to the *Awakening Song*, sharing stories from other regions, and challenging people to live up to the Covenant gods' example.

The Covenant is a pantheon of deities with a particular interest in Godsbreath. They have varied alignments and interests. This local pantheon is for you to define and might include gods appropriate to your campaign's setting or deities unique to Godsbreath.

Shared Stories

Stories are the glue that binds Godsbreath together, tying its people to their ancestors who helped shape this land and passing down traditions and beliefs through all the generations since. Most people here begin conversations with "give a listen" or "tell me true" before exchanging stories—the more captivating, the better. Although this sometimes encourages exaggeration, Godsbreath's people believe you can hear truth in the telling of any tale, and all enjoy the art of a well-crafted boast.

Stories of all kinds are shared around the evening fire in the heart of each community, while folk dine on roast rabbit and hog, spoon bread, hominy, rice and gravy, corn pone, or crawfish stew. Especially captivating tales might be memorialized on a grass-woven story basket from the Nightwater Isles or added to a Ribbon family's fireside quilt, creating invaluable heirlooms protected at all costs. Truly extraordinary stories might even be captured in song by one of the Proclaimers of the Covenant. Having a story chosen is a great honor and can make alliances and invitations to adventure easier to come by.

Names

Most folk in Godsbreath go by a single name—often a nickname picked up in their youth instead of their given name—preceded by an honorific reflecting their age, profession, or standing in the community. Those too young to have an honorific may be addressed without one, though it's often wise for strangers to use a courtesy honorific—Miss, Mister, Cousin—as a sign of respect. The following are examples of common given names in Godsbreath:

Feminine. Aba, Bilah, Diya, Emilene, Essie, Sukie

Masculine. Cato, Ellis, Kumber, Mobe, Saffran, Sogo

Gender-Neutral. Deland, Holston, June, Madel, Winter

Surnames. Godskith, Grayshore, Hilltop, Longkin, Riveridge

Legends of Godsbreath

Most people in Godsbreath worship one or more of the Covenant gods, who worked together to bring the first folk to this new land. Over long generations since, these deities have stood united as the guardians of Godsbreath. But of late, they have begun to work independently to recruit and reward their own followers. Through recent prophecies known only to themselves, the members of the Covenant have learned the blood of a deity is needed to revitalize the soil of the Ribbon and stave off potential famine across Godsbreath. In response, the gods are becoming more active, shoring up their power to avoid becoming this necessary sacrifice.

Adventures in Godsbreath

Consider the plots on the Godsbreath Adventures table when planning adventures in Godsbreath.

Godsbreath Adventures

d4	Adventure
1	A pack of giant coyotes (**dire wolves**) ventures far from the Rattle, threatening harvests in the Ribbon. The pack's leader is a particularly vicious, red-furred specimen. The characters are hired to end the creatures' threat.
2	The water subsides from Cradlelace Lake, revealing a hidden house haunted by a long-limbed phantom who keeps her family of spirits trapped. A mysterious message reaches the characters, entreating them to free the captive souls.
3	A **ghost** visits the characters and claims her tragic life and death were purposefully erased from the *Awakening Song* by the people of Promise. She can't rest until her story is restored.
4	The characters discover a lost part of the *Awakening Song* that hints at what might restore fertility to the Ribbon: the lifeblood of one of the Covenant gods. One of the gods responds to this discovery, hoping to either suppress this information or act on it.

Characters from Godsbreath

If players want to create characters from Godsbreath, consider asking them the following questions during character creation:

Who in your family was memorialized in the *Awakening Song*? Why do you love or hate that your family is connected to this regional memory? Is the song true? Do you think you will be memorialized in the song?

Have you spent a harvest season in the monster-filled Rattle? How did you respond to the threats of that region? Have you come close to losing anyone you cared about there?

Do you feel close to the gods of the Covenant? Why do you feel like you have this connection? How do you honor or otherwise interact with these deities?

Soul Shaker

A grasping mass of Humanoid limbs, a soul shaker is an obsessive claimer of corpses and collector of body parts. These nightmarish creatures arise from ghoulish collections of severed limbs exposed to necromantic energies or when numerous crawling claws form a cooperative relationship.

Most of a soul shaker's victims have their vitality drained and their flesh pulverized by its many arms. However, should a soul shaker encounter someone with an impressionable mind, the creature attempts to charm the individual, using them as a lure to tempt others into its hunting grounds.

If defeated, a soul shaker disperses into several skittering, animate limbs. The terror can only truly be vanquished by destroying these disembodied appendages. If more than one of these pieces escape, the soul shaker reforms over the course of days and begins hunting once more.

Soul Shaker
Large Undead, Typically Chaotic Evil

Armor Class 13 (natural armor)
Hit Points 76 (8d10 + 32)
Speed 20 ft.

STR	DEX	CON	INT	WIS	CHA
20 (+5)	8 (−1)	18 (+4)	8 (−1)	11 (+0)	14 (+2)

Damage Resistances necrotic
Damage Immunities poison
Condition Immunities charmed, exhaustion, frightened, grappled, paralyzed, petrified, poisoned, prone, restrained
Senses blindsight 60 ft. (blind beyond this radius), passive Perception 10
Languages telepathy 60 ft.
Challenge 4 (1,100 XP)   **Proficiency Bonus** +2

Enthralled Lure (1/Day). The soul shaker can cast the *geas* spell, requiring no spell components and using Charisma as the spellcasting ability (spell save DC 12).

Reconstruction. When the soul shaker is reduced to 0 hit points, it explodes into 7 (1d4 + 5) **crawling claws**. After 6 (1d12) days, if at least two of those crawling claws are alive, they teleport to the location of the soul shaker's death and merge together, whereupon the soul shaker re-forms and regains all its hit points.

Unusual Nature. The soul shaker doesn't require air, food, drink, or sleep.

Actions

Crushing Grasp. *Melee Weapon Attack:* +7 to hit, reach 5 ft., one target. *Hit:* 14 (2d8 + 5) bludgeoning damage. If the target is a Medium or smaller creature, it is grappled (escape DC 15). The soul shaker can have only one creature grappled in this way at a time.

Bonus Actions

Consume Vitality. The soul shaker targets a creature it is grappling. If the target is not a Construct or an Undead, the target must succeed on a DC 14 Constitution saving throw or take 7 (2d6) necrotic damage. The target's hit point maximum is reduced by an amount equal to the necrotic damage taken, and the soul shaker regains hit points equal to that amount. This reduction lasts until the target finishes a long rest. The target dies if its hit point maximum is reduced to 0.

TOM BABBEY

THE FIEND OF HOLLOW MINE

AN ADVENTURE FOR 4TH-LEVEL CHARACTERS

A DEADLY MAGICAL CURSE CALLED SERENO is killing people in the arid borderlands around the city of San Citlán. After an encounter with an outlaw in the village of Milpazul, the characters learn the source of the curse is a tlacatecolo—a shape-shifting fiend. Fearing for the folk under her protection, the outlaw directs the characters to the ghost town of Hollow and its abandoned mine, where she believes the creature lurks.

When the characters explore the mine, they find a connection to a humble home in the city of San Citlán, where they learn the tlacatecolo is controlling a troubled young man named Serapio. Amid the celebration known as the Night of the Remembered, the characters must find Serapio, confront the evil within him, and destroy it if they can.

BACKGROUND

Twenty years ago in San Citlán, an ambitious sorcerer named Orencio made a bargain with the demon lord Pazuzu to gain magical power, a deal that resulted in the deaths of many of his peers. Months later, Orencio's partner, Rosa, found evidence of the profane oaths he had sworn, revealed his crimes, and witnessed his execution.

After his death, Orencio bargained with Pazuzu to avoid eternal suffering. The demon lord allowed Orencio to remain in his court and serve him in exchange for the soul of the sorcerer's firstborn child, to be taken when the child reached the age of twenty. The sorcerer agreed, believing he had no children. He didn't realize Rosa had borne him a son, Serapio, a few months after his death.

As Serapio's twentieth birthday approaches, Pazuzu's power begins to consume the young man. While waiting for Serapio's final fall into corruption, the demon lord sent a faithful worshiper named Itzmin del Prado to watch over the youth. Itzmin works to convince Serapio to accept Pazuzu's power in exchange for undoing the affliction that has transformed the young man into a fiend. Serapio clings to his humanity, unaware of his part in Itzmin's plans to spread a curse across San Citlán.

PRONUNCIATION GUIDE

In Citlanés, the language spoken alongside Common in the region around San Citlán, vowels with an acute accent indicate stress on their syllable, the letter ñ sounds like the *ny* in *canyon*, *ch* is pronounced as in *charity*. The San Citlán Pronunciations table shows how to pronounce key names in this adventure.

SAN CITLÁN PRONUNCIATIONS

Name	Pronunciation
Doña Estela	doe-nya ehs-TAY-la
Doña Rosa	doe-nya ROH-sa
Evaristo	ay-vah-REES-toh
Itzmin del Prado	EETS-meen del PRA-doh
Los Gavilanes	los gah-vee-LAHN-es
Milpazul	mil-PAH-zul
Olvidado	ohl-vee-DAH-doh
Orencio	oh-REN-cee-oh
Paloma	pah-LOH-mah
Rufina	roo-FEE-nah
San Citlán	san see-TLAHN
Serapio	say-RAH-pee-oh
Sereno	say-RAY-noh
Teocín	tay-oh-SEEN
Tlacatecolo	tlah-kah-tee-KOH-loh

SETTING THE ADVENTURE

San Citlán and its borderlands can appear in any setting. The following are suggestions for contextualizing the adventure in a wider world:

Through the Radiant Citadel. Characters traveling from the Radiant Citadel arrive near the Ruisenor Peaks, a few hours travel from Milpazul. You can use the "San Citlán Gazetteer" section at the end of this adventure as a starting point to detail the region however you please.

GHOULS DRAG A FRESH VICTIM INTO THE DEPTHS OF HOLLOW MINE.

Eberron. San Citlán might appear between the Blade Desert and Endworld Mountains in eastern Khorvaire, a location that might lead you to add more elves and dinosaurs into the mix, given the proximity of Valenar and the Talenta Plains.

Forgotten Realms. This adventure could easily be placed on the edge of Anauroch, potentially along either the Graycloak Hills or Desertmouth Mountains. The lands east of Tethyr or the mountainous reaches of Chessenta might also accommodate this rugged region.

CHARACTER HOOKS

Consider the following suggestions to involve the characters in this adventure's plot:

The Dead Return. The characters are heading to San Citlán to enjoy the food, parades, and celebrations of the Night of the Remembered (see the accompanying sidebar)—and perhaps to reconnect with a departed ancestor or loved one.

Healing the Plague. The characters have a friend of a friend who lives in the village of Milpazul. This acquaintance writes to them, asking for help investigating a wave of strange ailments and fiendish attacks plaguing her community.

STARTING THE ADVENTURE

The adventure begins just outside the village of Milpazul, a tiny community a few hours' journey from the city of San Citlán.

Once the players are ready, describe their characters' approach to the village. Read or paraphrase the following description:

> Clouds rush overhead and dust swirls across the road to the village of Milpazul, which sits atop a hill overlooking a vast, semi-arid valley. The road ends at a wooden archway in a low, dry-stone wall that surrounds most of the settlement. As you near, a man on horseback spurs his mount and vanishes into the village.

The characters approach Milpazul at the same time as a group of bounty hunters searching for the outlaw Paloma. The man on horseback is the group's lookout; when he sees the characters, he assumes they're either a rival band of bounty hunters or Paloma's bandit allies. Characters who have a passive Wisdom (Perception) score of 12 or higher notice a trail of dust rising from the opposite side of the village, suggesting a group entering the community.

AMBUSH AT THE ARCHWAY

As the characters reach the archway entrance to the village, the character who has the highest passive Wisdom (Perception) score is the first to notice something is wrong:

> Within the waist-high village wall, a dozen or so wood-and-adobe houses surround a well. A worn-out sign hangs crookedly from the arch, proclaiming in fading blue paint, "Welcome to Milpazul," but that welcome is contradicted by angry voices and cries of pain coming from behind a building.

The bounty hunters have attacked several villagers who questioned their intentions. The other locals have retreated to their homes while several bounty hunter guards have set an ambush for anyone coming down the road, crouching low and hiding behind the wall near the archway.

A character who is looking for signs of trouble and succeeds on a DC 13 Wisdom (Perception) check notices villagers peering from their homes. A character who gets a 15 or higher on the check also hears movement behind the wall. As soon as the characters advance or attempt to fall back from the arch, the bounty hunters spring their ambush:

> Seven figures spring up from behind the wall, aiming longbows at you.
>
> "Clear out!" one of them shouts. "La Paloma pays for her crimes this day!" Without hesitation, they attack.

Seven bounty hunters (use the **scout** stat block) shoot from behind the waist-high wall, which grants them half cover against anyone attacking from the other side. They draw shortswords if the characters close for melee. If three of the bounty hunters fall, the survivors quickly retreat to their nearby **riding horses** and flee the village.

Characters can learn about Paloma and the crimes of which she is accused from any defeated bounty hunters who survive the fight (see the "Learning about Paloma" section). One of the bounty hunters who dies or is captured during the fight carries a wanted poster depicting a stern old woman with the name "Paloma" below the portrait and offering a 500 gp reward for her capture.

WELCOME TO MILPAZUL

Once the characters deal with the bounty hunters, a handful of locals thank the characters for their assistance and welcome them to Milpazul. Not everyone is enthused, though. Some villagers regard adventurers with distrust, fearing they'll bring more trouble.

ENTERING THE VILLAGE

As the characters progress into the village, read the following:

> In the distance, a slender figure tends to the wounded villagers, who respond with heartfelt gratitude. As the individual approaches, you realize they are more than simply thin—the figure is a skeleton clothed in a yellow-and-magenta dress, with many colorful bead necklaces hanging from the exposed vertebrae of their neck.
>
> "You must be parched after that fight," they say. "How about some drinks, friends? On the house!"

The name of the friendly skeleton is Rufina, and they own the village tavern. As thanks for dealing with the bounty hunters, Rufina invites the characters to the tavern for refreshments and rest, and happily helps acquaint the characters with the area.

RUFINA

Formerly a human, Rufina is now an olvidado—a deceased person who remained behind after the Night of the Remembered. Rufina doesn't know how or why they don't pass on to the afterlife. Although beings like Rufina are uncommon in the region, they're not unheard of, and the skeleton is a well-liked member of the community. Rufina is neutral good and uses the **commoner** stat block, but is Undead and doesn't require air, food, drink, or sleep.

Rufina has been sheltering Paloma in the cellar of the tavern; after witnessing the characters' prowess, the olvidado wonders if the adventurers might be able to help her.

LEARNING ABOUT PALOMA

While no one is willing to discuss Paloma's whereabouts, a character who succeeds on a DC 14 Charisma (Persuasion) check can gather the following information about the so-called outlaw from Rufina or the other villagers:

- Paloma is seen as a hero by the poor. Her band raids the estates and caravans of corrupt landowners and shares the captured wealth with folk who need it.
- She initially ran afoul of the law years ago when she was falsely accused of a crime.
- Paloma and her band were recently attacked by someone or something on the road. Most of the band were killed, but Paloma's body wasn't found.

CURSED VILLAGERS

As they walk through the village, the characters notice many locals huddled in corners, bundled in blanket-like sarapes and trembling with cold despite it being a warm but cloudy day. If asked about them, Rufina replies that these unfortunates have caught sereno, an ailment seemingly spread by bitterly cold winds. Folk who have fallen ill speak of those winds blowing mostly at night, and Rufina warns the characters against staying out after dark. Although no one in Milpazul knows it, the sickness stems from the youth Serapio, who has transformed into a tlacatecolo (detailed at the end of this adventure) and hunts at night.

A character who examines a villager with sereno and succeeds on a DC 14 Intelligence (Arcana) or Wisdom (Medicine) check determines that sereno is not a disease but a curse.

SERENO

Sereno is a deadly magical affliction that inflicts a supernatural chill on its victims and eventually kills them. A creature cursed with sereno is poisoned, can't regain hit points, and must make a DC 13 Constitution saving throw at the end of every hour, gaining 1 level of exhaustion on a failed save. The creature automatically succeeds on this saving throw if it is in sunlight. Sereno can be undone by magic that ends poison or disease, like *lesser restoration*, but only while the victim is in direct sunlight.

Sereno is inflicted by an insidious, shapeshifting fiend known as a tlacatecolo. If a tlacatecolo that afflicted one or more creatures with the curse dies, the curse ends for its victims. See the "Tlacatecolo" section at the end of this adventure for more details.

PULQUERÍA

The front wall of Rufina's tavern—called a *pulquería*, as it specializes in a local beverage called pulque—is plastered with portraits of missing persons and requests for help.

When the characters enter the tavern, read the following:

> The pulquería's walls are painted with murals that depict a series of armed conflicts, with locals celebrating victory at the end. A candlelit altar behind the bar includes a painted portrait of an elderly woman, which is surrounded by yellow marigolds and offerings of drinks and cactus fruits.
>
> Two dwarves seated at one of the three tables in the pulquería glance at you curiously.

The dwarves are revolutionaries (**veterans**) who hang out in the tavern to protect Paloma. They won't engage the characters unless Paloma or Rufina is threatened.

Rufina offers the characters pulque, an alcoholic beverage made from fermented agave sap and the only drink Rufina remembers how to make. The olvidado also offers cactus, beans, and tortillas to

PALOMA

ADRIÁN IBARRA LUGO

SERAPIO

any characters who are hungry and has a spare room if anyone needs to rest.

Characters who chat with Rufina learn the following:

- The mural was painted by Rufina and is an abstraction of San Citlán's history (detailed in the "San Citlán" section at the end of this adventure).
- The altar behind the counter is an *ofrenda*, a memorial made to commune with the dead during the Night of the Remembered festivities, which begins in the coming days and will continue for several nights. This ofrenda is dedicated to Rufina's late daughter, Carmen.

Meeting Paloma

As conversation dies down, Paloma emerges from a door leading to the cellar and approaches the characters. She is wrapped in a rebozo and suffers from sereno with 3 levels of exhaustion. If the characters threaten to take her for the bounty, the dwarf **veterans** rush to protect her, and Rufina warns the characters that not just the villagers, but the folk of the entire region, will turn against them if they proceed.

Paloma

Paloma (chaotic good, gnome **assassin**) leads a band of revolutionaries in the borderlands around San Citlán. She was falsely accused of rustling, defended herself from the unjust arrest, and was charged with attempted murder as a result. She fled to the Indigo Desert and joined an outlaw band, quickly climbing the ranks to become the leader. While traveling across the region, Paloma saw many injustices. She has recently allied with local revolutionaries opposing exploitation and corruption in the region, and she is already considered one of the revolutionaries' leaders.

Personality Trait. "I've seen much and have a story for every occasion."

Ideal. "I lost most of my life to others' corruption. I'll risk what I have left to bring an end to it."

Bond. "San Citlán is my home, and no one will ever drive me out of my own home."

Flaw. "I don't care who I endanger to further our cause."

Paloma's Request

Paloma explains to the characters that she needs the help of trustworthy adventurers to find the source of sereno and put an end to it. She goes on to share the following information:

- The sereno outbreak has killed many since it began a few months ago.
- One night while Paloma and three allies were traveling, trying to determine the source of the outbreak, a strange owl revealed itself to be a terrible fiend. They wounded the fiend, but it escaped.
- Two of her companions died in the battle. The third—a druid named Lope—died of sereno soon after. Lope had been researching the curse and believed the fiend they saw was behind its spread.
- Lope's research suggested killing the fiend will end the curse for all those suffering from sereno.
- Scouts have seen owls and strange figures going in and out of a mine near the supposedly abandoned mining town of Hollow.

The Hunt Begins

Paloma offers 100 gp per character for the party's assistance, and she gives them her *ring of jumping* if they agree to investigate the mine and slay the fiend if they find it. She gives them directions to Hollow, an abandoned settlement about 14 miles away and 4 miles north of San Citlán. She warns against going at night, lest the characters suffer her fate.

Rumors of Hollow

If the characters ask around Milpazul about Hollow, they learn the information at the start of the "A Town Called Hollow" section. Additionally, a local overhears their inquiries and shares a chilling story:

ADRIÁN IBARRA LUGO

> "I was riding by Hollow after dark, trying to get home, when I saw movement up by the old mine entrance. Two gaunt figures were dragging some poor soul into the mine—had it wrapped up tight. They looked like twin death, they did. I'll never forget their hissing and their slithering, horrid tongues. As a mercy, the body they were dragging looked like it was already dead. I rode on, I tell you. I didn't look back."

THE FIEND'S IDENTITY

The fiend that Paloma's band is searching for is Serapio, a taciturn young man who lives in San Citlán with his mother, Doña Rosa. The son of the evil sorcerer Orencio, Serapio suffers from the corruption of the demon lord Pazuzu and has transformed into a tlacatecolo (detailed at the end of the adventure). His fiendish nature compels him to spread his curse and feed on the afflicted. When he's himself, Serapio is terrified and doesn't understand why he's changing. When he's overwhelmed by fiendish influence, he's ruled by the evil of his new form.

FAMILY MATTERS

Serapio's mother, Doña Rosa, is unaware of her son's transformation and believes he's in some trouble that he's hiding from her. She never told him about his biological father, Orencio. Years ago, Rosa lived among the San Citlánian elite, but after Orencio's execution, she fled the city to escape his followers. Starting a new life, Rosa married a man named Evaristo who helped raise Serapio. Evaristo died three months ago from a sudden illness. In truth, Evaristo was the first victim of sereno. Soon after Evaristo died, when Serapio showed signs of his own strange affliction, Rosa decided to return to San Citlán to confront her past. She believes the cult Orencio was involved with is somehow responsible, but she's found no evidence of this thus far.

PAZUZU'S SERVANT

When the wicked sorcerer Orencio was executed, his protégé, Itzmin, made his own pact with Pazuzu. Two decades later, Itzmin has become a corrupt politician in San Citlán who serves Pazuzu as Orencio did, using the demon lord's favor to secure economic and political power. Under Pazuzu's guidance, Itzmin has befriended Serapio, arranging for the young man to get part-time jobs for a produce distributor and an ironworks warehouse he owns. As Serapio comes further under Pazuzu's control, Itzmin uses the youth's fiendish hunger to sow chaos in the borderlands.

A TOWN CALLED HOLLOW

The mining town of Pontezuela once thrived at the southern extent of the mountains known as the Silver Veins. That changed when the silver ore for which the range was named ran dry. Folks started referring to the mine as "hollow" for its exhausted resources, and discovery of monstrous bones in its depths inspired talk of the site being cursed. Nowadays, "Hollow" is the only name most people call the settlement and its mine. Both were abandoned years ago, making the mine a perfect place for Itzmin and Pazuzu's faithful to hold their secret meetings.

TRAVELING TO HOLLOW MINE

The journey from Milpazul to Hollow takes just over half a day at a normal pace. If you want to highlight the dangers of the borderlands, add an encounter or two along the way. **Perytons** are common threats in the region, and **ettins** sometimes descend from the mountains to raid farmsteads.

NIGHT TRAVEL

If the characters ignore Paloma's warning and travel at night, after a few hours of travel, Serapio sees them and flies overhead in his owl form. Though his mind is twisted by fiendish hunger, he is too wary to approach adventurers. A character who succeeds on a DC 14 Wisdom (Perception) check sees sudden movement in the darkness overhead as a spotted owl silently circles the party and then flies away.

HOLLOW

When characters approach Hollow, read the following description:

> A decrepit town spreads out along the road ahead, its weathered shacks creaking in the wind. A dozen or so armed figures move in and out of the structures, which appear long abandoned. An opulent coach, looking distinctly out of place, is parked amid the buildings with its curtains drawn.

The road leading to the buildings is littered with items abandoned by the former residents. The armed figures are twelve **bandits** working for Itzmin, who has been buying property in the area to control access to the mine. The bandits won't allow the characters to access the mine without their boss's permission. If any characters ask questions or make trouble, the bandits point them to the carriage.

If the characters approach the impressive carriage, Itzmin emerges.

ITZMIN

A spiteful tiefling in his late forties, Itzmin del Prado is a chaotic evil **cult fanatic**. He's also a politician and part of San Citlán's ruling council, the Trecena, where he serves as Councilor of Arms. The public gave him the moniker *Astaverde* (meaning "green horn") for his jadeite prosthetic horn.

Following the death of his mother, a celebrated military general, Itzmin squandered his family's fortune, and his family name became synonymous with disgrace. Desperate to regain his former glory, Itzmin sought the guidance of the cultist Orencio and forged his own pact with Pazuzu, offering his obedience in exchange for secrets that could be leveraged against San Citlán's elite.

Personality Trait. "I can't stand anyone treating me as their lesser."

Ideal. "I'll do whatever it takes to gain the upper hand in any situation."

Bond. "I must restore my family to its former glory."

Flaw. "I value prestige over security."

ITZMIN'S GOALS

Itzmin wants to use Serapio's corruption to advance Pazuzu's wishes. And the more chaos reigns in the borderlands, the less organized the revolutionaries can be, which benefits Itzmin's political agenda. He's currently in Hollow to cover his tracks by razing the town, caving in the mine, and destroying any evidence of the rites that have taken place there.

MEETING ITZMIN

Itzmin introduces himself as the owner of the mine and the township. He talks of hearing reports of a disease festering in town and says he plans to burn the abandoned houses to prevent it from spreading. He is dismissive of any suggestion that sereno isn't a disease. If the characters talk about entering the mine, Itzmin advises against it but doesn't stop them. If he is threatened in any way, he orders his bandits to attack and flees in his coach.

CAVE-IN!

At some point after the characters enter the mine, Itzmin's bandits detonate alchemical charges to collapse the entrance. Wherever the characters are in the mine, they hear a thunderous blast from above. If they return to mine's entrance, they find the cavern has collapsed, sealed by tons of impassable rubble. A character who is proficient with alchemist's supplies or who succeeds on a DC 12 Intelligence (Nature) check confirms that the collapse was deliberate.

To escape, the characters must find the alternative exit in the depths of the mine.

HOLLOW MINE

If the characters descend into the abandoned mine, they discover that it isn't empty and that the fiend they search for is at the center of a greater mystery.

HOLLOW MINE FEATURES

Hollow Mine has the following features:

Ceilings. Most ceilings are about 10 feet high, except for the ceiling in area H5.

Light. None of the mine's locations are lit unless otherwise indicated.

Wailing Wind. The structure of the mine and the elevation difference between its shafts funnels a strong wind through the tunnels. Gusts of air hiss and howl, imposing disadvantage on Wisdom (Perception) checks that rely on hearing.

HOLLOW MINE LOCATIONS

The following locations are keyed to map 4.1.

H1: MINE ENTRANCE

Loose planks cover the entrance to the mine. Once characters enter the mine, read the following text:

> The mine's entrance leads into a large cavern supported by wooden beams. At the chamber's center, a derelict wooden elevator rattles in the wind that rushes from the depths of a crumbling mineshaft.

The stone of the mine entrance cavern is crumbling badly, but a character who has the Stonecunning trait or who succeeds on a DC 16 Intelligence (Nature) check can tell the cavern is in no immediate danger of collapsing. See the "Cave-In!" section for details on how that might change.

Elevator. The elevator is rusted in place, and the shaft it once traversed is depicted as shaded spaces on map 4.1. A character who examines it and succeeds on a DC 15 Intelligence (Investigation) check recognizes that the elevator will collapse under any significant weight. If 100 pounds or more is placed on the elevator platform, it collapses. Any creature standing on the platform at the time drops 100 feet into area H5, taking 35 (10d6) bludgeoning damage from the fall.

Hidden Entrance. The people of Hollow sealed a tunnel leading to the mine's lower levels on the northwest wall after a number of explorers got lost in the mine. With a successful DC 12 Wisdom (Perception) check, a character perceives a section of the wall rattling in the wind, discovering a wooden door that was hidden behind a pile of rocks.

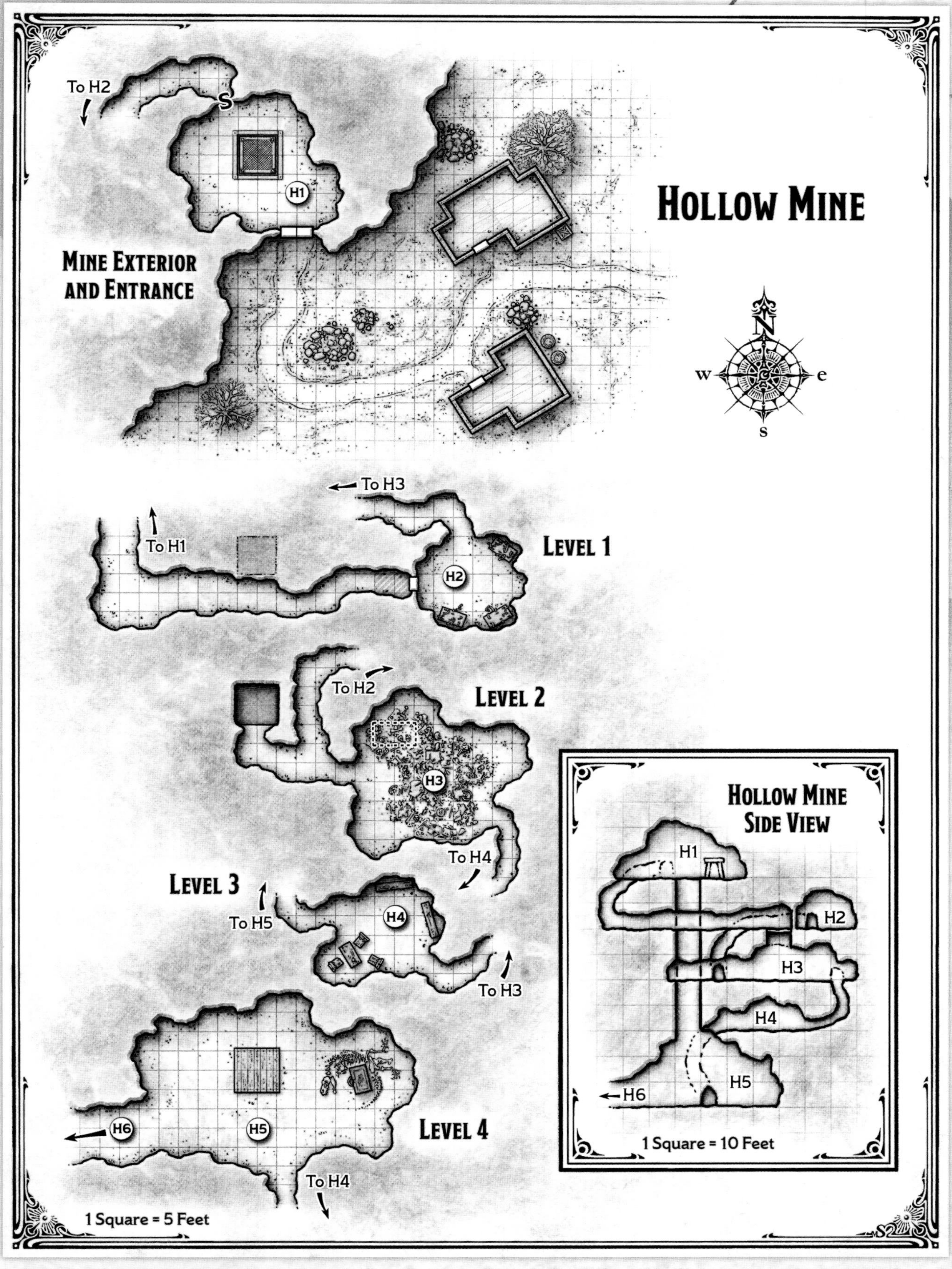

Map 4.1: Hollow Mine

To H2

S

H1

MINE EXTERIOR
AND ENTRANCE

HOLLOW MINE

N

W   E

S

To H3

To H1

LEVEL 1

H2

To H2

LEVEL 2

H3

HOLLOW MINE
SIDE VIEW

To H4

H1

LEVEL 3

To H5

H4

H2

To H3

H3

H4

LEVEL 4

H5

H6

H5

To H4

H6

1 Square = 10 Feet

1 Square = 5 Feet

H2: Teocín's Quarters

A makeshift wooden door blocks the entrance to this chamber. Candlelight shines through the cracks. A character who listens at the door and succeeds on a DC 13 Wisdom (Perception) check hears growling beyond it.

Passwall Trap. A 5th-level *glyph of warding* holding a *passwall* spell is inscribed on the floor in front of the door. Characters can spot the glyph with a successful DC 15 Intelligence (Investigation) check. If someone opens the door while standing on the glyph, the glyph triggers and casts its spell on the floor around it, opening a pit into area H3. Each creature standing in the shaded spaces in front of the door on map 4.1 falls 30 feet into area H3 and takes 10 (3d6) bludgeoning damage. The glyph's effects can be avoided by opening the door from a distance, which prevents the spell from being triggered.

Once the characters can see into this area, read the following:

> The floor of this chamber is slick with blood. Two of three tables have growling corpses strapped to them. A frenzied woman brandishes a knife as she undoes the straps.

This chamber is the workspace of Teocín, a **cult fanatic** dedicated to Pazuzu. As soon as the characters enter, Teocín releases the two **ghouls** on the tables and joins them as they attack.

Teocín. The cultist Teocín uses this laboratory to research ways to corrupt the magic of the Night of the Remembered. Itzmin has convinced Serapio that Teocín is trying to find a cure for him, so the young man leaves her alone. For months, Teocín's ghouls have killed animals, hunters, prospectors, and others wandering the borderlands so Teocín can study and raise the dead using profane knowledge she gleans from unholy rites.

If Teocín is captured, she says nothing to the characters, but they can learn of her goals, Orencio, and Pazuzu by looking through her notes—dozens of filthy, scrawl-covered pages strewn about the room.

Treasure. Teocín keeps the belongings of her victims in a chest: 2,500 cp, 950 sp, and jewelry and other trinkets worth 90 gp. She also wears a *periapt of health* to avoid the threat of disease that comes from working with the dead.

H3: Corpse Disposal

> The stench here is horrendous. Hundreds of humanoid and animal bones fill the chamber in charnel heaps.

Teocín uses this chamber to dispose of her failed experiments. Two **ochre jellies** feed on the remains and are dissolving meals deep under piles of bones. They emerge, oozing up through the bones, as soon as they sense movement.

If the mine entrance has not yet collapsed and all the characters are in or near this room, Itzmin detonates his charges (see the "Cave-In!" section earlier in the adventure).

H4: Serapio's Quarters

> Damaged furniture has been dragged into this area to create a study. Two bookshelves stand alongside chairs and a desk covered with papers. The rough cave walls feature gouges, as if some powerful creature dragged its claws across the stone.

Itzmin set up these living quarters for Serapio, hoping to entice him away from his mother and make the mine feel homier. Serapio is not present when the characters arrive but often isolates himself here to hide his monstrous shape. Silence and isolation calm him, as does his hobby of sketching. When the corruption becomes too much, Serapio scratches the walls with his fiendish talons.

Makeshift Library. The bookshelves hold a mix of fiction, histories, and more. A character who scans the shelves and succeeds on a DC 14 Intelligence (Investigation) check finds a *spell scroll* of *lesser restoration* and a book containing rituals for the *alarm*, *find familiar*, and *illusory script* spells.

Drawing Desk. Nubs of charcoal and drawings are scattered across the desk. The sketches range from mundane portraits and cityscapes to ghastly renditions of demonic faces with saucer-sized eyes. Any character who knows San Citlán recognizes the cityscape drawings as depicting features from San Citlán's Los Gavilanes district, the city's old town. If the characters don't know the city, a number of the drawings have the legend "Los Gavilanes" on them.

Characters looking through the drawings spot two things of note:

- One sketch depicts an elegantly dressed tiefling, whom the characters recognize as Itzmin if they met him outside.

- Numerous cityscapes show a distinctive vecindad, one of the manor houses converted into apartments that are common in Los Gavilanes. Many of these sketches bear the caption "Home" written in a shaky hand. This is the vecindad of Doña Rosa.

Hidden Locket. A character searching the desk's otherwise empty drawers finds half of a hinged silver locket wrapped in paper. The locket contains a tiny pencil portrait of a warmly smiling woman. The characters likely have no way of knowing it yet, but this is Serapio's mother, Doña Rosa. The other half of the locket is in Serapio's room in San Citlán.

H5: Wailing Cavern

The wailing wind that gusts intermittently through the mine rises to a continuous howl in this cavern. The elevator shaft in area H1 ends in this cavern's ceiling, and the elevator cage might have crashed to the floor below if the characters tried to use it.

> This sizable cavern's ceiling is thirty feet high, and strange symbols are scrawled across its walls. The skeletons of two huge creatures are here, one embedded in the east wall and the other coiled around an altar covered in filthy feathers.

Itzmin uses this cavern as a secret space to worship Pazuzu, performing rites that would draw attention in San Citlán.

Demonic Scrawls. The symbols scrawled across the walls are in Abyssal and represent omens and prophecies sent by Pazuzu to Itzmin. A character who understands Abyssal or succeeds on a DC 13 Intelligence (Arcana or Religion) check gleans that an innocent creature is being twisted into an envoy of Pazuzu and is spreading corruption through the region.

Dinosaur Skeletons. These giant skeletons were unearthed shortly before the silver in the mine ran out, inspiring talk that the mine was cursed. When Teocín first joined Itzmin here, she drew on the power of Pazuzu to turn these skeletons into guardians.

If a character approaches within 10 feet of the altar, the two skeletons animate and attack. They both use the **allosaurus** stat block, with these changes:

- They are Undead.
- They are vulnerable to bludgeoning damage, immune to poison damage, and immune to exhaustion and the poisoned condition.
- They have darkvision out to a range of 60 feet.

H6: Tunnel to San Citlán

> Eerie scrawls cover the walls of this long, straight tunnel. A breeze flows from that darkness, carrying a faint scent of smoke. Foul-looking feathers litter the floor, and claw marks gouge the stone walls.

This ancient tunnel runs south toward San Citlán. Itzmin, Teocín, and Serapio travel this passage from the city to the mine without attracting attention. After the demolition of area H1, this tunnel is the characters' only escape route from the mine.

The feathers here are unnatural, and any character who has proficiency in the Religion skill can tell they are from a fiendish creature. The claw marks match the marks in area H4. A character who can automatically sense direction or who succeeds on a DC 12 Wisdom (Survival) check knows the tunnel leads south toward San Citlán.

Dry Cenote

The tunnel leads the characters to a dry cenote in the district of Los Gavilanes within San Citlán. The cenote was mined when the city was first established, but these mines were abandoned centuries ago, leaving old scaffolding that can be used to climb approximately 100 feet to the surface.

Impoverished citizens dwell amid the scaffolding. They're surprised to see strangers emerge from the depths but don't bother the characters. If questioned about anything strange they might have seen, these locals prove tight-lipped. Should a character succeed on a DC 12 Charisma (Persuasion) check or offer at least 1 sp in exchange for information, someone admits having seen a strange spotted owl flying in and out of the cenote at night.

Night of the Remembered

Emerging from the cenote, the characters find themselves in San Citlán in the midst of the Night of the Remembered celebrations. The characters can make their way through the city without incident, but the festivities are unignorable.

> Colorful flowers and paper decorations hang between buildings, and delicious scents waft from the food stalls at every street corner. Locals wearing elaborate masks and costumes celebrate in the streets. Well-dressed skeletons walk alongside pompous-looking business barons, and mischievous children in devil costumes poke at onlookers with toy tridents.

A character who succeeds on a DC 14 Intelligence (History or Religion) check knows the costumes represent La Catrina, patron spirit of the city; Don Roque, a long-dead politician who became the satirical face of the government; and Los Diablitos, comical renditions of fiends from local fables.

THE FIEND'S TRAIL

While the characters explored Hollow Mine, a desperate Serapio watched the preparations for the Night of the Remembered in San Citlán. Overcome by guilt, Serapio managed to fight back his fiendish urges long enough to resume his human form. He confessed to his mother, then fled his home as he felt himself transforming again. For the better part of the day since, he has flown around in spotted owl form, trying to decide what path to take.

The characters can learn about his plight at Doña Rosa's vecindad, which they might find in multiple ways:

- A character who has a passive Wisdom (Perception) score of 12 or higher notices folk on the street pointing at the sky. If asked, the people say an owl has been flying over the district during daylight—a strange portent on the Night of the Remembered. The characters can determine the owl's course by succeeding on a DC 14 Wisdom (Perception or Survival) check, which leads them to Doña Rosa's feather-littered vecindad.
- A character can show the locket containing Doña Rosa's portrait to passersby. If they do so and succeed on a DC 14 Charisma (Persuasion) check, a character finds a local or recognizes the picture and provides directions to Doña Rosa's home.
- If the characters kept Serapio's cityscape drawings, they can use it to find the vecindad with a successful DC 14 Wisdom (Survival) check.

As the characters near the vecindad, folk on the street can direct the party toward the old manor house if the characters show them Serapio's sketches. If the characters found the half-locket in area H4 of Hollow Mine, they can use a *locate object* spell to find the other half of the locket once they are within 1,000 feet of the vecindad.

DOÑA ROSA'S VECINDAD

The old manor house stands on a quiet street. Read the following to set the scene:

> This large manor shows its age, but the building is well cared for and, like the rest of the city, cheerfully decorated for the impending festival.

THE LIVING AND THE DEAD CELEBRATE THE NIGHT OF THE REMEMBERED IN SAN CITLÁN.

> A colorful altar stands opposite the entrance, its tiers covered with sketched portraits. You hear sobbing coming from one of the apartments.

Most of the folk in the vecindad are celebrating, but Doña Rosa weeps alone in her apartment. Unless the characters attempt to sneak in, Doña Rosa hears them approach and opens the door.

Characters who saw Serapio's locket identify Doña Rosa as the woman in the portrait. If the characters are armed, she faces them defiantly, asking, "Are you here to kill my son?" The group's answer determines how she engages with them.

Doña Rosa

If the characters describe the creature they're looking for, Doña Rosa (neutral good, human **commoner**) invites them into her home and tells them there is much they don't know about this fiend. Use the following information to guide the conversation:

- The creature the characters hunt is named Serapio. He is Doña Rosa's son, not a monster.
- She had thought Serapio was ill, but he confessed his secret earlier that day and fled.
- Serapio's father, Orencio, was a sorcerer who consorted with demons. He was executed years ago after Doña Rosa exposed his deeds.
- Doña Rosa believes Orencio or the cult he served is responsible for Serapio's curse.
- She can share any of the details from the "Family Matters" section earlier in the adventure.

A Mother's Request. Doña Rosa asks the characters to spare Serapio and bring him to her, promising to look after him until she can find him help. She doesn't know where he has gone, though.

If the characters name or describe Itzmin, Rosa knows him as Serapio's employer. She doesn't trust him, as his friendliness rings false.

If the characters don't agree (or if they insist on killing the fiend), Doña Rosa orders them to leave. Learning more from her requires effective roleplaying to win her over, as well as a successful DC 13 Charisma (Persuasion) check.

Inside the Apartment

Doña Rosa's tiny apartment consists of a living room and a bedroom.

Living Room. A corner of the living room features an ofrenda with the portrait of a stern-looking man on top. If asked, Rosa identifies the man as her late husband and Serapio's stepfather, Evaristo. If a character treats her kindly or succeeds on a DC 12 Charisma (Persuasion) check, Rosa says that Evaristo died of an affliction the characters recognize as sereno, and that Serapio confessed to being inadvertently responsible.

Bedroom. The bedroom is split by a wooden screen with bedrolls on each side. The walls on Serapio's side are lined with drawings. The other half of his locket hangs on the wall near his bedroll. This is the top half, and no picture is inside.

Offerings for the Dead

After the characters speak with Doña Rosa, they see other residents of the vecindad pausing to decorate or say short prayers at the communal altar. These locals politely invite characters to help them.

Setting an Ofrenda. The shared altar has enough space for each character to set a small ofrenda. Locals guide them through the process:

- The altar must be decorated properly with candles and yellow marigolds (provided by the locals).
- While it is customary to have a portrait of the deceased on the ofrenda, it's not a requirement.
- Offerings might include any kind of food and drink that the deceased enjoyed in life or small curios.

A character who sets an ofrenda communes with the soul they're honoring and receives the Guidance of the Remembered charm.

ADRIAN IBARRA LUGO

Guidance of the Remembered. A deceased ancestor or loved one provides you with guidance, granting you insight via a charm (a type of supernatural gift detailed in the *Dungeon Master's Guide*). You can cast *speak with dead* during a long rest to contact the spirit of a friend or family member without that spirit's corpse. The spirit's answers to your questions manifest as whispers only you can hear. The charm does not function if the spirit you try to contact is Undead or was the target of *speak with dead* within the last 10 days. Once you use this charm, it vanishes from you.

ITZMIN'S MISSION

While the characters speak with his mother, Serapio meets with Itzmin at a metalworks Itzmin owns and recounts his confession to his mother. Itzmin reassures the youth that after he attends to some business, they can return to Hollow Mine. That unnamed business is the murder of Doña Rosa, whom Itzmin believes knows too much.

If Itzmin died or was captured in Hollow, one of his **cult fanatic** protégés meets Serapio in the warehouse and takes Itzmin's place in the following chase. The characters might recognize the protégé from Serapio's drawings, or Doña Rosa can identify them as one of Itzmin's people.

As the characters leave the vecindad, they spot Itzmin or his replacement approaching. As soon as he notices the characters, he flees.

PARADE CHASE

Itzmin tries to lose the characters by running into a crowd celebrating the Night of the Remembered—ultimately headed for the metalworks where Serapio hides. However, the characters can give chase.

After rolling initiative, each participant in the chase can take one action and move on its turn. Itzmin begins 120 feet ahead of the pursuers. Track the distance between Itzmin and the pursuers, and designate the pursuer closest to them as the lead. The lead pursuer might change from round to round.

DASHING

During the chase, a participant can freely use the Dash action a number of times equal to 3 + its Constitution modifier. Each additional Dash action it takes requires the creature to succeed on a DC 10 Constitution check at the end of its turn or gain 1 level of exhaustion. A participant drops out of the chase if its exhaustion reaches level 5, since its speed becomes 0. A creature can remove the levels of exhaustion it gained during the chase by finishing a short or long rest.

SPELLS AND ATTACKS

A chase participant can make attacks and cast spells against other creatures within range. Apply the normal rules for cover, terrain, and so on to these actions. Chase participants can't normally make opportunity attacks against each other, since they are all assumed to be moving in the same direction at the same time.

CHASE COMPLICATIONS

Complications occur randomly during the chase. Each participant rolls on the Parade Chase Complications table at the end of its turn. If a complication occurs, it affects the next chase participant in the initiative order, not the participant who rolled the die. The participant who rolled the die or the participant affected by the complication can spend inspiration to negate the complication.

PARADE CHASE COMPLICATIONS

d10	Complication
1	A 20-foot-tall, papier mâché skeleton puppet walks across the street. Make a DC 10 Dexterity saving throw to avoid being stepped on. On a failed check, you take 5 (2d4) bludgeoning damage and fall prone.
2	Fireworks go off nearby. Make a DC 10 Constitution saving throw. On a failed save, you are blinded by smoke until the end of your turn. While blinded, your speed is halved.
3	Centaur acrobats are performing in your path. Make a DC 15 Dexterity (Acrobatics) check. On a success, they lift you from the waist and speed you forward 30 feet. On a failed check, you fall prone.
4	Peaceful spectral dancers fill the street. Make a DC 15 Charisma (Performance) check to flow with their movements. On a failed check, they impede your sight and count as 10 feet of difficult terrain.
5	A religious procession blocks your way. Make a DC 10 Intelligence (Religion) check to recognize their customs and move respectfully among them. On a success, a thankful cleric casts *bless* on you. On a failed check, they cast *bane* instead (save DC 14).
6–10	No complication

ENDING THE CHASE

The chase ends when either side gives up the chase, when Itzmin escapes, or when the pursuers are close enough to catch Itzmin. If neither side gives up the chase, Itzmin makes a Dexterity (Stealth) check at the end of each round, after every participant in the chase has taken its turn. The chase's crowded surroundings give Itzmin advantage on this check. If the lead pursuer has proficiency in Survival,

Itzmin loses advantage. The check's result is compared to the passive Wisdom (Perception) scores of the pursuers.

If Itzmin is never out of the lead pursuer's sight, the check fails automatically. Otherwise, if the result of Itzmin's check is greater than the highest passive Wisdom (Perception) score, he escapes. If not, the chase continues for another round.

If the characters catch Itzmin, he tells them where Serapio is in exchange for his release. Should Itzmin escape, the character who has the highest passive Wisdom (Perception) score sees a spotted owl (Serapio in his owl form) overhead, watching Itzmin. They can follow the owl to the metalworks.

METALWORKS CONFRONTATION

The metalworks looks abandoned, and no employees are on site. Map 4.2 represents the structure. A double door is barred from inside, but Itzmin left a smaller door unlocked. When the characters enter, read the following:

> The warehouse measures about sixty feet by ninety feet and features a raised catwalk along two sides, accessible by ladders. Two fifteen-foot-diameter containers are suspended over the warehouse floor by chains, which run up and through a winch before descending to a mechanical control console atop the catwalk. Two doors near the console lead to other rooms.

SCRAP PILES

These large piles of scrap metal await separating and sorting and are difficult terrain. A character who studies or moves over a pile can see it contains mostly iron and a few scraps of low-quality silver (not enough to be valuable without hours of sorting).

HANGING CONTAINERS

The two huge suspended containers each contain more iron and silver scrap. A console on the catwalk controls both containers. A creature adjacent to the console can spend an action to throw a lever and tip either of the containers. If a container is tipped, the scrap metal within falls to the floor, dealing 14 (4d6) bludgeoning damage to any creature below it.

OFFICES

The two unlocked offices on the catwalk contain rough furniture, years-old business records, and mundane tools. If Itzmin reaches the warehouse, he ascends to the catwalk and hides in one of the offices, emerging and trying to escape only after he hears combat.

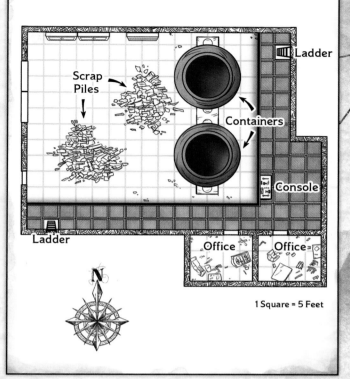

MAP 4.2: ABANDONED METALWORKS

FACING SERAPIO

When the characters arrive, Serapio the **tlacatecolo** (see the end of this adventure) is lurking on the catwalk. If Itzmin has been dealt with, the young man is struggling with his fiendish form, overcome by fear and rocking back and forth. If Itzmin reached the warehouse before the characters, Serapio is expecting danger and is ready to attack.

Talking Things Through. Trying to calm Serapio enough to talk to him requires convincing roleplaying and a DC 14 Charisma (Persuasion) check. If a character succeeds on this check before battle begins, Serapio temporarily overcomes the demonic influence afflicting him and reverts to his natural form, that of a human. He maintains this form for 1 minute, during which he begs the characters to find a way to end the curse afflicting him. After doing so, he transforms back into a tlacatecolo and attacks.

If Serapio attacks the characters before they can speak with him, a character can use an action to try to calm Serapio by making a DC 14 Charisma (Persuasion) check. Succeeding on this check once causes Serapio to hesitate, but he keeps attacking. Succeeding twice causes Serapio to regain control and transform back into a human (as noted above).

If Serapio throws off the demonic influence, and the characters attack or threaten him in any way, the fiend takes control of him again, causing him to transform back into a tlacatecolo and attack. Serapio can't be talked into transforming back into a human more than once.

Advantage and Disadvantage. If a character shows Serapio part of his locket, the young man's determination to fight the fiendish influence is bolstered, giving the characters advantage on checks made to convince him to stand down. If Itzmin is there, he goads Serapio to attack, giving the characters disadvantage.

FIGHTING THE FIEND
While Serapio is in his tlacatecolo form, he tries to remain airborne.

A character who has a passive Wisdom (Insight) score of 13 or higher can tell that the tlacatecolo's control of Serapio is not absolute and deduces that magic might disrupt that control. If Serapio is targeted by a *lesser restoration* or *remove curse* spell, the tlacatecolo is forced to leave his body for 5 minutes. During this time, the tlacatecolo becomes a separate entity that continues fighting. Serapio uses the **commoner** stat block and keeps out of battle.

If the tlacatecolo is reduced to 0 hit points while separated from Serapio, it is destroyed, freeing Serapio. If the tlacatecolo is slain while it's still in Serapio's body, his body retains its monstrous appearance as both the fiend and Serapio die.

CONCLUSION
If the characters bring Serapio to Doña Rosa alive, she weeps with gratitude and thanks them profusely. If Serapio is still under fiendish control, Doña Rosa seeks aid from the archmages of the Argent Congregation—the local academy of magic-users—who are able to put an end to his affliction and so end the curse on all victims of sereno.

If Serapio is slain while under fiendish control, the characters hear a blood-curdling scream as his soul is dragged into the Abyss. All the victims of sereno are immediately freed from the curse, but Doña Rosa falls into despair and refuses to speak to the characters again.

When the fiend is defeated, Paloma grants the characters their promised reward when they return to Milpazul. She also invites them to join her outlaw gang. The villagers freed from sereno's effects also express their gratitude to the characters.

SAN CITLÁN GAZETTEER
The stone-and-iron city of San Citlán stands at a confluence of ley lines, where the veil between the worlds of the living and the dead is thin. It's a place suffused with magic, where citizens commune with the dead in joyful festivals, and industrious minds create wonders of magic and technology. Despite San Citlán's rich culture and magical marvels, economic inequality is stark between the majority of its inhabitants and the wealthy landowners and technocrats who control the land's resources. These elite reap the rewards of progress with little regard for those left behind. As harsh as life can be for those in the city, the borderlands are harsher still. There, every day is a struggle to survive in the face of poverty, banditry, and drought.

A cosmopolitan trade hub, San Citlán is home to grand plazas, vibrant markets, and countless neighborhoods competing for space against towering industrial facilities. Smokestacks rise over cobbled streets. Silence is a commodity, as hammers ring out and forge fires roar in the city's ironworks at all hours.

Discontent among the common people has given rise to revolutionaries in the borderlands who are determined to fight the Trecena—the city's ruling council—to bring an end to corruption. Outrage recently reached a fever pitch as the city reels from political instability wrought by the death of a high-profile politician, Doña Estela. She was the longest-serving member of the Trecena, and rumors that magical resurrection will restore her to rule indefinitely have shattered the government's democratic facade. Discord brews among members of the Trecena, some of whom support Doña Estela's return while others vie for her coveted station.

FEATURES
Those familiar with San Citlán know the following facts:

Hallmarks. San Citlán is known for its magical industry but also its economic disparity. Its people maintain a strong bond with their honored dead.

People. The inhabitants of San Citlán typically have skin of light to medium brown, black hair, and dark eyes. Humans and dwarves are the most common folk in the city. A small number of intelligent Undead known as olvidados (detailed below) also reside here and are fully accepted as citizens.

Languages. The language of San Citlán is Citlanés, which is related to Tletlahtolli (the language of Tletepec; see the adventure "Trail of Destruction") and the language of previous colonizers. Most people also speak Common.

Noteworthy Sites

San Citlán is a land of contrasts. Lavish mansions cradle the wealthy while the poor scrape to survive. Purses are filled in lively markets and emptied in cantinas and wrestling rings. Massive industrial complexes loom over colorful homes in quaint streets and alleys.

Papalotlán Hill

This verdant hill at the heart of the city is the center of power and wealth. Councilors of the Trecena try to maintain order from the towers of the Crucible Court, the city's seat of government. Within the enchanted halls of the Argent Congregation, the minds behind San Citlán's progress prepare future generations of spellcasting adepts. The base of the hill teems with monuments, temples, and extravagant estates. These wealthy neighborhoods and aristocratic circles provide the backdrop for political and social intrigue.

Marfil Ironworks

The city's primary source of wealth is the industrial collective known as Marfil Ironworks, which processes local minerals using a mix of innovative technology and magic. The ironworks have many complexes across the city, and these labyrinthine facilities house all kinds of wondrous experimental creations.

Los Gavilanes

Los Gavilanes is the informal name given to San Citlán's old town. It's the most populous district, where ancient manors turned into collective living quarters are rented to industrial workers and their families. These buildings, known as *vecindades*, each house dozens of tenants and abide by complex internal community structures.

The Borderlands and Milpazul

The dry, rocky landscape outside San Citlán offers little in the way of comfort. Over half the city's workers live in these borderlands, while many more folk labor at mines and farms in the area. These communities have suffered neglect that has led to increased banditry on top of the usual attacks by monsters. One of the largest borderlands settlements, Milpazul, caters to travelers looking for shelter. It has acquired a reputation as a hub for mercenaries, as locals turn to *caporales*—traditional defenders on horseback—for security in the absence of city support.

Life in San Citlán

Molded through generations of cosmopolitan mingling, San Citlán's culture is ever-evolving but not without honored traditions.

Food and Recreation

Food is a particular point of pride in San Citlán, whose peoples use it to express their heritage. Local ingredients include agave, beans, cactus, chili peppers, maize, and tomatillos. These are combined with many imported goods to create dishes from painstakingly prepared stews such as hominy-and-meat pozole to ubiquitous snacks like tacos.

For city folk, many recreations relieve the pressures of daily life. Along with music and dance, ball games are a common pastime, ranging from ancient variations played with the hip to more contemporary kicking games. Wrestling evolved into its own form of theatrical entertainment: La Lucha, where luchadores don colorful masks, adopt epic personas, and battle using acrobatic maneuvers.

Faith and Festivals

Worship is ingrained in city culture, and major religions have temples ranging from grandiose to quaint. "Don't piss outside the cantina lest you soil a temple" is a local saying that both offers etiquette advice and references the city's many centers of worship. La Catrina—believed to be death herself—is the patron spirit of the city. She is a capricious figure who wishes to be celebrated rather than feared.

Map 4.3: San Citlán and Borderlands

SAN CITLÁN AND BORDERLANDS

THE SILVER VEINS

RUISEÑOR PEAKS

INDIGO DESERT

IXHUATEPEC MOUNTAINS

MANZANARES

MILPAZUL

MAGUEY VALLEY

N

HOLLOW

1 Mile

THE GROVEL

RINCONES

SAN CITLÁN

ONYX SPRINGS

CALAVERAS RIVER

ONE FLINT SIERRAS

While numerous festivals are held throughout the year, the most splendid and anticipated is the Night of the Remembered, a celebration that evolved from ancient funerary rites and draws on the magic of the city. During this night, people can be visited by deceased loved ones if they honor them with an ofrenda: food and drink enjoyed in life, among other traditional offerings, presented on elaborate altars that guide souls back to the world. The days leading up to this event are marked by colorful citywide parades that display San Citlán's diverse culture.

OLVIDADOS

In rare circumstances, the deceased remain in San Citlán as Undead following the Night of the Remembered. Known as *olvidados*, or "forgotten," these intelligent Undead often take the form of sapient, peaceful skeletons or spirits. Most retain the memories and personality they had in life, but they have no recollection of the afterlife.

GOVERNANCE AND GROWTH

San Citlán is governed by the Trecena, a council consisting of thirteen elected representatives. The ability to vote for these representatives is limited to landowners and their descendants, those who serve in the military, graduates of the Argent Congregation, and those who make a considerable contribution to the city's economy.

In recent decades, the city has undergone significant transformations marked by great discoveries attributed to the Argent Congregation. Doña Estela, a dwarf landowner who held a seat in the Trecena for more than fifty years, was the congregation's founder and is credited with San Citlán's economic rise. However, her focus on progress and city aesthetics has drawn heavy criticism, as the majority of the populace lives in poverty. The seat of Councilor of the Foundry remains vacant following Doña Estela's recent death, as it has become clear that the oligarch intended to be resurrected to continue her rule indefinitely.

NAMES

Those native to San Citlán often have up to three names: a given name and two family surnames, inherited from their parents. The following are common names in San Citlán:

Feminine. Citlali, Estela, Guadalupe, María, Quintina, Xóchitl

Masculine. Alejo, Cuauhtémoc, Eladio, Fortino, Pedro, Tenoch

Gender-Neutral. Azul, Centli, Cruz, Izel, Paz, Quetzal

Surnames. Apanco, Caloch, Infante, Moreno, Salazar, Xicoténcatl

LEGENDS OF SAN CITLÁN

According to the tale of San Citlán's founding, an explorer named Citlali became lost in the valley of the Calaveras River. After wandering for days, Citlali saw an elegantly dressed skeletal figure trailing behind her, never moving too close or straying too far. She tried to flee, but the figure always caught up. When she turned and followed her pursuer instead, the skeleton led Citlali to a hidden cenote. Citlali dove in to assuage her thirst, and when she resurfaced, the skeletal figure was gone.

Observing that the area was rich in precious minerals, Citlali returned home and convinced others to join her to settle the valley north of the cenote and the mountains now known as Citlali's Rest. Citlali grew old, and the skeletal figure returned to take her, but the settlement remained. It was named in her honor, with Citlán roughly translating to "the place near Citlali." People began calling the skeletal figure La Catrina for her elegant clothing.

San Citlán's history is rife with conflict. After years of failed invasions over its first century of existence, the city was overcome and occupied by a colonizing force. Colonial rule lasted for two hundred years and ended in a bloody series of conflicts called the Wars of Separation. In the aftermath, the folk of San Citlán held their first elections, finally looking forward to a time of peace. The wars have left scars, turning previously fertile lands barren and driving away the fey that once inhabited the region—some say forever.

ADVENTURES IN SAN CITLÁN

Consider the plots on the San Citlán Adventures table when planning adventures in San Citlán.

SAN CITLÁN ADVENTURES

d4	Adventure
1	A revolutionary asks the characters to rid a mine connected to Los Gavilanes of **ankhegs** so it can be used to smuggle information out of the city.
2	Intrigued by Marfil Ironworks' signature magical bodyguards (**helmed horrors**), a wizard named Montesco hires the characters to capture one.
3	A spectral olvidado named Don Edelmiro hires the characters for protection after a band of criminal **thugs** raid his estate. He's convinced his descendants are behind the attack.
4	A street child named Anita approaches the characters for help. Her friends were taken by a **banshee** that wanders the streets near the Calaveras River at night.

CHARACTERS FROM SAN CITLÁN

If players want to create characters from San Citlán, consider asking them the following questions during character creation:

Where do you stand in society? San Citlán's economic inequality shapes the lives of its people. Are you one of the privileged or one of the destitute? If you're privileged, do you have a vote? If destitute, do you live in or outside the city?

Whom do you honor with your ofrenda? Most in San Citlán eagerly look forward to the Night of the Remembered so they can commune with their loved ones. Do you? What does your ofrenda look like, and who is it for?

Does tradition color how you adventure? Are you familiar with the ways of an adventuring caporal or lifestyles that give you a close connection to your steed and the open road? Do you have experience as a larger-than-life luchador wrestler— maybe even wearing a signature mask?

BRIAN VALEZA

TLACATECOLO

Appearing as plague-stricken, bipedal owls, tlacatecolo sow sickness and feed on the suffering of mortals. These fiends spread an affliction that leaches heat and life from the living, dispersing it upon winds that rattle like a gasp from a frozen body. Sunlight staves off the disease, but those affected rarely survive the dark of night.

TLACATECOLO
Medium Fiend (Demon), Typically Neutral Evil

Armor Class 13
Hit Points 78 (12d8 + 24)
Speed 30 ft., fly 30 ft.

STR	DEX	CON	INT	WIS	CHA
12 (+1)	17 (+3)	14 (+2)	10 (+0)	15 (+2)	10 (+0)

Saving Throws Dex +6, Con +5
Skills Perception +5, Stealth +6
Damage Resistances cold, poison
Condition Immunities poisoned
Senses darkvision 120 ft., passive Perception 15
Languages Abyssal, Common
Challenge 5 (1,800 XP)   **Proficiency Bonus** +3

Magic Resistance. The tlacatecolo has advantage on saving throws against spells and other magical effects.

ACTIONS

Multiattack. The tlacatecolo makes two Talon attacks.

Talon. *Melee Weapon Attack:* +6 to hit, reach 5 ft., one target. *Hit:* 8 (1d8 + 3) piercing damage plus 14 (3d8) poison damage.

Change Shape. The tlacatecolo magically transforms into a Medium owl, while retaining its game statistics (other than its size). This transformation ends if the tlacatecolo is reduced to 0 hit points or if it uses its action to end it.

Plague Winds (Fiend Form Only; Recharge 5–6). The tlacatecolo emits a chilling, disease-ridden wind in a 60-foot line that is 10 feet wide. Each creature in that area must succeed on a DC 13 Constitution saving throw or take 26 (4d12) cold damage and become poisoned.

While poisoned in this way, the creature can't regain hit points. At the end of every hour, the creature must succeed on a DC 13 Constitution saving throw or gain 1 level of exhaustion. If the creature is in direct sunlight when it makes this saving throw, it automatically succeeds on the save.

If the creature is targeted by magic that ends a poison or disease, such as *lesser restoration*, while the creature isn't in direct sunlight, the effect does not end.

WAGES OF VICE

AN ADVENTURE FOR 5TH-LEVEL CHARACTERS

W HEN THEY STUMBLE UPON A MURDER, THE characters are caught up in the plots of a vengeful killer targeting the heirs of the city of Zinda's rulers. During the boisterous citywide festival known as March of Vice, the characters must find the killer and reveal the fiendish power that serves her.

BACKGROUND

The wealth of Zinda is defined by the jeli flower. This opalescent moonflower has graceful pink leaves and wide petals, and it's used to produce a sweet black wine. The flower was brought to the land several years ago and flourished, now growing exclusively around Zinda.

The March of Vice festival originally honored the city's entire wine trade, but jeli wine has recently become the focus of the centuries-old tradition. Zinda's recent prosperity hides a dire secret, however. Five years ago, the Kings of Coin—Zinda's rulers—established a covenant with a witch named Proud Edun. She used her magic to create the jeli flower, a crop with fantastic commercial value. In exchange, the six Kings of Coin were to give her their firstborn children to serve as apprentices. At the suggestion of one of their members, Myx Nargis Ruba, the Kings of Coin betrayed Proud Edun and murdered her instead of giving up their heirs.

For five years, the Kings of Coin have reaped the benefits of Zinda's prosperity, and Proud Edun's daughter, Kala Mabarin, has plotted her revenge.

PRONUNCIATIONS

The Zinda Pronunciations table shows how to pronounce names and words in this adventure.

ZINDA PRONUNCIATIONS

Name	Pronunciation
Amos Nir	AH-mohs neer
Azra Nir	AH-zrah neer
Jacopo Ain	yak-KOH-poh ayn
Jeli	JEH-lee

Name	Pronunciation
Kala Mabarin	KAH-lah MAH-bah-reen
Myx Nargis Ruba	mix nar-GEESE ROO-bah
Samira Arah	suh-MEER-uh AH-rah
Zenia Ruba	zen-EE-AH ROO-bah
Zinda	ZEEN-duh

SETTING THE ADVENTURE

Use the following suggestions to help contextualize Zinda in a wider world:

Through the Radiant Citadel. Characters traveling from the Radiant Citadel arrive in a jungle clearing 2 miles from Zinda's walls. Use the "Zinda Gazetteer" section at this adventure's end to provide further details about the surrounding lands.

Forgotten Realms. A trade city known for its wealth and magic, Zinda could find a home along the coasts of Amn or near Dambrath.

Greyhawk. Zinda might be found among the Holds of the Sea Princes or in the Lordship of the Isles.

CHARACTER HOOKS

Consider the following ways to involve characters in this adventure:

Celebration. Zinda's March of Vice is famous throughout the region. An influential ally of the characters requests they attend and, while they're there, purchase a bottle of jeli wine to be used as a gift in a diplomatic negotiation.

Obvious Suspects. The heirs of Zinda's rulers have been targeted by a murderer. Captain Adann, a leader of Zinda's anti-aristocrat group called the Bloodletters, seeks the characters' help in preventing blame from falling on his organization.

Old Secrets. Madame Samira Arah, one of Zinda's rulers, believes her fellow Kings of Coin are engaged in a deadly conspiracy. Through an anonymous agent, Samira hires the characters to come to Zinda and uncover what secrets her peers hide.

PRINCE OF VICE, AZRA NIR, LEADS ZINDA'S ANNUAL MARCH OF VICE FESTIVITIES— UNAWARE HE'S JUST ONE TARGET OF A KILLER.

STARTING THE ADVENTURE

The adventure begins with the characters traveling through the rain forest near Zinda, following a caravan of merchants. Read the following description to set the scene:

> Heat rises from the jungle floor and clings to the broad leaves in the canopy above. Ahead, an elephant sways drowsily. Its rider groans and stretches, and then rejoins the ululating marching chant.
>
> As the forest thins, the gleaming gates of the trade city of Zinda appear a mile ahead.

The road through the jungle is narrow, forcing the caravan to march single file along its trails. The other travelers are in high spirits, offering food and water to anyone who needs it. They also share the following information:

- The March of Vice is a ten-day festival of drinking, debauchery, shows, and sales.
- Revelers wearing feathered masks and beaded gowns make merry through day and night in celebration of the city's prosperity.
- The travelers can also share any details about Zinda from the "Zinda Gazetteer" section at the end of this adventure.

THE RIVER OF GOLD

The trail from the northwest widens as it reaches the city, feeding into the River of Gold, a thoroughfare paved with yellow potsherds. The caravanners cheer loudly as they enter the fields around the city and the bustling community comes fully into view. At Zinda's open gates, agents of the city collect a toll of 5 sp per entrant or goods of equal value. The tax collectors are in good spirits, so a character who succeeds on a DC 15 Charisma (Persuasion) check can convince a tax collector to allow the group free entry.

As the characters enter the city, read the following description:

> Beyond the city gates, the golden road continues amid silk-draped booths and squat buildings with conical roofs. The chatter of merchants and cheerful youths rings out along the road. Folk sell colorful flowers, beaded charms, and other wares from woven baskets atop their heads, while street performers spin in tight circles, waving long silk streamers.

Hundreds of revelers, merchants, jeli wine vendors, and entertainers pack the River of Gold. Buildings bear brightly painted signs and are covered with colorful vines bearing lush flowers. Beyond the crowds, the characters can see the bustling city center called the Court of Flowers, lined with tropical trees whose branches droop to the pavement.

A Grim Discovery

As the characters make their way from the River of Gold to the Court of Flowers, they pass a shadowed alley. Glancing down it, the character who has the highest passive Wisdom (Perception) score sees a still figure surrounded by spilled gold coins and slumped against the wall, head tilted to stare at them.

Characters who investigate find a dead dwarf wearing lavish robes. Nearby are 20 gp fallen from an open pouch the dwarf wears. His body shows no wounds, but a character who makes a successful DC 12 Wisdom (Medicine) check finds signs of poison. If the check succeeds by 5 or more, the character confirms that the dwarf was killed by burnt othur fumes (a poison detailed in the *Dungeon Master's Guide*). The dwarf has been dead for 5 minutes and thus is beyond the help of a *revivify* spell.

Characters who search the alley confirm it is a dead end, and the shop doors along it are all locked. There is no sign of any other creature in the area.

The characters currently have no way of learning that the dwarf was murdered by the vengeful Kala Mabarin, who got close enough to him in the crowd to poison him, then led him to the alley to die.

Guilt by Association

Before the characters conclude their investigation of the body and the alley, three **veterans** wearing gold filigreed armor shout for the characters to stay where they are, attacking if the characters flee. These veterans were hired by Madame Samira Arah, the newest member of the Kings of Coin, to protect the dwarf, but they lost sight of him during the celebrations.

The alley is only 10 feet wide. Each veteran fights until reduced to 10 hit points, then flees. The veterans stand down if all the characters surrender or if a character uses an action to explain they had nothing to with the dwarf's death and succeeds on a DC 14 Charisma (Persuasion) check. A character has disadvantage on this check if the group has wounded any of the veterans.

First Blood

After the last veteran is defeated or once the veterans stand down, read the following:

> A tall elf woman wearing a sumptuous gown appears at the mouth of the alley, shaking her head. "Jacopo, you fool, I hope your last March of Vice was worth it."

MADAME SAMIRA ARAH

> A smile touches her lips as she takes you in. "These guards are members of the Silent Verse, protectors in my employ. I apologize for their overzealousness. Seeing how you handle yourselves, though, I might be able to better apologize with an offer of employment."

The woman introduces herself as Madame Samira Arah, the newest member of Zinda's ruling council, the Kings of Coin (see the "Zinda Gazetteer" section).

Madame Samira Arah

Madame Samira Arah (neutral, elf **spy**) joined the Kings of Coin within the last year. She was the chosen heir of the King of Coin she replaced but not part of their family (an important detail as it relates to Kala Mabarin's vengeance). Her peers' embrace of the status quo frustrates her grand plans for making Zinda even more prosperous. Samira plots to usurp the leadership of the Kings of Coin from Grand Messer Amos Nir and claim rulership of the city. Samira is sharp and severe, and she presents herself as haughty and imperturbable.

Personality Trait. "I deserve only the best."

Ideal. "Someone must always command. Why not the one with the most ambition?"

Bond. "The common folk are sheep to be led, and I am the capable shepherd."

Flaw. "Why should I settle for less than everything?"

SAMIRA'S OFFER

Samira instructs any remaining veterans to deal with Jacopo's body quietly and to alert the other Kings of Coin. She then leads the characters to a small café at the edge of the city's central market, where she has a private room. After offering the characters jeli wine, she explains who she is and answers their questions. Use the following details to guide the conversation:

- Madame Samira Arah is the head of the Jewelers' Trade, the guild for those who craft and deal in gems and jewelry.
- Due to her experience protecting the valuable assets of her guild, she also acts as the security specialist for the Kings of Coin, controlling enforcers known as the Silent Verse.
- The murder victim is Jacopo Ain, eldest son of King of Coin Massimo Ain.
- Jacopo was under protective guard in response to a recent attack against the family member of another King of Coin. But he slipped past his guardians, intent on reveling amid the March of Vice.
- Last night, Zenia Ruba—the eldest daughter of Myx Nargis Ruba, another of the Kings of Coin—was attacked and nearly killed. Samira doesn't know if the attacks are related but fears they might be.

Samira wants to hire the characters to question Zenia and discover any information tying her attack and Jacopo's murder to Grand Messer Amos. Though she controls the Silent Verse, Samira fears some of its agents are loyal to Amos. A group of capable adventurers seeking information might yield the results she needs. In return for their assistance, Samira offers the characters 200 gp each. She's a shrewd bargainer but can be coaxed to increase her offer to 300 gp each if a character succeeds on a DC 18 Charisma (Persuasion) check.

If the characters agree to Samira's terms, she warns them to be discreet. The Kings of Coin took great pains to keep the attack on Zenia quiet for fear of jeopardizing the success of the March of Vice. Jacopo's death will likewise be concealed until the festival is over. She then provides directions to an establishment owned by Zenia's family, a tavern called the Thornapple, where Zenia is under guard. Zenia's directions avoid several streets closed by festivities and lead through the city market.

Samira also gives the characters a rose-shaped token that confirms the characters are her representatives. She tells them she will be among the celebrants on the city's main thoroughfare, the River of Gold, until the March of Vice begins.

ON THE HUNT

Seeking Zenia at the Thornapple gives the characters their first opportunity to explore Zinda. With the March of Vice occurring soon, people are in high spirits. Characters who move about the crowds, visit local vendors, or seek to learn more about recent events in Zinda each hear a rumor from the Zinda Rumors table. Each rumor also notes whether it is true or false.

ZINDA RUMORS

d6	Rumor
1	A witch is keen to collect coven members from the heirs and families of the Kings of Coin. (False)
2	Foul spirits known as biza haunt the forest and sometimes tempt innocent souls with secrets of evil magic. (True)
3	The March of Vice is an opportunity to cast off past mistakes and start anew. (True)
4	A half-wolf, half-human figure wanders the streets at night. This figure looks strikingly similar to Grand Messer Amos Nir, but the Kings of Coin refuse to investigate. (False)
5	A diviner revealed that the firstborn children of the Kings of Coin are in danger of having their souls stolen for mysterious reasons. (True)
6	Grand Messer Amos Nir plans to retire imminently and will name his son, Azra, to lead the Kings of Coin in his place. (True)

MAYHEM IN THE MARKET

As the characters move through the market, a stocky woman in green pantaloons and a yellow tunic irritably elbows her way past them. This is Kala Mabarin—one of Zinda's spirit shepherds, known as daturas—who has returned to the city after years of living alone in the jungle. Kala moves hurriedly through the crowd. Aside from her rudeness, there's nothing remarkable about Kala at the moment, but characters who notice her now might recall spotting her later when they hear descriptions of the woman. The milling crowd stymies characters who try to pursue Kala, even as a more pressing distraction arises.

The characters won't realize it yet, but Kala has just targeted another scion of the Kings of Coin, Arel Avim. She has used a poison of her own design to make an innocent merchant attack the local lordling.

KALA MABARIN

Kala Mabarin

Kala Mabarin (neutral evil, human **druid**) is a
skilled herbalist and datura, a protector of the spirits of the land. After years in the wilderness, she
has returned to Zinda intent on vengeance. Kala
entered into a pact with a biza, a type of vengeful
spirit versed in sinister magic. In exchange for
Kala murdering people for the biza to feed on, the
spirit taught her how to make a powerful poison to
facilitate her revenge. Now Kala uses what she has
learned to placate the biza and wreak havoc on the
Kings of Coin who murdered her mother—particularly targeting their adult, firstborn heirs. Her deep
rage at the Kings of Coin and Zinda is rivaled only
by her joyful reverence for the spiritual world.

Breath of Vengeance

Moments after Kala pushes past the characters,
read the following text:

> Shrieks of fear rise from an herb vendor's stall nearby.
> The crowd shifts as panicked people flee the scene.

The characters see the herbalist who works the stall
coughing as he attacks a man on the ground. Characters who have a passive Wisdom (Perception)
score of 14 or higher also notice a dissipating pink
cloud around the figures.

Seeing this, the horrified crowd stampedes. Each
character in the market must succeed on a DC 14
Dexterity saving throw or take 3 (1d6) bludgeoning
damage from the crush.

Poisoned Merchant. The merchant uses the
veteran stat block, except his only weapon is a
makeshift club—treat it as a longsword that deals
bludgeoning damage. He initially focuses his attack
on the fallen man but randomly attacks any creature
within reach. The merchant has been affected by a
poison made by Kala called biza's breath (see the
sidebar). A character who succeeds on a DC 14 Wisdom (Medicine) check notices that the man's glassy
eyes and puppet-like movement suggest he has been
drugged in some way. A *protection from poison* spell
or similar magic ends the effect on the merchant.

Victim. The man the merchant is attacking is
named Arel Avim. He uses the **noble** stat block, has
0 hit points, and is dying.

After the Attack

Once the merchant is dealt with, several people
move to help the wounded man, Arel Avim. One of
them is Captain Adann, who has neatly trimmed
facial hair and wears a red vest. He's a leader of the
anti-aristocrat group called the Bloodletters. Before
the party can get Arel back on his feet, several soldiers sweep in and take him and the merchant into
custody. These soldiers wear the same gold filigreed
armor as the Silent Verse members the characters
encountered earlier.

If asked, Captain Adann explains that the
wounded man is Arel Avim, son of the King of
Coin Messer Solenn Avim. Arel is sympathetic to
the Bloodletters' cause, much to his father's disap-
proval. Adann can also share any information from
the "Zinda Gazetteer" section about the Bloodletters. Ultimately, the Bloodletters aren't involved with
the attack on Arel.

If the characters ask Adann or others about a figure wearing green and yellow hurrying away from
the scene, several people report seeing such a person near the herbalist's cart just before she bumped
into the characters, but she is long gone. If the characters didn't notice Kala earlier, Adann mentions
seeing someone matching her description behaving
suspiciously just before the attack.

The Thornapple

Once things are under control in the market, the
characters can continue to the Thornapple. When
they enter, read the following description:

Although the building is packed with people, the Thornapple's baked clay walls create a cool interior. Dozens of tables are filled, and a huge stage across from the entrance is being set for a performance. From behind a long, well-stocked bar, a comfortably dressed orc gives an enthusiastic wave and says, "Welcome friends, and a blessed March of Vice to you! How can your cousin Nargis help you tonight?"

The tavern's proprietor, Myx Nargis Ruba, entertains customers from behind the bar.

Characters who survey the crowd and succeed on a DC 14 Wisdom (Perception) check note several armed figures focusing more on the tavern patrons than their drinks. These are guards of the Silent Verse assigned by Samira to watch over Nargis and Zenia.

Myx Nargis Ruba

Myx Nargis Ruba (neutral evil, orc **noble**) is one of Zenia's parents and also a King of Coin. Nargis is overseer of the Tavern Keepers Trade and spends much of their time at the Thornapple, the centerpiece of their family's fortune.

When the Kings of Coin made their bargain with the witch Proud Edun to magically cultivate the jeli flower, Nargis convinced the other Kings of Coin they could save their firstborn children by murdering the witch. For five years, Nargis took great pride in the city's success, but the attack on Zenia threatens to expose their lies.

Nargis is a stylishly dressed, middle-aged orc with a stout build. They switch between a posh Zindanese accent and a laborer's gruff lilt depending on whom they talk to.

Personality Trait. "I consider all to be my dearest companions unless proven wrong three—perhaps four—times."

Ideal. "Family is more important than all the gold in Zinda."

Bond. "I would cheat and kill to keep my daughter with me, but I fear I will lose her as a result."

Flaw. "I have taken the easy way out before, and I would happily do it again."

Nargis's Story

Myx Nargis Ruba plays the part of the friendly tavern keeper perfectly. If the characters strike up a conversation without initially revealing that Samira sent them, Nargis is happy to gossip and to brag about the tavern, being one of the Kings of Coin, and that they've arranged a performance from the renowned Diva Luma. A character who succeeds on a DC 14 Wisdom (Insight) check intuits that something weighs heavily on Nargis's mind, though the tavern keeper won't say what (see "Nargis's Confession" below).

If asked about the attempt on Zenia's life, Nargis remains tight-lipped until the characters provide Samira's token and reveal their mission. In response, Nargis acknowledges the guards and says keeping Zenia in the tavern with a crowd of witnesses should make another attack less likely. Nargis then points out where Zenia sits at a corner table.

Meeting with Zenia

Two Silent Verse **guards** sit at a table near the stage with Zenia, but they depart to allow the characters to sit if they see Samira's token. The tables near hers are packed with revelers, but the din of conversation makes it easy to talk without being heard.

Zenia greets the characters warmly. She is a grayskinned orc **commoner** with her hair braided in elegant loops. She has an easygoing demeanor but is clearly nervous. Zenia is thrilled to meet adventurers and asks about the characters' work and travels. She admits to considering the adventuring life herself but knows that Nargis would never allow it.

If asked about the attack on her, Zenia shares what happened. Based on the characters' questions, use the following details to guide the conversation:

- Zenia was shopping along the River of Gold, escorted by several of her family's servants, when she suddenly felt ill.
- A cloud of pink ash appeared around her, and her servants began attacking her and each other.
- Zenia remembers a figure bumping into her before she felt ill.
- Zenia describes feeling sick during the attack, but says the sensation faded swiftly.

A character who succeeds on a DC 14 Wisdom (Medicine) check suspects Zenia might have been poisoned but shook off the effects. Characters who specifically ask about a woman matching Kala's description and who succeed on a DC 14 Intelligence (Investigation) check cause Zenia to recall that the figure who bumped into her matches that description. Zenia doesn't know who the woman is, though, and can't name her.

Attack of the Divas

While the characters talk with Zenia, they hear raucous voices at the door.

> Performers in bright feathers and shimmering silk flood into the tavern, laughing bombastically. The crowd, including Zenia, responds with great enthusiasm.
>
> "That's Diva Luma and the Elucidarium Divas!" Zenia says, nodding to the dark-skinned woman leading the group, whose outfit is all sequins and bright feathers.
>
> The divas wave and proceed to the stage. There, Diva Luma pulls a small silk bag from her belt and hurls its contents upward, standing amid a rain of colorful glitter as the performance begins.
>
> A moment later, the diva's expression changes. Diva Luma grins cruelly, slips off her heeled shoes, and leaps toward Zenia.

Myx Nargis Ruba

Kala has been lurking near the Thornapple, looking for opportunities to strike at Zenia. She found her opportunity with Diva Luma, tainting the diva's glitter—a feature of the diva's performances—with rage-inducing biza's breath.

Diva Luma uses the **assassin** stat block, but her only weapon is her wicked, high-heeled shoe, which functions as a Shortsword attack without poison. The other two divas use the **scout** stat block and attack only with broken bottles that function the same as their Shortsword attack. As the divas are all under the effects of biza's breath, they each randomly make one melee attack against Zenia or a character on their turns. All three divas fail their saving throws to resist the poison affecting them for three rounds. On the fourth round, they overcome the effects of biza's breath and groggily stop attacking.

In the aftermath of the battle, characters who inspect the stage, the divas, or their glitter and succeed on a DC 12 Wisdom (Perception) check see the glitter left a film of pink ash on the divas and the floor around them. A character who examines the pink ash and succeeds on a DC 14 Wisdom (Medicine) check suspects this is some manner of poison.

Nargis's Confession

In the aftermath of the fight, terrified patrons clear the tavern. A distraught Nargis embraces Zenia and takes the blame for the attack. Characters can convince Nargis to reveal more through roleplaying or by succeeding on a DC 12 Charisma (Intimidation or Persuasion) check. Use the following points to guide Nargis's confession:

- Nargis confesses that their greed and arrogance doomed the firstborn children of the Kings of Coin.
- The jeli flower is the magical creation of a witch named Proud Edun. The Kings of Coin negotiated with the witch, promising their firstborn children would be her apprentices in exchange for the jeli flower and the wealth it would bring.
- Nargis talked the other Kings of Coin into murdering Proud Edun to break the bargain. After calling the witch to a secret meeting, they murdered her.

Learning about Kala Mabarin

When the effects of the poison end, Diva Luma and her fellow entertainers apologize profusely, explaining they weren't in control of their bodies. If asked about what happened to them prior to going on stage, the performers recall that just before they entered the tavern, a datura introduced herself and offered Diva Luma a fine sachet of glitter as thanks for many inspiring performances. The entertainers confirm that the woman was wearing green pantaloons and a yellow tunic if asked. If a character succeeds on a DC 14 Intelligence (Investigation) check, they

KN11O

get Luma or one of the other performers to recall that the datura boldly and purposefully introduced herself as Kala Mabarin.

Nargis Knows. If Nargis hears the name Kala Mabarin, the tavern keeper begins to weep. Nargis tells the characters that Proud Edun had a daughter by that name, but she was lost in the jungle years before the Kings of Coin bargained with Proud Edun. Nargis begs the characters to find Kala and put an end to whatever she's scheming.

Following Up. Several folks outside the Thornapple recall seeing a figure matching Kala's description heading toward the pier.

PERIL AT THE PARADE

The March of Vice parade begins as the characters make their way to the pier. The parade runs down the River of Gold and ends at the jetty. As the characters come to the city's central thoroughfare, read or paraphrase the following description:

> The streets are alive with joyful music and exuberant festival-goers watching an oncoming parade.
>
> An open carriage drawn by an ox leads the procession. The carriage bears a large man wearing a white mask and vines of jeli flowers. He waves to the adoring public as figures in gowns and head scarves the color of jeli flowers march after him, sweeping the ground in wide strokes with handmade brooms.

The parade is a splendid affair, and the streets are flooded with revelers. Nearby, locals call out to the man in the carriage—calling him the "Prince of Vice"—to attract his attention. A character who asks a bystander about the significance of the Prince of Vice, or who succeeds on a DC 14 Intelligence (History) check, learns the details from the "March of Vice" section at the end of this adventure. Revelers can also point out that the Prince of Vice is Azra Nir, the son of Grand Messer Amos Nir, the eldest member of the Kings of Coin.

Characters who follow the parade or search the pier for Kala wind up near the jetty as the parade reaches the end of the thoroughfare.

PARADE AMBUSH

As the parade nears the jetty, read the following description:

> Grasping weeds and vines erupt from the cobblestone street beneath the carriage at the head of the parade. The ox pulling the cart panics, causing the vehicle to careen into a post covered in decorations. The vegetation then wraps around the cart's wheels and the closest bystanders. A pair of revelers produce weapons, revealing themselves to be guards protecting the Prince of Vice.

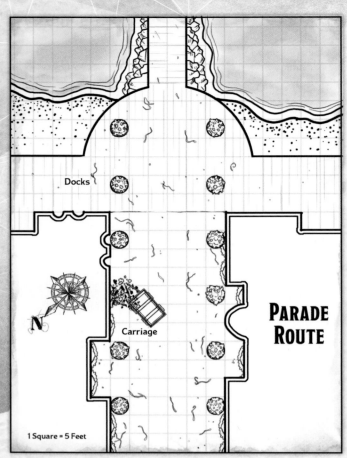

Docks

N

Carriage

PARADE ROUTE

1 Square = 5 Feet

MAP 5.1: PARADE ROUTE

As bystanders flee the area, the character who has the highest passive Wisdom (Perception) score spots a figure in green and yellow throwing something toward the cart. An instant later, a cloud of pink ashes bursts from a sachet, striking the two guards.

KALA'S ATTACK

The parade route appears on map 5.1. The characters are either at the northwest or south side of the map, depending on their path from the Thornapple to the pier. The guards and Azra Nir cluster around the crashed carriage, while Kala starts on the side of the map farthest from the characters.

Azra Nir. Azra uses the **acolyte** stat block and is surprised during the first round of combat. He seeks only to escape the chaos.

Guards. The two **guards** are affected by the poison biza's breath (detailed in a sidebar earlier in this adventure). They automatically fail their saving throws to end the poison's effect. The guards make one melee attack against a randomly determined creature within reach each round for 1 minute before the poison's effect ends.

Kala. Kala uses the **druid** stat block and has already cast *barkskin*, giving her AC 16. She keeps her distance from the poisoned guards as she tries

to kill Azra Nir using *produce flame* and *thunderwave*. She has three more doses of biza's breath, but they are prepared for use in combat.

Negotiating with Kala. A character can use an action to explain what they learned from Nargis about how Kala's mother was wronged and attempt a DC 16 Charisma (Persuasion) check. On a success, Kala stops attacking for 1 round. If a character succeeds on this check a second time, Kala stops attacking and agrees to discuss bringing her mother's murderers to justice without further bloodshed.

SPIRIT OF VENGEANCE

If Kala is reduced to 0 hit points or apprehended, she calls out to the biza she made a pact with. If the characters convince Kala to call off her attack, this breaks her pact with the spirit, which has the same effect as her calling it. In either case, the biza appears above Kala at the start of the following round and attacks the characters.

The biza uses the **wraith** stat block but does not have Sunlight Sensitivity.

As the biza attacks, it calls out and curses the names Amos Nir, Nargis Ruba, and the others listed in the "Kings of Coin" section later in this adventure. Samira Arah is omitted and spared the biza's ire, as she's only recently joined the council. Characters who've heard these names or who succeed on a DC 12 Intelligence (History) check recognize them. The biza goes on to accuse the Kings of Coin of killing it, revealing that it is the spirit of Proud Edun—a fact Kala never learned.

CONCLUSION

Samira appears on the scene soon after Kala and the biza are defeated. Along with several Silent Verse guards, Samira quickly restores order. Azra Nir thanks the characters just before Samira has her guards move him somewhere safer.

If the characters defeat Kala and the biza, they can reveal what they've learned to Samira. Exposing the bargain the Kings of Coins made and Proud Edun's murder will bring turmoil to Zinda. Samira asks the characters not to share what they've learned until she determines how to respond.

If Kala survived, Samira is determined to bring her to justice but fears that the other Kings of Coin might seek revenge. At your discretion, Samira might have her guards spirit Kala away to a secret location, or she might ask the characters to take her to a safe place outside Zinda, like the Radiant Citadel. Either way, Samira will decide how to punish Kala and the Kings of Coin for their crimes.

Whatever the outcome, Samira pays the characters the amount agreed upon at the start of the adventure, and she throws in a *bag of holding* filled with six flasks of jeli wine worth 25 gp each.

Zinda Gazetteer

Zinda is a city of spiraling marble towers and turrets, of universities and guildhalls, and of specialty shops lining paved streets. Far below the balconies, the Court of Flowers and the pier ring with the merry laughter and the songs of laborers. Year round, Zinda's plazas and parlors are full of academics, merchants, and pilgrims. But for ten days in the summer, the March of Vice draws even larger crowds as the city celebrates the local wine trade—specifically, the jeli wine that has made Zinda the wealthiest city in the land. Zindanese citizens garb themselves in brightly colored costumes and feathered headdresses and indulge in feasting, song, and dance.

After its recent years of prosperity, a cloud has settled over the city. Political dissidents are rumored to disappear from their beds as the Silent Verse, the enforcers of the ruling Kings of Coin, stalk the streets. The newest member of the Kings of Coin, Madame Samira Arah, grows restless with ambition and regularly hires mercenaries and spies to investigate her rivals' secrets. The Bloodletters laborers' union opposes the leadership of the aristocracy at every turn. And beneath it all, the dire secret on which Zinda's prosperity was built waits to be exposed.

Features

Those familiar with Zinda know the following facts:

Hallmarks. Zinda's people are known for cultivating the jeli flower, which features prominently in the annual March of Vice celebration.

People. Humans make up the majority of Zinda's population and have skin tones ranging from light brown to black. Their hair grows in spiral curls; most grow it long and wear it tucked beneath a headscarf topped by a wide-brimmed hat (if married) or set in scalp-hugging braids (if unmarried). Elves and halflings are also frequently seen in Zinda, along with other nonhumans.

Languages. All Zindanese citizens speak Common and N'warian. Many Zindanese also speak Draconic, since the power and wealth typically attributed to dragons are considered virtuous to the Kings of Coin.

Noteworthy Sites

In addition to its robust agricultural holdings, Zinda is home to magical universities, conservatories, museums, and other centers of the arts.

Court of Flowers

The Court of Flowers is the vibrant heart of commerce and art in Zinda. The district hosts streets lined with multiple palatial homes, towers with overflowing gardens, and museums. Performers gather here throughout the day, and merchants keep their shops open day and night. Most of the city's guilds—known in the city as trades—keep their headquarters among the district's towers. Artisans are expected to register with the headquarters of the appropriate trade and support the furthering of their craft.

Covenant

Hunched over brass cauldrons in their manor-like headquarters, members of the Covenant of Magic—an exclusive circle of traditionalist mages—preside over festivals, weddings, funerals, and similar events. Most covenant members are elderly; several have great-great-grandchildren who lead their own trades or are Kings of Coin. Their power stems less from magic and more from their far-reaching connections.

Elucidarium

The bardic college of Zinda, the Elucidarium, is the extravagant home of the famous divas of Zinda. Draped in bright silk and exuberant florals, the building is made of sculpted glass set with sparkling gemstones. Inside, musicians, dancers, orators, and thespians hone their talents. In addition to these public skills, students can also study spy-craft and information brokering. Those who visit looking for training in the arts might find themselves embroiled in the machinations of ruthless social climbers.

Jeli Gardens

The great gardens that spread to the west of the city are the source of Zinda's wealth. Many Zindanese laborers tend the jeli flowers that grow there, living in wood-and-stone huts in the heart of the gardens. These velvety flowers were discovered several years ago and can't be successfully cultivated elsewhere. Why Zinda is the only place where jeli flowers can grow is a mystery, but this single crop now supplies the city with raw materials for wine, dye, fabric, and paper. Gardeners occasionally fall prey to wicked spirits, zombies, and green hags that lurk in the jungle beyond the city, as Zinda has no standing army to protect these outlying regions.

LIFE IN ZINDA

Art, commerce, and magic fill the lives of Zinda's people and touch on every aspect of society.

THE BLOODLETTERS

Clad in aprons stained with jeli dye, Bloodletters proselytize a life free from oppression by the elite. The group's name originates from its members' desire to drain the greed from Zinda like blood from a wound. Under the leadership of Captain Adann, the group works in open defiance of the Kings of Coin. The Bloodletters' attacks upon the Court of Flowers and sabotage of the jeli gardens make the group a frequent target of the Silent Verse.

CLASS DIVIDE

Zinda has a stark class divide. The city's wealthy citizens live in large homes and revere academia, a strong work ethic, and wealth. Members of less affluent families sleep together in cramped quarters and often hold multiple jobs to survive. The rich feast on goat, fish, and mutton; wear gold and silk; and drink from spotless glass flutes while boasting of their academic achievements and frivolously displaying magic. The poor eat grains and roots served on palm leaves spread upon straw floors.

FAITH AND ANCESTORS

Though Zinda welcomes the practices of all citizens, the city's one common faith involves the daturas, also known as spirit shepherds. Daturas speak for and protect the spirits of the jungle. A datura might go years without meeting another member of the order, spending their life escorting caravans, performing exorcisms, and guarding sacred reaches of the forest. Others are hired to escort mourners to the sites of rare silk cotton trees, where the bereaved hang tokens for their recently departed ancestors. In some homes, particularly among the wealthy, whole rooms might be given over to altars intricately decorated to honor a family's ancestors.

MARCH OF VICE

During the height of summer, the people of Zinda celebrate the cultivation of the jeli flower with a multiday carnival. Built on traditions celebrating the city's wine trade, the March of Vice is overseen by the Prince of Vice—an organizer and theatrical figure. Chosen by the Kings of Coin, the masked Prince of Vice marches in the parade every evening. The parade is followed by the Covenant of Magic, magic-using elders who wave fans and brooms, symbolically sweeping Zinda's sin into the sea. On the tenth night, the Prince of Vice steps into the sea and sheds their mask, bringing the festivities to a close.

KINGS OF COIN

The Kings of Coin are the ruling council of Zinda, a collection of six elders from affluent families that represent specific trades. Their meetings occur weekly at the gilded collection of offices and towers known as the Vault of Justice. The following individuals currently hold positions on the council:

Grand Messer Amos Nir is head of the Kings of Coin and represents the Jeli Trade. He is the wealthiest, most influential leader in Zinda.

Madame Kit Mata represents the Grocers' Trade.

Madame Samira Arah is the newest member of the Kings of Coin. She represents the Jewelers' Trade and oversees the Silent Verse as head of security for the Kings of Coin.

Messer Solenn Avim represents the Weavers' Trade.

Myx Nargis Ruba represents the Tavern Keepers' Trade.

Myx Massimo Ain represents the Smiths' Trade.

The Kings of Coin keep order using their vast wealth, their societal influence, and the Silent Verse—the rulers' police force. The Silent Verse protects the Kings of Coin, collects information, and issues shadowy threats to keep political rivals in line.

NAMES

Zindanese of all origins receive their given name on the tenth day after their birth. The family gathers at this time, and the elders choose an appropriate ancestor's name to bestow upon the child. The following are examples of common names:

Feminine. Inyz, Larisa, Onika, Tanea
Masculine. Emran, Jacapo, Melo, Solenn
Gender-Neutral. Amal, Elar, Jari, Pirro
Surnames. Ain, Aran, Haro, Nir, Sur
Titles. Madame, Messer, Myx

LEGENDS OF ZINDA

In the oldest legends, spirits of the jungle and ocean worked together to create Zinda where fire once met the sea, creating the black volcanic sand above which the city stands. These beings raised stone buildings from the earth, shifting rivers and trees to accommodate them. Satisfied with their creations, the ancestral apparitions welcomed the first Zindanese. Lately, the datura who walk the jungles warn that these spirits are agitated and seek appeasement from Zinda for its avarice.

The festival called the March of Vice shares similar supernatural origins. Tales tell of wicked spirits corrupting the people before being cast into the sea by a parade of elders. This legend is commemorated every summer through the March of Vice, with the members of the Covenant of Magic assuming the mantle of the elders.

MAP 5.2: ZINDA

ADVENTURES IN ZINDA

Consider the plots on the Zinda Adventures table when planning adventures in the city.

ZINDA ADVENTURES

d6	Adventure
1	Madame Nasana Lar hosted an exquisite banquet for her rival Elucidarium divas, then the guests transformed into **zombies.** Diva Lar needs help clearing her home and her name—supposedly having had nothing to do with her guests' fates.
2	Myx Janisa Davi, an **archmage** of a school called the Arcane Coterie, has chosen their apprentice: a youngster in the city's laborer district. The apprentice has disappeared, and Janisa seeks assistance locating them.
3	The notorious giant caiman called Tikoloshe (**giant crocodile**) has wrecked many ships bound for Zinda. The Kings of Coin hire the characters to slay the deadly—and perhaps possessed—beast.
4	The lover of one of the Kings of Coin is revealed as a member of the Bloodletters. The paramour now needs help escaping the city ahead of Silent Verse **assassins.**

d6	Adventure
5	Locals are disappearing while swimming in forested pools near Zinda. Evidence suggests they have been kidnapped by a cabal of **sea hags.**
6	A massive silk cotton tree with a fiendish aura attracts a host of **banshees.** A datura seeks help in appeasing these mournful spirits.

CHARACTERS FROM ZINDA

If players want to create characters native to Zinda, consider asking them the following questions during character creation:

Are you affiliated with any of the organizations in Zinda? Do you belong to the Bloodletters or the Silent Verse? Should laborers be permitted the same rights as plutocratic rulers?

How do you celebrate the March of Vice? Do you revel with friends and local laborers? Do you attend galas among the wealthy? Do you perform in sequins and feathers as a Elucidarium diva?

What do you know of the forest's spirits? Have you trained as a mystical datura to hear spirits' voices and learn their ways?

SINS OF OUR ELDERS

AN ADVENTURE FOR 6TH-LEVEL CHARACTERS

A BELOVED FOLK HERO OF THE CITY OF Yeonido was wronged by the royal family and died in shame. Unable to rest peacefully, she returned as a spirit called a gwishin and became convinced that the city she had dedicated her life to had forgotten her. Now the powerful spirit spreads a mysterious fog across the land that drains the memories of Yeonido's people so they aren't even aware of their own ruin.

BACKGROUND

For decades, Dae Won-Ha dedicated her life to Yeonido, serving as a magistrate and protector as the city-state developed into a hub for trade. As Yeonido's population exploded after years of prosperity, Won-Ha ensured that the city was expanded with care for the wilderness, and the lower-class laborers and artisans of Yeonido reaped the benefits of the city-state's success. The common people cherished her, but the attitude of others was not so kind.

In time, merchants seeking to line their pockets began to embezzle government funds. City planners accelerated expansion into the forest without care for sustainability, and the local nobility began to monopolize the benefits of the booming economy. Whenever Won-Ha protested, royal advisor Young-Gi—the brother of Queen Young-Soo—dismissed her concerns and undermined her authority. Eventually, political tensions turned the folk hero into a figure of infamy. Meanwhile, Young-Gi publicly gave Queen Young-Soo credit for all of Won-Ha's achievements, ensuring that the queen's legend would never fade, while Won-Ha was forgotten. Unable to bear the lie swallowed by her beloved people, Won-Ha grew ill and died. She passed on with no money, no clan, and no deeds credited to her name.

When Queen Young-Soo died ten years ago, a monument to her was unveiled in the city's Park of the Elders. The next night, Won-Ha rose as a type of ancestral spirit called a gwishin and began haunting the monument. When no family claimed the spirit as their descendant, the city's spirit arbiters—magistrates responsible for rogue gwishin—tried to quell the angry spirit. As a former magistrate herself,

though, Won-Ha's spirit managed to avoid the spirit arbiters and is growing in power.

Just as Won-Ha was intentionally removed from Yeonido's story during her lifetime, her gwishin believes she has been forgotten by the city's people. In response, Won-Ha's gwishin has cursed the city's people, causing them to forget the source of the ruin she brings down upon them.

PRONUNCIATIONS

The Yeonido Pronunciations table shows how to pronounce names that appear in this adventure. In Halri, the local language, *g* at the start of a syllable is pronounced as in *goat*, *i* is pronounced as the *ee* in *seek*, *o* as the *o* in *code*, and *u* as the *u* in *rule*.

YEONIDO PRONUNCIATIONS

Name	Pronunciation
Bi Chin-Hae	bee chin-hay
Da Ju-Won	dah joo-wan
Dae Won-Ha	day wan-ha
Gwishin	gwee-sheen
Hwang Jung-Soon	h-wah-ng juh-ng-soon
Jin-Mi	jeen-mee
Kun Ahn-Jun	kun ahn-june
Nah Dae-Shim	nah day-sheam
Yeonido	yeohn-ee-doh
Young-Gi	yung-gee
Young-Soo	yung-soo

SETTING THE ADVENTURE

Use the following suggestions to help contextualize Yeonido in a wider world:

Through the Radiant Citadel. Characters traveling from the Radiant Citadel arrive only a few miles outside Yeonido. If you wish to further detail the city and its surroundings, use the "Yeonido Gazetteer" section at the end of this adventure.

Dragonlance. Either the island of Enstar or the New Coast region could host Yeonido. The distant relationship between the people of Krynn and

MONSTERS AND WILD BEASTS MYSTERIOUSLY
APPEAR TO MENACE THE PEOPLE OF YEONIDO.

their gods could be another reason why some of the city's dead have difficulty finding peace.

Forgotten Realms. The city of Yeonido could appear at the northeast edge of the Gulthmere along the Sea of Fallen Stars, making it an isolated but growing trade city at the edge of a vast wilderness.

CHARACTER HOOKS

Consider the following ways to involve characters in this adventure:

Festive Homecoming. Every spring, the people of Yeonido gather to encourage a bountiful harvest during the weeklong Dan-Nal Festival. The characters' families or friends invite them to visit for the festival.

Friend of Ahn-Jun. A character has a connection to Magistrate Kun Ahn-Jun, perhaps knowing them as a family friend or having helped them obtain supplies for Yeonido in the past. When Ahn-Jun has strange experiences no one else remembers, the magistrate asks that character to come to Yeonido to investigate.

Lost and Forgotten. Someone the characters know has died mysteriously in Yeonido, and no one knows why. The characters go to the city to learn more about this tragedy.

CYCLE OF DREAD

A bitter spirit and strict local traditions trap Yeonido in a cycle of quiet suffering. While spirits called gwishin are well known among the city's populace, social mores prevent people from speaking openly about their dead ancestors. One vengeful gwishin takes advantage of this custom to torment the city.

GWISHIN

Gwishin are the spirits of those who were wronged in life and died without receiving justice. They are intimately connected to Yeonido and the traditions of the city itself. While some manifest as Undead creatures, others are spiritual forces that seek to express an unfulfilled desire or familial shame.

Reputation is of paramount importance to the people of Yeonido, who adhere to strict social norms to avoid bringing shame to their clan. If a family member dies and becomes a gwishin, the burden is on the clan to appease the spirit. Asking for help would require the family to publicly acknowledge the missteps that created the gwishin—which is considered more shameful than the peril an unchecked gwishin might cause. But a gwishin's power grows over time, making it important for these troubled spirits to be quelled quickly.

Gwishin of Dae Won-Ha

The rage of Won-Ha's gwishin has gone unchecked for decades and is focused on the statue of Queen Young-Soo in the Park of the Elders. Throughout the adventure, the characters can obtain relics connected to the memory of Won-Ha. These objects can help the characters establish a connection to Won-Ha's spirit and potentially put the gwishin to rest.

Won-Ha's spirit manifests its power throughout Yeonido in two ways.

Spirit Fog. Won-Ha's gwishin can cause fog to lightly obscure the city within 1 mile of the Park of the Elders. The fog lasts for 5 minutes, though the gwishin can disperse it sooner. The gwishin can summon this fog up to three times per day.

Faded Memories. When the summoned fog fades, each creature of the gwishin's choice within the fog must make a DC 16 Wisdom saving throw. On a failed save, the creature is cursed and permanently loses its memory of the fog and what happened within, its mind filling in the gap in time. Creatures that can't be communicated with telepathically are immune to this effect. A *remove curse* or *greater restoration* spell cast on an affected creature restores its true memory. The gwishin typically manipulates only the memories of Yeonido's residents, not those of visitors.

Yeonido Customs

A character who wants to understand more about Yeonido's customs related to gwishin and the dead can learn the following by asking the city's residents or by succeeding on a DC 12 Intelligence (History) check:

- Yeonido's people are expected to present a brave face regardless of what hardships they're facing personally.
- Talking about another person's mishaps in public brings great shame to that person. To be good neighbors, people don't speak openly about others' troubles. This reluctance to speak of others' hardships makes talking about gwishin taboo.
- Residents of Yeonido readily assist their neighbors and help one another if asked, but also go to great lengths to ignore—or plausibly not see—things that might be embarrassing to others.
- To speak ill of the royal family—particularly the popular Queen Jin-Mi—is to betray a profound trust.

If a distasteful topic is broached with a citizen of Yeonido, conversation turns awkward. Most people try to change the subject unless they are pressed, and then they speak vaguely or in hypotheticals.

Starting the Adventure

The adventure begins as the characters near the walls of Yeonido. Read or paraphrase the following description as the party draws close to the city gates:

> The curving walls of the city of Yeonido come into view. Atop the walls, tall, colorful flags and ribbons flutter from poles. Traders, guards, and workers come and go through a grand gate, passing from the surrounding farmlands into the maze of graceful structures beyond. As you watch, a pale mist rises from within the city. It drifts through the gates and breaks over the walls as if the entire city were exhaling one great breath.

The fog emanating from within Yeonido encompasses the city, lightly obscuring every street and building, including the interiors. This fog is unnatural, which a character who succeeds on a DC 12 Intelligence (Nature) check realizes. The *detect magic* spell also reveals that the fog emanates an aura of enchantment magic.

As the characters near the city gate, they notice the guards and other travelers are bewildered by the strange weather but do their best to ignore it or joke to hide their insecurity. If asked about the fog, locals say they've never seen anything like this.

The characters have no way of knowing it, but this fog is created by Won Ha's gwishin (detailed in the "Gwishin of Dae Won-Ha" section).

Peril in the Fog

Soon after the characters arrive at the gate, three hostile **gargoyles** swoop down to menace the people nearby. The gargoyles all resemble the same fierce-looking woman with a mouth full of fangs, claw-like nails, and feathered wings. Two **guards** cover the retreat of panicked locals as the gargoyles attack traders' wagons or anything that threatens them. The gargoyles fight until destroyed, and they dissipate into mist when defeated, leaving no remains behind.

The fog covering the area vanishes 1 minute after the gargoyles appear. If the gargoyles are still alive, they vanish along with the fog.

Fading Mists

As the fog fades, the guards and other locals menaced by the gargoyles look momentarily perplexed by where they are and any damage that's been done around them, but then stoically go about their business again as if nothing had happened. If asked about the fog, the monsters, or other occurrences within the fog, they react with bewilderment. Locals have had their memories altered as detailed in the "Gwishin of Dae Wong-Ha" section—but the characters aren't affected. Locals don't fixate on the characters' confusing questions or any strangeness affecting anyone nearby, as is local custom (see the "Yeonido Customs" section). The *detect magic* spell reveals that locals—in fact, almost all the creatures in Yeonido—radiate an aura of enchantment magic, an effect of the curse affecting their memories. There is one exception to this.

DISTRESSED MAGISTRATE

As the characters question the locals or otherwise demonstrate that they've experienced a strange event, a local magistrate notices them. The magistrate approaches if the characters react to this scrutiny or as the characters prepare to leave the gate.

> An official wearing a red and blue outfit embroidered with phoenix designs approaches. "I apologize for my impertinence," they say, "but I have an odd question I have to ask. Have you just suffered an unusual experience?"

The magistrate is Kun Ahn-Jun, the only person in Yeonido who isn't affected by Wong-Ha's curse.

KUN AHN-JUN

Magistrate Kun Ahn-Jun (neutral good, human **noble**) is a rising star in Yeonido's city bureaucracy despite their unassuming presence. They are humble and shy but show their inner strength during crises. Thanks to their *ring of mind shielding*—a gift from their mother, who was also a magistrate—they have not been affected by Wong-Ha's curse, as the spirit can't telepathically alter Ahn-Jun's memories. Ahn-Jun treasures the ring and usually keeps it invisible—a property of the ring—while wearing it. The magistrate takes little solace in this protection, though, as they don't know what's befallen the city or why, and they fear the strangeness is all in their own mind.

Personality Trait. "Please let me know how I can help. I'll do my best!"

Ideal. "I know who I am, and I know my limits."

Bond. "Magistrates should do everything in our power to serve those who need assistance."

Flaw. "I have to check to reassure myself that my work has been done right, even if I just checked."

MAGISTRATE
KUN AHN-JUN

SOLE WITNESS

Ahn-Jun is quietly distraught about the events affecting Yeonido. They can't make sense of what's happening and fear they're suffering visions or worse. If the characters claim to have seen the fog and creatures within it as well, Ahn-Jun is relieved and shares the following details with the party:

- No one else in the city has seen the fog, but it's been rising and falling multiple times every day for weeks.
- The fog used to occur only every now and then, but it has been growing more frequent.
- Ahn-Jun has tried to tell people about it but is always ignored.
- Strange monsters have slain people in the fog. Those who've witnessed the tragedies are shocked anew by the sight of bodies when the fog dissipates. The deaths are always considered accidents or bizarre but isolated incidents.
- If the characters don't already know about the city's customs, Ahn-Jun shares the details in the "Yeonido Customs" section and notes that these mores contribute to locals' willingness to overlook the strangeness afflicting the city.

NIKKI DAWES

After sharing these details, Ahn-Jun asks the characters to help them uncover what mysterious magic is afflicting Yeonido and can pay each character 250 gp. Ahn-Jun also promises to inform the city's rulers of the characters' service.

WHERE TO INVESTIGATE

Once the characters agree to assist Ahn-Jun, the magistrate notes three locations the characters should investigate:

Construction Site. Located outside the city walls where the Tiger District abuts the nearby forests, this construction site has suffered numerous attacks and unexplained setbacks.

Park of the Elders. Several attacks have occurred at this royal park in the Haetae District.

Tea Shop. The city's oldest tea shop is located in the Phoenix District. Two nobles were found wounded and nearly dead outside it only a few days ago.

Ahn-Jun can offer directions to all of these locations. While Ahn-Jun's job prevents them from traveling with the characters, the characters can contact the magistrate by speaking with the guards at the Seat of Dragons, the city's center of government.

EXPLORING YEONIDO

The characters can explore Yeonido and visit the locations Ahn-Jun directed them to in any order. Use the "Yeonido Gazetteer" section to detail locations beyond the investigation sites. The city as a whole is depicted on map 6.1.

TIGER DISTRICT

The Tiger District is a relatively new part of the city and is still undergoing construction, particularly along the forested stretch being cleared to the northwest. Even though the locals don't recollect the fog and beast attacks that Wan-Ha's gwishin uses to impede their work, they're aware that accidents, vandalism, and missing workers delay construction.

When the characters visit the area near the forest, they find a large construction site full of scaffolding and equipment. Laborers clear stumps and raise the frames of new houses while armed guards keep an eye on the nearby forest for signs of trouble.

Shortly after the characters arrive, Overseer Hwang Jung-Soon, the official in charge of the site, approaches them.

WHAT THE OVERSEER KNOWS

Hwang Jung-Soon (lawful good, human **guard**) is friendly and speaks evenly, but she's frustrated by her site's setbacks and is protective of her workers. She wants to know what the characters' business is at the potentially dangerous construction site and asks them to leave if they seem to simply be sightseeing. If the characters openly carry weapons, she's hopeful that they've been hired by the magistrates to investigate the recent accidents at the site.

If asked, Jung-Soon doesn't know anything about the fog, strange events, or attacks on the camp. However, characters who succeed on a DC 14 Wisdom (Insight) check sense that she's holding back something in her response. Those who push her by succeeding on a DC 14 Charisma (Persuasion) check get Jung-Soon to share some of the strangeness she's experienced, like finding dents on her weapons or personally suffering inexplicable minor wounds at random—unknown to Jung-Soon, these are the results of defending her work site from creatures appearing amid the fog.

Jung-Soon can also share the following details:

- Her laborers are in constant fear. They think some creature or gang is trying to harm them. No one's seen anything, but accidents and sabotage are common.
- She's frustrated with the city's magistrates, believing they're failing to protect her people.
- Dangerous animals live in the nearby forests, particularly tigers, and she has guards to keep such threats at bay. Regardless, she doesn't think animals are to blame for the danger around the work site.

Talk of sabotage is Jung-Soon and her workers' way of explaining what's happening to them. The strangeness at the work site is a result of the memory-affecting fog and creatures under the control of Wong-Ha's gwishin. If the characters ask to see any damaged equipment or Jung-Soon's scars, they bear what look like claw marks. A character who succeeds on a DC 12 Intelligence (Nature) check thinks the marks are from large feline claws.

WORK SITE ATTACK

During the conversation with Jung-Soon, the character who has the highest passive Wisdom (Persuasion) score is the first to notice fog drifting into the work site from the southeast. A round later, the work site is lightly obscured by the fog.

A moment after the fog rises, four tigers (use the **saber-tooth tiger** stat block) appear from the direction of the forest. These hostile tigers are 12 feet long and have blue-tinged fur. The site's workers and hired guards flee upon seeing the tigers, but Jung-Soon stands her ground. The tigers attack her or any creature that appears to be a greater threat.

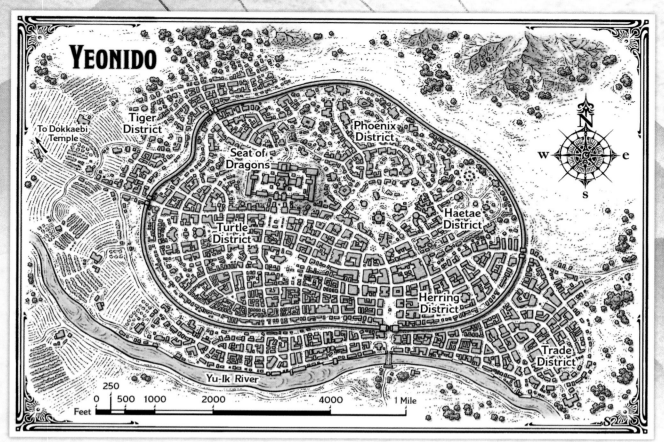

Map 6.1: Yeonido

Defeating the Tigers. The tigers discorporate into fog if defeated. They also vanish, along with the fog, 5 minutes after the fog appears. Before the last tiger vanishes, it retreats, heading toward the forest north of the construction site and a path hidden there (see the following section).

After the Attack. When the fog vanishes, neither Jung-Soon nor the workers recall the fog or tigers.

SHRINE OF THE HERO

An overgrown path heads into the forest near the construction site. A character might discover it by following a fleeing tiger or by investigating the tree line and succeeding on a DC 14 Wisdom (Perception) check.

The path is made of worn, muddy stones, and it leads 400 feet into the forest. It ends at a rocky pedestal bearing a slab of marble covered in moss and a simple stone lantern. A faint blue flame glows within the lantern.

Moss Slab. The moss on the slab can be cleared to reveal an inscription that reads "Dae Won-Ha, Warrior for the People" in both Common and Halri (the local language of Yeonido). Characters who succeed on a DC 18 Intelligence (History) check recognize the name as an obscure magistrate from Yeonido's past. Few others recognize the name, but Ahn-Jun does if asked (see the "Lingering Memories" section). Anyone who recognizes the

name also knows it's odd that such a figure would have a shrine dedicated to them—an honor usually awarded only to heroes.

Lantern. The lantern bears a magical flame that emits dim light for 10 feet and no heat. The *detect magic* spell reveals that the candle has an aura of evocation magic. If the name Dae Won-Ha is spoken within 10 feet of the candle, it momentarily flares in intensity. The lantern also flickers if brought within 10 feet of the teacup from the Phoenix District or the amulet Young-Gi carries (see the "Phoenix District" and "Estate Gardens" sections). The lantern can be moved and weighs 3 pounds. If the lantern is brought before the gwishin of Dae Won-Ha in the Park of the Elders, the spirit might be convinced the people of Yeonido still remember her.

PHOENIX DISTRICT

The oldest area in the city, the Phoenix District is adjacent to the royal palace known as the Seat of Dragons, and it is populated exclusively by nobles and the wealthy elite. Despite locals not recollecting the attacks in the area, the people know many have been harmed on the streets and fear that some gang or murderer is at large. The tea shop the characters are looking for is famous and is easy to find by asking any passerby.

The Tea Shop

The oldest tea shop in Yeonido was simply called the "Tea Shop" when it was built hundreds of years ago, and so it remains known to this day. The shop is decorated with hundreds of teacups arrayed on shelves; many cups bear the names of famous past patrons, adventurers, nobles, and royals.

The owner, a talkative, neutral human **noble** named Bi Chin-Hae, greets everyone who enters, offering to prepare them a pot of buckwheat or jujube tea. Chin-Hae grows taciturn if asked about the recent attack near his shop or the troubles in the city, speaking about these events only in vague terms—he doesn't want the area around his shop to be considered dangerous. A character who purchases a pot of tea for 2 sp or who succeeds on a DC 12 Charisma (Persuasion) check can convince Chin-Hae to mention that the two nobles attacked near his shop were named Nah Dae-Shim and Da Ju-Won and that they often play the game of baduk at the nearby baduk hall, a raised courtyard that's the social center of the Phoenix District.

Outside the shop, no evidence of the recent attack remains.

Baduk Hall

The baduk hall is three blocks away from Chin-Hae's tea shop. Characters who have proficiency in Performance know baduk is a game of strategy played on a board using black and white pieces. Additionally, baduk halls are popular gathering places, particularly for old or noble families.

At the baduk hall, dozens of pairs of players concentrate at tables covered in circular, black and white pieces. Hall guards or attendants can easily direct the characters to Dae-Shim and Ju-Won.

Nah Dae-Shim, a dwarf man, and Da Ju-Won, a human woman, are in the middle of an intense game. Both are neutral **nobles**. They're not unfriendly, but they're not interested in talking at the moment. The pair are happy to talk after their game—but it will take 3 hours to reach its conclusion. A character who succeeds on a DC 16 Charisma (Persuasion) check convinces the nobles to take a break from their game to talk. Alternatively, a character who watches their game and succeeds on a DC 16 Wisdom (Insight) check can point out strategic opportunities in the game to both sides, causing the game to conclude in 10 minutes.

Talking with the Nobles

When they're ready to talk, Dae-Shim and Ju-Won call for rice wine and ask the characters their business. The pair willingly share any of the following details.

- During a visit to the Tea Shop after dusk about a week ago, Dae-Shim and Ju-Won were both nearly killed.
- They both recall seeing a strange woman lingering near the shop.
- The next thing either of them remembered, they were waking up. Passersby found them near the shop and summoned a priest to aid them.

Neither of the nobles knows who the woman was, and they have no memory of the fog. However, if a character succeeds on a DC 14 Charisma (Persuasion) check, one of the nobles reluctantly reveals they think she was a gwishin. They can provide any of the information in the "Gwishin" section earlier in this adventure, but they don't like talking about such things. The nobles don't know why such a spirit might be lurking around the tea shop, but they suspect the proprietor Chin-Hae would know.

Back to the Tea Shop

If the characters return to the Tea Shop and ask Chin-Hae about the spirit seen around his shop, he claims to know nothing about that. If pressed, though, he shares the following information:

- He has seen a spirit that resembles a long-dead but regular customer who was famous in her time: Magistrate Dae Won-Ha.
- He has infrequently glimpsed the spirit near his shop, but also once at the Park of the Elders when he was walking home around midnight.
- Dae Won-Ha was an active magistrate and hero of the people, responsible for many social works.
- She was ultimately overshadowed by the last queen, Young-Soo. Chin-Hae doesn't know what happened to her after that.

As he explains this, he fetches a pair of teacups from a shelf. The cups are a set and bear the names Young-Gi—the uncle of the current queen and brother of Young-Soo—and Won-Ha. As the cup bearing Won-Ha's name is taken down, it glows with a faint blue light and pulses every time the name Won-Ha is spoken within 10 feet of it. It also flickers if brought within 10 feet of the lantern from the Tiger District or the amulet Young-Gi carries.

Chin-Hae allows the characters to borrow the cup if they ask. If the cup is brought before the gwishin of Dae Won-Ha in the Park of the Elders, the spirit might be convinced the people of Yeonido still remember her.

If asked about Young-Gi, the shop owner shares that the elderly noble still occasionally visits the shop, but he is retired and spends much of his time at home. If the characters choose to visit Young-Gi, proceed with the "Estate Gardens" section.

HAETAE DISTRICT

The Park of the Elders, in the Haetae District, is a beautiful public space devoted to walking and peaceful contemplation. It features a stately monument to the late Queen Young-Soo, aunt to Queen Jin-Mi. Read the following description if the characters visit this statue:

> The monument depicts a regal dragonborn seated on an ornate throne, a vision of wisdom and grace. She cradles a large scroll in one arm and raises the other hand as if about to speak. Stone plaques set into the statue's foundation are engraved with Queen Young-Soo's many achievements.

A character who reads the plaques and succeeds on a DC 20 Intelligence (History) check recalls that many of the queen's accomplishments echo those of the obscure magistrate Dae Won-Ha. If asked, Ahn-Jun also notes the overlap with the magistrate's efforts (see the "Lingering Memories" section).

If the characters arrive before speaking with Young-Gi, the park is lovely but empty. After they've learned more about Dae Won-Ha as part of their investigation, they encounter her gwishin here, as detailed in the "Spirit of the Past" section.

ESTATE GARDENS

Former royal advisor Young-Gi spends little time at the great palace known as the Seat of Dragons these days, instead enjoying retirement in the gardens of his small estate, where the Phoenix District meets the Haetae District. The characters might learn about Young-Gi from Chin-Hae at the Tea Shop or by speaking with Kun Ahn-Jun. Four **guards** at the gate to Young-Gi's estate prevent strangers from meeting with the nobleman uninvited, but Ahn-Jun can provide the characters with a message to win them a meeting. Alternatively, a character who succeeds on a DC 16 Charisma (Intimidation or Persuasion) check convinces the guards to let them see Young-Gi.

When the guards admit the characters, they escort the characters to the estate's gardens. Read the following when the characters enter:

> Trees hide the estate's walls from view, creating the illusion of being in a forest clearing. A pond dominates the center of the garden, with a pavilion overlooking the water. The place is a serene sanctuary, hidden from the clamor of the surrounding city.

A few moments later, an elderly dragonborn man enters the garden. This is Young-Gi.

YOUNG-GI

As the uncle of the current queen, Jin-Mi, and brother of the previous queen, Young-Soo, Young-Gi (neutral, dragonborn **noble**) is accustomed to wealth and privilege. A life spent enjoying his status has made him charming and personable but also haughty. As he ages, however, he remembers the few true friends he once had and regrets how he treated Dae Won-Ha.

YOUNG-GI

The elderly dragonborn's red scales aren't as lustrous as they once were, and he wears fine silk robes to compensate.

Young-Gi is also a victim of the gwishin's curse, so he doesn't recall the fog or the threats that appear within. But as he knew Dae Won-Ha and personally downplayed her achievements, he knows much about her past. He's not eager to reveal it, though.

Personality Trait. "Thank you for speaking to me. I promise you my full attention."

Ideal. "There is nothing more important than family, don't you think?"

Bond. "I hope the people will remember me as a hero."

Flaw. "Some members of my family waste their privilege and influence. I don't."

Forgotten Secrets

Young-Gi is calm and charismatic, and he listens intently when the characters speak. Because the elderly dragonborn is secure in his position, he isn't worried about the characters' visit. If they mention Dae Won-Ha, he's surprised and grows reflective. He shares his memories only if the characters present him with the lantern from Dae Won-Ha's forgotten memorial or her teacup, or if a character succeeds on a DC 12 Charisma (Persuasion) check. If convinced to speak about his old friend, he shares the following information:

- Dae Won-Ha was a brilliant magistrate and hero of the people. Much of the prosperity and equality Yeonido now enjoys is due to her work.
- Few remember Won-Ha's efforts, attributing them to Young-Gi's sister, the former queen, Young-Soo.
- Although the people once honored Won-Ha, the magistrate died in relative obscurity.

The Forgotten Magistrate. If Young-Gi is asked why Won-Ha was forgotten, he's reticent to answer. Through roleplaying or by succeeding on a DC 14 Charisma (Persuasion) check, a character can convince the noble to confess the following truths:

- He was personally responsible for undermining Won-Ha's work and crediting her successes to his sister, Queen Young-Soo. He did this not out of malice, but out of devotion to his family and the crown, believing any individual who the people place above the ruling class must be treated as a threat.
- He regrets what he did, but he has never worked up the courage to make amends to Won-Ha's spirit. He fears doing so will tarnish his sister's memory and, by extension, his niece's rule.

The Forgotten Spirit. If the characters try to convince Young-Gi that something strange is happening in the city, he's not surprised. He doesn't recall the fog, but he's seen Won-Ha's gwishin several times at the royal park called the Park of the Elders, specifically late at night near the statue to his sister Young-Soo. Since Won-Ha had no surviving family members, he finds it conceivable that her gwishin could have lingered for years since her death, growing powerful enough to affect the city. Young-Gi has called on spirit arbiters to investigate the park in the past, but they found nothing.

The Forgotten Amulet. Young-Gi encourages the characters to seek out the spirit at the Park of the Elders around midnight. If they agree, he produces a tarnished gold amulet with Won-Ha's name etched on it. This was one of her symbols of office, a memento of their former friendship that he's kept for years. If brought near the lantern from the Tiger District or the teacup from the Phoenix District, the amulet faintly glows. If the amulet is brought before the gwishin of Dae Won-Ha in the Park of the Elders, the spirit might be convinced the people of Yeonido still remember her.

LINGERING MEMORIES

Once the characters have visited some of the sites above, they'll likely learn the name Dae Won-Ha or Young-Gi, but they might not discover who these individuals are or how they relate to the city's past.

At any point, the characters might visit Kun Ahn-Jun at the Seat of Dragons. If asked about Dae Won-Ha, the magistrate doesn't recognize the name but can research her history. After four hours, the magistrate returns with the following facts:

- Dae Won-Ha was a celebrated magistrate in her time.
- The people of the newly constructed Tiger District built a small shrine honoring her in a nearby grove.
- She was close with the noble Young-Gi.
- Her career faltered, eclipsed by the successes of the renowned Queen Young-Soo.

If the characters ask about Young-Gi, Ahn-Jun also shares the following information about him:

- He's an elderly noble who lives at the edge of the Phoenix District.
- He's the brother of the last queen, Young-Soo, and the uncle of the current queen, Jin-Mi.
- Ahn-Jun can arrange for the characters to speak with him if they please.

Ahn-Jun knows nothing about any glowing antiques the characters might find or what use they have.

If the characters need any other pointers to put together the pieces of Dae Won-Ha's past or direct them toward seeking the spirit at the Park of the Elders at midnight, use Ahn-Jun to nudge them in the right direction. The magistrate has heard rumors

FROM THE PARK OF THE ELDERS, DAE
WON-HA'S SPIRIT SPREADS HER INFLUENCE
ACROSS THE CITY THAT FORGOT HER.

of a gwishin that lingers near the statue of Queen
Young-Soo in the Park of the Elders, but they volunteer this information only if the characters have
visited the other locations in the city and don't know
what to do next.

SPIRIT OF THE PAST

Once the characters learn about Dae Won-Ha and
that her gwishin often appears at the Park of the
Elders near the statue of Queen Young-Soo, proceed with this final encounter. This area is depicted
in map 6.2.

Won-Ha's spirit waits until midnight before appearing. When the characters are near the statue at
midnight, read the following description:

> The beauty of the park changes as fog spreads from
> the base of the monument to Queen Young-Soo.
> Something shapeless and malevolent wraps itself
> around the statue, coalescing as a robed figure that
> shrieks in pain and rage.

A mysterious fog covers the park, lightly obscuring
the area. The gwishin of Dae Won-Ha manifests
from the fog at the base of the statue as a **ghost**. She
appears as a middle-aged woman with dark hair
and mournful features. Two **gargoyles** emerge out
of the mist along with the spirit; like the gargoyles
from the start of the adventure, they bear Won-Ha's
face. Once defeated, these creatures discorporate
into fog. Won-Ha's gwishin reappears 24 hours later,
though, and continues to imperil the city until she is
put to rest.

MEMORIES OF DAE WON-HA

Despite being driven by sorrow and rage, the
gwishin of Dae Won-Ha is willing to speak to the
characters. Her initial communication is limited to
mournful statements like "They've all forgotten me"
and "I was nothing, I am nothing—soon they'll be
nothing." To engage with Dae Won-Ha meaningfully,
the characters must present evidence that people
still remember her—particularly by showing her
mementos from her life: the lantern from the Tiger
District, the teacup from the Phoenix District, and
the amulet Young-Gi kept safe.

PARK OF THE ELDERS

Gardens

Statue of
Young-Soo

1 Square = 5 Feet

W   E
N
S

If the characters present one or more of these tokens, or they attempt to speak with the dead and succeed on a DC 16 Charisma (Deception or Persuasion) check, the gwishin is calmed enough to talk; see "Conversing with the Gwishin." Additionally, depending on how many tokens the characters present, the following effects occur:

One Token. The gargoyles vanish into the mist.
Two or More Tokens. In addition to the gargoyles' disappearance, the fog fades from the park.

If the characters present no tokens and don't speak with the spirit, the gwishin and the gargoyles attack.

CONVERSING WITH THE GWISHIN

If the characters speak with Dae Won-Ha's gwishin, she can tell them the information in the "Background" section. She's angry that the city she dedicated her life to has forgotten her. She uses her accursed fog to make Yeonido's people suffer but forget why, leaving them with only pain and quiet confusion.

PUTTING THE GWISHIN TO REST

Once the characters have learned Dae Won-Ha's story, they can convince her gwishin she hasn't been forgotten in one of two ways.

Presenting Some of the Tokens. The characters can prove the people of Yeonido still remember Dae-Won by presenting any of the three tokens of remembrance and succeeding on a DC 16 Charisma (Deception or Persuasion) check. If the characters present two tokens, they have advantage on this check. If the characters fail this check (or haven't obtained any of the tokens yet), the gwishin attacks. If the characters succeed on this check, the gwishin makes them promise to spread the truth of her works and Young-Gi's role in hiding her successes across Yeonido. Should the characters do this, the gwishin finds peace, and neither she nor the fog returns. If they refuse or don't uphold their promise within a few weeks, her threat continues.

Presenting All the Tokens. If the characters present three tokens, the gwishin marvels that she hasn't been forgotten and thanks the characters. Before she vanishes for good, she provides the characters with the following charm (a type of supernatural gift detailed in the *Dungeon Master's Guide*).

Memory of the Ancestors. This charm calls the spirit of one of your ancestors to inhabit one weapon of your choice and watch over you. A weapon in your possession becomes a *weapon of warning* for the next 9 days. The charm then vanishes from you, and the weapon returns to normal.

CONCLUSION

Once Dae Won-Ha's gwishin is reassured that she hasn't been forgotten, the memory-affecting fog ceases to appear and the curse afflicting the people of Yeonido ends, restoring their memories. The characters might have more work to do to finally lay the gwishin to rest, such as reminding the city of Dae Won-Ha's historic role in the city's ascent to prosperity. Kun Ahn-Jun can help the characters with this and suggests restoring the magistrate's shrine outside the city and circulating records of Won-Ha's works. Ahn-Jun might also arrange a meeting with Queen Jin-Mi, who supports restoring knowledge of Dae Won-Ha's deeds.

If the characters don't follow through with their promise to the gwishin, the fog and mysterious attacks continue across the city.

Once the gwishin is put to rest, Ahn-Jun makes Queen Jin-Mi aware of the characters' role in saving the city. The Queen meets the characters, hailing them and Ahn-Jun as heroes and rewarding each party member with 500 gp rather than the 250 gp Ahn-Jun originally offered.

MIKE SCHLEY

Yeonido Gazetteer

The people of Yeonido, the City of Judgment, pride themselves on upholding tradition. Thousands of years ago, the great dragon Mireu entrusted the founders of the city-state with a mandate to forge and lead a great civilization. Yeonido's people took the dragon's words to heart, establishing a reverence for fealty and order that has remained steadfast through the centuries. Two main beliefs form the foundation of Yeonido society: that structure is key to all things, and that adherence to familial duty trumps all but one's devotion to the royal family.

But those noble traditions have a troubling side: the disquieting ancestral spirits called gwishin that refuse to leave the world behind. When a citizen of Yeonido dies feeling wronged or knowing that they've harmed others, they return as one of these spirits. It's up to the spirit's family to resolve the injustice and bring peace to the gwishin, allowing it to move onward. If a gwishin is allowed to endure, it grows ever more dangerous.

In recent years, some in Yeonido have begun to challenge the cultural reverence for ancient traditions, creating unease and discord. It may be no coincidence that gwishin are appearing more frequently than ever before, but it's unclear if more citizens are dying with unfinished business or if something more sinister is at work. Some even believe that the royal family has lost the trust of the great dragon Mireu. Everyone has an opinion, but no one knows how to restore harmony in Yeonido.

Yeonido Features

Those familiar with Yeonido typically know the following details:

Hallmarks. Yeonido is known for its citizens' familial loyalty and reverence for tradition, as well as for ancestral spirits called gwishin.

People. Humans and dragonborn are the most populous folk in Yeonido. Humans from Yeonido are primarily dark-haired and dark-eyed, and dragonborn have colorings based on their bloodlines, most commonly red or blue-green scales.

Languages. The city's official language is Halri, a language related to Draconic, though all citizens are also fluent in Common.

Noteworthy Sites

The city-state of Yeonido is nestled among fertile hills and deep forests. Though many dangerous beasts dwell in those lands, farming villages surround the walled city of Yeonido itself, supporting the city and benefiting from its protection.

The Seat of Dragons

In the center of Yeonido stands the Seat of Dragons, the palace that houses the royal family and government. The outer palace walls are a brilliant red, and the drawbridge over the moat is always open to allow citizens to enter. Important ceremonies take place in the castle courtyard, where Queen Jin-Mi can often be seen greeting her people.

Though the Seat of Dragons has no magical wards protecting it, gwishin never enter the palace grounds. Some speculate that this is because the Pearl of Mireu—a legendary gift the draconic founder of Yeonido granted to its people—is hidden somewhere in the palace.

Yu-Ik River

The Yu-Ik River flows just outside Yeonido's walls and is an essential part of the city. The riverbank holds a bright community of market stalls, colorful art, traders, peddlers, tinkers, and vendors of food and drink. On official holidays, people gather along the riverbank to tie ribbons on tree branches, play games along the shore, and celebrate with good food. However, these gatherings sometimes turn ugly, with fights breaking out due to muggings and territorial disputes arising among merchants. Cautious vendors often hire guards to protect them from trouble.

Dokkaebi Temple

Not far from the city, this cursed temple sits on a cliff above a majestic waterfall. Foolhardy children dare each other to spend the night within the forbidding temple—a challenge that has sometimes proven fatal. The temple is brilliantly painted with a thousand colors and marked with hundreds of spiritual seals. Although the site is rumored to be filled with treasures, only the most reckless thieves consider breaking in, for countless gwishin rage there each night, their screams echoing for miles.

Life in Yeonido

The people of Yeonido are proud of their traditions and welcoming to those who respect their ways.

Structured Society

Yeonido's residents believe in sacrifice for the good of the community. One must work selflessly, listen to one's elders, and act according to one's status for Yeonido to prosper. Structure is the central pillar of society. Class structure and family structure are key components of life within the city. Change is possible, but usually only when it's driven by members of the royal family or the noble clans. Queen Jin-Mi sits at the apex of the social order, followed by the noble elite, the various ranks of government magistrates, and the heads of each familial clan.

Clans and Identity

Clans live in compounds that often hold every member of the family, organized with its own hierarchy and led by a designated elder. But clans extend beyond families, often adopting outsiders who take up permanent residence in the city-state. When people meet, they exchange clan information before personal details, and the few folk in the city who have no clan—whether they were ejected from a clan or never adopted into one—are viewed with sympathy.

When people marry—whether for love or for social or political reasons, both of which are considered equally valid—they must choose which partner's clan they will belong to after the union. In rare cases, a new couple decides to establish their own clan, though they often face judgment from their birth clans.

Rule by Magistrates

The city-state of Yeonido is ruled by the beloved Queen Jin-Mi, a dragonborn said to be descended from the city's founder and first ruler, the dragon Mireu. The bureaucracy surrounding her consists of officials known as magistrates, who govern the city-state and enforce its laws. Those who aspire to become magistrates must undergo the exams—known collectively as the Test of Ascension—that take place each spring. These tests are notoriously difficult, and typically only those wealthy enough to afford time to study and special tutoring pass. Still, many less affluent but dedicated students have used this path to change their social status. Even non-citizens are allowed to take the test if they show proper respect for the process.

Queen Jin-Mi

Spirit Arbiter

Magistrates called spirit arbiters specialize in bringing an end—peaceful or otherwise—to rogue gwishin. They investigate the appearance of these spirits, soothe them, and then attempt to right the wrongs that hold them in the world. If left with no recourse, spirit arbiters destroy gwishin, but they seek to avoid doing so. These somber magistrates are known for the traditional, broad-brimmed black hat, called a gat, that they each wear as part of their uniform.

Names

Family comes first in Yeonido, and thus an individual's clan name is spoken before their given name. The royal family is an exception—they have no clan name, since it is expected that everyone should know them at first glance.

Given names in Yeonido typically have two syllables. Within each clan, siblings and cousins of the same generation often share one syllable of their name. For example, a couple might have a son named Ji-Min and a daughter named Ji-Yun. The head of the clan chooses each new child's name. The following are examples of common Yeonido names:

Clan Names. Bae, Chun, Ha, Ju, Seong
Feminine. Gyung-Won, Hana, Ji-Yun, Su-Min, Yun-Hi
Masculine. Do-Won, Gang-Min, Habin, Ji-Min, Oh-Seung
Gender-Neutral. Haneul, Han-Sol, Ji-Su, Si-Won, Yu-Min

Legends of Yeonido

According to the oldest tales, the Dokkaebi Mountains rose above a world shrouded in mist. All lands were bleak and terrifying in those days, cloaked in endless darkness. Those who had hope in their hearts set their sights on the Dokkaebi Mountains and traveled to the foothills, praying that something would save them.

Three great dragon siblings saw the penumbral world and descended from the heavens. The dragon Mireu gave the mortals at the Dokkaebi Mountains a divine gift—a pearl infused with the dragon's own heavenly power, which drove back the mist. Mireu's people formed the city of Yeonido, while the other two dragons established the lands of Xing and Umizu. Tales say that the Seat of Dragons in Yeonido is still home to Mireu's pearl, proof of the city's divine origins. However, if the pearl exists, its location is a secret fiercely guarded by the royal family.

The story of Yeonido's origins is often accompanied by the cautionary tale of the first gwishin. Her name has since been stricken from all records, but she was the sister of a king. Jealousy grew in her heart, and she raised her hand against her sibling. For this crime, she was struck down by Mireu, and a sickly monster appeared in her place.

Adventures in Yeonido

Consider the plots on the Yeonido Adventures table when planning adventures in Yeonido.

Yeonido Adventures

d8	Adventure
1	A magistrate in Yeonido has information the characters need, but she will share it only with characters who have passed the Test of Ascension.
2	Mercenaries capture a group of spirit arbiters trying to deal with a murderous gwishin (**ghost**). These mercenaries were hired by enemies of Yeonido seeking to undo the city from within.

d8	Adventure
3	Cunning **spies** are breaking into the homes of magistrates across the city, looking for proof that the Pearl of Mireu is hidden under the royal palace.
4	A **young red dragon** appears, claims to be the dragon Mireu, and demands offerings for its ages of protection. The characters are hired to verify or debunk the dragon's claims.
5	All except one member of a local clan are replaced by **doppelgangers**. Those who live near the clan have noticed them acting differently, but no one wishes to speak ill of them.
6	The characters are hired by a family to protect the gwishin haunting its members, whom they've come to a peaceable arrangement with, from spirit arbiters insistent on exorcising it.
7	The answer key for the upcoming Test of Ascension has been stolen. Unless someone quietly retrieves the key and determines who was responsible, the exams will be canceled and the city thrown into an uproar.
8	A tragic fire claims the lives of fifteen members of a Yeonido clan. The lone survivor begs the characters for help dealing with the fifteen gwishin (**specters**) that arise in the aftermath.

Characters from Yeonido

If players create characters from Yeonido, ask them the following questions:

What is your social class and clan? Is your family part of the nobility or the working class? Do you want to change your status? Are you an active member of your clan or have you left it behind?

Do you have a special role in the city's hierarchies? Are you a member of the royalty? Did you or do you hope to pass the Test of Ascension and become a magistrate? Are you an arbiter who deals with spirits?

How have gwishin affected you? Did a member of your family return as a gwishin? Did your family deal with their own gwishin, call aid in dealing with it, or let it linger? Did a gwishin of another clan teach, harm, or otherwise interact with you?

GOLD FOR FOOLS AND PRINCES

AN ADVENTURE FOR 7TH-LEVEL CHARACTERS

A TUNNEL COLLAPSE TRAPS MINERS DEEP within the Goldwarren, the great mine complex of the city-state of Anisa. But even more concerning, a survivor of the disaster reports being attacked by a creature thought to be long extinct. The characters must aid in rescuing the miners, but to do so they'll have to work alongside the rivals Prince Simbon and Prince Kirina—both of whom see the disaster as a way to influence their chances of claiming the imperial throne.

BACKGROUND

The three city-states of the Sensa Empire—Anisa, Niba, and Tarikh—compete for Empress Inaya's favor, hoping the empress will choose her heir from among their own royal families. This competition plays out in the cities' gold mines as each city vies for wealth and economic influence. But the Aurum Guild, to which most of the miners belong, holds great power over the city-states as the source of their wealth. Any young royal seeking consideration as the empress's heir must court the guild's favor.

The mines of Anisa, known as the Goldwarren, are extraordinarily efficient, but yesterday a tunnel collapsed, trapping seven miners inside. Amid efforts to reopen the mine entrance, a survivor claims to have seen a bizarre, many-limbed monster.

King Diara of Anisa has sent his eldest son, Prince Simbon, to take charge of the rescue mission. Diara hopes to raise Simbon's profile, thus gaining the empress's attention and securing Simbon as her successor. Unfortunately, the Aurum Guild favors Prince Kirina of Niba as its candidate for imperial heir, and he's intent on aiding the rescue mission.

PRONUNCIATION GUIDE

The Sensa Empire Pronunciations table shows how to pronounce many of the names in this adventure.

SENSA EMPIRE PRONUNCIATIONS

Name	Pronunciation
Anisa	ah-NEE-suh
Aurumvorax	au-rum-VOR-ax
Awa	AH-wah
Diara	dee-AHR-uh
Inaya	ih-NAI-uh
Kedjou Kamal	KED-joo cam-ALL
Kirina	keer-EEN-uh
Niba	NEE-buh
Sainesha	sai-NESH-uh
Simbon	SIM-bun
Sundasha	soon-DAH-shuh
Tarikh	tar-EEK
Uzoma Baten	oo-ZOH-muh BAH-ten
Zahra	ZAHR-uh
Zihaya	zi-HA-ya

SETTING THE ADVENTURE

Use the following suggestions to help contextualize the Sensa Empire in a wider world:

Through the Radiant Citadel. Characters who visit Sensa by traveling through the Radiant Citadel arrive near the city of Anisa. Use the "Sensa Empire Gazetteer" section to further detail the region.

Eberron. At a distant edge of the Menechtarun Desert on Xen'drik, Sensa could be a secluded oasis of peace amid the famously dangerous continent.

Forgotten Realms. The Sensa Empire might lie near to or within the desert of Anauroch. If placed at the edge of the great desert, it could be a rich trade partner to surrounding lands. If hidden deeper within, it might be a land of near-legend.

CHARACTER HOOKS

Consider the following ways to involve characters in this adventure:

Business Call. A character knows Uzoma, overseer of the Goldwarren, personally or through business dealings at the Radiant Citadel. She invites the

PRINCE KIRINA FENDS OFF AN ATTACK BY
TWILIGHT DUNE SCORPIONS.

characters to Anisa to discuss a trade opportunity, but a mine collapse occurs just before they arrive.

Imperiled Experts. The people of the Sensa Empire are famed as goldsmiths and jewelers. If the characters need a valuable object appraised or repaired, the Aurum Guild of Sensa can provide peerless experts. When the characters seek them out, they're distracted by a calamity.

Royal Attendants. King Diara of Anisa has heard about the characters and hopes they might guide his directionless son Prince Simbon. When the characters arrive, the king asks the characters to help Simbon resolve the Goldwarren disaster.

STARTING THE ADVENTURE

After arriving in Anisa, the characters overhear that the city's famed gold mine, the Goldwarren, has collapsed. Nearby, people are gathering to hear news of the missing miners, and two local princes will be speaking. Characters who ask questions about the situation among the gathered people can learn the following information:

- The Goldwarren is Anisa's famous gold mine. It's run by a group called the Aurum Guild.
- At least seven miners are trapped in the mine.
- Prince Simbon, the son of Anisa's king, is not widely respected in the empire.

- Prince Kirina comes from the neighboring city of Niba. He's a charismatic figure who's well-liked by the Aurum Guild.

Feel free to supplement this information with any details you wish to share about Anisa or the Aurum Guild from the "Sensa Gazetteer" section at the end of this adventure.

RIVAL PRINCES

When the characters arrive at the square, read or paraphrase the following:

Locals crowd a shaded square, listening to a fervent argument between two well-dressed human men wearing dark colors and gold jewelry.

"This isn't your place, Prince Kirina!" one man shouts. "This isn't your city! The trapped miners are my responsibility. As soon as the entrance is cleared—"

"But these are my people!" Kirina interrupts. "I value the friendship of the Aurum Guild, and I stand with my friends in their time of need. But don't worry, Prince Simbon. We can find something safe for you to do while we bring our missing family home."

Voices in the crowd rise as they declare support for one prince or the other. Most of the folk wearing the grimy tunics of miners are impressed when Kirina speaks, while the Anisan city folk shout agreement when Simbon speaks. As the debate continues, a muscular dwarf miner carrying a polished copper pick approaches the characters. This is Uzoma, the overseer at the Goldwarren.

OVERSEER UZOMA

Uzoma Baten (lawful good, dwarf **guard**) was selected as the Goldwarren's overseer due to her compassion and diligence. She sees this position as the highest possible honor and strives daily to be worthy as she labors alongside her fellow miners. Determined to do right by them, Uzoma doesn't hesitate to challenge orders she deems unfair—even if those orders come directly from King Diara.

Personality Trait. "I'm happiest when I'm working with my hands."

Ideal. "Though I might have more responsibility, I'm no better than anyone else who works in the Goldwarren."

Bond. "I would die to protect the miners of the Goldwarren."

Flaw. "I have to prove that I deserve my position."

MEETING UZOMA

Uzoma bluntly notes that she's looking for adventurers. She hopes to hire the characters to head into the mine and rescue the trapped miners, offering 300 gp to each character.

Uzoma also fills the characters in on the tension in the crowd:

- The folk of the Sensa Empire are loyal to the empress and their own city-states in equal measure. As such, most folk of Anisa favor Prince Simbon as the would-be heir to Empress Inaya.
- The Aurum Guild has thrown its support behind the more adventurous Prince Kirina of Niba, so many of the miners in the crowd favor him.
- Simbon has technically been given charge of the rescue mission by his father, King Diara. However, the prince seems rattled by the responsibility.
- Kirina has been in the city on private business for weeks, but he made a very public appearance after the accident at the mine. He's taken it on himself to volunteer for the rescue mission.

Once the characters agree to the mission, or if they want to learn more before signing on, Uzoma says she has someone she wants them to meet—a young miner who saw monsters in the mine before making his escape. She motions for the characters to follow her through the crowd.

PRINCES AND SCORPIONS

As Uzoma leads the characters through the crowd, they notice movement in the shadows across the street. Read the following description:

> Shouts ring out at the crowd's edge as massive, glowing scorpions rush from a shadowed alley. Prince Kirina draws a sword and races forward, while Prince Simbon hesitates before following.

The crowd flees, leaving only the characters and the princes to face five **giant scorpions**. Uzoma stands back and watches as the encounter unfolds.

The princes are friendly toward the characters and are quick to ally with them. Both use the **veteran** stat block, but they have only AC 11 and their Multiattack and Longsword actions. If a prince is reduced to half of his hit points or fewer, he uses the Dodge action to avoid taking further damage.

The scorpions are hostile and of a rare, fluorescent breed known as twilight dune scorpions. Any character who succeeds on a DC 16 Intelligence (Nature) check knows this and that the scorpions rarely venture from the deserts' depths.

The scorpions vanish when killed. A character who succeeds on a DC 12 Intelligence (Arcana or Religion) check realizes this is the mark of a magically summoned creature. A character familiar with conjuration magic recognizes that summoning giant scorpions in such numbers far exceeds the power of the *conjure animals* spell or other common magic.

In the aftermath of the battle, both princes thank the characters for their assistance.

KIRINA, PRINCE OF NIBA

As the eldest son of the king of Niba, Kirina (chaotic evil, human **veteran**) was raised knowing he might be named heir to the land's ruler, Empress Inaya. His childhood was filled with trips to her palace, the Azure Dome. In time, Kirina grew close to the empress. He came to see Inaya as a benevolent aunt, and his place as her heir seemed assured. Yet, as Kirina grew to adulthood, the empress didn't name him as her successor, a decision he came to resent.

Now, Kirina has made an alliance with the scheming High Priest Kedjou. They've used Kedjou's magical experiments to manufacture a calamity at the Goldwarren and to summon the giant scorpions. They plan to use these perils to establish Kirina as a hero in the eyes of the people and an obvious choice to be the empress's heir.

Personality Trait. "It's excusable to take abhorrent actions in pursuit of a higher goal."

Ideal. "Sometimes it's necessary to hurt those I love to accomplish my goals."

Bond. "I've devoted my entire life to becoming Empress Inaya's heir."

Flaw. "I'll stop at nothing to attain the throne."

SIMBON, PRINCE OF ANISA

Prince Simbon (neutral, human **veteran**) is loyal to Empress Inaya. His family seeks to ensure she chooses him as her heir, though he has never aspired to the position. But if one of Anisa's own were to rule the empire, it would be a point of pride for the whole land—so Simbon feels obligated to act as though he wants to be Empress Inaya's heir. In reality, Simbon believes his poor tactical mind and hedonistic bent make him a lackluster candidate.

Personality Trait. "I was raised to rule not only Anisa, but the entire Sensa Empire. Would that it were not so."

Ideal. "If you can't be who they want you to be, the least you can do is fake it."

Bond. "I respect my father even as he grovels to the empress on my behalf."

Flaw. "I don't want the life I'm supposed to want."

SEARCHING THE ALLEY

After the battle, characters who investigate the alley the scorpions originated from can make a DC 14 Intelligence (Investigation) check. If they succeed, they find a partial series of smeared magical runes drawn on the alley wall. A character who succeeds on a DC 12 Intelligence (Arcana or Religion) check knows that the runes are related to conjuration magic but can tell nothing more.

DEATH IN THE MINES

Soon after the giant scorpions are defeated, the crowd throngs Prince Simbon and Prince Kirina, lauding their heroics and asking what they'll do next. Uzoma ignores the chaos and, when the characters are ready, guides them to a young human at the crowd's edge whom she introduces as Awa—a young miner who escaped the Goldwarren. At Uzoma's prompting, Awa shares the following story:

- Awa and the rest of his crew—including his mother—were working a new excavation when it collapsed.
- Awa and the others were trying to escape when a snarling, eight-legged beast appeared.
- The beast would've killed Awa, but his mother, Zihaya, defended him. The creature attacked her in turn and dragged her away.
- In the chaos, Awa was separated from the others. He made his way to the entrance and was the last miner out before the entrance collapsed. No one else from his crew escaped.

If pressed, Awa can detail the creature that attacked him further (see the "Aurumvoraxes" section at the end of this adventure). A character who succeeds on a DC 16 Intelligence (Arcana or Nature) check recognizes the creature as an aurumvorax, a predator that eats precious metals but is thought to be extinct in the region.

After Awa shares his experience, Uzoma tells the characters how King Diara has been pushing to increase output at the mine to please Empress Inaya, excavating newer tunnels so quickly there's not time to fully reinforce them. The Aurum Guild has been warning of the potential for collapses within the mine, but has been ignored.

NEXT STEPS

As the characters finish their conversation with Awa, shouting among the princes' supporters causes Uzoma to intervene:

> "That's enough! All this talk is wasting breath. The crews at the entrance should have it cleared and shored up by day's end. We'll sort out who's on the rescue team then. But for now ..."
>
> As Uzoma speaks, Kirina and Simbon both step up, interrupting her to announce they'll gladly take a place in the rescue party. Their followers begin arguing again until Uzoma blows a piercing whistle.

OVERSEER UZOMA

> "If you want to help, stop arguing and do what I need you to do. Prince Kirina, you'll come to the Goldwarren with me. Prince Simbon, go find out what could be waiting for us in the mine. These adventurers will go with you. Let's get this done."

High Priest Kedjou

Uzoma tasks Simbon and the characters with seeking out Kedjou, a high priest visiting Anisa Academy. Kedjou has a rich understanding of the Sensa Empire's history and might know what lurks in the mine. Even if the characters already suspect aurumvoraxes, Kedjou can relate more about their history and how they were once removed from the region.

To the Academy

Prince Simbon escorts the characters to Anisa Academy, a ten-minute walk through the city. He's personable and speaks plainly, saying Kirina only seeks to make himself a hero to gain favor with the wealthy Aurum Guild. It's clear Simbon is frustrated, but characters who succeed on a DC 15 Wisdom (Insight) check recognize his complaints conceal jealousy of the well-liked rival prince.

Anisa Academy

The campus of Anisa Academy consists of buildings clustered around a wide courtyard. It's crowded with students, professors, and Acolytes of the Faceless Prophet—the Sensa Empire's clergy—milling between buildings. As the party seeks out Kedjou, Prince Simbon shares the following information:

- Kedjou has been in residence at the academy for only the past week. Visits from the high priest are rare.
- According to Simbon's friends, the entire campus is abuzz with speculation that Kedjou came to the academy to conduct secret research.

Finding Kedjou requires the characters to spend an hour asking around Anisa Academy or to succeed on a DC 14 Charisma (Persuasion) check while engaging with academy faculty. They eventually learn that Kedjou has taken up offices on the top floor of the academy's library.

Audience with the High Priest

When Simbon and the characters arrive at the library, a librarian ushers the group to Kedjou's private room on the library's top floor. Outside, two **guards** stand alert. Within, open tomes and scrolls lie spread across several tables, and Kedjou makes no effort to hide any of his notes, haughtily assuming no adventurer riffraff will understand it. Behind a screen in the corner stands a bed, suggesting the room doubles as Kedjou's quarters.

High Priest Kedjou

Kedjou Kamal (neutral evil, human **priest**) was raised in an orphanage run by the Acolytes of the Faceless Prophet (detailed in the "Sensa Empire Gazetteer" section) and has long coveted power. As high priest, Kedjou does little to combat allegations of the Acolytes' corruption—and in fact, he's behind much of that corruption. He is single-mindedly focused on securing an advisory position to Empress Inaya's heir. This mission has brought him into a pact with Kirina, Prince of Niba. The prince has offered Kedjou the position the priest seeks if he helps Kirina take the throne.

Barbs and Beasts

Kedjou expresses delight at seeing Prince Simbon and respectfully greets the characters. Characters who succeed on a DC 14 Wisdom (Insight) check sense animosity toward Prince Simbon. In the course of the conversation, Kedjou discreetly mocks the prince, going so far as to sympathize with Simbon about how straining it must be to busy himself among the common rabble or visit a library.

If told about the creatures in the mine, Kedjou believes the description matches that of monsters called aurumvoraxes, but he declares this is impossible as they're long extinct in the region. He can share the following details about the creatures:

- Aurumvoraxes are gold-eating predators that once claimed all the mines of the Sensa Empire as their territory. They were hunted down by Emperor Kassa a millennium ago. The creatures were eradicated from the region, and none have been seen since.
- Kedjou doesn't believe Awa's story. If any of the creatures had survived the purge, their hunger for gold would have revealed the creatures long ago.

If pressed to suggest what else might be in the mine, Kedjou flounders, then suggests it could be nothing more than overgrown rats.

SUMMONING SECRETS
During the conversation with Kedjou, characters who have proficiency in the Arcana or Religion skill catch sight of interesting details in the notes spread around the room. The notes suggest Kedjou is researching a unique conjuration spell. A character can steal a page from the notes by succeeding on a DC 12 Dexterity (Sleight of Hand) check. If they fail, the character still pockets the page but draws Kedjou's attention. The priest curtly declares he needs to get back to his studies and dismisses the group.

Any character who later spends at least 15 minutes investigating Kedjou's notes can make a DC 14 Intelligence (Arcana or Religion) check. If the check succeeds, the character realizes the priest is investigating how to summon powerful creatures and cause them to linger for longer than usual.

PUSHING KEDJOU
Characters might challenge Kedjou on his animosity toward Prince Simbon or question whether the priest's research is related to the giant scorpions appearing in the city. Kedjou initially denies any such suggestions, but a successful DC 14 Charisma (Persuasion) check or suitable roleplaying convinces Kedjou to admit he dislikes Simbon. He believes that if Simbon wins the empress's favor and is named heir, it will be because of Anisa's wealth, not because Simbon deserves the position.

Despite this being said to his face, Simbon chuckles awkwardly and doesn't defend himself except to say that everyone's entitled to their opinion. Kedjou requests the characters leave soon after.

If pressed about the scorpions, Kedjou insists the characters leave, not wanting to reveal that he was involved in summoning the creatures and the aurumvoraxes in the Goldwarren—as the characters later discover.

If the characters refuse to leave when Kedjou requests, he summons his guards, who escort the party out of the building.

SUPPORT FOR PRINCE SIMBON
After leaving the library, if a character asks Simbon about Kedjou's insults or assessments of his leadership potential, the prince tries to shrug it off. He also doesn't think much of his future as a leader. Through roleplaying or by succeeding on a DC 14 Charisma (Persuasion) check, a character can encourage Simbon to take his role as someone the people look up to more seriously. Doing so earns the characters Simbon's respect and influences the prince's willingness to speak out later in the adventure (see the "Beyond the Gold Warren" section).

TO THE GOLDWARREN
Whatever the outcome of the encounter with Kedjou, Prince Simbon suggests the group head to the Goldwarren, which lies a few hours north of Anisa. He doesn't relish the idea of venturing into the tunnels, but he truly wants to help those trapped within. He also hates the idea of Kirina starting the search effort without him.

Unless the characters have other pressing business in the city, Simbon calls for a coach to convey them there. He opposes any talk of breaking into Kedjou's quarters or harming the high priest, both of which would be scandals for Simbon's family.

THE GOLDWARREN
The Goldwarren's main entrance is wide enough for two carriages to drive through side by side; the mine then branches into a labyrinth of tunnels. When the party arrives at the Goldwarren, read or paraphrase the following description:

> Golden statues of royals smile down on visitors from atop the impressive, multistory entrance to the Goldwarren. While rubble spills from the open gates leading into the mines, a path has been cleared through it into darkness. Adjacent to the ornate entryway are several modest offices, bunkhouses, and workspaces.

A crowd gathers around the mine's huge entrance tunnel. Nearby, Uzoma and Prince Kirina watch as miners inspect the new posts shoring up the damaged tunnel. Uzoma welcomes the characters and asks them to enter the mine and find the missing miners. Both Prince Kirina and Prince Simbon plan to join the characters and won't be dissuaded.

Uzoma won't join the expedition but coordinates the rescue and rebuilding efforts; she notes that the missing miners should have been working in the tunnels south of a prominent junction. She provides the characters general directions to reach the section of the mines worth investigating.

ARGUING PRINCES

Simbon and Kirina join the characters for their expedition. To highlight the tension between them, describe the princes insulting each other using the following summaries for inspiration:

Connections to the Throne. Simbon mentions how close Kirina once was to Empress Inaya, pondering aloud what the prince might have done to earn the empress's disfavor.

Favored of the People. Simbon idly speculates that Kirina is interested in the Aurum Guild's support because he's so unpopular in Niba and needs to seek out the best friends money can buy.

Strength of Arms. Kirina reminisces about his past adventuring missions, downplaying Simbon's own combat experience.

KIRINA'S SECRET

During the expedition, Prince Kirina seeks opportunities to look heroic and undermine his rival, Prince Simbon. There's currently little evidence of Kirina and Kedjou's involvement in the Goldwarren's collapse, but Kirina carries with him a copy of the runes the high priest uses in experimental summoning rituals. Prior to the scorpion attack in Anisa, Kirina painted the runes from this paper in a nearby alley, preparing it for the priest's magic. In the course of the expedition into the Goldwarren, if Kirina falls prone, is rendered unconscious, or at another opportune time, this paper slips from his clothes. A character who succeeds on a DC 12 Wisdom (Perception) check notices the dropped paper before Kirina does. Alternatively, a character who sees Kirina drop the paper and recover it can steal the page from Kirina with a successful DC 14 Dexterity (Sleight of Hand) check.

If asked about the paper, Kirina is dismissive, claiming to have found it on the street. This copy of the runes might become useful evidence of Kirina's wrongdoing during the adventure's conclusion.

GOLDWARREN FEATURES

The stone tunnels and caverns of the Goldwarren have the following features:

Ceilings. The ceilings of the mine are 15 feet high.

Floors and Walls. The once-smooth walls have buckled after the recent tremors; the patches of rubble shown on the map are difficult terrain.

Gleaming Gold. Faint veins of gold lace the mine's walls. Mining or collecting ore worth 1 gp takes over an hour of effort.

Light. Metal torches set into wall brackets line the main junctions and turning points of the mine tunnels. However, their oil hasn't been replenished since the collapse, leaving the mine's tunnels and caverns in darkness.

Statues. The Goldwarren is a working mine but also a cultural site for Anisa's people. Immovable golden statues of Anisan royals (marked as stars on the map) smile from pedestals along the walls.

GOLDWARREN LOCATIONS

The following locations are keyed to map 7.1.

G1: JUNCTION TUNNEL

After a short, cautious march from the mine entrance, the party reaches a large junction with a turntable where mine cart tracks lead into side tunnels: two leading north, two leading east, and two leading south. Rockfalls have sealed off both tunnels leading east and one of those leading north. One tunnel leading north and both tunnels stretching south—one of which Awa escaped from—are still open. Read the following text as the characters approach:

> Just in front of a massive mine track turntable that fills the junction, a body lies splayed on the rocky ground. Even at a distance, it's clear this miner died not from falling rubble, but from terrible slashing wounds.

As the party approaches the turntable, characters who have a passive Wisdom (Perception) score of 14 or higher hear skittering emanating from a nearby tunnel. Characters who have lower scores are surprised when several many-legged creatures hurtle out of the northwest passage. These five **aurumvoraxes** (detailed in the "Aurumvoraxes" section at the end of this adventure) are hostile and rush to attack.

Track Turntable. The mine track turntable can be controlled from a panel at its center, but it was damaged during the cave-in. A character who uses an action to operate the simple controls causes mechanisms below to screech as the entire turntable shakes—trying to rotate, failing, then halting. Every creature on the turntable except the operator must succeed on a DC 16 Dexterity saving throw or fall prone. Creatures with more than two legs have advantage on this saving throw.

Summoned Fury. When an aurumvorax is reduced to 0 hit points, it vanishes. If they did not already deduce this during the scorpions' attack, characters who succeed on a DC 12 Intelligence (Arcana or Religion) check know that this is the mark

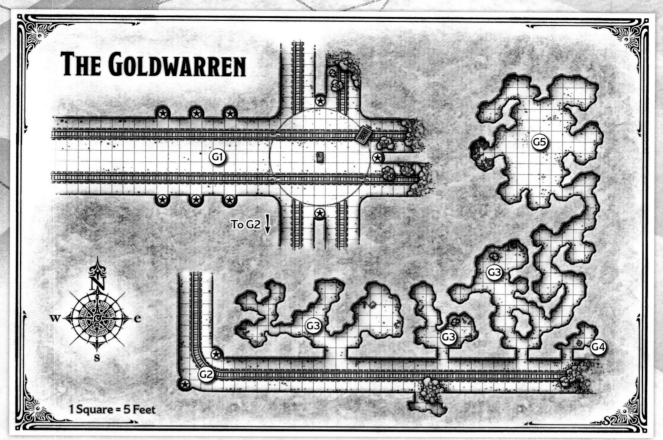

THE GOLDWARREN

To G2 ↓

1 Square = 5 Feet

MAP 7.1: THE GOLDWARREN

of a magically summoned creature, but also know of no spell that summons such creatures.

Miner Body. The body on the ground is that of a missing miner named Enwa, who was killed by an aurumvorax attack. If a character casts the *speak with dead* spell on the corpse, all its answers support Awa's story from the "Death in the Mines" section.

Multiple Paths. Awa wasn't sure which of the southern tunnels he fled through. Characters who search the area and succeed on a DC 14 Wisdom (Survival) check see that numerous aurumvorax claw marks lead from the southwest tunnel. If the characters head down that tunnel, they reach area G2 after 5 minutes of walking. If they follow any other tunnel, they reach a dead end after 10 minutes and have a 50 percent chance of encountering two **aurumvoraxes** gnawing on a seam of gold ore. These aurumvoraxes fight to the death and vanish when reduced to 0 hit points.

G2: SOUTHWEST TUNNEL

Warped cart tracks run down the center of this worked stone tunnel. Here and there, rockslides cover the floor where segments of wall have given way. Openings into rough-hewn caves line the northern wall.

Characters who have a passive Wisdom (Perception) score of 14 or higher notice signs of combat and bloodstains along the tunnel. Characters who have the Stonecunning trait can confirm that the tunnel is not in danger of collapsing, despite the crumbled walls.

The tunnel ends in a rockfall that would take days to clear. The entrance to area G4 is partially obscured by these rocks. Only a character who investigates this rockfall or succeeds on a DC 16 Wisdom (Perception) check notices the opening.

G3: NEWLY DUG CAVERNS

These three caverns are recent excavations seeking new profitable veins of gold. Use some or all of the following encounters in these caverns, depending on how quickly you want to reach the final showdown with the aurumvoraxes.

Danger Signs. A large red *X* is painted next to one cave entrance, a warning from the mining crew formerly working here. Inside the cavern, three patches of green slime cling to the ceiling (see the "Dungeon Hazards" section of the *Dungeon Master's Guide*) and drop on characters who wander in.

Dangerous Joke. The back wall of one cavern has collapsed—seemingly on top of a miner, though their boots are the only part of their body still visible. In truth, this rockfall happened months ago, and the boots were carefully stuck into the rubble as a joke by the crew working the wall. A character who succeeds on a DC 12 Intelligence (Investigation) check discovers the nature of the prank; a character who have a background in mining or with the Stone-cunning trait has advantage on the check. Anyone attempting to free the "body" must succeed on a DC 14 Dexterity saving throw to avoid taking 7 (2d6) bludgeoning damage from falling rubble.

Lounging Lizard. A friendly **giant lizard** lairs in one cavern. It was partly tamed by the miners and allowed to hunt rats and other vermin. The lizard charges the characters as soon as it spots them but doesn't attack immediately. Characters who succeed on a DC 14 Intelligence (Nature) check realize the creature is tame and hungry. The lizard attacks the characters only if they injure it, or if it's not placated with offerings of food.

G4: Abandoned Excavation

This small area shows signs that excavations were started here before being abandoned. At the far end of the chamber, a glowing gray stone protrudes from the rough ground. This *stone of controlling earth elementals* formed naturally via elemental magic, and the miners left it untouched until its power could be assessed. It can be removed from the rock surrounding it with a successful DC 16 Strength check, made with advantage by a character using a miner's pick or similar tool.

G5: Aurumvorax Nest

A tunnel dug by claws, not pick and shovel, extends from the easternmost of the newly dug caverns. As the characters approach, they hear sounds of movement from the large cavern beyond. This is the nest of the aurumvorax pack, including five **aurumvoraxes** and an **aurumvorax den leader** (detailed in the "Aurumvorax" section at the end of this adventure). Characters who want to sneak up on the aurumvoraxes can attempt a group DC 13 Dexterity (Stealth) check. (Assume one prince succeeds at the check and the other fails, canceling each other out.) With a successful group check, the aurumvoraxes are surprised.

When the characters enter the chamber, read the following description:

> The walls of this chamber are crudely dug and covered with scratches—particularly around seams of glistening ore. A half dozen deep alcoves circle a broad, open space. Two bodies lie in the center of the chamber.

As in earlier encounters, the conjured aurumvoraxes fight to the death and vanish when reduced to 0 hit points.

The bodies here are those of two of the missing miners. They both bear many claw and bite marks.

The Price of Power. During the fight, Prince Kirina tries to eliminate Prince Simbon as a rival. Kirina antagonizes one or more aurumvoraxes, then slips behind the other prince, leaving the monsters to attack Simbon. The character who has the highest passive Wisdom (Perception) score sees Kirina intentionally endanger Simbon.

Survivors. Three survivors—including Awa's mother, Zihaya—are holed up in an alcove to the west. They have blocked the alcove entrance with crates and mining gear. The aurumvoraxes ignore them while they remain out of sight. Each survivor uses the **commoner** stat block.

Suspicious Runes. Characters who investigate the area where the survivors were hiding can make a DC 14 Intelligence (Investigation) check. If they succeed, they find a series of runes drawn on the cave wall with chalk. If the characters found the runes in the alley after the scorpion attack, they recognize these being nearly identical. If they didn't, a character who succeeds on a DC 12 Intelligence (Arcana or Religion) check knows that the runes are related to conjuration magic but can tell nothing more.

Beyond the Goldwarren

Once the characters have found them, any survivors are eager to leave the mine. Before they do, Zihaya or another survivor whispers that they saw a stranger with long braided hair and colorful robes in the mines before the collapse. The stranger was drawing the runes in the cavern where the survivors were hiding—the survivor points them out if the characters haven't already noticed. If the characters describe Kedjou to the survivor, the miner supposes the high priest could be the person they saw.

Confronting the Prince

The characters might confront Prince Kirina over his attempt to harm Prince Simbon or any other evidence they've discovered. He answers questions confidently, deflecting accusations while smugly claiming no responsibility. Characters can press Kirina on these details by making a DC 14 Charisma (Intimidation or Persuasion) check. If the characters encouraged Prince Simbon to take his role more seriously in the "Support for Prince Simbon" section, Simbon vows to use his influence to reveal Kirina's goals—this gives characters advantage on this check. If one or more checks succeed, the characters coax the following information out of Kirina:

- Both the giant scorpions and aurumvoraxes were conjured by Kedjou to let Kirina play the part of the hero and increase his chances of becoming the empress's next heir.

- At Kirina's behest, Kedjou crafted the ritual that brought the aurumvoraxes to the Goldwarren.
- In exchange for positioning Kirina to become Inaya's heir, Kedjou expects to influence Kirina's policy decisions once Kirina becomes emperor.

If confronted with his responsibility for the miners who died for his charade, the prince merely shrugs. He blames the Aurum Guild for the shoddy conditions that caused the collapses, conveniently ignoring anyone who points out that the burrowing aurumvoraxes clearly contributed to them.

The Expedition's End

When the characters emerge from the Goldwarren, Uzoma and a crowd of miners flock around the group and hustle off any survivors to have their wounds tended to. Uzoma is quick to thank the characters and pay them. If either of the princes or all the survivors were killed, a second expedition is sent into the mines to recover the bodies.

Exposing the Enemy

If the characters mention Prince Kirina endangering Prince Simbon to Uzoma, she's surprised and listens to their story. Kirina denies the allegation, claiming the characters are in league with Simbon. With little patience for bickering amid her other duties, Uzoma quickly dismisses the distraction.

However, if the characters reveal that Prince Kirina and High Priest Kedjou were responsible for the aurumvoraxes' appearance and back up their claims with evidence, such as the matching symbols from the cave and Prince Kirina's or Kedjou's notes, Uzoma believes them and is outraged. Prince Kirina's confidence rapidly flags, and he makes a weak attempt at excuses, claiming the characters are lying on Prince Simbon's behalf.

If the characters encouraged Prince Simbon to take his role more seriously in the "Support for Prince Simbon" section, Simbon speaks out against Kirina, cutting through his excuses. If they didn't, a character must succeed on a DC 12 Charisma (Intimidation or Persuasion) check to undermine Kirina's defense.

If Kirina's excuses are believed, he swiftly leaves the area and, soon after, returns to his home city of Niba. Otherwise, with Prince Simbon's support, Uzoma throws status to the wind and orders her miners to lock Kirina in a nearby office while she summons the guards.

AWA IS AMBUSHED BY AN AURUMVORAX IN THE DEPTHS OF THE GOLDWARREN.

Conclusion

After Kirina's formal arrest, Uzoma demands an immediate investigation of High Priest Kedjou's lodgings to confirm the characters' claims. Bolstered by Prince Simbon's influence, she drives immediate action. The characters might join her, Simbon, and a group of guards in a surprise visit to Kedjou's chambers, where the high priest is caught off guard. His research notes—matching the runes in the Goldwarren—are discovered. The high priest is quickly taken into custody.

In the aftermath of Kirina's and Kedjou's arrests, Prince Simbon thanks the characters for supporting him and revealing Prince Kirina's plot. He rewards them with two of his family's treasures, an *adamantine chain shirt* and a *ring of warmth* emblazoned with the sunburst symbol of Anisa—Simbon says the ring carries with it the warmth of his homeland's sun and his family's friendship. It's also clear that Simbon is impressed with Uzoma. Together the pair might become a force to be reckoned with in Anisa and beyond.

If Kirina and Kedjou's plot isn't revealed, Kirina's rise in influence continues. Knowing the depths of his rival's treachery, Prince Simbon might request the characters' aid in exposing the rival prince's future plots.

Sensa Empire Gazetteer

The Sensa Empire runs on gold. Its three principal city-states—Anisa, Niba, and Tarikh—were each built around gold mines, and as their wealth has grown, so has their population, influence, and foreign trade. Most of the empire is arid and difficult to cultivate, so the regions between the city-states are sparsely inhabited and often lack the resources available in cosmopolitan areas. Still, the city-states and the outlands are tied together by Empress Inaya's rule, with each city governed autonomously by a hereditary monarch subject to the empress's ultimate authority.

Though the Sensa Empire is known as a peaceful realm, it faces a rocky transition of power. The next ruler is traditionally chosen from among the three city-states' royal families, excluding the direct descendants of the current ruler. But for years, Empress Inaya quietly made it known that she planned to appoint her own son to follow her—and in so doing, seemingly brought down a legendary curse that claimed the lives of her husband and eldest son. When the grieving empress announced she would appoint her successor from among the royal families of Anisa, Niba, or Tarikh as tradition dictated, the rulers of the city-states began to fight for favor—and competition for that favor is brutal.

Features

Those familiar with the Sensa Empire know the following facts:

Hallmarks. The empire is a collection of cosmopolitan city-states known for its expert goldsmiths and fabulous wealth.

People. Most residents of the region are dark-skinned humans with brown eyes and tightly coiled dark hair. These features are shared by dwarves and elves in the region.

Languages. Sensan is the native language of the region, and most imperial citizens also speak Common.

Noteworthy Sites

The Sensa Empire is structured around the three city-states of Anisa, Niba, and Tarikh, each a wealthy oasis in an arid and unforgiving landscape.

Anisa

The city-state of Anisa, in the east of Sensa, is ruled by the aging King Diara. Thanks to the wealth of the Goldwarren mine, the city's gold production far outpaces that of its neighbors. The people value education highly, and the city is home to Anisa Academy, the only university in the empire. Politically, the city has enjoyed years of peace under King Diara's rule, but many dread his inevitable retirement. While the king's heir—his oldest child, Simbon—waffles on how seriously he takes his responsibilities, Diara's daughter, Zahra, seeks to replace her brother as heir to the throne.

Niba

The city-state of Niba lies along Sensa's southeastern coast. Ruled by Queen Sainesha, the city is known for its grand bazaars and for being home to some of the most talented goldsmiths in the region. Entertainment in the form of cafes, theaters, and raceways is also central to life in the city. Among Niba's many celebrities is the queen's firstborn and heir, the ambitious and charismatic Prince Kirina.

Tarikh

The city-state of Tarikh lies in Sensa's northwestern reaches, nestled against jagged peaks. Its young ruler, King Sundasha, balances commercial needs and the local environment, as the city's scattered oases provide it with some of the only arable land in the region. While much of this land provides for the empire's people, a significant fraction is used to grow feed for the city's prized herds of camels. Tarikh also hosts the Seven Stairs, the headquarters of the Acolytes of the Faceless Prophet.

THE AZURE DOME

The deep-blue dome of Empress Inaya's coastal palace holds the seat of the Sensa Empire's power. Within the Azure Dome, the empress meets with her councilors and entertains the rulers of her three city-states. Merely entering the Azure Dome is considered a high honor for citizens of the empire.

The Azure Dome's legendary security couldn't protect Empress Inaya's husband and eldest son, Salaba and Shayan, from dying under unusual circumstances. Both passed away in their sleep after a state dinner—as they were in perfect health, it's believed they were poisoned by an unknown hand.

TOMB OF THE FACELESS

Half a day's ride north from Tarikh, the Tomb of the Faceless stands alone in the desert. A site of ritual pilgrimage and worship, the tomb is a large golden dome without an entrance that holds the Prophet's bones. The Prophet was a respected scholar and reformer adamant that her persona not eclipse her teachings. She insisted that after her death her followers not repeat her name or depict her face in art. Today, the faithful leave offerings of gold and salt at the site, which are collected at dusk by the clergy known as the Acolytes of the Faceless Prophet.

According to the acolytes who tend the tomb, learning the Prophet's name grants forbidden and dangerous power. Every so often, someone attempts to break into the tomb in search of clues to the Prophet's identity—a crime punished by permanent exile from the empire.

LIFE IN THE SENSA EMPIRE

Those who live in the Sensa Empire or who travel through the land experience its wealth, both in riches and deep traditions.

AURUM GUILD

Gold mining is a respected career, crucial to the empire's prosperity. Those who work with the riches of the earth number among the land's most respect artisans and have few peers. To support its members, the Aurum Guild allows miners and craftspeople to build social and professional connections, better their craft, and organize for improved labor conditions. Each city-state has its own chapter of the guild that pushes back when local rulers make unfair demands of miners for personal benefit—often placing the guild in conflict with those rulers.

LIFE AND LEGENDS

The empire is known for its rich tradition of oral storytelling, in which traveling historian-storytellers known as griots pass down tales from generation to generation. The most common tales are of Emperor Kassa, who founded the Sensa Empire after

PRINCE SIMBON

defeating the now-extinct aurumvoraxes—gold-eating predators—that once plagued the region.

The arid land of the Sensan Empire has inspired simple fashions, and Sensans of all genders wear loose cotton tunics, trousers, dresses, or caftans to stay cool. The region's deserts provide limited opportunities for agriculture. While spices and preserved foods are frequently imported, ocean-caught whitefish and locally grown plantains, cassava, and yams serve as staples of the Sensan diet.

SPLIT RULE

The Sensa Empire's three city-states are hereditary monarchies united into a coalition under the empress's control. Historically, rather than a single imperial line controlling the throne, each empress or emperor selects an heir from among the eldest children of each city-state's monarch. While no law prevents rulers from selecting their own children as heirs, few do so, fearing they'll fall victim to a terrible curse. Heirs are usually chosen based on merit.

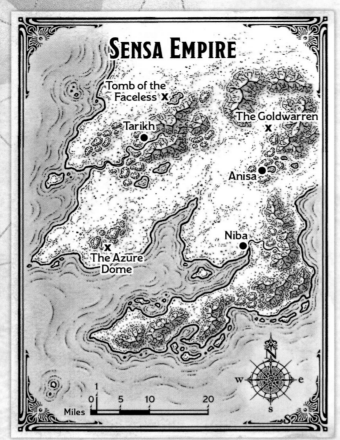

Map 7.2: Sensa Empire

Wealth of the Empire

With gold abundant in the Sensa Empire, there's no lack of lucrative, respected jobs in the mines, though the work comes with occupational hazards. But the wealth of the empire often draws threats. Banditry is an ongoing problem, and sometimes diplomacy is all that prevents raids from neighboring territories.

Names

Sensan names are typically drawn from significant locations connected to the parents' relationship, the pregnancy, or the child's birth:

Feminine. Aisha, Ayaan, Daniya, Fiza, Imani, Kinza, Laila, Sabah, Tania, Zakia

Masculine. Abdu, Dakhil, Ehan, Fahim, Haji, Jamal, Kasim, Mahdi, Omar, Zaid

Gender-Neutral. Akua, Azmi, Ijal, Jami, Maheen, Neeya, Rafi, Razan, Ula, Zuha

Surname. Abiodun, Buhle, Chike, Emem, Nnadi, Okiro, Zivai

Adventures in the Sensa Empire

Consider the plots on the Sensa Empire Adventures table when planning adventures in the region.

Sensa Empire Adventures

d4	Adventure
1	Increasingly dissatisfied with the investigation into the death of her husband and son, Empress Inaya seeks adventurers to find new leads.
2	A deadly illness, introduced by **bandits** to weaken trade, ravages camels throughout the empire. Empress Inaya hires the party to learn who paid the bandits and whether the ailment can be cured.
3	Caravans traveling between Niba and Anisa have recently come under attack by **air elementals**. A consortium of merchants hires the party to escort a caravan and deal with the threat.
4	King Sundasha of Tarikh declares his city-state independent of the Sensa Empire, using magic to line his borders with **giant scorpions**. Empress Inaya hires the characters to secretly infiltrate Tarikh and make the rogue king see sense.

Characters from Sensa

If players want to create a character from the Sensa Empire, consider asking them the following questions during character creation:

What city-state do you originate from? Are you staunchly loyal to your home city? If you grew up in the hostile outlands, how did your family survive?

Have you worked with the earth or its riches? Mining and goldsmithing are respected work in the Sensa Empire—are you experienced with such work? Do you bear scars from such labor? If you avoided it, why?

How does gold impact your life? The Sensa Empire's prosperity comes at a price—have you experienced these costs personally? Have you ever been targeted by bandits? Are there any resources you want or need that can't be bought?

Aurumvoraxes

An aurumvorax is an eight-legged, badger-like hunter. These aggressive omnivores attack any prey they think they can best, ambushing even creatures double their size. They supplement their diets with metal, whether it's worked or ore, and they have a particular taste for gold. This diet lends aurumvorax fur its golden sheen.

Alone or in small groups, aurumvoraxes dig deep in search of precious metals. Such exploration often leads them into conflict with subterranean settlements. As defenders of such communities often wear metal armor, aurumvoraxes prioritize attacking armored foes—whether that armor is metal or not.

AURUMVORAX

Early in life, aurumvoraxes cooperate with siblings and their den leader parents, digging tunnels in search of metal and other burrowing prey. As they grow to adulthood, aurumvoraxes hunt on their own, carving out territories they viciously defend.

AURUMVORAX DEN LEADER

Aurumvoraxes that feed on a steady supply of precious metals gradually grow in size. These aurumvoraxes are faster and deadlier than others of their kind.

AURUMVORAX DEN LEADER
Medium Monstrosity, Unaligned

Armor Class 16 (natural armor)
Hit Points 52 (8d8 + 16)
Speed 40 ft., burrow 20 ft.

STR	DEX	CON	INT	WIS	CHA
18 (+4)	14 (+2)	14 (+2)	3 (−4)	13 (+1)	8 (−1)

Saving Throws Str +6, Con +4
Skills Perception +3, Stealth +4
Condition Immunities petrified
Senses darkvision 60 ft., passive Perception 13
Languages —
Challenge 4 (1,100 XP)   **Proficiency Bonus** +2

Pack Leader. The aurumvorax's allies have advantage on attack rolls while within 10 feet of the aurumvorax, provided it isn't incapacitated.

Tunneler. The aurumvorax can burrow through solid rock and metal at half its burrowing speed and leaves a 5-foot-diameter tunnel in its wake.

ACTIONS

Multiattack. The aurumvorax makes one Bite attack and two Claw attacks.

Bite. *Melee Weapon Attack:* +6 to hit, reach 5 ft., one target. *Hit:* 13 (2d8 + 4) piercing damage. If the target is a creature wearing armor of any type, the aurumvorax gains one of the following benefits of its choice:

Frenzy. The aurumvorax has advantage on attack rolls until start of its next turn.
Invigorate. The aurumvorax regains 6 (1d8 + 2) hit points.

Claw. *Melee Weapon Attack:* +6 to hit, reach 5 ft., one target. *Hit:* 11 (2d6 + 4) slashing damage. If the target is a Large or smaller creature, it is grappled (escape DC 14). Until this grapple ends, the aurumvorax can't use its Claw attack on another target, and when it moves, it can drag the grappled creature with it, without the aurumvorax's speed being halved.

AURUMVORAX
Small Monstrosity, Unaligned

Armor Class 15 (natural armor)
Hit Points 36 (8d6 + 8)
Speed 30 ft., burrow 20 ft.

STR	DEX	CON	INT	WIS	CHA
14 (+2)	13 (+1)	12 (+1)	3 (−4)	12 (+1)	6 (−2)

Saving Throws Str +4, Con +3
Skills Perception +3, Stealth +3
Condition Immunities petrified
Senses darkvision 60 ft., passive Perception 13
Languages —
Challenge 2 (450 XP)   **Proficiency Bonus** +2

Tunneler. The aurumvorax can burrow through solid rock and metal at half its burrowing speed and leaves a 5-foot-diameter tunnel in its wake.

ACTIONS

Multiattack. The aurumvorax makes one Bite attack and two Claw attacks.

Bite. *Melee Weapon Attack:* +4 to hit, reach 5 ft., one target. *Hit:* 6 (1d8 + 2) piercing damage. If the target is a creature wearing armor of any type, the aurumvorax regains 4 (1d6 + 1) hit points.

Claw. *Melee Weapon Attack:* +5 to hit, reach 5 ft., one target. *Hit:* 5 (1d6 + 2) slashing damage. If the target is a Medium or smaller creature, it is grappled (escape DC 12). Until this grapple ends, the aurumvorax can't use its Claw attack on another target, and when it moves, it can drag the grappled creature with it, without the aurumvorax's speed being halved.

TRAIL OF DESTRUCTION

AN ADVENTURE FOR 8TH-LEVEL CHARACTERS

Disaster might strike at any moment, a truth the characters learn soon after arriving in the volcanic region of Tletepec. The town of Etizalan reels from monstrous attacks and unexplained earthquakes, leading the community's leaders to send for aid. When these requests go unanswered, the townsfolk enlist the characters to seek answers. The party must cross a region in the throes of volcanic upheaval and locate a shrine known as the Gate of Illumination. There the characters must placate a fiery creature awakened from its age-long slumber or face region-wide devastation.

BACKGROUND

Volcanic eruptions have been devastating the region around the town of Etizalan. Ordinarily, scholars called the Watchers of the Ashes predict volcanic eruptions and warn local folk, mitigating loss of life. Lately though, more and more eruptions evade detection.

Ameyali, one of Etizalan's leaders, believes the gods have grown angry and seeks to placate them. She has collected offerings from her town's people and now heads to the shrine known as the Gate of Illumination to pray for an end to the danger.

Unknown to Ameyali, dangerous Elemental creatures roam the land. Salamanders and fire snakes serve Izel, a powerful creature known as a tlexolotl. Tlexolotls, long thought to be myths, slumber within the volcanoes of Tletepec. So long as the tlexolotls are dormant, the volcanoes they slumber in are quiet. When they awaken, the volcanic dangers across Tletepec increase.

Izel, finding himself the only one of his kind active in the region, seeks to awaken his fellow tlexolotls. The salamanders allied with him are stealing offerings meant for the gods and plan to offer them to sleeping tlexolotls to rouse the creatures. If large enough offerings are made, the tlexolotls are sure to awaken, unleashing volcanic devastation.

PRONUNCIATION GUIDE

In Tletlahtolli, the language spoken alongside Common in Tletepec, when *tl* appears at the end of a word, it creates a sound like the *tl* in *subtle*, *brittle*, or *rattle*. The Tletepec Pronunciations table notes how to pronounce key names in this adventure.

TLETEPEC PRONUNCIATIONS

Name	Pronunciation
Ameyali	ah-meh-YAL-ee
Etizalan	ay-tee-zah-LAHN
Itzimico	eet-see-MEE-kaw
Izel	EA-sehl
Ollin	OHL-een
Tletepec	thle-TEH-pek
Tletlahtolli	thleh-thlah-TOLL-ee
Tlexolotl	thleh-SHAW-lotl
Tonalli	taw-NAH-lee
Xind	SHEEND
Xocopol	shaw-KAW-pole
Xoxotla	shaw-SHAW-thlah

SETTING THE ADVENTURE

Use the following suggestions to help contextualize Tletepec in a wider world:

Through the Radiant Citadel. Visitors from the Radiant Citadel arrive in Tletepec north of Etizalan and begin their investigation there. You can use the "Tletepec Gazetteer" section at the end of this adventure as a starting point to detail the region.

Forgotten Realms. The region of Tletepec might sprawl among the Peaks of Flame in Chult or the Firesteap Mountains east of the Lake of Steam.

Greyhawk. Tletepec could easily exist in the volcanic region where the Hellfurnaces meets the Amedio Jungle, just south of Cauldron. It could also be added as one of the Olman Islands.

SALAMANDER RAIDERS AMBUSH AMEYALI'S
CARAVAN ON THE ROAD NEAR ETIZALAN.

CHARACTER HOOKS

Consider the following ways to involve characters in this adventure.

Elemental Attacks. Ameyali, the assembly chief of Etizalan, requests aid to defend her city from attacks by hostile elemental creatures. By the time the characters arrive, though, things have grown far more dire.

Natural Disaster. A devotee of a nature god asks the characters to visit Tletepec and learn what methods the locals use to placate their tempestuous gods. The characters' contact hopes these techniques can be used to calm natural upheavals in other lands.

Prepared for the Worst. The Shieldbearers of the Radiant Citadel hire the characters to visit Tletepec to verify rumors that the region is becoming dangerous, so they can prepare for an influx of refugees. They suggest the characters start their investigations near Etizalan.

STARTING THE ADVENTURE

The adventure begins as the characters approach the town of Etizalan. Before they reach the community, they encounter a caravan being raided. Read or paraphrase the following description:

> The road weaves through a stretch of rain forest that flanks a deep valley, drawing near the town of Etizalan. Past a bend, smoke rises through the trees and shouts ring out. An overturned wagon lies in the road, and through the smoke you can see people being attacked by serpentine creatures wreathed in flame.

Two **fire snakes** and two **salamanders** have ambushed three travelers from Etizalan. The three travelers use the **priest** stat block and fight to defend a wagon full of food, flowers, and colorful crafts. If the characters defend the travelers, the Elemental creatures focus their attacks on the newcomers.

The area within 25 feet of the overturned wagon is obscured by smoke, which can be dispersed by a strong wind in 1 round. Flames burn in the forested area on either side of the 15-foot-wide road. Any creature who enters the burning forest must succeed on a DC 14 Constitution saving throw or take 10 (3d6) points of fire damage. The fire produces a great deal of smoke but will burn out in the wet forest in about 10 minutes. A character who succeeds on a DC 12 Intelligence (Nature) check realizes the flames won't spread far.

After the Battle

Once the characters deal with the vicious Elementals, their problems aren't over. The ground heaves as a small earthquake ripples through the area. Characters must succeed on a DC 12 Dexterity saving throw to keep their footing. The sound of wood splintering and trees falling echoes from deeper in the forest, but the tremor soon passes.

In the aftermath of the battle and earthquake, the travelers are thankful for the characters' help. Their leader introduces herself as Ameyali.

Ameyali

Ameyali (neutral good, human **priest**) has lived in Etizalan for years. After fire elementals destroyed her birth village and killed her parents, neighbors took her in and moved to Etizalan. There she learned a sense of community and acquired a strong desire to help others. As a youth, her aptitude with tools and weapons led her to train with the inventors known as the Shapers of Obsidian in Itzimico. She returned to Etizalan as an adult to ensure her birth village's fate would never befall her new home. Her many useful inventions impressed the people of Etizalan, and she eventually became a local leader.

Personality Trait. "I like building things. Seeing a complete work after hours of placing pieces is wonderful."

Ideal. "I want my inventions to ensure fewer children lose their parents."

Bond. "I always wear the necklace my adoptive sister gave me. When I feel anxious about a project, I hold the necklace to give me confidence."

Flaw. "The world disappears when I'm focused. I often don't notice people talking to me at such times."

Ameyali's Request

Ameyali can use her magic and three *potions of healing* she has to heal wounded characters. She gladly gives the characters any unused potions, sharing her wish that these items will keep the brave travelers safe.

While her companions right their cart, Ameyali can answer the characters' questions. She then asks if her caravan might travel back to Etizalan with them. Along the way, she shares the following information:

- The region around Etizalan is suffering a spate of earthquakes and incursions from fiery monsters.
- Three days ago, Ameyali sent four of the town's best warriors to seek insight from the Watchers of the Ashes. They dwell at the Twin Gods Observatory, a site of volcanic study that normally warns

Etizalan of impending earthquakes and eruptions. The warriors have not returned.

- Ameyali and her fellow travelers intended to look for the warriors and then take offerings to the Gate of Illumination, a shrine to the gods, in hopes of placating them and quelling the earthquakes.
- The group has traveled only a couple of miles from Etizalan, and the journey has already proven more dangerous than expected. For their safety, her group must abandon its mission.

Once the characters and Ameyali reach Etizalan, she thanks them again and asks if they'll do her another favor. She's still concerned about her town's warriors. She asks the characters to go to the Twin Gods Observatory and find out what happened to them. In return, she offers to pay the characters 400 gp each, and they will have earned the gratitude of her people.

If the characters have questions about monsters in the area or how to prepare for the journey, Ameyali suggests they talk to other locals (see the following section).

Exploring Etizalan

The town of Etizalan has seen better days. Although its colorfully painted stone homes and shady, tree-lined streets are welcoming, an air of urgency lingers over the community. Many of the stalls in the town's paved central market are closed as locals shore up buildings damaged by the recent earthquake or reinforce the town walls.

Enough local shops are still open that the characters can find any common goods they seek. A local inn called the Jolly Cotinga can also host guests, giving them a place to stay and a delicious meal of rice, fruit, and smoked turkey for 1 gp.

Characters who speak with the locals about threats in the area each learn one of the following pieces of information:

- Most of the creatures attacking the area are salamanders or fire snakes that dwell near volcanoes. They don't usually attack settlements.
- The earthquake the town recently suffered is the fourth this month. Earthquakes aren't uncommon, but this is far more than usual.
- A fire giant named Xocopol roams the territory around Etizalan and its volcano, and the folk of the city know to avoid him.

When the characters are ready to depart, Ameyali provides a map of the region outlining the path to Twin Gods Observatory.

THE WAY UP

The path to Twin Gods Observatory snakes through the rain forest, then climbs into the hills near the Twin Gods Volcanoes. Trails along the river flowing out of Atialli Lake lead to the town of Xoxotla, about 17 miles away. From there, paths lead another 9 miles to the observatory. The whole trip takes just over a day to complete at a normal pace.

VOLCANIC THREATS

Volcanic activity increases as the awakening of the tlexolotl Izel affects the region. While the characters travel, the earth occasionally shakes anew. During the journey, roll on the Volcanic Awakening table every 12 hours or whenever you desire. You can also have two **salamanders** ambush the party as these volcanic events take place.

VOLCANIC AWAKENING

d4	Connection
1	A fumarole opens alongside the road, venting noxious gases 25 feet in all directions. Each creature in the area must succeed on a DC 14 Constitution saving throw or take 10 (3d6) poison damage.
2	Falling ash lightly obscures the characters' surroundings for the next hour.
3	The ground suddenly collapses, creating a 30-foot-deep fissure that's 120 feet long and 20 feet wide. The gap severs the road ahead of the characters.
4	The earth cracks, revealing magma flowing below. A **fire snake** rises from the crack and attacks the first creature it sees before retreating after 1 round.

XOXOTLA

Xoxotla is the largest community in the Tletepec region. Characters might stop, rest, and resupply here, safe from fiery threats or monster attack. See the "Tletepec Gazetteer" section at the end of this adventure for more details on Xoxotla.

DARING DANCER

As the characters are leaving Xoxotla, an impossible figure to ignore hails them. This is Ollin, a tiefling performer with turquoise patterned skin. They're headed the same direction as the characters and are eager to travel with the party, both for company and protection. The dancer is kind-hearted but has an over-the-top stage persona they rarely let slip. In return, they offer to be the characters' guide and good luck charm on the road. Even if the characters don't accept Ollin's company, the performer is traveling in the same direction and tags along anyway. Ollin keeps their distance only if threatened or rebuffed in extremely clear terms.

OLLIN

Ollin is a chaotic good tiefling. They use the **priest** stat block but have Performance +3 rather than Persuasion, and they can speak Common; Ignan; and the local language, Tletlahtolli.

Ollin is a bombastic, traveling dancer who enjoys participating in local celebrations and entices Tletepecs to dance their cares away. Ollin uses their skillful dances and optimistic view of the power of the gods to lighten others' hearts. With the increasing dangers in the region, Ollin has decided to head to Twin Gods Observatory on behalf of Tletepec's people and personally find out how to stop the problem. The performer knows the value of a good supporting team, though.

Personality Trait. "I love to help people and am not afraid to take on tasks I don't know how to do. I'll figure it out!"

Ideal. "I want my public to forget their worries for a moment, letting me guide them to a happy place."

Bond. "I want to spread the smiles I see on the faces of those I entertain."

Flaw. "My stage persona cloaks my insecurities. Sometimes I go to extremes to keep up this facade."

OLLIN

Twin Gods Observatory

> Above the trees on the rocky slope ahead rises a tower covered in elaborate carvings of local animals and majestic mountains. Beyond it, smoke rises from a volcanic peak.

Twin Gods Observatory is home to a group of scholars and regional guardians called the Watchers of the Ashes. These scientists observe and record the behavior of Tletepec's volcanoes, predicting eruptions and warning locals before danger strikes. The Observatory itself is a narrow, 120-foot-high tower.

Meeting the Watchers

When the characters arrive, three Watchers (neutral, human **acolytes**) greet them with a hint of disdain. The Watchers explain they are aware of the unusual volcanic activity and are doing their best to determine the cause, but their work will proceed faster if they're not interrupted. They initially claim to know nothing about warriors from Etizalan.

A character who succeeds on a DC 14 Charisma (Intimidation or Persuasion) check convinces a Watcher to behave more hospitably, whereupon the acolyte shares the following information:

Tonalli

- The observatory has been besieged by inquiries from across the land seeking answers the scholars don't have.
- Dozens of volcanoes are showing activity across Tletepec, which is unprecedented.
- The acolyte doesn't recall warriors from Etizalan arriving, but the Watchers' leader, Tonalli, might.
- Tonalli has been tirelessly observing the volcanoes from atop the observatory.

Regardless of the acolytes' attitudes, the characters are free to enter the tower.

Inside the Observatory

The interior of Twin Gods Observatory is hollow, with a spiral stone staircase rising to a roof with a commanding view of the region. Carvings along the observatory's interior depict volcanic events and smoke formations, which the Watchers consult to inform their predictions. The stairs leading to the top of the tower are shallow and have no railing, winding around an open, 15-foot-wide, central space. The stairs count as difficult terrain and, following the steps, the route from the bottom of the tower to the top is 200 feet long.

A character who spends at least 5 minutes examining the carvings inside the observatory and succeeds on a DC 16 Intelligence (Investigation) check notes a carving of a gigantic, frilled reptile bursting from an exploding volcano. If asked, any of the Watchers identify this creature as a mythical being called a tlexolotl, a spirit said to sleep in volcanoes. Most Watchers don't believe tlexolotls are real.

Disaster Strikes

When a character climbs to at least half the height of the observatory—whether using the steps or via another method—the structure begins shaking, and a crack like a thunderclap sounds from below. Anyone outside the observatory sees the structure sway, while those inside feel the floor pitch beneath them. Creatures on the stairs inside the tower must succeed on a DC 16 Dexterity saving throw or fall. Unless characters have been tracking their ascent, assume they've climbed 60 feet when the earthquake hits, causing them to take 21 (6d6) bludgeoning damage and knocking them prone if they fall.

Countdown to Ruin. After the initial quake, have characters roll initiative to emphasize the urgency of the situation and track their movement through the tower. Twin Gods Observatory will collapse after 6 rounds or whenever feels appropriately dramatic. Emphasize the tower's precarious state by describing the continued swaying of the building and crumbling of walls.

Tonalli. The leader of the Watchers, Tonalli (lawful neutral, dwarf **priest**), is on the rooftop when the

structure begins to collapse. He survives only if the characters reach the roof and encourage him to flee back down the stairs immediately or save him via some other method. Desperate to escape, he eagerly follows the characters' instructions.

Collapse. When the tower collapses, each creature in or atop Twin Gods Observatory must make a DC 16 Dexterity saving throw. On a success, a creature falls from its current height and takes 1d6 bludgeoning damage for every 10 feet it fell, but lands free of the collapsing structure. On a failed saving throw, the creature takes the falling damage and an additional 17 (5d6) bludgeoning damage, and the creature is buried under rubble. A creature buried in this way is blinded, restrained, and has total cover. It can try to dig itself free as an action, ending the blinded and restrained conditions on itself and crawling to the surface with a successful DC 16 Strength (Athletics) check. A creature that fails this check three times can't attempt to dig itself out again.

A creature that is neither restrained nor incapacitated can spend 1 minute freeing another creature buried in the rubble. Once free, that creature is no longer blinded or restrained by the collapsed structure.

IN THE RUINS

As dust rises from the ruins of Twin Gods Observatory, the earthquake ceases. All of the Watchers survived, with the possible exception of Tonalli. If the characters didn't rescue Tonalli, the other Watchers soon find his body. They entreat the characters to rush the dead scholar back to Xoxotla, where he can be resurrected.

Once saved or revived, Tonalli is thankful for the characters' help. If the characters explain why they came, Tonalli tells them what he knows:

- Ameyali's warriors arrived three days earlier.
- At the time they arrived, Tonalli didn't have any theories about what was causing the eruptions, but he knew they were strongest near the volcano called Jademount.
- Tonalli sent the warriors to the Gate of Illumination, a shrine to the gods on Jademount, to see if they could learn anything more. They haven't returned.
- Just before the observatory collapsed, Tonalli's research into the tower's writings and signs in

the surrounding lands convinced him that the cause of the eruptions is a tlexolotl—a spirit of the volcanoes.

- Tales say many of the volcanoes in Tletepec have tlexolotls dwelling within them. Tonalli believes these volcanic spirits are all gradually awaking at once—which in turn increases the activity of their volcanoes.
- Based on his observations, Tonalli believes there's already an awakened tlexolotl near where the volcanic disturbances began: Jademount.

Tonalli regrets sending Ameyali's people to the Gate of Illumination—he didn't realize the danger. He asks the characters to travel to the shrine to check on the warriors and seek signs of the tlexolotl.

Traveling to the Gate

Tonalli or other locals can easily mark a trail on the characters' map leading to the Gate of Illumination, a well-known sacred site. The route from the ruins of Twin Gods Observatory leads 9 miles back to Xoxotla. From there, it follows the Atialli River 18 miles to the shrine. At a normal pace, the journey takes a little over a day.

As the characters travel, volcanic events continue to rock the region. Consult the "Volcanic Threats" section earlier in the adventure for dangers that might occur. Additionally, at a point between the Xoxotla and the shrine, the characters come upon the aftermath of a battle.

Ashen Battlefield

Four bodies lie where they've fallen on the road ahead, all showing burn marks and spear wounds. Broken arrows and fragments of a shattered wooden cart are strewn about.

The four bodies were human travelers from the town of Itzimico who were headed to Twin Gods Observatory to seek answers about the growing volcanic disturbances from the Watchers of the Ashes. Like Ameyali's warriors, they carried offerings of fruits and crafts, but those have been stolen. A character who investigates the bodies and succeeds on a DC 14 Wisdom (Perception) check finds burns on them and sizable, snakelike tracks nearby, suggesting the travelers were killed by salamanders. The tracks lead toward the Gate of Illumination, with a few dropped prickly pears along the path—offerings the raiders stole.

Giant's Wrath

As the characters prepare to move on, a roar comes from a forested rise over the road. The towering figure of a fire giant pushes through the trees toward the characters. "Go back!" he yells in Common. "Abandon your offerings! You know not what you do!"

This is the **fire giant** Xocopol, whom characters might have learned about in Etizalan. Xocopol is neutral. He wields a massive hammer, which deals bludgeoning damage but is otherwise identical to a fire giant's Greatsword attack. He can speak Common, Giant, and Tletlahtolli.

Xocopol isn't interested in fighting unless he's attacked first, but he blocks the characters' way and tries to frighten them into returning the way they came. Calming the giant and convincing him to talk requires either a successful DC 14 Charisma (Persuasion) check or appropriate roleplaying.

If the characters convince Xocopol to talk, he shares the distressing information he has recently learned.

What Xocopol Knows

Like many of his kin, Xocopol dislikes the tendency of Humanoids to build settlements near the volcanic mountains. The awakening tlexolotls, however, have made the small folk of these lands the lesser of two evils. Xocopol's people have long known about the tlexolotls that slumber deep in the region's mountains and don't consider them myths.

If the characters calm Xocopol and explain they aren't headed to the Gate of Illumination to make an offering, the fire giant stops threatening them and shares the following information:

- Tlexolotls dwell deep in volcanoes. When their sleep is disturbed, volcanic eruptions often follow.
- The tlexolotl that inhabits Jademount has awakened. Xocopol has seen it moving inside the volcanic pool connected to the Gate of Illumination.
- Salamanders and fire snakes serve this tlexolotl. They have been stealing offerings meant for the gods and are carrying them back to Jademount.
- Xocopol doesn't know why the tlexolotl is hoarding offerings, but he has seen salamanders going to volcanoes throughout the region with them.

Xocopol doesn't know much more. While he's happy to fight any salamanders he encounters, he's too large to slip into the Gate of Illumination and find out what's happening there. If the characters are willing to do so, Xocopol offers to travel with them and defend them along the way.

GATE OF ILLUMINATION

The Gate of Illumination is a centuries-old shrine consecrated to the gods of nature, fire, and renewal. It's cut into the slope of the Jademount volcano and tunnels to the lake of magma within the caldera. The slopes of Jademount are steep and treacherous to climb, making passage through the shrine the most direct route to the volcano's interior. Traditionally, offerings of flowers, fruits, and crafts are brought here and to similar shrines to thank the gods for their bounty, as the volcanic pools are viewed as passages to the gods' realm.

As the characters near the Gate of Illumination, read the following text:

> A well-traveled trail climbs into the mountains, the haze of volcanic smoke hanging overhead. The path ends at the entrance to a cavern carved with images of divine figures and gigantic lizards amid cracking mountains, clouds, and geometric flourishes. Crimson light emanates from within, and the smell of sulfur is thick in the air.

Characters who noticed the tlexolotl carvings at the Twin Gods Observatory recognize similar imagery here. A character who succeeds on a DC 16 Intelligence (Nature or Religion) realizes the carvings depict reptilian spirits that dwell in volcanoes.

GATE OF ILLUMINATION FEATURES

The following features are common to all areas of the shrine:

Ceilings. Ceilings throughout the shrine are 10 feet high.

Heat and Gas. The air in the shrine is heavy with smoke and heat. The shrine's magic keeps the temperature at 90 degrees Fahrenheit, despite its proximity to the volcano's magma. This same magic prevents volcanic gases from posing a threat, but these gases still lightly obscure every area within the shrine.

Illumination. Veins of magma thread the walls and fill magical lanterns throughout the shrine, illuminating each area with dim light.

GATE OF ILLUMINATION LOCATIONS

The following locations are keyed to map 8.1.

I1: CAVE ENTRANCE

A 30-foot-long tunnel leads from the entrance of the shrine to its main chambers. Magical decorations look like veins of magma flowing through the walls, but they're cool to the touch and don't seep into the room. A character who has the Stonecunning trait can tell the passage isn't natural and was constructed using magic (no check required).

I2: HALL OF HISTORIES

> Bright murals cover the walls of this broad, pillared hall, depicting people through the ages receiving blessings from the gods. A stone double door stands at the far end of the room, while stairs rise to the west and another hall opens to the east.

People who bring their offerings to the gods prepare their prayers in this area, meditating on the blessing they want. A **salamander** and four **fire snakes** are in this room. The salamander stands guard before the door to area I5, while each fire snake lingers near one of the room's pillars. These creatures are hostile and attack any strangers that enter the room.

Door. A narrow, 10-foot-tall stone double door bars the way to area I5. A character must succeed on a DC 14 Strength (Athletics) check to open the door. As the door opens, it grinds nosily, alerting any creatures in this room and areas I4 and I5.

Murals. The murals covering the walls depict several myths known throughout the region. Any of the legends mentioned in the "Tletepec" section at the end of this adventure might be represented here, such as the tale of the two lovers.

Dying Dancer. If Ollin didn't join the characters in Xoxotla, the dancer came to the shrine on their own and fell victim to the salamander and fire snakes. The dancer has 0 hit points, is unconscious, and will die if they don't receive healing within the next hour.

I3: Blessings Memorial

> Murals of people making offerings to the gods cover this room's walls. At the chamber's center stand three statues on short pedestals: one of a tiefling, one of a dwarf, and one of a human, all in poses of supplication. Two of the statues—the tiefling and the human—appear to be missing something.

This room memorializes some of the greatest offerings made to the gods, as well as legendary figures who made earnest sacrifices and were rewarded. The three statues at the room's center have inscriptions written in the local language, Tletlahtolli, that include the following details:

Leuchis. At the north of the room, this white stone statue depicts a tiefling offering a sculpted ring to the heavens. His other arm is bent as if holding something, but it is empty. An etching at the base of the statue reads, "Leuchis, who traveled on the wind."

Lilva. In the middle of the room, this red stone statue of a dwarf holds a large urn as if about to take a drink. An etching on the statue's base reads, "Lilva, who brewed the waters of the gods."

Pattox. At the room's south, this blue stone statue of a human holds up a seed, offering it to the heavens. His other arm is crooked, as if holding something that's missing. The etching at the foot of the statue reads, "Pattox, who brought the rain with a seed."

A character who succeeds on a DC 12 Intelligence (History or Religion) check recognizes these statues as devout figures from local legends who earned the favor of the gods. If Ollin is with the party, they can also share this information.

The statues are magical, but their power was disrupted when the urns held by two of the statues were removed. They're currently in areas I4 and I5. Only the urn on the statue of Lilva remains; inside the urn is a worn, stone cup.

If the empty white urn is placed back upon the statue of Leuchis, the urn fills with nonflammable oil. If the empty blue urn is placed back upon the statue of Pattox, the urn fills with water. Both urns magically fill in this way once per week.

If the contents of the white and blue urns are poured into the red urn, they create a bright red magical fluid that is equivalent to three *potions of resistance* (fire).

I4: Raided Memorial

> Shelves are carved into this room's walls, their contents swept onto the floor, reduced to shards of shattered pottery and heaps of ashes. A mural on the north wall depicts erupting volcanoes and smoke in the shape of tiny people drifting into the sky. Beneath the mural, a salamander lies curled in a corner.

This room held the ashes of priests who sought to be interred near the gods, along with small remembrances for the dead. Salamanders have raided this room and thrown most of the memorial items into the volcano, leaving little behind.

The salamander resting here is named Xind, and it was wounded during an encounter with Xocopol.

Xind the Salamander. Xind is a **salamander** with 1 hit point and no will to fight. Upon seeing the characters, it throws up its hands and says in Ignan, "I give up." In return for being left alone, Xind is willing to tell the characters about Izel's plan to collect offerings and cast them into volcanoes across the region, waking dozens of other tlexolotls. It can also relate any other detail of the Izel's plot from the adventure's background.

Mural. A character who succeeds on a DC 14 Knowledge (Religion) check recognizes that the mural depicts a local myth about the Ashrise, a period when all the volcanoes in the area will erupt, devastating the region. If Ollin is with the group, they can also explain the mural's significance.

Treasure. A character who spends at least 5 minutes sifting through the debris finds a sand-colored pouch embroidered with colorful, geometrically stylized animals. This is a tan *bag of tricks*. Any creature created by the bag looks artistically stylized in a manner similar to the embroidery on the bag. This doesn't affect the creatures' statistics.

An intact white stone urn lies near the mural. This urn is part of one of the statues in area I3.

I5: Preparation Room

> Crates and heaps of supplies surround a stone altar with a flame burning in a depression at its center. Stone double doors lead to the north and south. The door to the north is carved with the image of a frilled, lizard-like creature amid flames.

The salamanders serving Izel have brought the stolen offerings here. One **salamander** is currently organizing the offerings. It attacks any strangers who enter the chamber.

Altar. The stone altar is consecrated to the gods of fire and nature. A candle-sized flame burns in a bowl-sized depression upon its surface. The flame is magical and relights after 10 seconds if extinguished.

Gate. A 10-foot-tall stone double door bars the way to area I6. A character must succeed on a DC 14 Strength (Athletics) check to open the door. As the door opens, it grinds nosily across the ground, alerting any creatures in this room and area I6.

Offerings. The offerings consist of foodstuffs and colorful crafts with little monetary value. The edges of the room hold hundreds of pounds of such goods, all of which are flammable. If purposefully set aflame, all of the offerings burn up in less than 10 minutes. A character who succeeds on a DC 14 Wisdom (Perception) check notices a blue stone urn amid the offerings. This urn is part of one of the statues in area I3.

Offering with Intention. A character who succeeds on a DC 12 Intelligence (Religion) check knows locals value the intention behind the offerings they make more than an offering's monetary value. A small offering made with an earnest prayer to the gods is considered greater than a valuable offering made while going through the motions of piety. Should the offerings in this room be burned or thrown into the volcano along with a prayer to the gods, every character that participates in making the offering gains advantage on their next saving throw as a minor blessing. Destroying these offerings undermines Izel's plan, as the offerings are consecrated to the gods and can't be used to coax forth other tlexolotls.

I6: Caldera

> The masonry of the shrine gives way to the natural formation of the volcano's caldera. A blast of heat and gas billows off the lake of magma roiling here. At the magma's edge stands a pair of ornate altars carved of obsidian. Nearby, four humans are slumped against the west wall, their arms dangling from rusty manacles. Beyond, sooty rock juts into the molten lake. Something moves amid the lava.

The magmatic pool at the heart of Jademount is the lair of the **tlexolotl** (detailed at the end of this adventure) named Izel. The tlexolotl resents any interruptions to his plans. The four humans chained to the wall are the missing warriors from Etizalan.

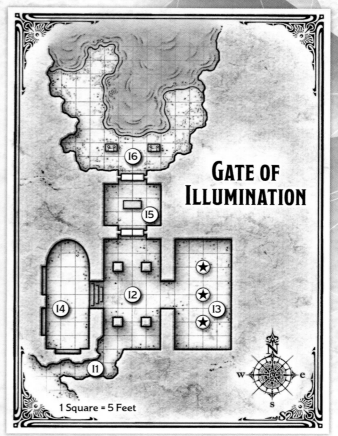

MAP 8.1: GATE OF ILLUMINATION

Izel. Izel emerges from the lava and speaks in Ignan, demanding the characters leave. If the characters don't respond, he attacks. If they do, he's willing to converse with them and explain the following:

- Izel awoke several months ago and can tell that the other tlexolotls dwelling in volcanoes across the region are still asleep. Izel treats these other tlexolotls as his family.
- Izel has instructed his salamander servants to make offerings at the volcanoes where his family dwells and wake them. So far the salamanders have made some small offerings, causing other tlexolotls to stir.
- Izel doesn't understand or care that the awakening tlexolotls endanger the region's populace. The Elemental has little experience with Humanoids or the concept of mortality.
- The magma vents beneath the volcano connect to the Elemental Plane of Fire. Izel convinced the awed salamanders on the other side to assist him. He knows nothing of the vicious attacks they've conducted to fetch offerings for him.

Through convincing roleplaying or by succeeding on a DC 20 Charisma (Persuasion) check, a character can talk Izel out of his plans and persuade him to send his salamander allies away. Any such negotiation needs to account for the fact that Izel will be

MIKE SCHLEY

lonely if this happens. If Ollin is with the party, they volunteer to stay at the Gate of Illumination—Ollin believes keeping Izel content is important and wants to help keep the region safe (they also like the idea of having a regular audience).

Lava. A creature that enters the lava in this area for the first time on a turn or that starts its turn there takes 55 (10d10) fire damage.

Missing Warriors. The four missing warriors from Etizalan found their way to the Gates of Illumination and would have been killed by salamanders if Izel hadn't been curious about them. The tlexolotl can't understand them, so it has had them manacled to the western wall. If asked, they explain that the tlexolotl didn't harm them—it seemed curious about them, not hostile. The warriors use the stat blocks of **scouts**, but their weapons have been destroyed and they each have 1 hit point remaining. Their manacles have no locks, as the salamanders melted them closed. Each manacle has AC 19, 10 hit points, and immunity to poison and psychic damage, or can be broken as an action with a successful DC 18 Strength (Athletics) check.

Treasure. The obsidian altars are bare except for four ruby-encrusted torch sconces, two on each altar. The sconces are easily removed, and each is worth 750 gp.

CONCLUSION

After the characters defeat or placate Izel, the remaining salamanders and fire snakes in the region return to the Plane of Fire. Without offerings being made to awaken the region's other tlexolotls, the volcanic threats cease, and the characters find their travels back to Etizalan free of volcanic dangers. If the warriors from Etizalan survived, they ask to accompany the characters.

Back in Etizalan, Ameyali is eager to hear the characters' story. So long as the volcanic threats to the region have ended, she rewards the characters with 250 gp each regardless of whether her town's warriors survived. If the warriors did survive, through, local children also show the thanks of the whole community by gifting the characters a local treasure, an axolotl-shaped *decanter of endless water*.

If the characters fail to stop Izel's plan, the tlexolotl completes his offerings, and volcanoes across Tletepec begin erupting as numerous other tlexolotl awaken—some larger and more powerful than Izel. How the characters contribute to saving the region could be the focus of future adventures.

TLETEPEC GAZETTEER

In Tletepec, it's said ancient heroes transformed themselves into volcanoes long ago and now keep vigil over the land. The region's inhabitants view these volcanoes as sacred sites and believe their offerings pass through the volcanoes' flames into the realms of the gods beyond.

Tletepec is surrounded by mountains that enclose lush forests and open valleys. The history of Tletepec is a cycle of destruction and rebirth: ashfall and lava lay waste to the earth, and forests regrow from the fertile soil destruction leaves behind. The locals settle these fertile areas, founding new villages and cities as the landscape changes.

Tletepecs fear a long-prophesied devastation, a time known as the Ashrise, when all the regions' volcanoes will erupt. Scholars like the Watchers of the Ashes look for signs of this doom and seek ways to prevent it. Others wish to use the threat of destruction for their own nefarious ends.

FEATURES

Those familiar with Tletepec know the following facts:

Hallmarks. Tletepec is known for its cycles of destruction and rebirth. The people of the land live alongside dangerous volcanoes and make communal offerings to the gods to prevent eruptions.

People. The population is mostly humans and dwarves with brown skin and dark hair. Tieflings are common in many settlements and often have skin tones evocative of minerals or gems. Other folk are rarer and are most commonly visitors.

Languages. The language of Tletepec is Tletlahtolli, but people also know Common.

NOTEWORTHY SITES

Volcanic eruptions and earthquakes constantly change the landscape of Tletepec, moving landmarks and destroying roads. Yet, several noteworthy sites have endured for generations.

XOXOTLA

Tletepec's capital city, Xoxotla, is a refuge for those forced to evacuate settlements elsewhere in the region. Its founder, Meztli, sought a safe place for her family and made a significant offering to the gods. In return, the gods created a stable plain where she built her new home. A group of guides and explorers called the Trail Keepers base their operations in Xoxotla. From here, the group keeps paths across the region safe and clear. They are often at odds with fire giants that dwell among the volcanoes, who claim that their homes were destroyed when the gods moved mountains to create Xoxotla's plain.

MAP 8.2: TLETEPEC

ITZIMICO

As volcanic ash drifts into the sea, it turns the coastal waters of the Obsidian Gulf dense and acidic, making docking a challenge. The magical piers of the town of Itzimico filter the seawater and allow ships to dock safely—for a moderate fee. Captains who avoid docking here often find their boats stuck in the water and at the mercy of the fire giants and dangerous beasts along the coast.

The city is controlled by the Shapers of Obsidian, a group of scholars who create magic inventions that protect the city. These scholars constantly test new magic on the city's walls, which are designed to protect against lava rivers and ash storms. They are always willing to reward those brave enough to help them try out their newest inventions.

TWIN GODS OBSERVATORY

This observatory stands on the slopes of the Twin Gods Volcanoes. From here, members of a group called the Watchers of the Ashes study the surrounding volcanoes and seek to predict disasters before they strike. Centuries of records and myths are etched into the observatory's walls. The oldest Watchers claim all the information necessary to predict and prevent the Ashrise is recorded here.

LIFE IN TLETEPEC

The volcanoes of Tletepec are a fact of life. Most locals live their lives focused on the promise of what's to come, not impending doom.

FAMILY AND HOME

Family is a cornerstone of Tletepec society. From birth, Tletepecs are surrounded by family and are protected by their neighbors. People help each other and their community, and they are fond of saying, "Strangers are just family you haven't met."

Tletepecs build villages near the land's many volcanoes, but travel between villages can be challenging, as the dirt paths that connect them often shift or are blocked. Therefore, Tletepecs make great efforts to sustain the common culture and values that unite them, embodying that culture in their food and festivals. Spicy dishes are a specialty; the hotter the feeling on the tongue, the more delicious the food is considered. Peppers appear in every meal in a variety of forms. Festivals often feature turkey covered in molli, a thick, sweet-spicy sauce made from a mix of peppers, seeds, and cacao. Most Tletepecs have a sweet tooth, especially if it involves cacao. Regional candy combines the sweet and spicy flavors of local fruits, and Tletepecs enjoy watching foreigners react to these unique tastes.

Leadership

Each Tletepec village is ruled by a rotating assembly, a group of five rulers led by an assembly chief. The chief is chosen through a series of trials that vary from village to village, ranging from tests of knowledge to trials of physical prowess. In earlier days, villages that fought over resources were quickly wiped out, while those whose people cooperated survived and grew, so cooperation has become the central tenet in Tletepec.

Offerings and Celebrations

Offerings are an integral part of life and religious celebrations in Tletepec. Twice a year, every village assembles a communal offering to the gods to request blessings, chief among them protection from disaster. The gathered offerings are carried by a caravan of walkers and wagons to a shrine at the nearest volcano, accompanied by a priest to perform the offering. Villagers with individual requests might follow the caravan to make their own offerings. These offerings—typically consisting of foodstuffs and colorful crafts—are dropped into the volcano, where it's believed they're conveyed to the realms of the gods.

On the travelers' return, villagers celebrate for several days, thanking the gods for their help. Event preparations begin many days in advance and involve the entire village. At the end of the festival's final night, villagers light the fire eagle: a fireworks-filled eagle effigy whose burning signifies the offerings given and whose light represents the blessings from the gods.

Watchers of the Ashes

The Watchers of the Ashes are a religious coalition dedicated to appeasing the gods and monitoring the land's volcanoes. Watchers look for signs of imminent volcanic eruptions from the observatories the order builds and maintains, measuring and interpreting every smoke ring, ash storm, and tremor to keep the folk of Tletepec safe. The order also watches for signs signaling the disastrous Ashrise and researches ways to prevent it.

Names

Most names in Tletepec have meanings drawn from words in the Tletlahtolli language related to nature. Many Tletepecs change their name on reaching adulthood, choosing a new name that reflects their accomplishments or aspirations. The following are examples of common names in Tletepec:

Feminine. Tzalanti, Xochitl, Yeyetzi, Yul
Masculine. Mixtli, Tequihua, Tonalli, Yoali
Gender-Neutral. Ameli, Chamani, Citlalli, Quetzalli, Sinti, Tenampi, Tlalli, Yoltzin
Surnames. Aca, Atzin, Coyac, Pale, Temich, Tepoz, Xopa, Zaca

Legends of Tletepec

Long ago, two lovers led their people away from war and conflict, looking for a new place to settle. They and their people were starving by the time they arrived at a peaceful but infertile land. The lovers offered themselves to the land, fusing their souls to create the two oldest volcanoes in what is now Tletepec, but the land remained barren. Desperate, the people offered everything they had to the spirits in the volcanoes, even the last of their food. The spirits accepted this offering in the name of the gods and blessed the land. Since then, the people of Tletepec have offered a portion of what they have to the volcanoes to maintain these blessings.

It's said that when the lovers became volcanoes, their memories of mortal life began to fade. When they forget their past completely, Tletepec will be destroyed by the Ashrise, a chain volcanic eruption that will cover the land in lava and ash. The Ashrise is certain to destroy everything in Tletepec, even as it plants seeds for a new civilization to grow.

Adventures in Tletepec

Consider the plots on the Tletepec Adventures table when planning adventures in Tletepec.

Tletepec Adventures

d4	Adventure
1	An aggravated **fire giant** prevents a caravan bearing offerings from leaving a village. The locals hire the characters to placate the giant.
2	Someone from Etizalan turns to stone after making an offering to a nearby volcano. Ameyali hires the characters to find out why.
3	A volcano freezes mid-eruption. The Watchers ask the characters to escort them to the volcano so they can interpret this unprecedented omen.
4	A Watcher tasks the characters with capturing a **tlexolotl** (see below), which he hopes to interrogate regarding the omens of the Ashrise.

Characters from Tletepec

If players want to create characters from Tletepec, consider asking them the following questions during character creation:

What offerings have you made to gods? Did you regret the loss of your offering? Did you receive the blessing you sought? Did you expect this or not?
Have you had to flee a natural disaster? What happened? Did you lose something while fleeing? What happened to your friends and family?
Have you trained with the Watchers of the Ashes? Do you seek omens in smoke or disasters? Do you seek evidence of some coming doom?

TLEXOLOTL

Huge Elemental, Typically Neutral

Armor Class 15 (natural armor)
Hit Points 104 (11d12 + 33)
Speed 40 ft.

STR	DEX	CON	INT	WIS	CHA
25 (+7)	10 (+0)	17 (+3)	7 (–2)	13 (+1)	9 (–1)

Damage Immunities fire, poison
Condition Immunities paralyzed, petrified, poisoned
Senses darkvision 120 ft., tremorsense 120 ft.,
　passive Perception 11
Languages Ignan
Challenge 10 (5,900 XP)　　　　**Proficiency Bonus** +4

Fire Aura. At the start of each of the tlexolotl's turns, each creature within 10 feet of it takes 7 (2d6) fire damage, and flammable objects in that aura that aren't being worn or carried ignite. A creature that touches the tlexolotl or hits it with a melee attack while within 5 feet of it takes 7 (2d6) fire damage.

Illumination. The tlexolotl sheds bright light in a 30-foot radius and dim light for an additional 30 feet.

Regeneration. The tlexolotl regains 10 hit points at the start of its turn. If the tlexolotl takes cold damage or is immersed in water, this trait doesn't function at the start of the tlexolotl's next turn. The tlexolotl dies only if it starts its turn with 0 hit points and doesn't regenerate.

ACTIONS

Multiattack. The tlexolotl makes one Bite attack and one Tail attack.

Bite. *Melee Weapon Attack:* +11 to hit, reach 10 ft., one target. *Hit:* 12 (1d10 + 7) piercing damage plus 18 (4d8) fire damage.

Tail. *Melee Weapon Attack:* +11 to hit, reach 10 ft., one target. *Hit:* 11 (1d8 + 7) bludgeoning damage plus 14 (4d6) fire damage. If the target is a Large or smaller creature, it must succeed on a DC 19 Strength saving throw or be pushed up to 10 feet away from the tlexolotl and knocked prone.

Pyroclasm (Recharge 5–6). Gouts of molten lava erupt from the tlexolotl's body. Each creature in a 30-foot-radius sphere centered on the tlexolotl must make a DC 15 Dexterity saving throw. On a failed saving throw, a creature takes 21 (6d6) fire damage and 21 (6d6) bludgeoning damage. On a successful saving throw, a creature takes half as much damage.

TLEXOLOTL

Tlexolotls are gigantic, salamander-like creatures that slumber deep in the magma of dormant volcanoes. A tlexolotl drowses amid the molten depths for centuries, rising only rarely to gorge itself on massive amounts of animal and plant life before returning to its slumber. Should a tlexolotl's sleep be disturbed—whether by intruders in its volcanic lair or the eruption of its molten home—the lava-drenched brute emerges in a rage, rampaging forth until its belly is full and its volcano is quiet once more.

Despite a tlexolotl's destructive prowess, the land around its volcano is often naturally abundant. It's common for those who live nearby to honor the tlexolotl as a protector of the land, as the ash it creates rejuvenates the soil and encourages life to flourish.

BRIAN VALEZA

IN THE MISTS OF MANIVARSHA

AN ADVENTURE FOR 9TH-LEVEL CHARACTERS

THE FINAL DAY OF THE SHANKHA TRIALS unfolds in the city of Sagorpur. But the joy of this most auspicious competition turns to terror as the city's great river swells in a destructive wave—sweeping away both the trials' champion and the sacred trophy. The characters join the effort to rescue those lost and seek out an ancient corruption that has returned.

BACKGROUND

Shankhabhumi is a forested swampland where three great city-states thrive on solid ground created by the graces of the riverines, sapient river spirit guardians. Each riverine is the patron spirit of a river, which shares its patron's name. The riverines of the four largest rivers in this land—Iravati, Mehul, Joltara, and the now-lost Adirohit—raised the islands on which the great cities sit. In exchange, the people of Shankhabhumi pay homage to the capricious riverines through the Shankha Trials.

There were originally four cities in Shankhabhumi, but the city of Manivarsha was destroyed during the Shankha Trials five hundred years ago. Manivarsha's patron riverine, Adirohit, vanished, and his river dwindled into dozens of swampy streams. Manivarshi citizens who were away from home were forced to adopt new lives in the other three cities, but the memory of the lost city of Manivarsha remains.

No further catastrophes happened for centuries. But now the conclusion of the most recent Shankha Trials has attracted the attention of a sinister figure from Shankhabhumi's past. This is the ancient, fiend-tainted athlete Jijibisha Manivarshi, a wicked soul whose desire for eternal honor directly caused the destruction of Manivarsha. Having lived a cursed life as a pride-obsessed fiend in the depths of the swamps for centuries, Jijibisha has recently heard of a rival that threatens to claim her title as the greatest Manivarshi athlete of all time. Her delusions insulted, Jijibisha prepares to use the power of a trapped riverine to claim both the honor and the life of this year's champion.

PRONUNCIATIONS

The Shankhabhumi Pronunciations table shows how to pronounce key names in this adventure.

SHANKHABHUMI PRONUNCIATIONS

Name	Pronunciation
Adirohit	add-ear-OH-hit
Amanisha	uh-MA-nee-SHA
Ashwadhatu	ASH-woh-DHA-tu
Bhatiyali	BHA-tee-UH-li
Dukha	DOO-ka
Iravati	EE-ra-WO-tee
Jijibisha	JEE-jee-BEE-sha
Joltara	jol-tuh-RA
Kubjhatika	CUB-ja-TEE-ka
Majhi	MA-jee
Manivarsha	MO-nee-VER-sha
Mehul	MAY-hull
Plabon	PLUB-on
Riverine	RIH-ver-EEN
Sagorpur	SHUG-or-poor
Shankhabhumi	SHANK-uh-VOO-mee
Tinjhorna	TEEN-jor-na
Tippurika	TIP-poo-ree-ka

SETTING THE ADVENTURE

Use the following suggestions to help contextualize Shankhabhumi in a wider world:

Through the Radiant Citadel. Characters traveling from the Radiant Citadel arrive just outside Sagorpur. If you wish to further detail that region, use the "Shankhabhumi Gazetteer" section at this adventure's end as a departure point.

Eberron. Shankhabhumi could appear as its own island between the continents of Khorvaire and Xen'drik. Alternatively, it could be a hidden nation in Xen'drik, east of Dread Lake.

Forgotten Realms. Shankhabhumi might be found in the jungles south of the Shining Sea, near Chult, or as its own island west of Lantan.

A DEVASTATING WAVE FROM THE IRAVATI RIVER CRASHES UPON THE RIVERINE TEMPLE IN SAGORPUR.

CHARACTER HOOKS

Consider the following ways to involve characters in this adventure:

Event Guards. Judges overseeing the Shankha Trials want to make sure the important event goes smoothly. They hire the characters to serve as bodyguards for visiting athletes.

Holy Waters. The characters or their allies need a magical reagent or blessed water and believe the riverines of Shankhabhumi can provide it. When the characters arrive in Sagorpur, though, the city is swept up in the final days of the Shankha Trials. Members of the local riverine temple will provide these waters only after the upheaval surrounding the trials is ended.

THE SHANKHA TRIALS

Characters who come to Shankhabhumi learn the following details about an exciting event called the Shankha Trials:

- The Shankha Trials are a spectacle of art and athleticism. They take their name from shankha shells—the shells of conch mollusks—which feature in Shankhabhumi's legends and are an icon of the land.

- These contests are held over a twelve-day period every twelve years.
- Competitors come from all three of Shankhabhumi's city-states, and they include some folk descended from survivors of the ruined city of Manivarsha.
- Contests include boatbuilding, boat racing, cooking, dancing, shankha diving, and swimming.
- The contests honor the region's riverines, spirits who hold power over the region's many rivers.
- One contestant among three dozen emerges victorious and claims the great conch-shell trophy known as the Riverine's Shankha to grace their home city until the next competition.

STARTING THE ADVENTURE

The adventure begins as the characters are in the city of Sagorpur for the end of the competition called the Shankha Trials. Use the "Character Hooks" section to determine why the characters find themselves in the city, and the "Shankhabhumi Gazetteer" section at the end of this adventure to further detail the city. Read or paraphrase the following when you're ready to begin:

AMANISHA
MANIVARSHI

The city of Sagorpur is teeming with onlookers enjoying the Shankha Trials. The final event of this great competition is being held next to the temple to the riverine Iravati, an ancient burnt-clay edifice adorned by images of lilies and spirits that peek from behind moss and vines. Countless spectators fill the surrounding streets and line the river.

If the characters don't already know the information in "The Shankha Trials" section, now's a perfect time for them to learn it. This might be related by a friendly ally or enthusiastic locals in the crowd.

The crowd has assembled for the final event of the Shankha Trials, where a popular young prodigy—the dancer Amanisha Manivarshi, called Nisha by her fans—is about to perform. Her name passes through the crowd with a buzz of excitement. The characters have a clear view of her performance. Read the following description for those who watch:

Amanisha's performance is breathtaking, but it carries an edge of sadness. As she dances, an announcer explains that her performance represents the story of the city of Manivarsha's mysterious destruction and of the anguish carried by Nisha and all those Manivarshi who will never return to their ancestral home. As the dance ends, a tumultuous cheer rises from the crowd.

A character who succeeds on a DC 10 Wisdom (Insight) or Charisma (Performance) check realizes that Nisha's dance was outstanding and captured something meaningful to many people in the crowd. Some viewers wipe the edges of their eyes.

After brief deliberations, the trial judges produce a great conch shell trophy, the Riverine's Shankha. A judge bows, then beckons Nisha forward. Amid cheering and fanfare, she accepts the trophy and takes her place as the newest champion of the Shankha Trials.

STORM OF DESTRUCTION

As Nisha raises the Riverine's Shankha above her head and the Shankha Trials conclude, read the following description:

Thunder rings out as the sky fills with clouds. From the formerly calm river, a surge of water rises, forming a towering wave that flings boats onto the banks. The massive wave crests in a mighty swell crashing toward the crowded shore and riverine temple.

The characters have a moment to react to the sudden disaster. The plaza surrounding the riverine temple is thousands of feet long and packed with people. There's little the characters can do to stop the sudden wave, but quick thinking or magic—such as teleporting atop surrounding buildings or a precisely timed *control water* spell—might spare the characters and those around them.

When the wave crashes on the plaza, each character must make a DC 15 Strength saving throw. Those who fail take 9 (2d8) bludgeoning damage and are knocked prone. Those who succeed take half as much damage and aren't knocked prone. This damage is less in other parts of the great plaza but causes chaos across the open space, smashing vendors' stalls, harming hundreds of people, and leaving behind a foot of standing water that turns the area into difficult terrain.

MASS DESTRUCTION

The wave has caused utter devastation across the plaza, and hundreds of people rush to escape. Roll on the Wave Chaos table one or more times to see what perils confront the characters.

WAVE CHAOS

d6	Encounter
1	A stall selling mango drinks has collapsed. A character must succeed on a DC 14 Strength (Athletics) check to free the frantic, trapped vendors.
2	An overly helpful local insistently tries to get the frailest-looking character to flee with them.

d6	Encounter
3	An elder has fallen down. They're bruised and separated from their family. A character must succeed on a DC 16 Wisdom (Perception) check to find the lost family amid the chaos.
4	A desperate local searching the ground for the 20 sp they lost in the wave is in danger of being trampled by those fleeing. A character can cause the local to stop searching and move to safety by replacing the lost silver pieces or succeeding on a DC 14 Charisma (Intimidation or Persuasion) check.
5	Drifting debris smashes into characters on the ground, each of whom must succeed on a DC 14 Dexterity saving throw or be knocked prone.
6	The wave washes a hostile **swarm of poisonous snakes** into the nearby crowd.

Chaos at the Temple

After a few rounds of contending with the destruction, the character who has the highest passive Wisdom (Perception) score sees the following scene:

> At the base of the temple, creatures of living water attack people trying to flee.

A hostile **water elemental** and two **water weirds** with heads shaped like king cobras attack anyone who comes near the temple.

A character who succeeds on a DC 14 Intelligence (Religion) check realizes the water creatures are defenders of the temple. A character who uses an action and succeeds on a DC 16 Charisma (Intimidation or Persuasion) check convinces the confused creatures to stand down; the Elementals then dissolve back into the waters within the temple.

Survivors at the Temple

Once the temple's guardians are dealt with, several people emerge from within the temple. These are Shankha Trials contestants and judges, including the temple's leader, High Riversinger Plabon Bhatiyali—a 200-year-old, chaotic good, halfling **priest**. Many are wounded, but thankfully everyone is alive. However, both Amanisha Manivarshi and the Riverine's Shankha trophy are missing. Plabon approaches the characters, and he says:

> "The river came for Amanisha and the Riverine's Shankha. The wall of water descended and flowed around us, seeking Amanisha as she tried to help others to safety. It seized her and the trophy, then pulled them both away!"

The Riversinger's Fears

Plabon is soft-spoken but insists on sharing what he witnessed with the characters. Use the following points to guide the conversation:

- Plabon is one of the judges of the Shankha Trials.
- Although riverines hold the power to control river water, Plabon doesn't believe this disaster is the doing of Iravati, the spirit of Sagorpur's river.
- Plabon felt a deep jealousy in the storm and the river. He fears that today's destruction might be linked to the catastrophe that befell the city of Manivarsha.
- Tales of Manivarsha's ruin tell of a sudden storm and a huge wave that rose above the swamp forest, then consumed the city.
- He believes Amanisha is the key to understanding what happened and wants the characters to find her.

Plabon offers the characters 400 gp each if they will find and return Amanisha. If the characters balk, other judges—influential locals and senators of the city—add to the reward, increasing it to 500 gp each in treasures and trade goods, as well as 20 acres of fertile farmland outside the city.

If the characters accept, Plabon admits the task won't be easy; the flooded swamp forests of Shankhabhumi are vast. He encourages the characters to find a boat and a guide who can take them upriver to search for Amanisha.

Before the characters leave, Plabon gives one of them a small shankha shell from the temple. This shell functions as a *stone of good luck*.

Venturing from Sagorpur

The swamp forests of Shankhabhumi defy attempts to map them. Travelers along the rivers must rely on experienced navigators to guide them. As the characters prepare to head upriver to find Amanisha, they learn many of the city's watercraft were damaged by the disastrous wave. Even if they have their own vessel, they'll still need to hire a navigator for it.

Characters who search along the rivers' edge find the city's river boats in disarray after the disaster. However, as they search, a boat pulls into the harbor. This is the vessel of a skilled majhi—or navigator—named Dukha Majhi Sagorpuri. He has just arrived back in the city.

Dukha Bhatiyali

Dukha Bhatiyali is an experienced majhi. Although he appears human, his colleagues and passengers don't know he's a **weretiger** (neutral). While several bands of such lycanthropes dwell deep in the swamp forests of Shankhabhumi, Dukha left his tribe and is trying to live as a human. He roams the rivers around Sagorpur in human guise and subjects anyone who accompanies him on his expeditions to endless tales of forest lore.

Personality Trait. "I know everything there is to know about the swamp forests!"

Ideal. "Outside the cities, the land should be held in harmony between people and the riverines."

Bond. "I will protect my people's territory, but I want to live on my own terms."

Flaw. "I see danger everywhere."

Way of the Waters

If the characters seek to hire Dukha, he offers to guide them for 100 gp. A character who haggles and succeeds on a DC 14 Charisma (Persuasion) check convinces him to reduce this price by 25 gp. Once a deal's been made, he shares these details:

- Dukha was traveling toward Sagorpur when the wave struck.
- While approaching, he saw a current of water sparkle with an eerie green light and sweep away from the city. He has seen that same glowing ripple recently along local tributaries of the Iravati River. The first time he saw it was twelve days ago, the first day of the Shankha Trials.
- He followed the glowing ripples, tracing them along a small river called the Tinjhorna.
- Near a series of waterfalls, Tinjhorna the riverine warned Dukha to stay away, accusing mortal folk of unleashing tainted magic upon his waters.
- Dukha can share any of the details in the "Riverine" section at the end of this adventure.

Dukha suggests taking the characters to that same series of waterfalls on the Tinjhorna River in the hope of learning more from the riverine. He has little further information and, at this time, he doesn't share that he's a weretiger.

Dukha's boat is a narrow, flat-bottomed skiff with room for the characters but little else. It moves at a rate of 1½ miles per hour. The majhi is ready to head off whenever the characters please.

Contacting the Riverine Iravati

The characters might attempt to contact Iravati, the riverine guardian of the river that flows past Sagorpur. The riverine, like the river, is listless and slow to act. No calls or offerings made to Iravati provoke the riverine into appearing.

Dukha
Bhatiyali

The Swamp Forest

Dukha pilots his skiff to the mouth of the Tinjhorna River, a journey that takes 10 hours in his boat. From there, the journey to the waterfalls takes an additional 10 hours. Travel through the swamp forest is smooth until the ship reaches the Tinjhorna River's wilder and narrower waterways. For every 3 hours the characters spend traveling on the Tinjhorna River, or whenever you please, roll on the River Journey Encounters table to see what occurs.

River Journey Encounters

d10	Encounter
1–2	It rains heavily. For the next hour, the boat and its surroundings are heavily obscured. Roll again on this table, ignoring another result of 1 or 2.
3	The current increases along a narrow stretch of the river. Dukha urgently asks the characters to help row the boat upstream. All of the characters must succeed on a DC 10 Strength (Athletics) check. The boat loses a half-hour of progress for every failed check or character who doesn't assist.

d10	Encounter
4	A mangrove-shaped **treant** blocks the path forward. The treant moves only if the party listens to its hour-long ode to the swamp, or if a character succeeds on a DC 18 Charisma (Persuasion) check to convince it to let the skiff pass.
5	A **spirit naga** appears and asks where the characters are heading. It offers to give a single character its magical treasure, a *pearl of power*, if that character is brave enough to let it bite them three times.
6	Six swamp spirits (use the **mud mephit** stat block) emerge from the river, demanding that the characters hand over their shiniest valuables. They can be driven off with force or a successful DC 14 Charisma (Intimidation) check.
7–10	No encounter

FALLS CLEARING

As the characters approach the series of waterfalls, read the following description:

> A gradually increasing roar drowns out the rain forest sounds long before the river turns, revealing a series of parallel waterfalls cascading from a ridge that runs alongside the river. A chain of sparsely forested islands lies along the far side of the river opposite the base of the falls.

Dukha explains this is where he met the riverine Tinjhorna. He moors the boat amid the islands opposite the falls so the group can attempt to call upon the riverine—and to keep it safe in case the spirit proves hostile.

As Dukha ties up the boat, characters who succeed on a DC 14 Wisdom (Perception) check notice several pairs of green, feline eyes watching from amid the island's foliage. Upon being noticed or soon after the characters land on the island, three hostile **weretigers** in hybrid form emerge with longbows drawn. They gauge the party's intentions for 1 round before attacking. A character who talks to the weretigers during this round can convince them not to attack by succeeding on a DC 16 Charisma (Intimidation or Persuasion) check. Even if the weretigers do attack, a character who spends an action can attempt this check, convincing the weretigers to stand down if they're successful. All the weretigers flee from combat when any of them are reduced to 10 hit points or fewer.

Dukha's Role. Dukha tries to stay out of this conflict, but he doesn't want to see his fellow weretigers harmed. If the weretigers attack, Dukha shouts for the lycanthropes to fall back, telling them the characters come in peace. If the fight lasts more than 2 rounds, Dukha shifts into his hybrid form and fights alongside the characters until the other weretigers are driven off. If he does so, he resents the characters' lack of diplomacy and does not aid them in future battles. However, if he doesn't have to, he appreciates the characters' respect for the creatures of the forest and aids the party in any future conflicts where they need aid.

TIGER TALK

If the characters converse with the weretigers, or if they run the weretigers off and then question Dukha, it becomes clear that Dukha and the weretigers are familiar with each other. Dukha or the weretigers share the following information:

- This area is the weretigers' territory, and they have noticed unnatural changes to the flow of the river.
- The weretigers think that the people of Sagorpur have caused the disturbance.
- They seek to protect their territory from anyone who would harm it or the riverine Tinjhorna.
- The weretigers haven't seen the riverine Tinjhorna since he confronted Dukha, but the riverine often frequents the pool atop the falls.
- If he hasn't already, Dukha reveals he is a lycanthrope and was raised among the weretigers who dwell in the forest.

After conversing with the characters, the weretigers encourage the party not to linger in their territory; then they depart. Dukha makes no apologies for hiding his true nature and encourages the characters to continue their search for the riverine Tinjhorna atop the falls.

HEADWATER POOL

From where Dukha moors his boat, the characters can follow an indirect but mostly dry path to the cliffs the parallel waterfalls cascade down. Climbing the slippery, 20-foot-tall rock face around the waterfalls requires a successful DC 12 Strength (Athletics) check. Those who fail the check fall 10 feet into the water. If more than one character falls, a **swarm of quippers** takes notice and attacks.

When the first character reaches the top of the waterfalls, the following scene unfolds before them:

> The adjacent waterfalls are fed by a broad, shallow pool surrounded by ancient mangrove trees. Twenty feet away, a young man with green skin walks atop the water, speaking softly while slowly circling two churning pillars of glowing green foam.

Tinjhorna the **riverine** (detailed at the end of this adventure) is speaking in Aquan and trying to calm a pair of **water elementals** corrupted by the strange magic afflicting his river.

Characters who succeed on a DC 12 Intelligence (Arcana) check recognize the frothing pillars as water elementals. Characters risk provoking the Elementals if they're noisy or approach without caution. Characters who approach carefully and succeed on a DC 15 Intelligence (Nature) or Charisma (Persuasion) check to calm the creatures aid Tinjhorna in pacifying the Elementals, and a moment later, the creatures vanish. If the characters are aggressive, the water elementals are startled and attack.

The pool is 4 feet deep and is difficult terrain.

Speaking with Tinjhorna

Tinjhorna is a youthful, neutral riverine who appears as a soft-spoken young man with long hair. His river was one of many waterways created in the geological fallout after the destruction of the city of Manivarsha and the great river Adirohit. Although he dreams of one day being a mighty river, his

TINJHORNA
THE RIVERINE

dream is imperiled by the strange magic infecting his waters.

Tinjhorna thanks the characters for their help and eagerly converses with them. Use the following points to guide the conversation:

- A week or so ago, Tinjhorna felt an ancient power affecting his river, as if something were moving through the waters to the southwest.
- There's little in that direction except for a haunted area called the Forest of Hands.
- The Forest of Hands occupies much of the same land as the vanished Adirohit River and the disappeared city of Manivarsha.
- The magic Tinjhorna felt has angered many inhabitants of the surrounding swamp forest. He has his hands full trying to calm them.
- Tinjhorna has seen no evidence of the lost dancer Amanisha, but he asks the characters to seek out the source of the magic affecting his river.

If the characters agree to help the riverine, he thanks them and gives them a *potion of healing* (superior). The riverine offers to watch over the characters if they wish to rest near the falls but won't travel with them, as he must attend to the disturbed creatures along his river's length.

Forest of Hands

From the waterfalls, the journey to the Forest of Hands takes 10 hours. Dukha continues to serve as the characters' navigator, regardless of the events at the waterfall. For every 3 hours the characters spend traveling on the Tinjhorna River, or whenever you please, roll on the River Journey Encounters table in "The Swamp Forest" section.

When the characters reach the Forest of Hands, read the following description:

> The scent of the swamp takes on the sweet stink of rotting flesh. Trees with drooping limbs stand amid the river, their branches like hundreds of gray hands and their dangling leaves like long, leathery fingers.

Characters who succeed on a DC 14 Intelligence (History or Nature) check recognize the region's notorious angul trees, plants that stink of rotting flesh and drip crimson sap. The trees are harmless, but many travelers find the long, finger-like leaves gliding over them as they pass beneath more than a little disconcerting.

The journey through the Forest of Hands lasts 3 hours. Roll for or choose an encounter from the Forest of Hands Encounters table after every hour of travel.

THE SWAMP FORESTS OF SHANKHABHUMI HOLD
EQUAL MEASURE OF BEAUTY AND DANGER.

FOREST OF HANDS ENCOUNTERS

d4	Encounter
1	Three clots of animate angul tree sap (use the **black pudding** stat block) attack from underwater.
2	Spectral boats appear through the trees. Dukha or a character who succeeds on a DC 14 Intelligence (History) check knows these phantoms are travelers who were lost when Manivarsha was ruined. The spirits are unnerving but harmless.
3	Fog rises and lightly obscures the forest. Through it, two **will-o'-wisps** try to lead the characters into the path of a hostile **hydra**.
4	A **fomorian** hermit blocks the boat's passage. It demands the characters cook a meal for it, or it will eat them. It likes only disgusting food.

FOREST HEART

Pushing through the Forest of Hands eventually brings the characters to a clearing at the forest's heart. This area is depicted on map 9.1. Read the following description when the characters arrive:

> Several slow-moving waterways convene at a rocky island covered in moss and ruined stones. Atop it stands the blackened, rotting stump of a great tree. On the stump, Amanisha Manivarshi lies motionless.

The water in this area is 10 feet deep (see the *Player's Handbook* for details on swimming). The island rises gently to the north and south, while on its east and west sides, 10-foot-high bluffs rise from the river. Characters who succeed on a DC 18 Wisdom (Perception) check notice the island's rocks look like pieces of an ancient structure.

Amanisha (neutral good, human **spy**) is unconscious. She currently has no weapons and 5 hit points. Magical healing or a successful DC 20 Wisdom (Medicine) check restores her to consciousness. Characters who look for her trophy from the Shankha Trials, the Riverine's Shankha, don't see it.

AMANISHA MANIVARSHI

Amanisha Manivarshi is an accomplished dancer and the most recent champion of the Shankha Trials. Known as Nisha to her friends and fans, she is a charming young woman whose Manivarshi ancestors settled in Tippurika after their home disappeared. Nisha uses the last name "Manivarshi" out of respect for her family and heritage.

Personality Trait. "Many see my focus and assume I'm not approachable. But I welcome new friends."

Ideal. "I will make the city of my birth and descendants of Manivarsha proud by bringing home the Riverine's Shankha."

ALFVEN ATO

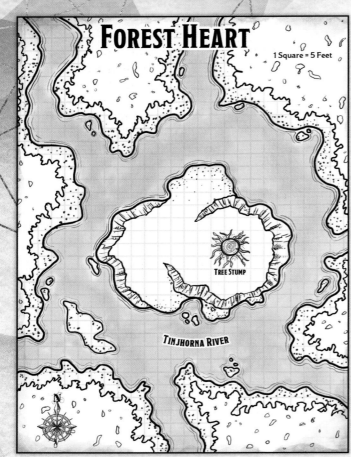

FOREST HEART

1 Square = 5 Feet

TREE STUMP

TINJHORNA RIVER

MAP 9.1: FOREST HEART

Bond. "The folk of the Manivarshi diaspora cling too much to memories. I will give them something new to celebrate."

Flaw. "I am both a child of Tippurika and a descendant of Manivarsha. I am quick to hold a grudge against those who tell me I have to be one or the other."

PRISONER OF THE PAST

Nisha awakens in a fog, confused and disoriented. She calms down if the characters assure her that they've come to help. Nisha shares the following information:

- The wave that smashed Sagorpur seized Nisha and the Riverine's Shankha, then dragged them here.
- Once here, Nisha was attacked by a monstrous woman with gray skin that oozes crimson ichor, like the surrounding forest's angul trees. The fiend seized the Riverine's Shankha, declaring it belonged to her.
- The fiend claimed this place marks the edge of the ruins of lost Manivarsha.
- The fiend said that if Nisha thinks she's Manivarshi, then she can be a prisoner here for the rest of her days.

JIJIBISHA'S VENGEANCE

Jijibisha Manivarshi, a vicious soul from the land's past, lurks in the nearby forest. Long ago she made a deal with wicked otherworldly forces that gave her longevity and fiendish powers, a bargain that ultimately resulted in the ruin of Manivarsha. She is behind Amanisha's capture and is loath to let her prisoner escape.

Before the party can complete their conversation with Amanisha, the effects of Jijibisha's *wall of fire* spell spring up, separating as many characters from their boat as possible. Read the following description:

> A woman with tattered, ancient robes and skin the color of a drowned corpse walks out of swamp at the south edge of the island.
>
> "Welcome, visitors! I am Jijibisha Manivarshi—I'm sure you've heard of me. I know you've come to steal my trophy," the woman says, holding up the Riverine's Shankha. "But I am the last champion of Manivarshi to win the Riverine's Shankha—not this upstart. It cost me everything, but my victory is eternal!"

Jijibisha Manivarshi uses the **ultroloth** stat block, but she has access to only the *wall of fire* spell and the at-will spells from her Innate Spellcasting trait. Despite her fiendish powers, she looks like an ancient, withered human.

After she finishes speaking, Jijibisha attacks. She attempts to use her Hypnotic Gaze to turn Dukha and Amanisha against the characters. While she fights, Jijibisha mocks the characters, claiming to be the last champion of Manivarsha and the only Manivarshi who can rightfully claim the Riverine's Shankha. If Jijibisha is separated from the Riverine's Shankha, she has disadvantage on ability checks and attack rolls until she regains it. She fights to the death.

A character who succeeds on a DC 20 Intelligence (History) check has heard of Jijibisha Manivarshi and can confirm that she was favored to win the Shankha Trials the year Manivarsha was destroyed.

ADIROHIT'S RETRIBUTION

When Jijibisha Manivarshi is destroyed, all is silent for a moment before a voice drifts from beneath the tree stump at the center of the Forest Heart.

> "You out there!" calls a voice from beneath the tree stump. "Has that horror been banished? Is she finally gone? Set things right. Set me free!"

If the characters respond to the voice, the speaker shares the following information:

- The voice says he is Adirohit, the riverine of the lost Adirohit River, which once nourished the great city of Manivarsha.
- Adirohit has been locked away for hundreds of years beneath a mighty mangrove that once adorned a temple built in his honor—ever since the Shankha Trials that precipitated the destruction of Manivarsha.
- Jijibisha trapped him here using her fiendish power and forced him to cause the flood in Sagorpur.
- Now that Jijibisha is gone, touching any blessed shankha to the tree stump will release him.

Using either the Riverine's Shankha or the magical shankha Plabon gifted the characters releases Adirohit. However, Amanisha urges the characters to consider cautiously.

Through roleplaying or by succeeding on a DC 12 Charisma (Persuasion) check, a character can convince Adirohit to reveal the following details:

- Long ago, Jijibisha Manivarshi made a deal with a wicked god to give her fiendish powers that would ensure her victory in the Shankha Trials.
- Adirohit was outraged that humans would pervert the sacred trials and unleashed a flood to punish the whole city by sinking it into the swamp.
- Jijibisha Manivarshi survived, though, and declared herself winner of the trials.
- Jijibisha used her sinister powers to bind Adirohit within his ruined temple.
- Jijibisha was delighted that she would be the last Manivarshi to ever win the Shankha Trials—at least, until Amanisha's victory.

While Adirohit is a captive now and has been used by Jijibisha, he was not when he sank Manivarsha.

It's up to the characters to determine whether or not they free Adirohit. Amanisha has complex feelings about this, seeing Adirohit as a tie to her ancient people and one who could restore a measure of what was lost, but also a tempestuous being who destroyed her ancestors. She will not impede the characters no matter what choice they make.

Adirohit's Fate

If the characters free Adirohit, he emerges from the stump in a torrent of river water. He is an arrogant, chaotic neutral **riverine** (detailed at the end of this adventure) who looks like a muscular, middle-aged man with white hair and blue skin. He thanks the characters for their service and brings forth treasure to reward them with (see the following section).

Adirohit is unapologetic for his past deeds, even if Amanisha or others ask him to explain Manivarsha's fate. He's confident, though, that he can reestablish his river and that soon enough humans will build a new, greater city on its banks. He invites the characters to rest here under his protection and tell him how the world has changed. Amanisha has no interest in doing this, though—what Adirohit did to Manivarsha fills her with anger. Feel free to roleplaying the contentious dynamic between Amanisha and Adirohit, or encourage the characters to choose sides, as much as you please.

Ultimately, the riverine allows the characters to leave whenever they like but insists on rewarding them for freeing him before they do.

Treasure

Using his magic, Adirohit causes the following treasures to rise upon a geyser from the ruins beneath the island, bequeathing them upon the characters:

- A fist-sized sapphire worth 6,000 gp
- An emerald *elemental gem* that conjures a water elemental that resembles Adirohit
- An intricately carved jade statuette depicting a muscular version of Adirohit, worth 500 gp
- A waterproof sack containing a length of the finest silk bastra, embroidered with pearls worth 250 gp

Conclusion

The journey back to the Tinjhorna River is uneventful. The riverine Tinjhorna is enthusiastic to hear about the characters' journey and thanks them for investigating. When the characters return to Sagorpur with Amanisha and the Riverine's Shankha, they receive a hero's welcome, along with the rewards Plabon and the other trial judges promised. Depending on Adirohit's fate, only time will tell how the riverine could change the waters of the swamp forest or whether he is lost forever.

Shankhabhumi Gazetteer

Shaped and defined by its rivers, Shankhabhumi is a dynamic floodplain surrounded by mountains and crisscrossed by waterways. Most of the land is covered in swamp forests infested with unknown perils, except for three city-states that stand proudly on broad islands of miraculously dry land. The islands on which the cities of Ashwadhatu, Sagorpur, and Tippurika stand were each granted to the people by a different riverine, and at the heart of each city is a temple dedicated to that city's patron riverine. A fourth city, Manivarsha, was destroyed in a cataclysm five hundred years ago.

Each city spreads out in concentric circles from its riverine temple. The innermost circle holds the city's senate house, main market, and academy, as well as the houses of wealthy citizens. Past these lie modest residential neighborhoods and trade wards. At its edges, each city slopes down to submerged rice fields before dissipating into the swamps. The skies of Shankhabhumi are eternally heavy with rainclouds, and even well-maintained buildings wear a fine coat of moss.

To experience Shankhabhumi at its finest, one must visit during the Shankha Trials, held every twelve years in one of the three cities. A twelve-day spectacle of skill and might, the trials feature contestants representing each city who entertain thousands of spectators. But the trials are more than a competition; they represent the origin story of the land and a pact endlessly renewed between the people and the riverines to whom the land belongs.

FEATURES

Those familiar with Shankhabhumi know the following details:

Hallmarks. This region is known for its isolated city-states separated by tangled swamps, and for the capricious river spirits that rule its waters.

People. Urban society is a mix of humans, halflings, elves, and dwarves. Skin tones in Shankhabhumi span shades of brown, and people have uniformly dark hair that ranges from wavy to very curly.

Languages. The folk of Shankhabhumi speak Common and Shankhi, the regional tongue.

NOTEWORTHY SITES

Hundreds of rivers flow through Shankhabhumi, creating natural paths to its three great cities.

ASHWADHATU

The Mehul River flows from the Nirjhar Highlands, through Ashwadhatu, and on to Dishahara Bay. The city of Shankhabhumi with the largest area of solid land, Ashwadhatu has long been the home of proud, traditionalist farmers, miners, and boatbuilders. More recently, metalworkers and inventors are fueling a growing industry, though some citizens dismiss them as eccentrics creating unnecessary, newfangled contrivances.

SAGORPUR

Sagorpur is the mightiest city of Shankhabhumi, having inherited that mantle when Manivarsha was ruined five centuries ago. The city lies where the Iravati River flows into Dishahara Bay, and its mainstay is sea trade. A wide array of goods can be purchased in the city's sprawling markets, and seafaring foreigners and inland travelers from Tippurika and Ashwadhatu mingle with locals in Sagorpur's numerous inns, playhouses, gambling dens, and restaurants.

TIPPURIKA

The city of Tippurika stands where the Joltara River flows from the Adhameru Mountains into a deep canyon, frothing with whitewater rapids. Tippuri citizens—a majority of them dwarves and halflings—are adept at climbing steep paths, traversing unstable rope bridges, fishing in mountain rapids, and exploring the inaccessible caves of the mountains. The city is known for its hill crops—particularly tea and timber. Locals take pride in their staunch courage and infuriating stubbornness in equal measure.

LIFE IN SHANKHABHUMI

Outsiders often refer to the people of Shankhabhumi collectively as "riverlanders," but the folk of the three city-states call themselves Sagorpuri, Ashwadhatuj, or Tippuri, and claim to have little in common with one another. However, that's an exaggeration; the people of Shankhabhumi share unifying traits and experiences.

CLOTHING AND ACCOUTREMENTS

The folk of Shankhabhumi favor clothing composed of lengths of cotton or silk cloth called bastras, which are wrapped around the body in various styles. These include the loose, voluminous drapes of a sedentary noble, the tight, ropelike wrap of a Shankha Trials contestant, and the practical, gathered garments of a laborer or river navigator.

Wavy or curly hair is common in the region; people rub it to a shine with coconut oil and wear it long or in thick plaits. Ornaments include conchshell bangles and hairpieces, as well as designs of white clay painted directly onto the skin. Gold and gemstone jewelry, a specialty of the ruined city of Manivarsha, is popular among wealthy citizens and often crafted by the descendants of artisans from the Manivarshi diaspora.

MANIVARSHI DIASPORA

The city-state of Manivarsha was destroyed five hundred years ago under circumstances that have never fully been explained. On the last day of that year's Shankha Trials, the city simply vanished, along with everyone there. A few survivors who were just outside the city at the time told of a towering wave along the Adirohit River that marked its demise; subsequent attempts to reach its former location found nothing but endless swamps. Citizens who were away from home were left stranded. Those survivors and their descendants assimilated into the other cities, bringing Manivarsha's traditions of gem-cutting and jewel-setting to their new homes. This jewelry is now common throughout the land, and many pieces are fantastically valuable.

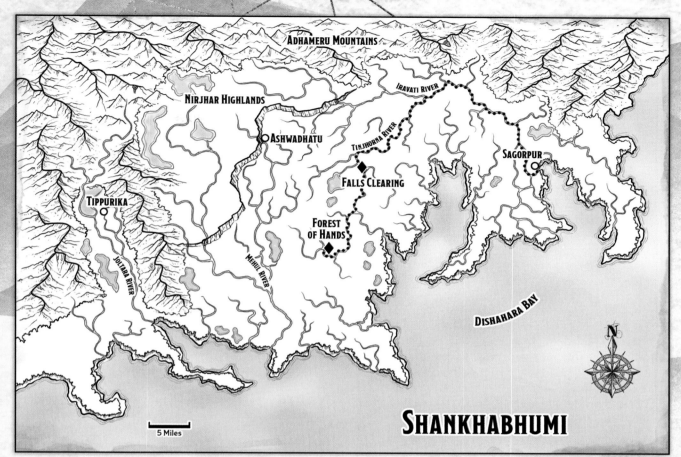

Map 9.2: Shankhabhumi

POWER AND POLITICS

Aside from their cultural rivalries, Sagorpur, Tippurika and Ashwadhatu rarely engage in major conflicts—living in a land that constantly changes with the caprices of the riverines is precarious enough. The shadow of the lost city of Manivarsha hangs over the remaining cities as a reminder that life in Shankhabhumi can easily be swept away.

Power in each city is shared between three factions—fifteen senators who officially govern the affairs of the city-state; a network of river-navigator majhis known as the Bhatiyali; and former Shankha Trials contestants who become famous public entertainers and heroes, if they don't become senators themselves.

RIVER BOUNTY

Every meal in Shankhabhumi includes fish, though each city proclaims its own style of preparing it to be the best. In fact, cooking is a competitive discipline at the Shankha Trials. Sagorpuri fish curries are fragrant with spices imported from foreign lands, while Ashwadhatuj cook their fish with locally farmed vegetables, and Tippuris ferment their mountain fish in tea.

SIGN OF THE SHANKHA

The shell of the conch mollusk, known locally as a shankha, is the eponymous icon of Shankhabhumi. The sizable Riverine's Shankha is the legendary shell trophy that circulates among the cities via the Shankha Trials, kept at the riverine temple in the current champion's city until that city hosts the next trials. Smaller shankhas are rare and precious, and they are often worn like pendants by those who can afford them. Shankha motifs decorate all riverine temples and adorn weaving, white-clay body art, jewelry, children's toys, pastries, and more.

NAMES

The given names of people in Shankhabhumi tend to be many syllables long and indicate the bearer's gender. Most folk use a last name based on their city of birth—Sagorpuri, Ashwadhatuj or Tippuri. The only exceptions are the descendants of Manivarsha (many of whom still use "Manivarshi") and majhis who take the last name "Bhatiyali." The following are common names in Shankhabhumi:

Feminine. Amrapali, Bhanumati, Jamdani, Phullora
Masculine. Anuttom, Chakrayudh, Rudrashekhar, Udayaditya
Gender-Neutral. Kheya, Kobi, Palki, Ulka

LEGENDS OF SHANKHABHUMI

The ancestors of the people of Shankhabhumi migrated here from other lands about a thousand years ago. They arrived to find swamp forests infested with monsters and other dangers—a land shaped by hundreds of riverines who were indifferent to the newcomers and their fates. Then the elven leader Kubjhatika killed a giant mollusk that attacked her people. After the battle, she carved the tale of her victory and her people's journey on a beautiful, red-ridged shell. This shell became the Riverine's Shankha. Kubjhatika offered it as tribute to the riverines, appealing to them for refuge amid the unforgiving land.

The four greatest riverines—Adirohit, Iravati, Mehul, and Joltara—each wished to claim the Riverine's Shankha as their own. Kubjhatika proposed the Shankha Trials to ensure it would circulate fairly. But since people who could barely survive in this unstable land couldn't put on such a spectacular event, Kubjhatika persuaded the riverines to each create a site for a great city. Thus, the riverines created the stable islands on which Manivarsha, Sagorpur, Ashwadhatu, and Tippurika would be built, and the histories of those great cities began.

ADVENTURES IN SHANKHABHUMI

Consider the plots on the Shankhabhumi Adventures table when planning adventures in Shankhabhumi.

SHANKHABHUMI ADVENTURES

d4	Adventure
1	A den of **cultists** high in the Adhameru Mountains worships a **spirit naga** and seeks to poison the riverine Joltara.
2	A Sagorpuri merchant has imprisoned a **marid** within a shankha and intends to use its powers to help create a new city—potentially creating conflict with the riverines of the existing city-states.
3	A hermit asks for help when a newly born **riverine** (detailed at the end of this adventure) appears in a stream near her home. The hermit fears the aggressive riverine of a nearby river will see the young spirit as a rival and harm it.
4	Dense swamp trees grow overnight among a city-state's farmlands. Thousands of acres of thriving agricultural land will decay unless the magic that spawned the forest is identified and destroyed.

CHARACTERS FROM SHANKHABHUMI

If players create characters from Shankhabhumi, consider asking them the following questions during character creation:

Which city do you come from? Were you raised in cosmopolitan Sagorpur, traditionalist Ashwadhatu, or hardy Tippurika?

Are you looking forward to the next Shankha Trials? Are the trials the best part of living in Shankhabhumi for you, or just a spectacular nuisance every twelve years? Have you participated in past trials?

Have you ever encountered a riverine? Did the unpredictable spirit harm you or bless you in some way? Have you seen the riverine since then? Do you now have a deeper connection to it?

RIVERINE

More than mere waterway guardians, riverines are embodiments of particular rivers. These spirits of nature take shape to defend their waters and interact with those who travel along their currents. From the waist up, riverines have skin the color of the waters they protect but are otherwise humanlike in appearance. From the waist down, they can manifest either humanlike legs or churning gouts of water. A riverine's personality reflects the nature of the river it arises from—some are lethargic while others are wild and reckless.

A RIVERINE'S LAIR

Some riverines enjoy reverence akin to worship. Their likenesses are cast as statues and housed in temples, and worshipers act as agents between the river spirits and the people who revere them. These temples often become the home of the riverine itself, serving as its lair, though other nexuses of power along the river's path—such as its source or a significant waterfall—can also be used as lairs by a riverine.

A riverine encountered in its lair has a challenge rating of 13 (10,000 XP).

LAIR ACTIONS

On initiative count 20 (losing initiative ties), the riverine can take one of the following lair actions; the riverine can't take the same lair action two rounds in a row:

Phantasmal Mist. The riverine creates fog around a creature it can see within 120 feet of it. The target must succeed on a DC 17 Wisdom saving throw or take 5 (1d10) psychic damage and be frightened of the riverine until the end of the target's next turn.

River's Fury. The riverine conjures swampy ground that briefly covers the ground in a 20-foot square the riverine can see within 120 feet of itself. That area becomes difficult terrain until initiative count 20 on the next round. Any creature, other than the riverine, that enters the affected area or starts its turn there takes 7 (2d6) cold damage.

REGIONAL EFFECTS

The region containing a riverine's lair flourishes under the magic of the riverine's presence, which creates one or more of the following effects:

Clearwater Sight. The waters of the river serve as a conduit for the riverine's consciousness. As an action, the riverine can cast the *clairvoyance* spell, requiring no spell components, targeting any point along the river it's connected to.

River's Bounty. Freshwater fauna and flora reproduce rapidly and thrive in the waters within 1 mile of the riverine's lair. Foraging in these waters yields twice the usual amount of food.

Spirit Guidance. Tracks appear along the banks of the river within 6 miles of the riverine's lair. The tracks lead to potential shelters and safe passages across the river's waters, while also leading away from areas that the riverine prefers to remain undisturbed.

If the riverine dies, the flora and fauna return to normal levels, and its river dries out over the course of 1d10 days. All other effects cease immediately.

RIVERINE

Large Fey, Any Alignment

Armor Class 14
Hit Points 204 (24d10 + 72)
Speed 30 ft., swim 60 ft.

STR	DEX	CON	INT	WIS	CHA
20 (+5)	19 (+4)	17 (+3)	12 (+1)	16 (+3)	21 (+5)

Saving Throws Int +5, Wis +7, Cha +9
Skills Insight +7, Nature +5, Perception +7
Damage Resistances acid, fire
Senses blindsight 60 ft., passive Perception 17
Languages Aquan, Common, Sylvan
Challenge 12 (8,400 XP)   **Proficiency Bonus** +4

Amphibious. The riverine can breathe air and water.

Legendary Resistance (3/Day). If the riverine fails a saving throw, it can choose to succeed instead.

ACTIONS

Multiattack. The riverine makes two Flood Strike attacks.

Flood Strike. *Melee Weapon Attack:* +9 to hit, reach 10 ft., one target. *Hit:* 14 (2d8 + 5) bludgeoning damage plus 10 (3d6) cold damage.

Spellcasting. The riverine casts one of the following spells, requiring no material components and using Charisma as the spellcasting ability (spell save DC 17):

At-will: *control water, fog cloud*
1/day: *greater restoration*

BONUS ACTIONS

Whirlpool Step. The riverine magically teleports to an unoccupied space it can see within 30 feet of itself. Both the space it leaves and its destination must be in or on the surface of water.

LEGENDARY ACTIONS

The riverine can take 3 legendary actions, choosing from the options below. Only one legendary action option can be used at a time and only at the end of another creature's turn. The riverine regains spent legendary actions at the start of its turn.

Whirlpool Rush. The riverine uses its Whirlpool Step. Immediately after it teleports, each creature within 5 feet of the riverine's destination space takes 5 (1d10) cold damage.

Raging Deluge (Costs 2 Actions). The riverine unleashes a torrent of river water in a 30-foot line that is 5 feet wide. Each creature in that area must make a DC 17 Dexterity saving throw. On a failed save, a creature takes 11 (2d10) bludgeoning damage and is knocked prone. On a successful save, a creature takes half as much damage and isn't knocked prone.

BETWEEN TANGLED ROOTS

AN ADVENTURE FOR 10TH-LEVEL CHARACTERS

WHEN A LEGENDARY DRAGON KNOWN AS A bakunawa appears and attacks a town that has long revered its kind, the characters are called upon to learn why it has gone on a rampage. They must track down the bakunawa and discover the reason for its ire before dragon hunters slay the sacred creature.

BACKGROUND

The bakunawa known as Pangil ng Buwan has long dwelled on the dangerous island of Lambakluha, once the holiest site on the Dayawlongon archipelago. Its dwelling lies before the great tree-temple called Bathalang Puno, a massive, mighty, sacred tree that was long ago burned by invaders. In the years that followed the tree's desecration, evil spirits infested the island. These foul spirits caused unnatural growths to manifest—spirit blisters that corrupt the land and its creatures. Gradually, this sickness encroached on Pangil ng Buwan's lair. While the ancient bakunawa slept, strangling roots enveloped it and poured poison into its being for centuries.

When Pangil ng Buwan awoke not long ago, its corruption caused it to hate all it once loved. After raging across Lambakluha, it sought its ancient spirit companion, Lungtian. But its one-time feelings of companionship has turned to rage, and it wreaks vast destruction in its search.

PRONUNCIATION GUIDE

The Dayawlongon Pronunciations table details how to pronounce key names in this adventure.

DAYAWLONGON PRONUNCIATIONS

Name	Pronunciation
Bakunawa	ba-coo-NA-wah
Bathalang Puno	bu-THA-lung POO-no
Binukot	BEE-nu-kut
Dayawlongon	dai-YOW-long-on
Kalapang	ka-la-PUNG
Lambakluha	lam-bak-LOO-ha
Lungtian	loong-TEE-an
Nimuel	nee-moo-EL
Ninuno	knee-NOO-noh
Pangil ng Buwan	pahng-IL nang BWONE
Paolo	PAO-low

SETTING THE ADVENTURE

This adventure and the islands of the Dayawlongon archipelago can appear in any setting. The following are suggestions for contextualizing the adventure in a wider world:

Through the Radiant Citadel. Characters traveling from the Radiant Citadel arrive in Dayawlongon near the town of Kalapang. While this adventure visits just two of the local islands, the "Dayawlongon Gazetteer" section provides context for further adventures you might have in the region.

Eberron. The eastern coast of Sarlona or the seas around Aerenal could incorporate the Dayawlongon archipelago, or the islands could be in a new chain convenient to your other adventures.

Forgotten Realms. Various islands in the Sea of Swords, such as those off the coast of Tethyr, could host the adventure's locations. The Dayawlongon archipelago could also be in the Sea of Fallen Stars, the Shining Sea, or elsewhere.

CHARACTER HOOKS

Consider the following ways to involve characters in this adventure:

Call of the Storyteller. Via a mutual connection, the characters receive a plea to come to Kalapang from a binukot, a regional bard who serves as a repository of Dayawlongon's history. This performer, Nimuel, seeks the help of experienced adventurers for a delicate mission with a handsome reward.

Monster Hunt. The characters hear rumors of a monster rampaging across the Dayawlongon archipelago. But soon after they arrive in the region, they receive word that the binukot Nimuel seeks a word with them, as not all is what it seems.

CLAUDIO POZAS

Rare Sighting. A scholar friend of the characters has heard that a bakunawa, an exceptionally rare type of dragon, has appeared on the Dayawlongon archipelago. They entreat the characters to go and fetch a scale from the creature. To start the characters' quest, the scholar points them toward a local expert, Nimuel, in the town of Kalapang.

STARTING THE ADVENTURE

The adventure begins as the characters approach Kalapang. As they draw near, they witness a calamity. Read or paraphrase the following text to set the scene:

> The trip to Kalapang has been uneventful, with travelers and trade wagons regularly passing. Soon the pale, vine-covered wall surrounding the town appears in the distance.
>
> Suddenly, from the clear sky crackles a bolt of lightning followed by a thunderous screech. Above the town circles a mighty draconic form—an iridescent creature wreathed in lightning and with multiple sets of wings. As smoke begins to rise from Kalapang, the creature dives toward the town.

The characters are still a mile from Kalapang when Pangil ng Buwan—a bakunawa (see the end of this adventure)—attacks. The attack is swift; the creature strafes the town, vanishes among the buildings for an instant, then soars away to the northwest. No matter what methods the characters use to reach Kalapang, the bakunawa has already departed by the time they reach town.

As the characters near Kalapang, they see people fetching water to put out fires and others tending to the wounded and scared. A character who asks these people what happened learns the following:

- A bakunawa came out of nowhere and attacked. Its lightning breath and brief rampage caused terror, fires, and ruin.
- A bakunawa is a kind of dragon said to hold power over the seas and skies.
- Dayawlongon was once protected by gigantic bakunawa, but they vanished long ago. Their smaller descendants are rare.
- Bakunawa are sacred in the region, though dragon hunters pursue rumors of them, hoping to sell their body parts for gold or as sacred relics.

Characters who help the locals are thanked, but the locals largely have the situation under control. The characters are allowed to enter the walled town unimpeded.

Destruction in Kalapang

As the characters enter Kalapang, read or paraphrase the following:

> The streets of Kalapang are filled with rushing people, some trying to douse smoldering rooftops, others tending to the wounded or to crying youngsters. Nearby, a row of homes lies in rubble. Iridescent blue scales are scattered amid the debris.
>
> A woman wearing a teal dress embroidered with golden constellations surveys the destruction. She waves in your direction, then approaches. "You arrived at a difficult time. I'd hoped to prevent exactly this," she says, gesturing at the fallen building. "I am Nimuel. Thank you for answering my call." The woman pauses, looking around at the chaos, before addressing you again. "Follow me. I know a place where we won't have to worry about others overhearing—and there's someone I need you to meet."

Before the characters can go with Nimuel, the character who has the highest passive Wisdom (Perception) score notices something moving amid the debris. A character who investigates realizes someone's trapped in the rubble. Clearing the rubble safely requires a character to make a DC 14 Strength (Athletics) check. On a failed check, they find one of the home's residents (a **commoner**) unconscious with 0 hit points. On a successful check, they find the resident coughing but largely unharmed. Whether found conscious or restored by healing, the resident thanks the characters. The resident can't reward the characters but speaks well of them to the whole neighborhood—a development that impresses Nimuel.

The Spirit and the Storyteller

Following the rescue, Nimuel asks the characters to follow her to a quiet, nearby courtyard shaded by an ancient salingbobog tree. When the group arrives, a figure steps from the base of the tree. This is Lungtian, a ninuno and Nimuel's partner. Light clothing of leaves and vines grows from Lungtian's body, and when Lungtian speaks, their voice sounds like rustling leaves. A character who succeeds on a DC 14 Intelligence (History) or Intelligence (Religion) check knows that a ninuno is a spirit of the land, similar to a dryad, who serves as an intermediary between the living and the gods. Nimuel or Lungtian shares these details if asked, along with any specifics from the "Life in Dayawlongon" section later in this adventure.

Nimuel

Nimuel (neutral good, human **mage**) is a binukot in Kalapang, a scholar who collects and orally shares the region's wisdom, laws, traditions, culture, songs, poetry, literature, and more. Though young, she is so distinguished that many come to her for guidance and for stewarding their own stories.

Personality Trait. "I seek to honor the gods with every song I sing and every word I speak."

Ideal. "The history of our land is rich with wonders and missteps. By sharing these truths, I can help create a greater future."

Bond. "My tie to Lungtian is special and brings me closer to the divine."

Flaw. "I would never question the will of the gods or their servants."

Lungtian

The ninuno Lungtian (chaotic good **dryad**) was once a human and one of the first binukots of Kalapang. In this earlier life, they fought to defend the land from invaders alongside Pangil ng Buwan and formed a deep friendship with the bakunawa. When Lungtian died, the gods brought their spirit back as a dryad-like ninuno.

Personality Trait. "I am devoted to whoever protects the land and its people."

Ideal. "The land and its ways must be defended, most of all those ancient beings—like bakunawa—who created all that exists today."

Bond. "My love for Nimuel makes me feel like my old self."

Flaw. "I compare all mortals I meet to the heroes I've known throughout my long life."

The Bakunawa's Wrath

Nimuel introduces Lungtian, then moves on to explain that the message she sent the characters arose from the ninuno's concern. The two share the following information:

- The bakunawa that attacked Kalapang is named Pangil ng Buwan, and it is one of the oldest of its kind. It fought against foreign invaders long ago and has never been hostile toward the land's people.
- Pangil ng Buwan was a friend to Lungtian, but the bakunawa disappeared more than two hundred years ago.
- A few weeks ago, Lungtian began having visions of corruption centered on the island of Lambakluha, once a holy place and now a ruined land. Pangil ng Buwan appeared in these visions, leaving Lungtian to believe the bakunawa still lives.
- Lungtian and Nimuel ask the characters to seek out Pangil ng Buwan, discover what's happened to it, and bring it peace.

- Nimuel offers the characters 600 gp apiece as a reward, while Lungtian promises them a divine blessing (see "Ninuno's Mark" in the adventure's conclusion).

Additionally, Nimuel and Lungtian can share any information from the "Dayawlongon Gazetteer" section later in this adventure. Before the conversation ends, Lungtian shares one more important piece of information:

> "During the attack, I could feel Pangil ng Buwan," Lungtian whispers. "There was a shadow in its spirit. Something poisonous and pulsing, a sickness I don't know. The bakunawa seemed to be fighting with itself. I believe that's why we've seen many injured but no dead among the rubble."
>
> Lungtian glances toward the street, still packed with wounded and scared people, then continues. "I want you to know and understand this—after today, I don't expect many to have the ears to hear such things."

LUNGTIAN

MISSION TO LAMBAKLUHA

If the characters agree to Nimuel and Lungtian's terms, Lungtian tells the characters that Pangil ng Buwan's home was once the island of Lambakluha. The pair originally wanted the characters to journey to the island and discover the source of Lungtian's visions along with any signs of Pangil ng Buwan. Now, this mission is even more urgent—the bakunawa must be found and calmed.

A sea voyage to Lambakluha would be perilous due to the raging whirlpools that separate the archipelago's islands, but the characters can reach Lambakluha in an easy two-day journey by traversing Flames Everlasting, one of the skybridges that connect the islands. This skybridge stretches from the island of Malabulak to Lambakluha, where Pangil ng Buwan once made its home in Bathalang Puno, a massive holy tree killed long ago. The island is largely deserted, but at the end of Flames Everlasting is a camp called the Final Steps of Courage, home to soldiers and scholars seeking to fight back the dangers infesting the island.

PREPARATIONS IN KALAPANG

Although Nimuel and Lungtian encourage the characters to depart for Lambakluha as swiftly as possible, the party can rest and resupply in Kalapang as long as the characters need. Pangil ng Buwan doesn't threaten the town again during this time.

Characters who explore the town find the people hospitable but distracted, fearing that the bakunawa might return at any moment. Most shops are closed, but the characters can find shops selling any item from the *Player's Handbook*. A local inn called the Root and Roost offers rooms for 1 gp a night. The price normally includes a hot meal, but with everything going on, the kitchen offers only a cold meal of mangoes and shrimp paste.

TRAVELING THE SKYBRIDGE

Journeying from Kalapang to the foot of the Flames Everlasting Skybridge takes only a few hours. Travel is quick along the main roads, and word of the attack on Kalapang has spread to the few travelers the party meets. Most people are headed away from Kalapang, believing the bakunawa will return.

As the characters near the skybridge, read the following description:

> A magnificent bridge arcs into the air, stretching high above the trees and over the sea beyond. The span soars without supports, its path bending in serpentine curves that stretch into the distance. The bridge is over a hundred feet wide, and statues of stern, draconic creatures adorn it.

HINCHEL OR

Flames Everlasting is typical of the skybridges that connect the islands of the Dayawlongon archipelago, though it's used less than the others. These legendary structures were created by draconic magic in the distant past and still feature prominently in local legends. Characters who succeed on a DC 14 Intelligence (History) check know the details about skybridges from the "Noteworthy Sites" section at the end of this adventure. Any travelers the characters pass are also happy to share these details.

Dragon Hunters

As the characters approach the foot of the skybridge, they find a group of five locals with horses resting and sharing a meal at the roadside. The five are well armed and look like hunters or adventurers. If the characters approach openly, the group's leader waves them over. When the characters are within earshot, the leader introduces himself as follows:

> "Hail travelers! I'm Paolo Maykapal, and judging by your road, I guess that you've come from Kalapang. Tell me, were you there during the attack? Are the rumors true? If Pangil ng Buwan has returned, I swear by all my ancestors that the monster will die by my hand."

Paolo is the group's leader, and he travels with four of his cousins: Dolores, Raqua, Senedicto, and Yomas. They were raised together and share Paolo's conviction that they must slay the bakunawa as vengeance for wrongs done to their clan. All five dragon hunters are lawful neutral humans. They use the **veteran** stat block with the following adjustments:

- They wear studded leather armor that gives them AC 13.
- Replace the Heavy Crossbow action with the action below.

Longbow. *Ranged Weapon Attack:* +3 to hit, ranged 150/600 ft., one target. *Hit:* 5 (1d8 + 1) piercing damage.

Paolo Maykapal

One of the city of Laguna's finest heroes, Paolo Maykapal has trained his entire life to kill bakunawa. He is warm and friendly but is uncompromising when it comes to carrying out his work. Now that Pangil ng Buwan has returned, his duty to the memory of his clan's founder and ancestors is clear. He's willing to engage in underhanded behavior to ensure he and his team succeed.

Personality Trait. "Everything I do and say has a purpose. I've no time for frivolities."

Ideal. "I want to be a living example of a true Dayawlongo: one who gives everything for family and country."

PAOLO
MAYKAPAL

Bond. "What I want matters less than what is good for my home."

Flaw. "I will use anyone who isn't part of my family as a means to an end."

The Dragon Hunters' Offer

Paolo and his group listen intently to anything the characters share and ask them about the bakunawa, what it looked like, and how it behaved. A character who succeeds on a DC 12 Wisdom (Insight) check can tell Paolo is trying to learn all he can about the bakunawa but is less concerned about Kalapang or its people.

If the characters don't share details of their experience with Paolo, he still recognizes them as adventurers and asks them to join his group as they head to Lambakluha to slay Pangil ng Buwan.

Even if the characters don't join the dragon hunters, Paolo eagerly discusses any of the following points:

HINCHEL OR

- Pangil ng Buwan was seen flying away to the southwest. Paolo and his group plan to follow via the skybridge.
- Paolo and his cousins hate Pangil ng Buwan due to the Maykapal Clan's blood feud with the bakunawa. During the region's last revolution against foreign aggression two hundred years ago, Pangil ng Buwan abandoned the defense of the city of Laguna. This resulted in the death of Urian, the founder of Laguna and the Maykapal Clan.
- Generations of Laguna hunters have grown up on stories of Pangil ng Buwan's betrayal. When Paolo heard word of a bakunawa seen in the skies over Dayawlongon, he began to seek the creature so he can settle his clan's blood feud.
- Paolo is also certain he and his group can make a profit from selling pieces of the bakunawa's corpse and would split the profits with the characters.

To anyone who speaks out against hunting the bakunawa, Paolo laughs and says:

> "Yes, yes. I hear those who speak of the monsters as though they're gods. But Pangil ng Buwan is a god who left my people, my city, the founder of my clan to die. Surely you understand my position?"

Nothing any character can say deters Paolo or his allies from their quest. If the characters decide to work with Paolo's group, the two groups travel to Lambakluha together. If the party chooses not to accompany Paolo and his group, Paolo politely wishes them safe travels but says nothing more of the dragon hunters' plans. His group then hangs back. They ultimately use *necklaces of prayer beads* from a bonesinger (see the following section) that they had previously aided to *wind walk* to Lambakluha and reach Bathalang Puno about the same time as the characters.

TRAVELING THE SKYBRIDGE

The journey across the Flames Everlasting Skybridge takes 36 hours, with the incredible bridge soaring 600 feet or more over forests, steep hills, and the sea. Like all the skybridges between the Dayawlongon islands, this bridge is well-lit by gentle magical light at night. It once featured way stations, but few travel to Lambakluha anymore, so the way stations are abandoned, and the party encounters few people during their travels. As the characters make their way to Lambakluha, roll on the Skybridge Sights table after every 12 hours of travel—or whenever you see fit—to determine what encounters they have.

SKYBRIDGE SIGHTS

d4	Encounter
1	Bonesinger (see below)
2	A small storm reveals itself to be a violent group of three **air elementals**.
3	A dead wyvern lies on the skybridge, its body scorched by lightning.
4	A curious and friendly **cloud giant** is surprised to see travelers on the skybridge and asks them at length about recent happenings in the lands below.

BONESINGER

As the characters travel the skybridge, they might encounter a lone old woman crouching near one of the draconic statues adorning the bridge, singing to it in a gentle voice. This is Ina (neutral good, human **priest**), a skybridge tender known as a bonesinger. She tends the magic that supports and protects Flames Everlasting and honors the many gigantic, ancient bakunawa whose bones are infused into the bridge.

Ina greets the characters courteously and warns them of the dangers of Lambakluha. The bonesinger has not yet heard of the attack in Kalapang and is horrified if the characters share the news with her. If asked about recent bakunawa activity, Ina says she's heard a bakunawa's call over the skybridge in the night, but she has seen nothing.

After conversing with the characters, Ina returns to her ritual song and invites the characters to join in. Any character can sing with her, but those who do so and succeed on a DC 18 Charisma (Performance) check impress the bonesinger. She thanks the first character to impress her by giving them her *necklace of prayer beads*. The necklace's beads look like tiny fangs and include a bead of *wind walk* and 1d4 other magic beads.

SIGHTING LAMBAKLUHA

A few hours before the party reaches Lambakluha, the party spots their destination:

> The mist on the horizon parts, revealing a gigantic tree thousands of feet tall, its highest branches hidden by clouds. The great tree's boughs are bent, barren, and lifeless.

A character who succeeds on a DC 12 Intelligence (History) check knows this tree is Bathalang Puno, one of the holy trees of the Dayawlongon archipelago that was burned by invaders long ago. Soon after the characters sight the tree, the stench of ash permeates the air.

LAMBAKLUHA

Once a verdant island with an expansive network of rivers and mangrove forests, Lambakluha is now a rank swamp. Tormented spirits haunt the island, especially its ruined communities, and their corruptive influence blights the surviving life. The island can be reached by two skybridges: Flames Everlasting, which the characters traveled, and Hope's Dagger, which leads to another island to the west.

Lambakluha is depicted on map 10.1.

THE FINAL STEPS OF COURAGE

As the characters pass the final bend of Flames Everlasting, read the following description of the skybridge's end:

> The skybridge descends onto a sizable island overgrown with tangled swamp vegetation and covered in a haze tasting of ash. A few acres at the skybridge's end have been cleared and surrounded by a wooden palisade. Within, simple wooden buildings and dingy tents form an encampment.

The camp is called the Final Steps of Courage, and beyond it spreads the blighted landscape of Lambakluha. The skybridge ends within the redoubt's wooden walls, which hold tents for a few dozen soldiers and scholars, as well as a mess hall and trading post. The camp's amenities are for those working there, but if the characters distinguish themselves as the soldiers' allies or succeed on a DC 14 Charisma (Persuasion) check with mess hall or trading post staff, they can use the facilities, too.

Should the characters follow the skybridge into the camp, four sentries (use the **veteran** stat block) armed with crossbows stop them and question them about their origins, business, and destination.

ATTACK ON THE FINAL STEPS

As the characters converse with the sentries, a horn sounds from the camp's south gate. The sentries run toward the opposite side of the camp while the camp staff scatter. If the characters follow the sound, they see several tortured-looking incorporeal Undead attacking the camp's south gate and soldiers making an organized defense. A moment later, whether the characters are near the gate or elsewhere, three **wraiths** that look like the spirits of burn victims close in on the characters and attack.

FLAMES EVERLASTING SKYBRIDGE STRETCHES OVER STEEP HILLS AND SEAS TO THE ISLAND OF LAMBAKLUHA.

WHAT THE SOLDIERS KNOW

If the characters defeat the wraiths, the camp's commander, Captain Atoy, thanks the characters and welcomes them to rest, eat, and resupply.

The soldiers and scholars of the camp are here in hopes of reclaiming Lambakluha and making it safe for resettlement. Their work is slow, as the tortured spirits of the land attack at random intervals. The soldiers are used to defending against spirits, but in recent weeks they've spotted flashes of blue lightning near Bathalang Puno, Pangil ng Buwan's storied lair.

If the characters explain to Captain Atoy or others in the camp that they're seeking Bathalang Puno and Pangil ng Buwan, the soldiers warn them of the danger, not just of the bakunawa but of the miles of swamp known as the Weeping Paths that the characters will have to traverse. If the characters ask anyone in the camp about what dangers they might face, the soldiers speak of Undead and of vicious vegetation.

Swapping Stories. The camp's inhabitants are starved for stories of the outside world. After the attack, several ask the characters to share a meal and tell them of their travels. If the characters agree, in the course of their discussions a soldier relates recent gossip about a scouting troop that returned from a ruin called Sorrow's Zenith and described strange vegetation that "breathed with hatred." No one in the camp knows more than this, as the scouts left the island weeks ago. However, the remaining troops can direct the characters to Sorrow's Zenith if the characters wish to investigate further.

THE WEEPING PATHS

When the characters leave the Final Steps of Courage for the Weeping Paths, read the following:

> Beyond the camp, the ash-heavy air closes in. Decay and ruin are everywhere, from the murky water flowing through the endless swamp to the mildewed vines and the rotting roots of swollen mangrove and banyan trees.

The Weeping Paths is a treacherous quagmire home to malicious spirits. The swamp and the overgrown hills beyond are difficult terrain. At a normal pace, it takes the party a full day to reach Bathalang Puno (24 miles away), or half a day to reach Sorrow's Zenith (12 miles away) and then two thirds of a day to reach Bathalang Puno (9 miles away; see the *Player's Handbook* for details on travel pace). The entire region is also lightly obscured by foliage and haze,

MAP 10.1: LAMBAKLUHA

causing creatures to have disadvantage on Wisdom (Perception) checks that rely on sight.

Threats lurk amid the wilds. For every 3 miles the party travels, roll on the Weeping Paths Encounters table.

WEEPING PATHS ENCOUNTERS

d10	Encounter
1–3	Miasma (see below)
4–5	A **wraith** appears and attacks the party. It looks like one of the characters, albeit covered in terrible burns.
6–7	Three **shambling mounds** emerge from a heap of rotting vegetation near a ruined statue and attack the party.
8–9	A fire-scarred **treant** awakens and attacks the characters, blaming them for the destruction of its home.
10	Voices of Flame (see below)

Miasma

The haze surrounding the characters coalesces into a dense, gray miasma. A minute before this occurs, characters who succeed on a DC 12 Wisdom (Perception) or (Survival) check notice the haze growing thicker and more pungent. If the characters notice, they can avoid the miasma by rushing out of the area. If they don't, a toxic, 20-foot-radius sphere surrounds a random character. Creatures in this sphere must succeed on a DC 15 Constitution saving throw, taking 21 (6d6) poison damage on a failure, or half as much on a success. The miasma is stationary and dissipates 1 minute later.

Roll on the Weeping Paths Encounters table again for another encounter that occurs soon after, re-rolling another miasma encounter.

Voices of Flame

Dozens of gray, spectral figures appear in the haze around the party and move along with them. The forms can't be harmed or warded away by any means. Soon after the shapes appear, the figures begin speaking as one, telling the grim fates of those who perished during the razing of Bathalang Puno. The figures relate terrible ends like burning alive in their homes or being crushed by massive, falling tree limbs. After the recitation of each grim fate, one of the forms bursts into flames and vanishes. After a minute, a voice from the haze asks each character, "Tell us. How did you die?" Characters who respond with a tragic tale, even a fictitious one, are unharmed. Characters who don't must succeed on a DC 15 Wisdom saving throw or burst into flames and take 35 (10d6) points of fire damage.

Sorrow's Zenith

Out of the way from the path to Bathalang Puno is a ruined temple called Sorrow's Zenith. If the characters visit the site, they notice an unusual growth covering a weathered statue. Read or paraphrase the following:

> An ancient statue of a bakunawa is cracked with age and covered with unusual vines. Amid a cluster of tangled roots, a blister-like growth heaves like a breathing thing and glows with a sickly light.

A character who studies the blister and succeeds on a DC 14 Wisdom (Perception) check realizes that the movement within the mass is the shifting of tiny, ghostly figures. A character who has proficiency in the Nature skill recognizes that these vines and the blister are unnatural. With a successful DC 18 Intelligence (Arcana or Religion) check made to examine the blister, a character determines the vines are drawing spiritual energy from the land and concentrating that energy within the blister. However, the nature and purpose of that magic are unclear.

The blister is a Medium object with AC 17; 30 hit points; vulnerability to fire and radiant damage; and immunity to acid, necrotic, and psychic damage. If destroyed, the blister bursts with a chorus of distant sighs. A moment later, a spectral figure appears.

Memory of Peace

If the characters destroy the spirit blister, the spirit of a ninuno appears and thanks them for releasing it from the bitter memories trapped within the blister. The spirit has forgotten its name, but it can share the following details:

- It was once a protector of Lambakluha and the temple that stood here, but when invaders burned the sacred tree Bathalang Puno and the surrounding city, the ninuno was overwhelmed by the pain of those who died.
- Angry spirits still haunt the island, their memories corrupting its vegetation and creatures.
- The spirit knows stories of Pangil ng Buwan, but fears that if the bakunawa went into dormancy on the island, wicked spirits could have corrupted it.
- The spirit encourages the characters to destroy any other spirit blisters they see and release the

A Spirit Blister at Sorrow's Zenith

spirits brooding within. It knows that the blisters are vulnerable to flames and divine light.

After conversing with the characters, the spirit vanishes.

ROOTS OF BATHALANG PUNO

The swamps grow drier and more densely forested within a couple miles of Bathalang Puno, with vines and mangroves ensnaring ancient, overgrown ruins. A character who succeeds on a DC 16 Intelligence (History) check knows that a great city once spread around the sacred tree; the crumbled structures are that city's ruins and the remnants of a destroyed skybridge called Moon's Respite.

Once the characters reach Bathalang Puno, they must still find Pangil ng Buwan's lair. Circling the great tree takes over an hour. But while searching for the lair, if a character succeeds on a DC 16 Wisdom (Survival) check, they find marks suggesting the passage of a massive creature and can follow that trail to Pangil ng Buwan's lair in 10 minutes.

If the characters are not traveling with Paolo and his group, a character who succeeds on a DC 14 Wisdom (Perception or Survival) check notices booted tracks headed in the direction opposite them—the wrong way around the massive tree. These are the tracks of Paolo Maykapal and his dragon hunters, who arrived ahead of the characters and who are also searching for the bakunawa.

FACING THE DRAGON HUNTERS

If the characters follow the dragon hunters, they catch up to them as the hunters conduct a stealthy—and slow—search. Paolo and his cousins are surprised to see the characters but aren't deterred from their hunt. If a character tells the dragon hunters that Pangil ng Buwan isn't behaving naturally and succeeds on a DC 18 Charisma (Persuasion) check, Paolo wants to see the bakunawa himself and will decide its fate then. If hostilities break out, the dragon hunters defend themselves, using the stat blocks of five **veterans** (see "The Dragon Hunters" earlier in this adventure).

THE BAKUNAWA'S LAIR

Map 10.2 represents Pangil ng Buwan's lair. When the characters arrive, read the following description:

> Charred roots the size of buildings surround an open clearing with a broad patch of blackened ground. Nearby lie pieces of a fallen skybridge. At the clearing's center, writhing vines with glowing, green veins wrap around the massive form of Pangil ng Buwan. These vines emanate from four green, blister-like growths entangled amid the great tree's roots.

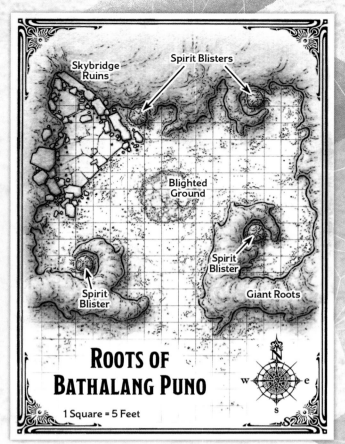

MAP 10.2: ROOTS OF BATHALANG PUNO

Whether the creature is alone or the dragon hunters are present depends on whether the characters found a direct path to the lair and whether they met the dragon hunters along the way. See "Dragon Hunters" below for more details.

Pangil ng Buwan (see the **bakunawa** stat block at the end of this adventure) is covered in vines but is not restrained. The creature is half awake, resting as the corrupt vines spread hateful thoughts into its mind. Once the bakunawa notices creatures in its lair, it attacks.

Calming the Bakunawa. Pangil ng Buwan isn't currently in control of itself and can't be reasoned with, as the spirit blisters in its lair cause it to see the party as the invaders of Lambakluha who haunt its dreams. The dragon's eyes glow with sickly green light the same color as the nearby spirit blisters. If a creature casts *dispel magic* (DC 15) or *greater restoration* on Pangil ng Buwan, the bakunawa is stunned until the end of its next turn, but then its rage surges anew. The only way to end Pangil ng Buwan's rampage is destroying the four spirit blisters in its lair.

Corrupted Ground. Gigantic roots surround the area where Pangil ng Buwan rests. The roots and the rubble of the fallen skybridge are difficult terrain.

At the center of the clearing, a patch of blighted ground marks the area of intense corruption where the bakunawa suffered years of nightmares. A creature that enters that area or starts its turn there is overwhelmed by visions of the burning of Bathalang Puno and must succeed on a DC 15 Wisdom saving throw or take 18 (4d8) psychic damage.

Spirit Blisters. Four spirit blisters have corrupted the bakunawa's mind. A character who investigates a blister can make a DC 14 Intelligence (Arcana) or Wisdom (Perception) check. On a success, they notice the glow of the blisters matches the glow of the bakunawa's eyes.

The blisters are Medium objects with AC 17; 30 hit points; vulnerability to fire and radiant damage; and immunity to acid, necrotic, and psychic damage. Pangil ng Buwan defends the spirit blisters and prioritizes attacking any creature that damages the blisters.

Dragon Hunters. If, after arriving at the great tree, the characters took the direct path to Pangil ng Buwan's lair, the bakunawa is alone when they arrive, but Paolo and his dragon hunters (five **veterans**; see "The Dragon Hunters" earlier in this adventure) arrive 3 rounds later. If the characters took an indirect path but didn't interact with the dragon hunters, the dragon hunters are already there and are about to attack.

Unless the characters have previously convinced Paolo to hold back, the dragon hunters immediately attack. Rather than rolling for the dragon hunters' attacks, assume any of the five dragon hunters not engaged in combat with the characters or otherwise prevented from attacking deals 10 damage to Pangil ng Buwan each round. If a character points out to Paolo that the spirit blisters are affecting Pangil ng Buwan and succeeds on a DC 20 Charisma (Persuasion) check, Paolo and his allies stand down.

Treasure. Pangil ng Buwan has a small hoard beneath the burnt tree roots. If the bakunawa is freed, it gives the characters its treasure in thanks. If it is slain, a character who succeeds on a DC 16 Wisdom (Perception) check notices the hidden cache beneath one of the giant roots. Pangil ng Buwan's treasure consists of 320 gp, 5,800 sp, three opal figurines of dugongs worth 150 gp a piece, an *arrow of dragon slaying*, a *necklace of adaptation*, and a *staff of the python*.

THE END OF DESPAIR

If Pangil ng Buwan is cleansed of the spirit blisters' corruption, the bakunawa thanks the party for saving it and shares the following information:

- Pangil ng Buwan recounts the details in the "Background" section.
- The bakunawa remembers Lungtian fondly and was able to stop itself from harming the people of Kalapang when it sensed the ninuno's presence.
- If the characters mention Laguna, Pangil ng Buwan expresses remorse for not being there when the city was attacked. The bakunawa and Urian Maykapal, Paolo's ancestor, were close friends, but the day prior to the attack, the two had a disagreement. Pangil ng Buwan left Laguna to clear its head and heard about the violence too late.

CONCLUSION

If the characters save Pangil ng Buwan, the bakunawa accompanies them back to Kalapang. Pangil ng Buwan apologizes to the townsfolk, explains the cause of the attack, and promises to aid in restoring the town. Nimuel and Lungtian reward the characters as promised, with Lungtian bestowing the Ninuno's Mark charm upon each of them (see "Ninuno's Mark" below).

If the party is unable to save Pangil ng Buwan, Nimuel and Lungtian accept their report of the corruption that destroyed the bakunawa, assigns them no blame, and pays them as promised. If Paolo's band slays the bakunawa and the characters leave them with its body, a week later the characters receive a parcel from Paolo with 150 gp and a bakunawa tooth for each character—their cut for assisting the dragon hunters or not standing in their way.

NINUNO'S MARK

A ninuno, one of the spirits of the Dayawlongon archipelago, grants you its insight as a charm (a type of supernatural gift detailed in the *Dungeon Master's Guide*). This charm allows you to cast either *augury* or *speak with plants* once per day. Once used three times, this charm vanishes from you.

Dayawlongon Gazetteer

For any first-time visitor to the archipelago of Dayawlongon, the skybridges are a stunning sight. Both roadways and refuges, with whole communities dwelling along some of the miles-long spans, these structures were built centuries ago with the help of great bakunawa—massive, serpentine dragons endemic to Dayawlongon's five main islands and dozens of smaller islands, which were much larger than the bakunawa that remain. The skybridges are the safest way to travel between many islands, high above the whirlpools that churn in the sea below. However, centuries of conflict have taken their toll on those structures; the great bakunawa whose bones and magic infuse them are long gone; and the artisan-warriors who maintain the bridges, known as bonesingers, are disappearing from history.

Dayawlongon has survived battles between its resident clans and the incursions of five foreign powers, and it has been independent and largely at peace for the last two centuries. In ages past, bakunawa served as mediators and defenders of the islands, but successive waves of invasion targeted the creatures, drastically reducing their numbers. Today, the islands' residents fiercely defend their home and seek to honor the history stolen by centuries of war.

Features

Those familiar with the Dayawlongon archipelago know the following details:

Hallmarks. The archipelago is known for the gigantic skybridges and sacred trees that tower over the islands. Serpentine Dragons called bakunawa, now rare, once defended the islands, and their bones and magic are infused into the skybridges.

People. Most Dayawlongos are human, with dark hair and brown skin. Eyes of yellow, green, or brown are most common. Dragonborn and tieflings are also indigenous to the archipelago; many Dayawlongo dragonborn have iridescent scales and serpentine features, and many tieflings have iridescent feathers.

Languages. Most folk in Dayawlongon speak Common and Snakesong, a dialect of Draconic that tales say was taught to the locals by bakunawa.

Noteworthy Sites

Dayawlongon is a tropical archipelago whose waters hold massive whirlpools that make boat travel between the islands challenging. Winding rivers, deep jungles, and mountains define its five major islands.

Kalapang

Kalapang, the largest community on the island of Malabulak, stands among verdant fields. The city is a blend of old and new, with ancient religious sites and relics of foreign rule constructed alongside newer structures built by traders and immigrants looking for security. Kalapang is welcoming toward foreigners and encourages visitors. Powerful clans and the mercantile ventures regularly hire adventurers for trade excursions and exploration—such as journeys to the island of Lambakluha.

Lambakluha

The island of Lambakluha is known as the "Vale of Tears" in Snakesong. It was once the holiest place in Dayawlongon, home to Bathalang Puno, a temple city nestled within the roots of a colossal banyan tree that shared the city's name. That great tree was said to be where islanders' souls went after death. Some of these souls transcended into ninunos—dryad-like spirits of the land who serve as stewards to the gods and resided in the surrounding lands. Colonizing invaders burned the great tree and razed Bathalang Puno, killing untold people and spirits alike. In the aftermath, Lambakluha became a cursed place, where spirits seethe in the land, spreading corruption across the island.

Decades ago, an expedition from Kalapang set up a camp on the island called the Final Steps of Courage, hoping to exorcise the land's tormented spirits. Thus far, these soldiers and scholars have made little progress toward their goal.

Skybridges

A gift from bakunawa to the first folk of the archipelago, the skybridges of Dayawlongon are magical feats of architecture that connect many of the region's islands. Travelers are common, and the most traveled skybridges hold small communities where they can rest and resupply. Legend holds that the bones of enormous bakunawa were infused into the skybridges in ages past, with the creatures' blessing. Only bonesingers, people chosen as stewards of the skybridges, know how to maintain the magic that keeps the skybridges safe.

Life in Dayawlongon

Several truths shape life on the Dayawlongon archipelago; some are deeply rooted traditions, and others have been molded by foreign influences.

Ancestral Strength

Reverence toward one's ancestors is deeply ingrained in Dayawlongo society, where a passion for the past is demonstrated by people's love for oaths, poetry, and song. Ancestors sometimes return as guardians called ninunos, spirits of the dead who have taken on new, dryad-like forms and serve as intercessors between mortals, the gods, and the land. Ninunos watch over their bloodlines, bestowing good fortune on pious descendants or curses upon those who put their own needs over those of the family and broader community.

Bonesingers

Artisan-warriors, bonesingers dedicate their lives to maintaining the skybridges. In the ancient past, bonesingers oversaw the final rites when great bakunawa died, then infused the creatures' bones into the magical bridges that unite Dayawlongon as one land. During the days of the first colonial incursions, bonesingers became Dayawlongon's earliest freedom fighters, but their victories came at a great cost. Many skybridges became battlegrounds, and countless allied bakunawa were lost. Today, the gigantic bakunawa of old are gone, and few of their smaller descendants remain. The loss of these great creatures and their magic prevents the creation of new skybridges.

Clans and Reputation

Dozens of clans unite families across the Dayawlongon archipelago. Marriages are unions of clans as much as unions between individuals. Adoptions, polyamorous relationships, and other generous family bonds create varied ways to join different clans. Clans have few proscribed roles for their members, with each group sharing responsibilities in ways that work for their members.

Reputation carries great value in Dayawlongon, and a person's reputation also shapes that of their loved ones in the eyes of peers. A Dayawlongo treats their best friend's children like their own offspring and curses the names of their enemy's family.

Debt of the Soul

One of the cornerstones of Dayawlongo culture is the concept of *utang ng loob*, a debt of the soul. If someone saves another from mortal peril or assists another at great cost to themself, a soul debt is formed between the people in question and their bloodlines. This debt holds throughout any number of generations until it is repaid. Failing to respect a soul debt is the deepest form of betrayal for Dayawlongos and the root of countless blood feuds.

Names

Traditionally, Dayawlongos have a personal name followed by a clan name. Personal names are varied and often reflect a characteristic that a ninuno connected to an individual or their family found desirable. However, some personal names are relics of colonization and have foreign origins. The following names are common in Dayawlongo:

Feminine. Asterio, Corazon, Flordeliza, Modesta, Sinta
Masculine. Amado, Estanislao, Gio, Joaquin, Mirikit
Gender-Neutral. Alon, Bulan, Dalisay, Melchor
Clan Names. Bahaghari, Dimansalang, Fabion, Posadas, Recio

Legends of Dayawlongon

Ancient belief states that all life on Dayawlongon is born from the spoken words of a poet goddess—known as Kamatayang-Langit—from which comes the people's deep reverence for poetry and song. This is why every community has one or more binukots, bards who serve as living repositories of art, culture, custom, and law. The death of a binukot can result in the loss of generations of history, as Dayawlongo tradition eschews writing stories or songs down. Bonesingers maintain that bakunawa are among the greatest binukots, their vast memories making them bearers of ancient truths.

Adventures in Dayawlongon

Consider the plots on the Dayawlongon Adventures table when planning adventures in Dayawlongon.

Dayawlongon Adventures

d4	Adventure
1	A merchant the characters know is being pursued by a vengeful ninuno (**dryad**) for her mother's broken oath. The merchant is desperate for the characters to intervene and placate the spirit.
2	A binukot named Panfilio offers to handsomely reward anyone who can impress them with a riveting tale of love and adventure from each of the archipelago's largest islands.
3	A **storm giant** has claimed a skybridge as her domain and refuses to let anyone cross, trapping the residents of an island to which the bridge connects.
4	A foreign trader has found a bakunawa egg and is waiting for severe weather to pass before leaving the islands with it. A bonesinger entreats the characters to rescue the egg.

Characters from Dayawlongon

If players want to create characters from the Dayawlongon archipelago, ask them the following questions:

What stories can you tell about yourself? Has a ninuno ever spoken to you? Is a particular song, poem, or tale the binukots tell your favorite? What stories do you want others to tell about you after your death?

What do you think of bakunawa? Does a bakunawa feature in your family's history? Do you believe bakunawa are creatures to be revered or monsters?

Are you trained as a binukot? Do you collect the stories of your people? Do you want to broaden your peoples' knowledge by collecting stories from distant lands and sharing them at home?

BAKUNAWA

Worshiped as draconic avatars of storm and tide, bakunawa soar over the archipelagos they call home. Iridescent scales crackling with lightning cover a bakunawa's fearsome serpentine body, and the sharp movements of its mighty wings echo with thunderous winds. Known for their mercilessness in battle, bakunawa swallow whole any who challenge them.

BAKUNAWA
Gargantuan Dragon, Typically Neutral

Armor Class 15 (natural armor)
Hit Points 150 (12d20 + 24)
Speed 20 ft., fly 60 ft., swim 60 ft.

STR	DEX	CON	INT	WIS	CHA
21 (+5)	12 (+1)	15 (+2)	14 (+2)	17 (+3)	16 (+3)

Saving Throws Dex +5, Con +6, Wis +7
Damage Resistances lightning, thunder
Senses blindsight 60 ft., darkvision 120 ft., passive Perception 21
Languages Celestial, Common, Draconic
Challenge 12 (8,400 XP)   **Proficiency Bonus** +4

Amphibious. The bakunawa can breathe air and water.

Legendary Resistance (3/Day). If the bakunawa fails a saving throw, it can choose to succeed instead.

ACTIONS

Multiattack. The bakunawa makes one Bite attack and one Storm Slam attack.

Bite. *Melee Weapon Attack:* +9 to hit, reach 10 ft., one target. *Hit:* 12 (2d6 + 5) piercing damage plus 7 (2d6) lightning damage. If the target is a Large or smaller creature, it must succeed on a DC 17 Strength saving throw or be swallowed by the bakunawa. A swallowed creature is blinded and restrained, and it has total cover against attacks and other effects outside the bakunawa. At the start of each of the bakunawa's turns, each swallowed creature takes 10 (3d6) lightning damage.

   The bakunawa's gullet can hold up to two creatures at a time. If the bakunawa takes 30 damage or more on a single turn from a swallowed creature, the bakunawa must succeed on a DC 16 Constitution saving throw at the end of that turn or regurgitate all swallowed creatures, which fall prone in a space within 15 feet of the bakunawa. If the bakunawa dies, a swallowed creature is no longer restrained by it and can escape from the corpse by using 15 feet of movement, exiting prone.

Storm Slam. *Melee Weapon Attack:* +9 to hit, reach 10 ft., one target. *Hit:* 9 (1d8 + 5) bludgeoning damage plus 5 (1d10) thunder damage, and the target is pushed up to 10 feet in a horizontal direction away from the bakunawa.

LEGENDARY ACTIONS

The bakunawa can take 3 legendary actions, choosing from the options below. Only one legendary action option can be used at a time and only at the end of another creature's turn. The bakunawa regains spent legendary actions at the start of its turn.

Nimble Glide. The bakunawa flies or swims up to half its speed. This movement doesn't provoke opportunity attacks.

Slam. The bakunawa makes one Storm Slam attack.

Lightning Strikes (Costs 3 Actions). The bakunawa arcs lightning at up to two creatures it can see within 60 feet of itself. Each target must succeed on a DC 15 Dexterity saving throw or take 22 (4d10) lightning damage.

SHADOW OF THE SUN

AN ADVENTURE FOR 11TH-LEVEL CHARACTERS

O N THE EVE OF A TRIENNIAL LUNAR FESTIVAL, a monster attack brings the characters to the attention of the Brightguard, holy enforcers in the city-state of Akharin Sangar. The characters are asked to act as an angel's agents and discover rebel plots before innocent blood is spilled. But soon the characters learn that in Akharin Sangar, nothing is as plain as day or night.

BACKGROUND

For about one week every three years, a mysterious lunar phenomenon bathes Akharin Sangar with light in the dead of night. Ancient magic causes the moon to blaze like the sun for a short while. Sangarians call this phenomenon Shabe Taabaan, or "Brilliant Night," and celebrate it with a multiday festival commemorating light's triumph over darkness. Atash, an angel who has ruled Akharin Sangar since he delivered it from catastrophe fifty years ago, suspends the city-state's nightly curfew in honor of the holiday. This year, however, celebrations are muted.

Recently, anarchists called the Ashen Heirs have tormented the city with propaganda and violence, seeking to incite rebellion against Atash. The Brightguard struggles to maintain law amid the havoc. Stretched thin, the order detains suspected resistance members and issues citations. This makes hiding in plain sight difficult for members of a more peaceable resistance group, the Silent Roar, that hopes to restore Sangarian society to its former glory.

PRONUNCIATION GUIDE

The Akharin Sangar Pronunciations table shows how to pronounce key names in this adventure.

AKHARIN SANGAR PRONUNCIATIONS

Name	Pronunciation
Afsoun Ghorbani	af-SOON ghor-bah-NEE
Akharin Sangar	ah-khar-EEN san-GAR
Artavazda	ahr-tah-vaz-DAH
Atash	ah-TASH

Name	Pronunciation
Avalin Sahar	a-val-EEN sa-HAR
Baadi	bah-DEE
Emad Farrokh	eh-MAHD fa-ROKH
Laleh Ghorbani	lah-LEH ghor-bah-NEE
Marzieh	mar-zee-YEH
Navid	na-VEED
Pari	pa-REE
Piruzan	pee-roo-ZAN
Ruz Bazaar	rooz bah-ZAHR
Shabe Taabaan	SHAB-eh tah-BAHN
Zolmate Shab	zohl-MAT-eh shab

SETTING THE ADVENTURE

Use the following suggestions to help contextualize Akharin Sangar in a wider world:

Through the Radiant Citadel. Characters traveling from the Radiant Citadel arrive just outside Akharin Sangar. If you wish to further detail this land, use the "Akharin Sangar Gazetteer" section at this adventure's end as a departure point.

Forgotten Realms. Akharin Sangar fits in well along any edge of the Calim Desert in Calimshan.

Greyhawk. The western edge of the Barrier Peaks and the Crystalmist Mountains hold many isolated, arid regions where Akharin Sangar might exist. Isolated reaches of the Bright Desert also make logical locations for the city-state.

CHARACTER HOOKS

Consider the following ways to involve characters in this adventure:

Friends of Afsoun. A character knows the famed actor Afsoun Ghorbani, head of the Silent Roar, or is connected to her via an acquaintance. She invites the characters to Akharin Sangar to help protect her people during Shabe Taabaan.

Impartial Guardians. Atash or a ranking member of the Brightguard invites outsiders to Akharin Sangar to supplement the city's guard during the

THE PLANS OF ASHEN HEIR ANARCHISTS GO AWRY WHEN A PURPLE WORM ERUPTS INTO THREE SUNS SQUARE.

festival. The group in power trusts that competent adventurers from outside the city will have no connection to the local revolutionary factions.

Midnight Sun. An ally of the characters has received permission to visit Akharin Sangar and witness a periodic event in which the moon shines like the sun. This ally asks the characters to escort them on a scholarly or religious expedition.

SPLITTING LOYALTIES

During the adventure, characters will ally with one of two factions: the Brightguard or the Silent Roar. The Brightguard approaches them first, but characters might change their loyalties. How the characters manage relationships with these factions affects how the adventure unfolds.

BRIGHTGUARD

Before Atash, the Brightguard was a fringe collective of devout protectors who vowed to defend Akharin Sangar from evil in the name of their deity, the Sunweaver. When the angel Atash—an agent of the Sunweaver—deemed service in the Brightguard a holy calling, the group's ranks swelled. Most members have unshakable resolve, but recent revolutionary acts have the order on edge. The Brightguard obeys Atash and, through him, the Sunweaver (see the "Akharin Sangar Gazetteer" section for details).

Motto. "All good acts take place under the sun."

Beliefs. The Sunweaver sets my path.

Goals. Maintain order under the enlightened direction of Atash.

Character Role. Characters who align with the Brightguard find the group earnestly seeks to enforce Akharin Sangar's laws and keep the city-state peaceful and pristine. At the behest of the group, the characters investigate the activities of the Ashen Heirs and come into contact with the Silent Roar.

SILENT ROAR

Members of the Silent Roar seek to return Atash to the Sunweaver and restore Akharin Sangar to a state of self-rule. Named for the lions that roam the lands beyond the city, the faction is secretly led by famed actor Afsoun Ghorbani, and its agents are largely chaotic good artisans, philosophers, and merchants who have suffered under Atash's isolationist policies. Silent Roar agents are usually patient and nonviolent, but they defend the order and its members like lions protect their prides. They resent other revolutionary groups whose violent ways cause the people to distrust the Silent Roar by extension. Many Silent Roar members romanticize Akharin Sangar's past even as they acknowledge that the city-state has faced dire problems and might not have survived without Atash's intervention.

Motto. "Protect the pride, preserve the city."

Beliefs. Atash has cost this once-great city-state its splendor.

Goals. Remove Atash and remake the city.

Character Role. After the Brightguard initially sets the characters on the path to track down disruptive anarchists, Afsoun's sister, Laleh Ghorbani, approaches the characters for aid. Characters who align themselves with the Silent Roar end up opposing Artavazda, an angel prominent in the Brightguard, as they try to free Afsoun.

Starting the Adventure

The adventure begins once the characters arrive in Akharin Sangar. The city is filled with locals anticipating the festival of Shabe Taabaan. Whether the characters seek accommodations, opportunities to shop, or a glimpse of the festivities, they soon find themselves in Three Sun Square. Once the characters arrive, read the following description:

> Hundreds of people flock to Three Sun Square in advance of Shabe Taabaan, the Brilliant Night. The crowded plaza is filled with colorful stalls and vendors hawking toys and keepsakes. Booths selling steaming rice, tangy stews, and sun-shaped desserts fill the air with delectable fragrances. Nearby, members of the Brightguard—Akharin Sangar's holy order of protectors—patrol the arched balconies of their headquarters, the Noble Jewel, and scan the crowd for trouble.

Give the characters the opportunity to explore the square. The people of Akharin Sangar are largely friendly and curious about outsiders. A passing member of the Brightguard might even introduce their order to the characters and ask the party to seek out the Brightguard if they ever need aid.

Once the characters have interacted with a few of the city's people, proceed with the following section.

Anarchist Outcry

> An ear-splitting crash pierces the air. Five figures wearing snarling, crimson masks clamber atop stalls, each raising a cone-like device to their mouth. Along with an irritating buzzing noise, the masked figures' voices emanate from the contraptions, amplified over the cacophony of the crowd: "Down with tyrants! Let the embers light the way!"

Five masked anarchists (use the **spy** stat block), members of a group called the Ashen Heirs, have interrupted the festivities to antagonize the

> ### Timing Shabe Taabaan
>
> Shabe Taabaan is meant to serve as a backdrop to the final encounter of this adventure. How many nights the moon glows like the sun over Akharin Sangar is left purposefully vague so you don't need to rush the climax to occur on a specific night.

Brightguard. As they do so, their attempts to stand atop stalls cause booths and tents to collapse, disrupting trade and imperiling vendors.

Each anarchist wears an intimidating mask sculpted to look like an efreeti and carries a device called a boomhailer. These sound-amplifying, clockwork funnels have the following properties:

- Any creature that speaks into the small end of a boomhailer has its voice amplified to be three times louder than normal.
- Poorly made devices, boomhailers function for 10 rounds before breaking.
- A boomhailer emits an irritating buzzing noise whenever it's used and for a minute afterward. The noise is harmless, but creatures sensitive to vibrations find it infuriating.
- A boomhailer is a Tiny object with AC 13, hp 5, and immunity to poison and psychic damage.

The Ashen Heirs decry the Brightguard as oppressive brutes masquerading as pious saints. While some onlookers may agree, no one is fool enough to draw attention to themself by openly supporting either side. While the speaker shouts, five members of the Brightguard (use the **guard** stat block) move toward the Ashen Heirs—one toward each anarchist—trying to make sure they don't hurt themselves or anyone else with their dramatics.

Caught in the Middle

The characters might decide to get involved in the conflict, perhaps by trying to subdue the Ashen Heirs or convincing them to run before they're arrested. In any case, harming a member of the Brightguard is a serious offense, a fact nearby locals warn the characters of if they draw their weapons.

The characters might also choose to avoid getting involved, as do most of the folk around them. If they don't act, new strife will involve them imminently.

Sensing Tremors

During the conflict, the Ashen Heirs continue decrying the Brightguard with calls of "Cast off your fetters!" and "Mortal life, mortal rule!" Regardless of whether the characters get involved, a character who succeeds on a DC 16 Wisdom (Perception) check feels an intensifying vibration beneath their feet. A character who succeeds on a subsequent DC 14 Intelligence (Nature) check realizes something is burrowing under the square.

PURPLE WORM ATTACK

As the altercation between the Ashen Heirs and the Brightguard comes to a head, read or paraphrase the following:

> Stone cracks and people scream as a massive, spiked worm erupts from the center of the square, catapulting booths and handcarts into the air. The monstrosity roars, spraying the scattering crowd with fist-sized globs of spittle. Guards shout for reinforcements.

The combination of noises from the large crowd and the disruptive vibrations of the boomhailers has enraged a **purple worm** dwelling deep below the city. It emerges and begins wreaking havoc on Three Sun Square, targeting the Ashen Heirs' boomhailers. When the Ashen Heirs see the worm racing toward them, they attempt to flee. The purple worm is irritated by the sound from the boomhailers and continues to attack until it devours the devices (and likely the Ashen Heirs holding them) or it is slain.

Map 11.1 depicts the area as the purple worm emerges. Stars mark the locations of Ashen Heirs. The fleeing crowd and scattered debris make the entire square difficult terrain.

DEALING WITH THE BOOMHAILERS

The purple worm thrashes its head as it rampages through the square. A character who succeeds on a DC 14 Intelligence (Nature) or Wisdom (Survival) check realizes the Ashen Heirs' devices are irritating the creature. Unaware of this, the Ashen Heirs cling to their buzzing boomhailers as they flee. A character who spends an action alerting an anarchist to the risk and succeeds on a DC 14 Charisma (Intimidate or Persuasion) check convinces that anarchist to drop their device. The purple worm ignores creatures that don't have a boomhailer and that don't threaten it. If all five boomhailers are destroyed, the purple worm retreats down the hole it created in the center of the square.

GUARDS

The guards who were trying to capture the Ashen Heirs shift to helping locals escape as soon as the purple worm appears. At the start of the fifth round, the angel Artavazda (a lawful good **pari**; detailed at the end of this adventure) appears at the southeastern corner of the square with ten members of the Brightguard (use the **guard** stat block). If the purple worm is still alive, Artavazda rapidly moves to slay it. If the characters defeat the purple worm before this, Artavazda arrives just as they do so.

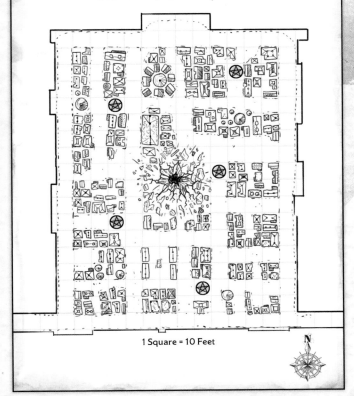

MAP 11.1: THREE SUN SQUARE

ANGELS IN THE AFTERMATH

After the purple worm is dispatched, the pari Artavazda introduces themself:

> A blue-skinned angel with four scarlet wings lands before you, accompanied by a gentle breeze. The angel wears a pointed, shimmering helmet and wields a flanged mace reminiscent of a blazing sun. "I am Artavazda," the angel announces, "harbinger of the Brightguard and Atash's righteous hand."

Artavazda saw how the characters distinguished themselves and offers to heal an injured character. The angel can answer questions about the Ashen Heirs, the Brightguard, or Atash (all are detailed in the "Akharin Sangar Gazetteer" section at the end of the adventure). If asked about the purple worm, Artavazda tells the characters such creatures are rare, calling the attack "a calamity incited by reckless souls." The angel converses with the characters for a moment before offering them a proposition.

Artavazda

When Atash came to Akharin Sangar, he was accompanied by a host of angels, the pari Artavazda among them. Artavazda has four narrow wings whose gradually shifting colors are reminiscent of a sunset. The pari's smooth, curly black hair is mostly hidden beneath a pointed gold helmet that frames a calm, pale-blue face and glowing eyes.

Artavazda embodies the Sunweaver in word and deed. Though Artavazda holds lawbreakers accountable for their crimes, the pari is a staunch believer in rehabilitation and leads a voluntary gardening program for those serving time, cultivating goodness in folk who have lost their way.

Personality Trait. "There is light in every soul. I am keen to purge the darkness that shrouds it."

Ideal. "Good and evil are as plain as day and night."

Bond. "It is my duty to protect Akharin Sangar according to Atash's law."

Flaw. "I am incapable of telling a lie. Truth doesn't hide in darkness."

Artavazda's Request

Artavazda explains that in the lead-up to Shabe Taabaan, the Brightguard has seen many disruptions. The angel asks the characters to work with the Brightguard until the festival ends a few days from now, protecting the people from dramatic displays that turn dangerous. Artavazda goes on to explain the following points:

- Though the angels who serve Atash are powerful, they are too few to support the Brightguard's rank-and-file members during times of trouble. With tensions between the Brightguard and rebel groups running high, Artavazda seeks assistance.
- Too often, rebels and Brightguard members are harmed during altercations. Artavazda wants those who oppose Atash's rule to have the opportunity to learn the error of their ways peaceably.
- The angel believes adventurers can be more creative—and more liberal with the truth—than the Brightguard, enabling such characters to learn more about rebels and prevent dangerous situations in ways the Brightguard can't.
- Artavazda offers each character 800 gp for their aid, plus the potential for additional work.

If the characters balk at working with the Brightguard, Artavazda doubles his payment offer. Should the characters still refuse, the pari understands but requests they visit the Ruz Bazaar to see the pain the Ashen Heirs are causing. Continue with "Afsoun's Arrest" but then skip the "Artavazda's Mission" section and move on to the "Ruz Bazaar" section. There, have agents of the Brightguard or Silent Roar entreat the characters to help prevent more violence.

Afsoun's Arrest

As things calm down in Three Sun Square, the Brightguard places any remaining Ashen Heirs under arrest. The Ashen Heirs are belligerent as they're arrested, proclaiming, "A few lost lives are nothing if it means the Brightguard falls!" Among the bystanders is the well-known actor Afsoun Ghorbani. While the characters converse with Artavazda, read the following text:

> Two white-and-gold-clad Brightguards question a calm elf woman with dark hair, sharp green eyes, and a pink tunic over a red dress. One guard and the blue-skinned angel Artavazda lock eyes, and the angel nods. The Brightguards place manacles on the elf.

If the characters inquire about the woman's detainment, Artavazda explains that she's an infamous agitator who's worth questioning about her involvement in today's incident. The pari adds that she will be released in time—if she's innocent.

If a character attempts to intervene, Afsoun (chaotic good, elf **archmage**) tells the guards she doesn't know the character while discreetly signaling to them not to escalate. If the characters ignore that signal, any threats or combat this close to the Brightguard's headquarters attracts four **devas**, who defuse the situation through moderation—and by disarming belligerents.

Artavazda's Mission

Artavazda is concerned that the Ashen Heirs are planning to further disrupt the celebration of Shabe Taabaan. That morning, Ashen Heirs attacked merchants in the Ruz Bazaar. The merchants said the Ashen Heirs were seeking a magic jar recently unearthed in the nearby desert. The timely appearance of the Brightguard drove the Ashen Heirs away before anyone was hurt.

If the characters accept Artavazda's offer to work with the Brightguard, the pari explains the situation:

> "Atash worries for the safety of his people. Today's incident comes on the heels of an Ashen Heirs assault at the Ruz Bazaar, which shows their threat is increasing. We've learned they're seeking magic they can use to disrupt Shabe Taabaan. If the Ashen Heirs are left unchecked, I fear Atash will cancel the celebrations and impose martial law until the rebels' threat is ended. Will you help me prevent this?"

If the characters agree to Artavazda's mission, the angel explains that the Brightguard inspected the bazaar after the morning's attack but didn't learn much. Artavazda requests that the characters investigate further to determine what magic the Ashen Heirs were seeking, learn how they plan to use it, and put an end to their threat—preferably by bringing their mysterious leader to justice. The angel then provides directions to the nearby Ruz Bazaar.

CHAOS AT THE BAZAAR

The Ruz Bazaar is a sprawling market as old as the city. The Ashen Heirs have been searching the bazaar recently, seeking a magic samovar. None of the merchants the Ashen Heirs shook down had the samovar, and the search was disrupted by the Brightguard just as the Ashen Heirs were interrogating a well-known rug merchant, Emad Farrokh.

RUZ BAZAAR

The main entrance to Ruz Bazaar is near Three Sun Square. When the characters enter the bazaar, read or paraphrase the following text:

> The covered stone halls of the Ruz Bazaar echo with the voices of merchants proclaiming the wonders of heady spices, fresh produce, and sun-themed Shabe Taabaan souvenirs.

Anything made or grown in Akharin Sangar eventually finds its way to the Ruz. Characters can purchase crafts, food, festive keepsakes, and any adventuring gear in the *Player's Handbook* at normal cost.

If the characters accepted Artavazda's mission, they can spend 10 minutes conversing with merchants to confirm the angel's story: four Ashen Heirs using magic threatened and attacked multiple merchants. If a character succeeds on a DC 14 Charisma (Intimidation or Persuasion) check or offers a merchant at least 1 gp, a merchant adds that the Ashen Heirs were looking for a magic vessel of some sort, and the last shop owner they attacked was Emad the rug merchant.

The characters can also learn about Emad by spending an hour investigating the bazaar. After doing so, have each character investigating the market make a Wisdom (Perception) check. The character who has the highest check notices a halfling merchant watching them from the doorway of one of the bazaar's shops. This is Emad, and he slips inside his shop as soon as he's noticed.

EMAD'S RUG SHOP

Emad is a middle-aged merchant (neutral, halfling **noble**) and the proprietor of a sizable black-market business. If the characters enter his shop, read the following text:

> The cramped, musty shop is filled with ornate rugs of many styles and designs. A brown-skinned halfling smiles and hops down from atop a stack of folded carpets beside the shop's wide-open doors. "Welcome! Does anything catch your eye?"

From the front of his store, Emad sells all manner of rugs. At the shop's rear, several hanging rugs hide a secret room containing Emad's stock of foreign goods. Most of these wares are mundane, but all have been deemed illegal by the Brightguard. Emad has survived decades of inspections thanks to his calm, friendly demeanor, but the Ashen Heirs' shakedown has rattled him.

Talking to Emad. If questioned, the merchant plays down the day's events but confirms the Ashen Heirs sought a magic vessel. He denies knowing anything about it, but a character who succeeds on a DC 16 Wisdom (Insight) check suspects he's lying.

Emad misses the time before Atash's rule when the bazaar was packed with shoppers from faraway lands. That was before Atash's stringent edicts limited visitors to the city. A character who succeeds on DC 16 Charisma (Persuasion) check can get Emad to reveal his illegal dealings. Characters dressed in a way that marks them as being from lands far from Akharin Sangar have advantage on this check.

Once Emad feels he can trust the characters—or is coerced—he reveals the following information:

- Emad smuggles luxuries and other contraband Atash and the Brightguard have outlawed.
- His smuggling business is dwindling, as his contacts fear provoking Atash or believe there's no money to be made in the isolated city.
- Emad recently received a strange samovar from a treasure hunter in the Burning Dunes. He knows the jar is magical, but he hasn't been able to sell it or even have it identified due to the increased presence of the Brightguard in the bazaar.
- With citizens being detained despite scant evidence of wrongdoing, Emad's usual clients and contacts are wary of being seen at his shop until things settle down.

Additionally, Emad will show the characters his secret room if he thinks they're interested in buying contraband.

Investigating the Shop. A character who inspects the goods piled in Emad's shop and succeeds on a DC 18 Intelligence (Investigation) check notes that the thick rugs hanging at the back of the shop have been moved more often than the goods around them. If these display rugs are moved, the door to the hidden chamber is revealed. Proceed with the "Backroom Thieves" encounter.

BACKROOM THIEVES

Whether Emad shows the characters his shop's secret room willingly or they find it themselves, there's a surprise waiting inside. Even if the characters don't seek out the room, the sound of something shattering inside reveals the room before they leave.

Two of the Ashen Heir **mages** who shook down local merchants earlier in the day have returned. When the mages threatened Emad before, one of them found the shop's secret room, but the Brightguard's arrival forced them to flee before they could investigate.

These two Ashen Heirs have squeezed through a window in the secret room that's disguised from the outside. They've riffled through the space and found not just the samovar they've been searching for but also a *carpet of flying* Emad has been trying to sell for months. The rug merchant foolishly scribed the rug's command word, "baalaa," on the carpet's tag.

Read the following text when the characters enter the secret room:

> This chamber's shelves sag under crates and curios. On the far wall, a narrow window opens into a cluttered alley beyond. Just outside, two figures wearing menacing scarlet masks kneel on a flying carpet, one holding an ornate samovar. They laugh as the carpet shoots down the alley.

BAZAAR CHASE

As the two masked thieves soar away on the carpet, the characters can give chase.

Give the characters a moment to spring into action and swiftly come up with their own ways to fly after the thieves. If they don't have a method of flying, Emad produces another *carpet of flying* and loans it to the characters. He is vocal about wanting both carpets and the samovar back. Each *carpet of flying* from Emad's shop measures 4 feet by 6 feet, has a capacity of 400 pounds, and has a flying speed of 60 feet. It can accommodate two Medium or Small creatures.

After rolling initiative, each participant in the chase can take one action and move on its turn. The Ashen Heirs begin 120 feet ahead of the pursuers and 15 feet off the ground. Track the distance between the Ashen Heirs and the pursuers, and designate the pursuer closest to the thieves as the lead. The lead pursuer might change from round to round.

As the Ashen Heirs seek to escape, one controls the carpet while the other casts spells at any pursuers in range.

DASHING

During the chase, a participant can freely use the Dash action a number of times equal to 3 + its Constitution modifier. Each additional Dash action it takes during the chase requires the creature to succeed on a DC 10 Constitution check at the end of its turn or gain 1 level of exhaustion. Unless it can move in some other manner, like riding a *carpet of flying*, a creature drops out of the chase if its exhaustion reaches level 5, since its speed becomes 0. A creature can remove the levels of exhaustion it gained during the chase by finishing a short or long rest. The Dash action cannot make a *carpet of flying* move faster.

SPELLS AND ATTACKS

A chase participant can make attacks and cast spells against other creatures within range. Apply the normal rules for cover, terrain, and so on to the attacks and spells. Chase participants can't normally make opportunity attacks against each other, since they are all assumed to be moving in the same direction at the same time.

CHASE COMPLICATIONS

Complications occur randomly during the chase for both the Ashen Heirs and the characters pursing them. Each participant in the chase rolls on the Bazaar Chase Complications table at the end of its turn. If a complication occurs, it affects the next chase participant in the initiative order, not the participant who rolled the die. The participant who rolled the die or the participant affected by the complication can spend inspiration to negate the complication. Unless otherwise noted, the events on the Bazaar Complications table affect a single creature; this should be the one controlling a *carpet of flying* if multiple creatures are on such a magic item.

BAZAAR CHASE COMPLICATIONS

d10	Complication
1	A taught line of pennants stretches across your path. You must succeed on a DC 10 Dexterity saving throw, or you fall 2d4 × 5 feet, taking 1d6 bludgeoning damage per 10 feet fallen and landing prone. If you are using a *carpet of flying*, any character on the same conveyance must also make this saving throw.
2	Choose to fly around or through a gap between bazaar stalls. If you fly around, the area counts as 10 feet of difficult terrain. If you fly through the gap, you must succeed on a DC 16 Dexterity saving throw, or you break through the stall and take 4d6 bludgeoning damage. If you are using a *carpet of flying*, any other character on the same conveyance must also make this saving throw.

d10	Complication
3	An overturned crate releases chickens and a cloud of feathers into the air. Make a DC 16 Wisdom (Survival) check to try to stay on course through the distractions. On a failed check, the obstacle counts as 10 feet of difficult terrain.
4	You pass through an arc of knives thrown by performing food vendors (+3 to hit, 4d4 + 1 piercing damage on a hit).
5	You fly through hanging textiles. Make a DC 14 Dexterity (Acrobatics) check to navigate the fabric. On a failed check, the path counts as 10 feet of difficult terrain.
6	Spices from an overturned stand fill the air. You must succeed on a DC 16 Constitution saving throw, or you are blinded until the end of your turn, roll on this table again, and immediately experience that complication. You can avoid rolling on the table again if you don't move this turn.
7–10	No complication

Ending the Chase

The chase ends when either side gives up the chase, when the Ashen Heirs escape, or when the pursuers are close enough to catch the thieves. If neither side gives up the chase, one Ashen Heir mage makes a Dexterity (Stealth) check at the end of each round in which the Ashen Heirs get out of the lead pursuer's sight, after every participant in the chase has taken its turn. The check's result is compared to the passive Wisdom (Perception) scores of the pursuers. If the result of the mage's check is greater than the highest passive Wisdom (Perception) score, the Ashen Heirs escape. If not, the chase continues for another round.

Questioning the Ashen Heirs

If the characters catch the Ashen Heirs, the mages tell the characters everything they know in exchange for being let go before the Brightguard arrives. They share the following facts:

- The Ashen Heirs were ordered to find the samovar and return it to their cell's hideout.
- Their hideout is an abandoned temple in the Old City.
- Their cell leader is a wise sage named Navid.

If a character succeeds on a DC 15 Charisma (Intimidation) check, the thieves also hand over their masks and share the passphrase required to access their hideout: "Let the embers light the way."

The Stolen Samovar

The stolen samovar is an *iron flask* containing a djinni. If opened, the samovar loses its magic (unlike a typical *iron flask*) and releases a friendly **djinni** named Baadi. Baadi is a bombastic fellow who offers to grant the characters a wish if they help him find his cousin—another genie who lives in Akharin Sangar—though Baadi doesn't know where he is or what name he's using. A character who succeeds on a DC 18 Wisdom (Insight) check notes that Baadi is bluffing and can't grant wishes. Baadi doesn't know that his cousin is the Ashen Heir leader, the efreeti Navid.

Returning to Emad

If the characters capture the Ashen Heirs, Emad gives them a *carpet of flying* as a reward—particularly if the characters don't reveal his illegal operations. If the mages escape, Emad promises to give the characters a *carpet of flying* if they retrieve and return the stolen samovar.

If the characters return the samovar without opening it, the halfling opens it while checking for damage and releases Baadi (see the previous section).

BRIAN VALEZA

To Navid's Hideout

The characters' next move is likely finding the Ashen Heirs' hideout so they can complete Artavazda's mission. If the characters lost the Ashen Heir thieves or otherwise aren't sure where to go next, they can spend 15 minutes asking locals if they saw a flying carpet and make a DC 12 Charisma (Persuasion) check. On a success, they get vague directions that bring them to an abandoned temple (see the "Ashen Heir Hideout" section).

The Lions' Plea

After contending with the members of the Ashen Heirs or completing their business with Emad, the characters are approached by a member of another revolutionary group, the Silent Roar, who has been observing the characters. The agent, a robed old human who uses the **spy** stat block, gives each character a piece of pistachio nougat candy wrapped in paper stamped with the symbol of the Ghorbani Bakery, a smiling manticore. The agent says that the characters' "old friend Laleh" is anxious to see them, then walks away.

If the characters follow the agent, they lose sight of him near the Ghorbani Bakery but spot the manticore symbol on the bakery's awning. Characters who succeed on a DC 12 Charisma (Persuasion) check can also convince a passerby to identify the manticore symbol as the symbol of the Ghorbani Bakery.

Ghorbani Bakery

Laleh Ghorbani's bakery is a two-story edifice west of Three Sun Square. Inside, Laleh is hard at work. She wears a flour-dusted apron with flower motifs. She has high cheekbones, smiling brown eyes, brown skin, and an ornate prosthetic arm.

Laleh Ghorbani

Laleh Ghorbani (neutral good, elf **scout**) uses her bakery as a safe house for the cell of the Silent Roar she leads with her sister, Afsoun Ghorbani. The gregarious baker delights in conversation and plumbs her customers for gossip that might be valuable to the Silent Roar. She distrusts those who enforce Atash's law without question.

Personality Trait. "I can't help but offer my guests food."

Ideal. "Change is like dough. It takes hard work to shape, but also time and patience for it to rise."

Bond. "My sister means the world to me. Her cause is my cause."

Flaw. "I sometimes freeze when faced with difficult decisions."

Talking with Laleh

When the characters enter the shop, Laleh presents them with a platter of desserts as she attends other customers. Once the other shoppers are gone, she locks the doors and apologizes for her strange invitation. Laleh is friendly toward the characters and guides the conversation to the following points:

- Laleh is the sister of Afsoun Ghorbani, who was arrested by the Brightguard in Three Sun Square.
- Afsoun secretly leads the Silent Roar, a coalition of rebels that seeks to nonviolently overthrow Atash and put Akharin Sangar's people in power for the betterment of the city-state.
- Although the Silent Roar are rebels, they're not affiliated with the destructive Ashen Heirs.
- Laleh has received word that Afsoun was not released after her questioning. Laleh seeks information on where her sister is being held.
- While Afsoun is in Brightguard custody, Laleh has assumed command of the Silent Roar.
- Laleh can share any information from the "Akharin Sangar Gazetteer" section.

LALEH GHORBANI

EKATERINA BURMAK

Laleh knows the characters have had dealings with the Brightguard, though she doesn't know the specifics. Regardless, she asks them to keep their ears opened for any information about her sister.

If the characters mention seeking the Ashen Heirs or their arrangement with Artavazda, Laleh offers assistance. The Ashen Heirs' recklessness endangers the work of the Silent Roar, and Laleh encourages the characters to put an end to the dangerous anarchists even if the characters aren't in league with the Brightguard. She promises that her agents will obtain any resources the characters need, such as the location of the Ashen Heirs' hideout, the passphrase to get in, or efreeti masks.

If the characters agree to help Laleh, she thanks them and says her agents will contact them later. Should the characters prove reluctant to help, Laleh tells them to think on what is right and promises to be in touch.

If the characters are forthright about working for the Brightguard, Laleh tries to recruit them as double agents. Should the characters stay loyal to the Brightguard, Laleh is disappointed but trusts them not to compound the tragedy her family suffered today. She still shares any information she has about the Ashen Heirs, seeking to put an end to their threat.

Ashen Heir Hideout

The Ashen Heir hideout is a crumbling, one-story temple located in the Old City. Captured Ashen Heir agents or Laleh Ghorbani might direct the characters to the location.

Read the following as the characters approach the site:

> A small, neglected temple stands within a courtyard surrounded by an iron fence and containing only dead overgrowth and a dry fountain full of garbage. A tower juts from the temple's roof; one of its walls bears tall vents to catch the wind.

A padlock holds closed a gate in the temple's 8-foot-tall fence, but it can be unlocked as an action with a successful DC 12 Dexterity check using thieves' tools or broken with a successful DC 18 Strength check.

Characters who succeed on a DC 16 Wisdom (Perception) check also notice that the double door leading into the temple has a sliding peephole.

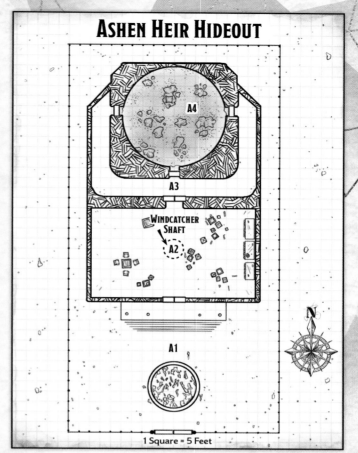

MAP 11.2: ASHEN HEIR HIDEOUT

Ashen Heir Hideout Locations

The following locations are keyed to map 11.2.

A1: Courtyard

The temple's courtyard lies in ruin, its stone paving overgrown with weeds. The fountain at its center is broken and filled with discarded furnishings.

Temple Entrance. The main door to the temple is made of solid wood and is barred from the opposite side. The door can be forced open with a successful DC 20 Strength check, but doing so alerts the Ashen Heir **veteran** guarding the door in area A2.

If the characters knock on the door or otherwise make themselves known, the guard slides open the peephole and checks to see if they're wearing the Ashen Heirs' distinctive efreeti masks. If they are, he then asks for the passphrase. If a character answers, "Let the embers light the way," the guard unbars the door and admits them. Even if the characters never learned the passphrase, a character who succeeds on a DC 18 Intelligence (Investigation) check recalls that this was one of the more prominent slogans the Ashen Heirs were shouting during the incident at Three Suns Square.

If the guard sees the characters aren't wearing efreeti masks or the characters offer the wrong passphrase, he slams the peephole shut and alerts the other Ashen Heirs in area A2.

Windcatcher. A sand-green windcatcher rises from the temple's roof and directs cool air through the building. The tower's vents are 50 feet from the ground and open into a 10-foot-wide shaft that descends into the center of area A2. This shaft is marked with a dotted circle on map 11.2. A character can climb the temple's walls and the tower's interior with a successful DC 14 Strength (Athletics) check.

A *glyph of warding* spell cast at 5th level is etched onto the south side of the windcatcher's interior. The first Small or larger creature that descends 10 feet down the shaft activates explosive runes. Any creature within 20 feet of the runes must make a DC 17 Dexterity saving throw. Creatures that fail take 31 (7d8) lightning damage, and then must succeed on a DC 15 Dexterity saving throw or plummet 40 feet to area A2, taking 14 (4d6) bludgeoning damage and landing prone. Creatures that succeed on the saving throw against the explosive runes take half damage and don't fall. In either case, all creatures in area A2 are alerted to the intruders' presence.

A2: Prayer Hall

> An unfinished mosaic depicting plants flourishing under a glowing moon adorns the walls of this prayer hall, though the mosaic is partially obscured by graffiti. Crates are strewn across the marble floor, and rickety scaffolding along the east wall serves as makeshift sleeping spaces.

This temple was once consecrated to a god other than the Sunweaver, but it was abandoned years ago and became home to Navid's cell of the Ashen Heirs. Characters can enter this area via the front door or the windcatcher tower above its 20-foot-high ceiling.

If the characters have not alerted the anarchists to their presence, four Ashen Heirs are here: a guard near the door (**veteran**), two more **veterans** playing cards, and an **assassin** resting on the scaffolding. So long as the characters wear efreeti masks and attempt to pass as members of the group, the Ashen Heirs treat them as fellow anarchists. These cell members don't know much about Navid's plans or the samovar some of them were sent to track down, but they know their leader has big plans.

If the characters attack or damage anything in the area, the Ashen Heirs turn hostile.

Scaffolding. Three sections of sturdy wooden scaffolding were here when the Ashen Heirs claimed the temple. The scaffolding now serves as a resting place for members of Navid's crew. Each section of scaffolding rises 10 feet high.

NAVID THE EFREETI IN HIS HUMAN DISGUISE

Treasure. The crates scattered through the room hold 500 gp worth of stolen goods, including numerous fine jars stolen from the bazaar. A character who succeeds on a DC 15 Wisdom (Perception) check while searching the scaffolding also discovers a set of *Nolzur's marvelous pigments*.

A3: Hallway

This hallway features mosaics depicting the cycles of the moon. If both **mages** from the bazaar escaped with the samovar, one is lingering here. If one or neither of the mages escaped, this area is empty.

A4: Selenic Garden

> Natural rocks jut from the sizzling, red-sand floor of this sweltering, domed chamber. Dust-speckled light streams from eight stained-glass magic lanterns set around the ceiling, each embossed with the phases of the moon. At the room's center, a brown-skinned man with glowing eyes reclines upon a cushion. An attendant wearing a mask designed to look like an efreeti's face stands nearby.

This cylindrical chamber once housed a lush garden, but Navid torched it to create more comfortable surroundings. The man here is Navid, leader of the Ashen Heirs, and his attendant is an Ashen Heir **mage**. The characters recognize the mage from the bazaar if either of those Ashen Heirs escaped; otherwise, he's a stranger.

THABISO MHLABA

Burning Sand. The sand here is difficult terrain. Any creature that enters the area of the sand or starts its turn there takes 7 (2d6) fire damage. Navid is immune to this effect, but his attendant keeps off the sand. A few large pieces of volcanic rock are scattered about the room and are safe to stand on.

Baadi the Djinni. If the characters failed to retrieve the stolen samovar during the bazaar chase, the **djinni** Baadi and the samovar are also present. If Baadi is here, read the following text after reading the initial boxed text:

> Several feet above the room's other occupants, an 8-foot-tall man with blue skin casually flies about the room. As he does, he peppers the reclining man with questions about sightseeing opportunities in the city.

Baadi is eager to learn about Akharin Sangar after his century of imprisonment, but Navid silences him with a wave when the characters appear. Baadi stays out of combat. His samovar is discarded among the rocks near where Navid sits.

If Baadi is with the characters or is released from the samovar here, Navid reveals his efreeti form and is delighted to see his cousin. Not wanting to have their reunion in front of strangers, both genies thank the characters for reuniting them, then use *plane shift* to catch up elsewhere. Navid might return to Akharin Sangar someday, but without their leader any remaining Ashen Heirs are no longer a threat.

Audience with Navid. Navid is an **efreeti** with the additional ability to cast *polymorph* (self only) at will. He's currently wearing his preferred disguise, that of a human man in black and crimson garb. Navid was in line to rule the region around Akharin Sangar before Atash deposed his father, forcing the efreeti prince into hiding. Now he plots in the shadows, disguised as a visionary who disdains authority.

If the characters don't attack immediately, Navid calmly asks why they've paid him a visit. If asked about the actions of the Ashen Heirs, Navid justifies them by pointing out the futility of serving either the Brightguard or the Silent Roar. He describes both organizations as preserving a crumbling husk of a city-state, stating that the only way to move forward is to start anew.

Navid attacks if threatened, revealing his true form. He fights until reduced to 50 hit points or fewer, at which point he uses *plane shift* to escape. His mage ally attacks along side him but surrenders if Navid is defeated.

Treasure. An iron chest is buried just beneath the burning sand. Any character who searches the room for treasure and succeeds on a DC 15 Intelligence (Investigation) check notes a patch of sand that was recently dug up. The iron chest can be exposed and opened by two or more characters working for 1 minute. The chest contains a gold crown inlaid with fire opals (worth 3,000 gp), a silvered sickle with a pearlescent pommel (worth 750 gp), and a *spell scroll* of *fly*. If the Ashen Heirs in the bazaar escaped on Emad's *carpet of flying*, the carpet is here as well.

AFTER THE ASHES

Once Navid is captured or otherwise dealt with, the characters can return to Artavazda at the Brightguard's headquarters—the Noble Jewel, near Three Sun Square. If the characters describe Navid in his efreeti form, Artavazda remembers the hot-headed efreeti prince, and the pari murmurs thoughtfully, "Blood doesn't make you royalty. Only light can do that." Ultimately, Navid's downfall puts the pari's mind at ease, and Artavazda rewards each character with a pink diamond worth 500 gp.

If the characters abandon Artavazda's mission or agreed to aid Laleh, she soon contacts them with an invitation to the Twilight Rose theater for that night. The theater's guards will admit the characters if shown this invitation.

A SECOND REQUEST

If the characters neutralized the Ashen Heir threat, Artavazda offers them a second assignment as thanks. If any aspect of the previous mission went awry, the pari offers this assignment as a chance for the characters to correct their missteps.

Artavazda has learned another group of rebels, the Silent Roar, is planning a gathering that night at the Twilight Rose theater. The Silent Roar's dedication to nonviolent protest makes it less of a threat than the Ashen Heirs, but Atash doesn't tolerate dissent. The pari knows if the Brightguard raids the meeting, the Silent Roar's members will scatter. Artavazda hopes the characters can gather intelligence on the group and its plans prior to the Brightguard raiding the theater. Artavazda promises another 500 gp per character as a reward for this assignment.

If a character tells Artavazda about their meeting with Laleh Ghorbani, the pari is delighted that they already have a connection with the Silent Roar—one they can use in the Brightguard's favor.

If the characters ask Artavazda for more information, the pari admits to working with vague information about the Silent Roar but insists the Brightguard is dedicated to keeping the people of Akharin Sangar safe from reckless revolutionaries, especially during Shabe Taabaan. If asked about Afsoun Ghorbani, the pari explains that the rebel is being held for questioning outside the city at a site called the Pedestal of Judgment.

If, during this conversation, the characters sever ties with the Brightguard in favor of helping the Silent Roar, Artavazda is clearly wounded and flies away rather than immediately acting against the characters; Laleh contacts the characters with an invitation to the Twilight Rose soon after. Otherwise, when the characters are finished conversing with the pari, Artavazda gives them directions to the Twilight Rose.

THE TWILIGHT ROSE

The Twilight Rose is a few minutes' walk from Three Sun Square. As the characters approach the theater, read or paraphrase the following text:

> Colorful geometric tiles emboss the exterior of this two-story circular theater. People pass along the street, but all is dark behind the boards that cover the structure's windows. A tattered awning shades the theater's stout wooden double door.

The Twilight Rose was shut down by the Brightguard years ago for hosting performances deemed immoral. Despite this, the building's doors are unlocked. Any character who listens at the theater's front entrance or investigates the windows can make a DC 15 Wisdom (Perception) check. On a successful check, the character hears a muffled voice within.

Characters who spend time surveilling the building see figures furtively open the front door and slip inside once every 10 minutes or so.

THEATER LOBBY

Four Silent Roar guards (**veterans**) sit amid several small tables and chairs drinking tea and watching the entrance. Behind them, thick curtains close off the entrance to the theater proper. The guards are indifferent toward those who show an invitation from Laleh and hostile toward other strangers. A character without an invitation can persuade the guards to let the party pass by succeeding on a DC 14 Charisma (Deception or Persuasion) check. Mentioning Laleh or showing goods from the Ghorbani Bakery grants a character advantage on this check. If a fight breaks out, Laleh appears on initiative count 0 of the first round and intervenes (see "Laleh's Plea" below).

A TIMELESS PERFORMANCE

As characters enter the theater, an actor is performing a monologue. Read the following description when they enter:

> A dozen people stand in the darkened wings of a stage lit only by candlelight. The thirty people in the audience watch an actor costumed as a royal perform an impassioned monologue.
>
> "We stand on a steep and dreadful precipice, but we can hide no longer," the actor proclaims. "Leap, my kindred! For our true home lies just beyond the darkness!"

The thirty audience members (**commoners**) in the theater assume the characters are simply latecomers and ignore their entrance. Should a character strike up a whispered conversation with an audience member, that local can share the following information:

- The actor on stage is an understudy for the famed actor Afsoun, whose incarceration has everyone on edge.
- The play being performed is called *The First Queen*, which tells the triumphant story of the first ruler of Akharin Sangar and the deliverance of her people from a fearsome demon.
- The play used to be a Shabe Taabaan tradition, but performances were outlawed by the Brightguard in one of Atash's earliest decrees due to the play's glamorized portrayal of secular rule.
- The Silent Roar secretly performs *The First Queen* in different spaces throughout the city. There's another performance coming up this evening.

The evening performance of *The First Queen* is the event the Brightguard plans to raid tonight. It's nothing more than a harmless cultural event, though.

Soon after the characters enter, Laleh Ghorbani appears near the characters.

LALEH'S PLEA

Regardless of the characters' reason for coming to the theater, Laleh commends the characters for finding her, saying their industriousness makes it clear that they're the best suited to help her. She's recently learned that Afsoun is still in Brightguard custody, being kept at a magical holding facility known as the Pedestal of Judgment, several miles outside the city. Laleh is eager to enlist the characters in a plan to save Afsoun.

If the characters agree to help Laleh, she goes on to explain that the Silent Roar has arranged a diversion in the city the following evening. Laleh expects this diversion will lead members of the Brightguard in the city to call upon those at the Pedestal of Judgment for support. This will leave the site where Afsoun is being held only lightly guarded. There's time before the plan is to commence, but when the characters are ready, she leads them to meet with a group of Silent Roar agents—see the "Pedestal of Judgment" section.

If the characters refuse Laleh's mission, she turns away without another word.

Regardless of how the characters interact with Laleh, the performance ends soon after, and the audience makes its way out.

ARTAVAZDA'S LAST MISSION

Upon learning that the Silent Roar is merely performing a banned play that evening, characters working with the Brightguard can report back to Artavazda at the Noble Jewel. The pari rewards each character with a ruby worth 500 gp.

If the characters don't reveal the imminent attempt to free Afsoun, the insightful Artavazda shares a concern about the likelihood of such a breakout. The pari asks the characters to go the Pedestal of Judgment and support the Brightguard members there in capturing alive any who attack the prison. Artavazda fears that if the Brightguard is guarding the platform, any Silent Roar members who appear will fight to the death, and Artavazda is eager to rehabilitate these largely nonviolent rebels.

In return for the characters' help in this endeavor, Artavazda offers to reward them with a gift from Atash himself and another 500 gp gem for each character.

PEDESTAL OF JUDGMENT

The Pedestal of Judgment is a stone disc whose ancient magic keeps it hovering high above the arid landscape approximately 5 miles outside Akharin Sangar. Atash built this site for use as a holding prison to ensure Brightguard headquarters would be seen as a place of justice, not punishment. The Brightguard brings detainees to this platform for questioning and temporary incarceration, suspending them in magical crystals that only Celestials can use the Pedestal to create. Prisoners remain here until they are freed or are sentenced and transferred to Zendaane Sabz, Atash's impenetrable Sky Prison.

PREPARING TO DEPART

The characters have likely been asked by Laleh Ghorbani or Artavazda—or both—to go to the Pedestal of Judgment. When the characters are ready to travel to the Pedestal of Judgment, either contact provides them with mounts.

If the characters are working with Artavazda, the pari grants each character access to a **pegasus** from the Brightguard's stables. Artavazda tells the characters to fly to the northeast and to stay visible. The angels guarding the Pedestal of Judgment will recognize the mounts and allow the characters access to the platform.

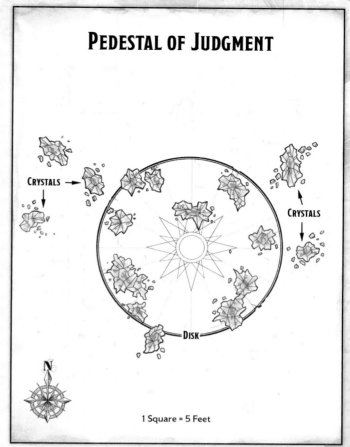

MAP 11.3: PEDESTAL OF JUDGMENT

If the characters joined forces with Laleh, she arranges a loan of mounts from the Tamers of the Winged Mane, a group of manticore riders in the nearby Heavenly Peaks. Laleh and her agents lead the characters to meet the tamer at the edge of the city. Each character is paired with one helpful, lawful neutral **manticore**. Before they depart, Laleh advises the characters to fly to the northeast to the hovering marble pedestal, flying low to stay out of view.

In both cases, the characters' ally encourages the party not to leave for the Pedestal of Judgment until the following dusk.

DOUBLE AGENTS

Depending on how the characters choose to operate, you might end up combining aspects of both Artavazda and Laleh's missions to the Pedestal of Judgment. Characters working with Laleh Ghorbani might pretend to serve Artavazda, hoping to lull the pari into a false sense of security that makes the rescue of Afsoun Ghorbani easier. Or the characters might pretend to aid Laleh, but then report the Silent Roar agents when they reach the Pedestal of Judgment. Just as the politics of Akharin Sangar aren't cut and dry, so might the characters' plans get complicated. Work with the characters to come up with a plan and be flexible with how the adventure's

SEAN MACDONALD

factions respond. Keep in mind, though, that it's unlikely the characters can please both the Brightguard and the Silent Roar with their deeds.

SITE OF JUDGMENT

The flight to the Pedestal of Judgment is brief, taking approximately an hour by manticore and a half hour by pegasus. The characters draw near to the Pedestal of Judgment shortly before the glowing moon of Shabe Taabaan rises in the heavens.

Map 11.3 depicts the Pedestal of Judgment. As the characters near the site, read the following description:

> The Pedestal of Judgment appears before the city has faded from view. The sixty-foot-diameter disc is made from golden rose marble and floats three hundred feet above the rocky ground. Green crystals hover near the disc, like jeweled spikes adorning a crown. A handful of similar crystals slowly orbit the disc, twinkling in the night sky.

If the characters are riding the Brightguard's mounts, two **devas** salute the characters and depart for the city—Artavazda has sent word informing these guards about the characters.

If the characters are coming to rescue Afsoun, there are no deva guards present, Laleh's diversion in the city having drawn them away from the platform.

PRISON CRYSTALS

Thirteen Sangarian **commoners** are frozen within the gold-banded, green crystals around the platform. These prisoners are a mix of criminals, resistance members, and ordinary citizens awaiting judgment. One crystal at the eastern edge of the platform holds Afsoun Ghorbani (chaotic good, elf **archmage**).

Each crystal is an immobile, Large object with AC 13, 25 hit points, and immunity to poison and psychic damage. Creatures inside the magic crystals are immune to all damage. A trapped creature is freed if its crystal is reduced to 0 hit points, or if the crystal is targeted with a *dispel magic* spell cast at 5th level or higher. The crystals leave their prisoners magically drained. If Afsoun is freed, she has 1 level of exhaustion and can only cast spells of 3rd level or lower until she finishes a long rest. She seeks to avoid combat unless the characters find themselves about to be defeated.

SUN CIRCLE

A 10-foot-diameter circle at the center of the platform is inscribed with writing in Celestial that glows with a warm orange hue. The glyphs read, "All good acts take place in the light." The circle acts as a permanent *zone of truth* (spell save DC 17) and is where detainees are questioned at dawn.

FALLING

A creature that falls from the platform or within 10 feet of it must make a DC 14 Dexterity saving throw. On a successful save, they grab onto one of the crystals hovering near or just below the platform. On a failed save, they plummet 300 feet to the ground, taking 70 (20d6) bludgeoning damage and landing prone.

FINAL CONFLICT

Depending on the characters' alliances, they might guard the platform or try to free Afsoun. Whether the characters are standing guard, attempting to free Afsoun, or scheming otherwise, soon after they're in position or their plan is in motion, they realize they're no longer alone. Read or paraphrase the following text:

> Twilight covers the land as the moon fills the sky. The moonlight suddenly disappears, shrouding the land in darkness. An instant later, with a burst of radiance, the moon returns. In the deepest night of Shabe Taabaan, daylight washes over Akharin Sangar.
>
> A shadow moves across the brightly lit platform. Overhead, silhouettes stand out against the radiant moon.

The identity of the creatures approaching depends on which side the characters are fighting, as detailed in "Fighting the Brightguard" and "Fighting the Silent Roar" below. Whichever enemies the characters face here, the stakes are too high for their foes to surrender or flee.

AERIAL COMBAT

The characters might use their mounts to fight foes in the air, using the mounted combat rules in the *Player's Handbook*. As intelligent creatures, the characters' mounts can act independently, but they also follow the characters' commands. A character's mount acts on its rider's turn.

If a character lands and dismounts on the Pedestal of Judgment, their mount takes to the sky during the next round, circling the platform until called.

AFSOUN GHORBANI,
IMPRISONED IN CRYSTAL

THABISO MHLABA

FIGHTING THE BRIGHTGUARD

If the characters seek to free Afsoun, the shadows overhead are the **pari** Artavazda and two Brightguard **knights** riding two **pegasi**. They appear 30 feet in the air above the center of the pedestal. Artavazda expresses genuine disappointment with the characters and chastises them for turning away from the path of justice. The pari asks that the characters and their allies surrender and face arrest. As the characters are involved in a crime by attempting to free someone Artavazda considers justly arrested, the pari is unlikely to be talked out of apprehending them. During combat, the knights attempt to shove characters off the platform whenever possible.

FIGHTING THE SILENT ROAR

If the characters are defending the Pedestal of Judgment for the Brightguard, they're confronted by three Silent Roar agents: two **veterans** riding **manticores**, and Marzieh, a **gynosphinx** ally of the rebels and friend of Afsoun. The Silent Roar members are loyal to Afsoun and are unlikely to be talked out of abandoning their leader—particularly after enacting a plan to liberate her.

CONCLUSION

After the battle, the characters can return to the city and report to whichever faction they chose before the final encounter.

RETURNING TO THE BRIGHTGUARD

If the characters are working for the Brightguard, Artavazda waits for them in a garden terrace atop the Noble Jewel. The pari is eager to hear how the characters' mission went and thanks them profusely for keeping Akharin Sangar safe. Artavazda promises that any foes the characters killed will be returned to life so they can face justice. The pari gives each character a sapphire worth 500 gp before producing a cloak made of flawless white feathers with a single golden feather that would sit high on the wearer's back. The cloak has the properties of *wings of flying*, and Artavazda explains that the golden feather is from the wing of Atash himself. Any Brightguard member will recognize the cloak's wearer as a friend of the Sunweaver and Akharin Sangar.

RETURNING TO THE SILENT ROAR

If the characters free Afsoun, the rebel leader accompanies them to the city to reunite with her sister. Though the Silent Roar has little money to offer, Laleh and Afsoun offer the party personal treasures as a reward. Laleh gifts them her *hat of disguise*, while Afsoun offers an *Ioun stone* of leadership. The sisters also promise the characters a lifetime supply of free treats from the Ghorbani Bakery.

Afsoun must lie low now that she has defied the Brightguard, but the Silent Roar as a whole is invigorated by their leader's recovery. The group redoubles its efforts to oppose the Brightguard and Atash.

WHAT'S NEXT?

Regardless of the characters' allegiance, their actions and the fallout of Afsoun's detainment or escape have broad implications for Akharin Sangar. The Silent Roar's resistance efforts increase in either case, causing the organization to become the Brightguard's greatest rival. If the characters remain in Akharin Sangar, Artavazda or the Ghorbani sisters seek to enlist them in the factions' conflict. As either the Brightguard continues to crack down on rebels or the Silent Roar encourages wider resistance, the characters are likely to be drawn into increasingly desperate conflicts, eventually coming to the attention of the land's ruler, Atash himself.

Akharin Sangar Gazetteer

From the turquoise spires of this holy city-state's oldest temple, a radiant angel watches over Akharin Sangar. His name is Atash. For many, his presence is a source of comfort: a promise of protection and guidance. But a growing proportion of Sangarians find his rule suffocating. The angel's word is law, his doctrine rigid, and his enforcement absolute.

Akharin Sangar is a vibrant city-state with a deep appreciation for art and tradition. It rests on a plateau beneath the Heavenly Peaks, a bulwark of rugged, snow-capped mountains that have protected their lands for centuries. Though most inhabitants reside in the city or the surrounding hills, more stalwart folk brave the Burning Dunes, where kenku scavengers scour the ruins of old civilizations and rocs soar over adobe settlements like massive vultures.

Akharin Sangar has all but closed its gates to the rest of the world. Outsiders often surmise the city-state is full of zealots as severe as the city's angel ruler. In truth, Sangarians are a friendly, hospitable people, eager to share their traditions with visitors and unhappy with Atash's embargoes and nightly curfew. A fellowship of artisans, philosophers, and merchants has formed a secret coalition known as the Silent Roar that seeks to oust Atash and revive the city by instituting rule by the people. Meanwhile, pernicious anarchists called the Ashen Heirs foment unrest, striving for change at any cost.

Features

Those familiar with Akharin Sangar typically know the following facts:

Hallmarks. Akharin Sangar is a theocracy presided over by Celestials. It's known for its isolation and history of political turmoil.

People. Sangarians are predominately human with brown or black hair and fair to rich brown skin tones. Dwarves, elves, halflings, and gnomes represent a little over one-third of the populace, and some in the city claim to have a touch of Celestial ancestry.

Languages. The primary language is Zabaani. Although all citizens also speak Common, the lack of visitors to Akharin Sangar means they have few chances to practice it. Celestial is also commonly spoken among Atash's followers and theologians.

Noteworthy Sites

The city-state of Akharin Sangar is steeped in proud traditions. While its city is a hub of culture, the surrounding lands are fraught with magic and danger.

Three Sun Square

Three Sun Square is an important hub whose three architectural marvels exemplify the pillars of local society—religion, government, and economy.

Avalin Sahar. The decorative turquoise-and-gold facade of the city-state's oldest temple, Avalin Sahar, beckons all to kneel in worship of the deity locally known as the Sunweaver.

Noble Jewel. Members of the Brightguard, a holy order of protectors and enforcers, call the Noble Jewel—once the royal palace—their headquarters. Occasionally, Atash appears on the palace's garden terrace to issue a proclamation, much like the rulers who preceded him.

Ruz Bazaar. Fragrant spices lure shoppers to the bustling Ruz Bazaar, a sprawling complex of vendors that hides an underground market.

Foothills of the Heavenly Peaks

The hills beneath the Heavenly Peaks are fertile, blessing farmers with bountiful harvests of juicy pomegranates, buttery pistachios, and crimson strands of saffron. Rebellion also flourishes, as the Brightguard has a smaller presence here, and the nation's curfew is not enforced. Free thinkers gather at aged teahouses, discussing philosophy as they sip from steaming cups, and acting as secret missionaries who dare to defy angelic law.

The Sky Prison

Deep within the majestic desert east of Akharin Sangar, the floating edifice of Zendaane Sabz, known more commonly as the Sky Prison, hangs over a lake of shattered glass. The prison is a crystalline hive peppered with demiplanes of divine judgment. Inside lurk potent evils banished by Atash, such as Faasadi the Rotten, an adult blue dracolich, and the ageless Chesmare, a beholder who can do nothing but admire her own reflection in a mirrored cell that neutralizes her power. Given Atash's intolerance for misconduct, the prison's population continues to grow, but now it fills with more ordinary folk guilty of lesser crimes.

Life in Akharin Sangar

Despite the rumors outside its borders, Akharin Sangar is markedly hospitable. By long-standing custom, every Sangarian is a potential host and must be prepared to entertain guests on short notice. Visitors are invited to relax on luxurious carpets adorned with colorful pillows while their host prepares them hot beverages—if not an entire meal.

EDUCATION AND ART

A thirst for knowledge permeates Akharin Sangar. Its many independent schools are free to teach broad curricula that beget a well-read populace, although the long list of censored works constrains opportunities for higher education, especially in philosophy and literature. The city-state cautiously embraces progress, adopting developments in magic and science as long as they don't contradict religious principles.

Akharin Sangar has a rich artistic heritage. Architecture is thoughtful and symbolic, and instruments like the barbat and kamancheh sweeten poetic lyrics with their unmistakable tones. Sangarian carpets exemplify the city-state's long history of vibrant textiles: painstakingly woven rugs are highly sought works of art. Some are even rumored to fly.

FOOD AND CLOTHING

Sangarian cuisine emphasizes savory, sweet, and sour flavors. When households entertain guests and during festivals, kabobs and hearty stews infused with saffron grace dinner plates alongside beds of rice. Bakers stay busy, filling bellies with chewy flatbreads and scrumptious pastries tinged with rosewater. But Sangarians know how to stretch small pots of a soup called aash to feed an entire family.

Clothing is generally modest, and Sangarians value fashionable dress. Men's attire consists of baggy trousers, handwoven shoes, and robes or tunics secured with wide cloth belts. Women typically dress in layers, sporting long, elegant skirts and blouses with heavy embroidery. Floral patterns are common regardless of gender, and colors range from vivid to muted depending on preference. Common headwear includes scarves, caps, and headbands with veiled hats.

LAWS AND SOCIETY

Unprepared visitors might find some aspects of Sangarian society unusually austere. Intoxicants are prohibited within the city, there's a strict curfew after sundown, and everyday interactions are tinged with restraint to steer clear of Atash's forbiddances. Sangarians reserve intimacy for family and close friends, lowering their social guard only in the comfort of their homes.

THE SUNWEAVER

Most Sangarians revere the Sunweaver—or pretend to. Locally, the Sunweaver's faith uses an upright torch topped with a blazing sun as its symbol. Activities halt during daily prayers, which take place at dawn, noon, and sundown. Though other faiths are tolerated, those faiths are sequestered in shrines on the city's outskirts. Public preaching is considered taboo, and unauthorized missionary work earns the ire of the Brightguard. The nature of the Sunweaver and whether they're a unique god or a regional name for another deity—like Dol Arrah or Pholtus (detailed in the *Player's Handbook*)—is up to you.

The Sunweaver holds ultimate authority in Akharin Sangar, which is a theocracy ruled by the god's self-proclaimed messenger. Atash interprets the Sunweaver's doctrine and encourages all citizens to cultivate light and warmth. The Sunweaver's clerics hold significant power. In addition to priestly duties, they act as government officials and judges, employing divination magic in audits and trials.

Those who break the law answer to the Brightguard. The religious order enforces the law without prejudice, though its ranks contain both tender-hearted civil servants and disciplinarians who relish chastising citizens for misdemeanors.

ATASH, RULER OF
AKHARIN SANGAR

Names

Sangarian names are drawn from lineage, religion, and literature and are often suffused with symbolism and history. The following names are common in the region:

Feminine. Forough, Mariam, Nazanin, Shohreh, Yasamin
Masculine. Amir, Bahram, Farshid, Hassan, Ramin
Gender-Neutral. Keyahnosh, Omid, Roshani, Shadan, Sorosh
Surnames. Farzaneh, Nasri, Pasdar, Rasul, Setar

Legends of Akharin Sangar

Akharin Sangar's most famous historical tale is an epic poem about its heroic founder, Piruzan. When Piruzan's people were tormented by the horned demon Zolmate Shab, she led them up the Heavenly Peaks in search of a land free from tyranny and darkness. The demon intercepted them at the summit, appearing in a pillar of smoke. Emboldened by the coming dawn, the first Sangarians prepared to make a last stand. With the power of the Sunweaver, Piruzan banished the relentless demon. She became queen of this new land and ruled for over three hundred years, never forgetting the Sunweaver's warmth.

Akharin Sangar flourished during the dynasties that followed but eventually succumbed to excess, corruption, and complacency. Darkness fell upon the city-state, and Zolmate Shab returned. As demons beset the city, Sangarians prayed to the Sunweaver, and Atash answered. After an earthshaking battle, the angel emerged victorious.

Afterward, Atash prophesied the return of Zolmate Shab, even stronger than before, if the people of Akharin Sangar fell from grace again. After fifty years of peace, though, most Sangarians have come to doubt the prophecy's legitimacy, and many question whether the angel's rigid control of the city-state is justified.

Atash

Atash (lawful neutral **solar**), the angelic ruler of Akharin Sangar, came to the city-state's aid when all hope seemed lost. After smiting Zolmate Shab's fiendish army with righteous fury, Atash elected to stay, believing his mission incomplete. In the early years of his rule, Atash walked among the common folk, performing miracles. Over time, he withdrew from his people, tired of witnessing them repeat their mistakes. He spends his days in contemplation, occasionally breaking his silence to address an increasingly distraught populace.

Atash possesses an ageless and inflexible perspective. Everlasting and seemingly emotionless, the angel answers complex problems with direct solutions. He believes that only by following his decrees can Sangarians prevent another demonic incursion. He deems those who oppose him outlaws.

Personality Trait. "I'm being tested. I've not heard the Sunweaver's voice since my rule began."
Ideal. "To disobey the Sunweaver is to protest truth."
Bond. "I must protect the people of Akharin Sangar, even from themselves."
Flaw. "The subtleties of mortal nuance are simply the repetition of mortal mistakes."

Adventures in Akharin Sangar

Consider the plots on the Akharin Sangar Adventures table when planning adventures.

Akharin Sangar Adventures

d6	Adventure
1	An **adult blue dragon** plagues the Burning Dunes with a magical sandstorm. Desert dwellers beseech the characters for aid.
2	A **marid** named Nedootash agrees to outfit the Silent Roar with valuable supplies if the characters complete three personal favors for the genie.
3	Before their execution, a coven of **night hags** prophesy that an angel-killing blade is hidden in an unholy subterranean temple. The characters are charged with finding the blade.
4	A **planetar** reveals itself to the characters and declares Atash a false emissary of the Sunweaver.
5	Possessed by a **shadow demon**, a high-ranking member of the Brightguard calls for the characters' arrest on charges of high treason.
6	Revolutionaries begin signing their graffiti with the symbol of the **beholder** Chesmare, a terror imprisoned in the Sky Prison. Astrologers approach the characters, afraid the sigils will set her free.

Characters from Akharin Sangar

If players want to create characters native to Akharin Sangar, consider asking them the following questions during character creation:

How have you been affected by the angel Atash's rule? What changes have you or your loved ones made in response to Atash's edicts? How has this theocracy benefited or harmed you?
Do you worship the Sunweaver? If not, do you make that known? How has this affected your life?
Do you behave differently in private than in public? Whom do you trust? Are you part of resistance efforts, or do you actively oppose them?

PARI

A pari is an angelic harbinger gifted with foresight. A visit from a pari is often a prophetic warning or portent of an event yet to come. Pari have pastel blue skin, wear robes and armor, and have two sets of wings with vivid red feathers sprouting from their back.

PARI

Medium Celestial, Typically Lawful Good

Armor Class 16 (breastplate)
Hit Points 180 (19d8 + 95)
Speed 30 ft., fly 90 ft.

STR	DEX	CON	INT	WIS	CHA
20 (+5)	20 (+5)	20 (+5)	20 (+5)	22 (+6)	22 (+6)

Saving Throws Con +10, Wis +11, Cha +11
Skills Insight +16, Perception +11
Damage Resistances fire, radiant; bludgeoning, piercing, and slashing from nonmagical attacks
Condition Immunities charmed, exhaustion, frightened
Senses truesight 120 ft., passive Perception 21
Languages all, telepathy 120 ft.
Challenge 13 (10,000 XP)　　　　**Proficiency Bonus** +5

Magic Resistance. The pari has advantage on saving throws against spells and other magical effects.

Unusual Nature. The pari doesn't require food, drink, or sleep.

ACTIONS

Multiattack. The pari makes three Mace attacks.

Mace. *Melee Weapon Attack:* +10 to hit, reach 5 ft., one target. *Hit:* 8 (1d6 + 5) bludgeoning damage plus 14 (4d6) radiant damage.

Disorienting Futures. The pari attempts to flood the mind of one creature it can see within 60 feet of itself with visions of the future. The target must succeed on a DC 19 saving throw or take 27 (5d10) psychic damage and have disadvantage on attack rolls until the start of the pari's next turn.

Spellcasting. The pari casts one of the following spells, requiring no material components and using Charisma as the spellcasting ability (spell save DC 19):

At will: *detect evil and good*
2/day each: *cure wounds* (as a 6th-level spell), *lesser restoration*
1/day each: *commune* (as an action), *dispel evil and good*

THE NIGHTSEA'S SUCCOR

AN ADVENTURE FOR 12TH-LEVEL CHARACTERS

AFTER EXPERIENCING A MYSTERIOUS haunting, the characters become embroiled in a quest to restore lost lore to the realm of Djaynai. As they journey from the misty coast of Djaynai to the phantasmagoric realm of Janya beneath the sea, the characters discover not all folk are of one mind concerning the mysterious Djaynaian teachings called the Blackmist Way and the Blackthrone Arts. Some believe these mystical practices and defensive martial strategies should be restored to reestablish the power Djaynai held in the past. Others believe they should only be used as the basis for new arts and then retired. Still others want the lost lore destroyed so Djaynai and Janya can break from the past that binds them. Ultimately, the characters must decide which path to follow and face a forgotten terror in the deepest reaches of the Nightsea.

BACKGROUND

In centuries past, the people of Djaynai employed mystical practices known as the Blackmist Way and defensive martial strategies called the Blackthrone Arts to protect their land. During a period called the Passage of Vultures, raiders assailed the nation and kidnapped its people. Many of those captured escaped into the ocean to found a new aquatic realm called Janya. These escapees included the most skilled practitioners of both arts, but the writings that recorded their lore were lost.

Recently, the People's Stewards, the leaders of Djaynai, enacted the Will of the Insurgent Tides, a collective vow to restore the glorious knowledge and traditions of Djaynai's past. As Atiba-Pa, leader of the People's Stewards, seeks aid in finding lost evidence of the Blackmist Way and the Blackthrone Arts, sinister forces near the undersea city of Janya have roused the spirits defending this lost wisdom. Now these wayward souls travel far to find aid in their homeland, hoping to prevent their people's ancient wisdom from being turned to wicked ends.

PRONUNCIATIONS

The Djaynai and Janya Pronunciations table shows how to pronounce names that appear in this adventure.

DJAYNAI AND JANYA PRONUNCIATIONS

Name	Pronunciation
Anadoua	ahn-AH-dwuh
Atiba-Pa	uh-TEE-buh-puh
Broumane	broo-MAH-nay
Chil-liren	CHILL-l'ren
Djaynai	JAY-nigh
Djeneba	jen-EH-buh
Girscamen	geer-SKA-men
Gurau	guhr-ROW
Haint	HAYNT
Janya	JAN-yuh
Kisaroua	kee-SAH-rwuh
Xoese-Addae	ZO-shee uh-DAY
Zisatta	zee-SAH-tuh

SETTING THE ADVENTURE

Use the following suggestions to help contextualize Djaynai and Janya in a wider world:

Through the Radiant Citadel. Characters traveling from the Radiant Citadel arrive in a clearing 5 miles upriver from Djaynai. If you wish to further detail these lands, use the "Djaynai and Janya Gazetteer" section at this adventure's end as a starting point.

Forgotten Realms. Djaynai could lie among the Nelanther islands or be a new island realm in the Trackless Sea.

Greyhawk. Consider setting Djaynai along the coast of Hepmonaland or as an influential land anywhere along the Azure Sea.

CHARACTER HOOKS

Consider the following ways to involve characters in this adventure:

CASTLE DJAYNAI MONITORS THE ARRIVAL OF TRAVELERS TO THE FOG-SHROUDED PORT OF DJAYNAI.

ZOLTAN BOROS

Ancestor's Invitation. A character's relative or associate is a local official who lives in Djaynai. This contact has received strange dreams in which the spirit of one of their ancestors tries to communicate with them. The contact asks the character to visit them in Djaynai to help them unravel the mystery of their ancestor's message.

Defending the Land. Djaynai's leaders often employ experienced adventurers to exchange knowledge and magic with Djaynaian scouts and defenders. Based on the characters' previous exploits, high-ranking Djaynaian officials request the characters share their expertise.

Lore Masters. An ally in Djaynai or someone who recently visited the city has heard talk of unusual sightings of spirits there. This ally connects the characters to an official who knows more about the spirit sightings and arranges for them to visit.

STARTING THE ADVENTURE

The adventure begins with the characters arriving in the city of Djaynai. Whoever arranged for the adventurers to come to the city has paid for their ship's passage, as well as for rooms at a fine inn on arrival. Read or paraphrase the following text:

> The ship passes through swirling fog that parts to reveal distant cliffs. A port emerges from the mist, nestled among mangroves. Elaborate mud-brick buildings in chalky pastel colors line the shore. A grand mud-brick castle bristling with wooden supports and adorned with pilasters dominates the skyline.

A porter cowled in flowing damask-and-linen fabric greets the characters and offers to escort them to their inn: Anadoua's Rest House, a well-appointed, two-story, mud-brick building painted pale blue. The characters have a full day to rest and explore Djaynai before they meet with the official who arranged their journey at Castle Djaynai. Map 12.1 depicts the central portion of the city of Djaynai, near where the characters are staying.

Anadoua, a friendly, well-dressed human woman, owns the inn and attends to the characters. Each is given a private room, and delicious meals are prepared and served in the common room. Anadoua is happy to share details from the "Djaynai and Janya Gazetteer" section or direct the characters toward the market for any mundane items they require.

THE RESTLESS DEAD

After the characters retire for the night, the quiet of Anadoua's Rest House is disturbed. Read or paraphrase the following text:

> Distant music provides an almost hypnotic undertone to a calm night. Then shouts ring out, shattering the peace. Someone's calling for help!

The characters can tell the shouts are coming from the inn's common room. Following the sound, the characters find the common room lightly obscured, filled with swirling mist. The haze makes the area feel like it's full of fog and floating on a stormy sea. Staff and other patrons who've stumbled out of their rooms are frightened by the sight.

Amid the mist are two terrified figures who cry out, saying "Please, they're coming after us!" and "We can't lose them again!" These **haints** (detailed at the end of this adventure) are spirits murdered during the Passage of Vultures. They've both taken on the lifelike appearances of the artisans they were in life and seek to escape the wicked souls who hold them captive in death. Their sorrow causes them to fear the characters are allies of the invaders who murdered them.

Before the haints can say much, or after 1 round of combat, a **wraith** that looks like a faceless sea raider manifests near them. This is the spirit of one of the wicked captors the haints are trying to escape. The wraith looks around, then signals toward the characters. If the haints haven't already attacked, they back away from the wraith and reluctantly join it in attacking the characters. All three Undead attack until the wraith is destroyed.

SPIRITS' PLEA

When the wraith is defeated, any surviving haints remain, lingering in the center of the common room. If both haints were destroyed, their voices emerge from silhouettes drifting in the lingering mist. The spirits apologize for any harm they caused and entreat the characters for help, sharing the following information:

- Their names are Derek and Violette.
- They were separated from their families and taken from their homes in Djaynai long ago.
- The ship they were on, the *Girscamen*, sank, and they were lost to the sea, along with important tomes they were protecting.

- Something wicked recently disturbed their remains and claimed the lore they were guarding.
- The wraith was one of the haints' captors. The haints are free now, but the tomes they protected are in danger.
- They entreat the characters to help them by finding their resting place and reclaiming the tomes. Only when that knowledge is safe can they find true peace.

Before the spirits can answer all the characters' questions, the mist filling the common room swirls faster, and the characters hear the distant sound of howling wind and pounding waves. The spirits cry out, "Something terrible threatens our precious lore. Please help us, or our people's secrets will be lost forever!" Then the mist roils away to nothing and the haints vanish. The common room returns to normal, but where the spirits vanished, two puddles of water remain, each forming a distinctive sigil. They're clearly visible for a minute before drying.

WHAT WAS LOST

Characters who succeed on a DC 16 Intelligence (Arcana or History) check recognize that the sigils represent the Blackmist Way and the Blackthrone Arts: two local traditions lost during the Passage of Vultures. Any local in the common room or resident of Djaynai who sees a copy of the symbols can identify them and share the basics about these lost traditions—as described in the "Background" section of the adventure.

The name *Girscamen* holds no meaning to anyone.

If questioned, Anadoua is baffled by what's occurred. No other spiritual manifestation has occurred at her inn during the thirty years she's owned it.

CASTLE DJAYNAI

The next morning, guards wearing long black tunics wait to escort the characters to their meeting at Castle Djaynai. The guards are members of Djaynai's elite reconnaissance patrol, called the Lightsea Lancers. They are formal and encourage the characters not to dawdle.

As the characters near Castle Djaynai, read or paraphrase the following description:

> The onyx-colored Castle Djaynai towers over the surrounding structures. It is built of mud bricks and studded with the projecting ends of wooden supports. Stern guards stand watch alongside an open gate.

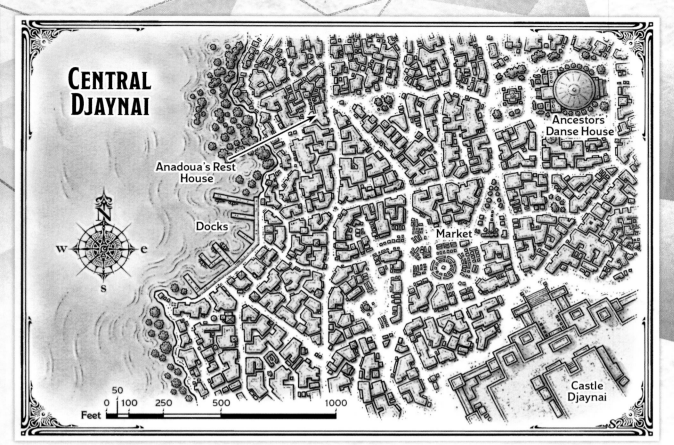

Map 12.1: Central Djaynai

MEETING ATIBA-PA

The characters' escorts lead them through magnificent corridors lined with glass-encased lights. Their trip ends in a tapestry-lined hall whose floor is covered in luxurious rugs. Instead of the official they expected to meet, they see a somber human man with gray hair wearing purple robes and sitting on a central rug among several books and sheafs of paper. As the guards retreat, the man introduces himself as Atiba-Pa, regent of the People's Stewards, and he thanks the characters for coming as he beckons them to join him.

ATIBA-PA

Atiba-Pa (lawful good, human **priest**) is a former Lightsea Lancer and Djaynai's current regent. He is known not only for his falcon-eyed shrewdness but also for his compassion and kindness.

Those close to him know he suffers bleak moods, during which it is challenging to obtain an audience with him. Yet during those times, he is still kind to those he meets, even as he speaks sparse and sorrowful words. Atiba-Pa fears that the Djaynaians' ancient traditions are lost forever, and that their loss puts his homeland at risk. Hearing of others' commitment to reclaiming lost lore acts as a balm for his bleak moods.

Personality Trait. "It isn't our way to simply treat guests with kindness. It is our way to welcome guests as family."

Ideal. "The nobility of each person's essence can never be sullied by the actions of others."

Bond. "It is my honor to serve my homeland. I will not pass beyond our borders for any reason."

Flaw. "I can't let them see me when I'm like this. The melancholy in my bones is mine alone to bear."

WILL OF THE PEOPLE'S STEWARDS

The characters originally planned to meet with a lower-ranked official of the People's Stewards. However, rumors of the events at Anadoua's Rest House reached Atiba-Pa, and he decided to meet with the characters himself.

Atiba-Pa quickly dismisses the characters' original mission in Djaynai and asks them to recount what they saw the previous night. A sheaf of notes before him makes it clear he has heard the story already, but he records any new details the characters share. When the characters' account is complete, Atiba-Pa pauses thoughtfully, then shares the following information:

- The spirits called haints aren't uncommon in Djaynai, as spirits born of sorrow were spawned all too frequently during the Passage of Vultures.
- The manifestation of the sigils connected to the Blackmist Way and the Blackthrone Arts is a noteworthy development, not seen elsewhere.
- The appearance of these symbols is timely, as Atiba-Pa and the People's Stewards believe now is the time to restore the traditions of Djaynai's past—an endeavor they refer to as the Will of the Insurgent Tides.
- If the characters haven't already learned about the Blackmist Way and the Blackthrone Arts, Atiba-Pa shares their history from the "Background" section.

Before continuing, Atiba-Pa pauses and patiently answers any of the characters' questions before moving on to propose a theory. In answering questions, he can share any information from the "Djaynai and Janya Gazetteer" section.

Atiba-Pa's Plan

Once the characters understand how meaningful Atiba-Pa finds their encounter, he proceeds:

> "For centuries, we have dreamed of reclaiming the Blackmist Way and the Blackthrone Arts so our people can defend their lands and our neighbors with all the strength of the past. I believe that you all have connections to Djaynai's ancestors ... perhaps your roots or something gained in your life's journey. This drew the spirits to you, and we must learn why."

Since hearing of the characters' encounter, Atiba-Pa has been engaged in research and verifying stories. Based on his investigations, he believes the following is true:

- The longship *Girscamen* was a raiding ship that captured Djaynaians took over and sank during the Passage of Vultures. The spirits the characters encountered likely died in the struggle before the ship sank.
- Two great stone tomes holding the collected lore of the Blackmist Way and the Blackthrone Arts were lost during the Passage of Vultures.
- The sigils suggest some connection between this lost lore and the *Girscamen*.
- The People's Stewards now hope the tomes were on the *Girscamen* and can be recovered from its wreck.

Regent Atiba-Pa

Atiba-Pa explains that he wants the characters to find the wreck and any hint of Djaynai's lost lore still aboard. In return for finding the ship and whatever it holds, he will reward them with 3,000 gp and whatever they originally came seeking.

The Regent's Mission

Atiba-Pa admits that finding the *Girscamen* won't be easy. No one in Djaynai knows where the ship sank. However, the People's Regents know the undersea folk of Janya have detailed records of wreck sites and other points of interest around their undersea city. A character who succeeds on a DC 14 Intelligence (History) check knows that Janya is an aquatic city populated by the Nightsea chil-liren, an aquatic people descended from the people of Djaynai. Atiba-Pa can also share this information and details about Janya from the "Djaynai and Janya Gazetteer" section. He solemnly speaks of the importance of recovering his people's lore:

> "The Blackmist Way and the Blackthrone Arts helped save Djaynai in the ancient past. Without that knowledge, who knows how we might fare if another threat comes to our shores? If you succeed in this mission, you will help ensure Djaynai's future by reclaiming the strength and traditions of the past." Atiba-Pa then mutters, "If the Night Revelers don't drag us into chaos first."

Characters who succeed on a DC 14 Intelligence (History or Religion) check know the Night Revelers are local philosopher-hedonists who embrace new ideals and oppose the People's Stewards. Atiba-Pa can also share this information. He clearly views the group as misguided and encourages the characters to avoid contact with them.

Making Preparations

To help with the characters' journey to Janya, Atiba-Pa is having a sailboat called the *Beden-Moon*, crewed by Lightsea Lancers, prepared to sail at dawn. He also provides each character with a necklace of black cowrie shells. The necklaces are magic items that provide the same benefits as a *cloak of the manta ray*, except each is activated or deactivated as a bonus action. The necklaces are historic relics of Djaynai, and Atiba-Pa expects to get them back when the characters complete their mission.

The characters are free to do what they please for the rest of the day, and Atiba-Pa has paid for their continued stay at Anadoua's Rest House. When the characters are ready to leave, Atiba-Pa thanks them warmly and summons guards to escort the group from the castle.

The Night Revelers

The characters are free to wander Djaynai while they prepare for their mission. At a point of your choosing, whether the characters are exploring the streets or resting at the inn, an agent of the Night Revelers visits them:

> A figure wearing pale-blue robes approaches, her face obscured by a diaphanous blue veil. "The People's Stewards have lost their way," she whispers. "Many speak of your mystic experiences last night, of what they might mean, and of what causes are championed by those seemingly at the center of them."

The whispering figure identifies herself only as "the Blue," and conveys the message that Djeneba of the Night Revelers has invited the characters to the Ancestors' Danse House for a meeting that night, at any time of the characters' convenience.

If the characters ask what Djeneba wants with them, the Blue says the meeting is to discuss the choice between "Atiba-Pa's folly and Djeneba's glorious revelry." The Blue then takes her leave.

If the characters ignore the summons, skip ahead to the "To the Nightsea" section.

Ancestors' Danse House

Anyone in the city can provide directions to the Ancestors' Danse House, and the characters find it easily. The structure is a combination mausoleum and dance hall, a place where the living can both honor the departed and celebrate.

When the characters arrive, the Blue is waiting for them. She leads them past a pair of sentries into the chalk-white, mud-brick structure. Read the following when the characters enter:

> A captivating drumbeat grows louder as the Blue leads you along a corridor set with archways, at the end of which a cavernous ballroom opens up. Half the space is filled with dancing people, but other figures stand along the sides, vigorously debating.
>
> The Blue leads you to a nearly seven-foot-tall figure draped in a complex arrangement of robes and sashes. Speaking in a beautifully sonorous voice, the figure greets you. "Welcome! I am Djeneba, and we have much to discuss."

Djeneba

Mysterious and bright, with a unique mind that rapidly jumps from one subject to the next, Djeneba (chaotic neutral, human **mage**) is the charismatic voice of the Night Revelers—and a person whose true identity is a mystery to all but the most devoted members of that anarchic group. Djeneba, who speaks with a honeyed tongue that makes others feel understood and embraced, has convinced an increasing number of Djaynaians to embrace the ways of the Night Revelers.

Djeneba is exceptionally tall and always adorned head-to-toe in elaborate layers of form-obscuring gray and blue fabric. All other aspects of Djeneba's appearance and identity are unknown.

Personality Trait. "People sometimes have difficulty following my rapid shift in thoughts."

Ideal. "Indulging in all of life's pleasures is the path to serenity and freedom."

Bond. "The best way to honor our ancestors is to build a new future."

Flaw. "I know my thoughts are hard to follow, but even unfocused minds hold value."

DJENEBA'S CURIOSITY

After leading the characters to a private corner of the ballroom set with fine couches, Djeneba speaks wistfully of the past and more animatedly of the present and future. Use the following points to guide the conversation:

- Ancient Djaynai was a wondrous place, its streets lined with alchemical lights and its people's hearts gilded with the peace of free living. But the past is gone, and it's not coming back.
- Too many in Djaynai focus on the glories of the past, obsessed with searching for ancient lore that might restore that glory. The Night Revelers seek to surpass the heights of ancient Djaynai with new traditions.

Djeneba asks the characters about the spirits they saw, but quickly grows bored and excitedly changes the topic. "We will speak more, friends, but first, let us partake in the night revelry!"

DJENEBA

THE NIGHT REVELRY

Djeneba dances into the crowd, away from the characters. Soon after, nearby musicians approach and encourage the characters to participate in the festivities with them, perhaps by dancing, drumming, or joining a group of Night Revelers in a vigorous debate.

Dancing. The dance of the Night Revelers involves graceful acrobatics and exuberance. A character who succeeds on a DC 10 Dexterity (Acrobatics) check performs the dance well. If the check succeeds by 5 or more, the character is lauded by the dancers around them, one of whom bestows the gift of a fine Djaynaian silk neck scarf.

Drumming. Joining in the percussion performance on one of the hall's large drums requires a character to make a DC 12 Charisma (Performance) check. A character who succeeds impresses their fellow musicians and is allowed to keep a small, resonant drum.

Debating. Debating Night Revelers engage in spirited arguments regarding gradations between states of anarchy and freedom. A character who engages them and succeeds on a DC 14 Charisma (Persuasion) check or a DC 14 Wisdom (Insight) check impresses the philosophers. If the check succeeds by 5 or more, the character stuns the group with some insight, and several philosophers ask the character to sign their favorite journals.

DJENEBA'S OFFER

After the characters interact with the Night Revelers or an hour passes, Djeneba circles back to them. If none of the characters interacted with the Night Revelers, or all the characters failed at their attempts to dance, drum, or debate, Djeneba admits having forgotten about the characters and invites them to leave—clearly, they aren't Night Reveler material.

If one or more characters succeed on their checks to dance, drum, or debate, Djeneba is impressed and pulls the characters aside to share the following information:

> "Word comes to Djeneba of meetings between the so-called People's Stewards and adventurers, yes? And whispers of sigils seen where the spirits of the past are wrought to life by ancient pain. Atiba-Pa knows those sigils as well as I. But I offer you a chance to turn from his empty past and help build the future for Djaynai."

Djeneba assumes Atiba-Pa hired the characters to seek the lore of the Blackmist Way and the Blackthrone Arts, and makes a counteroffer:

- If the characters find the lore of the Blackmist Way and the Blackthrone Arts, they should bring it to the Night Revelers instead of the People's Stewards.
- The Night Revelers hope to take these ancient traditions and forge them into something more powerful.
- With this new power, Djeneba promises the people of Djaynai will be so scintillatingly free that no marauder would dare come to their shores except to engage in the revelry.

Djeneba promises the characters a reward of 4,000 gp and a place of honor among the Night Revelers in return for the lore. If the characters seem reluctant to answer, Djeneba tells them to take their time. The leader offers the characters the use of private rooms in the Ancestors' Danse House, as well as a chance to join in the revelry until the night is spent.

If the party refuses the offer, Djeneba says the characters may yet change their minds if they see firsthand the pain the past carries with it.

To the Nightsea

However the characters spend the night, the same guards who took them to Castle Djaynai the previous morning come to Anadoua's Rest House at dawn to escort them to the docks to board the *Beden-Moon*. If the characters didn't stay at the inn, the guards find them on the street and hasten them to the ship.

Read or paraphrase the following description as the characters reach the docks:

> Beneath the pink dawn sky, a swift-looking, double-masted vessel floats in the aquamarine water. Two wiry figures wearing green-blue armor and matching silk cloaks stand on the deck. One looks dour, the other cheerful.

The boat is a beden-safar, a common vessel in Djaynai. The figures on board are Lightsea Lancers, skilled local scouts and sailors. They wear their hair in natural locs and have warm brown skin.

As the characters approach, the cheerful Lancer introduces himself as Gurau (neutral good, human **veteran**). He is friendly and explains that the two have been informed of the characters' mission and are eager to help. His brooding companion, Kisaroua (neutral good, human **veteran)**, encourages the characters to board swiftly so they can embark. Kisaroua is initially sour, but her mood lightens toward characters who help prepare the ship, which requires a successful DC 14 Strength (Athletics) check.

Once the *Beden-Moon* is underway, its journey takes two hours. During this time, the sailors can share with the characters any of the details about Janya from the "Djaynai and Janya Gazetteer" section.

Preparing to Descend

The *Beden-Moon*'s journey across the calm, shallow waters known as the Lightsea is uneventful. Eventually the water darkens as the ship crosses the edge of the continental shelf, entering the Nightsea. Gurau and Kisaroua furl the sails and drop a sea anchor at what Gurau calls the gateway to Janya, an area of glassy open water that Kisaroua identifies by careful compass and sun reckonings. Gurau offers to wait for the characters and hold on to any equipment the characters don't want to take underwater.

When the characters are ready to descend, Gurau explains what to expect.

- The descent to Janya is approximately 4,500 feet. This should take about 4 minutes for characters who have a swimming speed of 60 feet, or 15 minutes for those who don't have a swimming speed.
- Word has been sent ahead to Xoese-Addae, an emissary of the High Court that rules Janya. He'll meet the characters when they arrive.

Once Gurau has shared these details, Kisaroua has little patience for lingering. She gives the characters three *driftglobes* and encourages them to dive into the water. She pushes in characters who tarry.

Beneath the Waves

Schools of silvery fish swarm around the characters as they descend through the first few hundred feet of the Nightsea. Life in the sunlight zone begins to thin as the water changes from vibrant blue-green to deeper blue. Once the characters descend 500 feet, only dim light illuminates their surroundings. After the characters descend 3,000 feet, they enter an area of complete darkness.

Unless characters are aided by magic, such as the cowrie shell necklaces from Atiba-Pa, they can't swim for a full 8 hours per day. After each hour of swimming, a character must succeed on a DC 10 Constitution saving throw or gain 1 level of exhaustion. A creature that has a swimming speed can swim all day without penalty and uses the normal forced march rules in the *Player's Handbook*. The magic surrounding Janya protects visitors from being harmed or growing exhausted more swiftly because of the deep water's pressure and temperature.

Before proceeding with the following encounters, review the rules for underwater combat in the *Player's Handbook*.

Death Helms a Ghost Ship

After the party descends approximately 3,000 feet, the character who has the highest passive Wisdom (Perception) score spots something unexpected:

> The water begins to churn. From the darkness below glides a glowing, translucent longship, its oars bringing it just below you. A cloudiness covers the deck, swirling into forms vaguely resembling people. On the foredeck, a figure resolves from the cloudiness—a transparent, rough-looking sailor in crusty scale mail, whose eyes blaze.

The name *Girscamen* is plainly emblazoned on the ghost ship's hull. As the ship comes alongside the characters, the first mate (use the **wraith** stat block) is joined by four crew members who are little more than eerie light and drifting skulls (they use the **flameskull** stat block). At first, it appears they are searching for something—they're hunting for the haints that escaped them, Derek and Violette. Once they see the characters, however, the hostile Undead snarl challenges and attack.

Once the Undead are destroyed, the ghost ship breaks apart as if wrecked by a spectral storm and disappears.

Arrival in Janya

As the characters near the seafloor, a pearlescent haze cuts through the darkness. Below they see a shimmering dome of light, a great magical barrier that shelters the city below. As the characters pass through, read or paraphrase the following text:

> A majestic vista spreads beneath the dome: the undersea city of Janya. The city's dark towers are carved with circular windows and covered with designs marked by bioluminescent barnacles. People slip through open corridors between buildings, swimming high above the volcanic rock and coral of the seafloor below.

As the characters take in the beauty of the city, a figure approaches them.

Meeting Xoese-Addae

A figure with kelp-colored hair and stingray-colored skin approaches the characters, introducing himself as Xoese-Addae, an emissary of the High Court of Janya. Xoese-Addae is neutral good and one of the Nightsea chil-liren (see below). He greets the characters warmly, saying his friend Gurau sent word of their coming, and asks what brings them to the city.

THE SHADOWS OF AQUATIC RESIDENTS FLIT BENEATH THE IRIDESCENT MAGIC THAT PROTECTS THE UNDERSEA CITY OF JANYA.

Once the characters relate their story, Xo-ese-Addae ponders a moment. If the characters mention the phantom ship they encountered on the way to Janya, he is particularly concerned. Many of the wreck sites dotting the seafloor around Janya are known to be haunted, but he's never heard of similar manifestations in open water.

Xoese-Addae notes that if anyone has heard of ghost ships or knows if the wreck of the *Girscamen* is charted, it's Zisatta, who commands Janya's security force. He offers to escort the characters to the Cerulean Lyceum, Janya's great bardic college, where Zisatta and the other members of the High Court are attending a gala.

If the characters want to explore Janya, Xo-ese-Addae can guide the characters around the city before taking them to the Cerulean Lyceum. Use the "Djaynai and Janya Gazetteer" section to guide explorations of Janya.

NIGHTSEA CHIL-LIREN

Xoese-Addae or any of Janya's other residents can tell the characters that the undersea city of Janya is populated by descendants of Djaynai who escaped into the sea during the Passage of Vultures. The magic of Djaynaian transmuters and that of the Nightsea itself gave these people the ability to live beneath the waves. Now known as Nightsea chil-liren, the people of Janya look similar to the humans of Djaynai, but their brown skin is often tinged shades of gray, and eel-like fins run along their arms and legs.

Nightsea chil-liren use the **merfolk** stat block with the following changes:

- They have darkvision out to a range of 60 feet.
- Replace the Amphibious trait with the trait below.

Water Breathing. Nightsea chil-liren can breathe only underwater.

GALA AT THE CERULEAN LYCEUM

Xoese-Addae leads the characters to the Cerulean Lyceum, a series of vaulted, crystalline halls set around a broad quadrangle. When the characters arrive, the quad is filled with Janyans enraptured by the low-toned, hypnotic music of a group of bards.

Xoese-Addae leads the characters to a private audience suite overlooking the quad, occupied by a single Janyan wearing fine, billowing robes—this is Zisatta.

ZISATTA

The aloof Zisatta is a member of the High Court and commands Janya's security forces, called the Billowing Patrol for their sable robes that undulate like jellyfish. She is lawful neutral and one of the Nightsea chil-liren (see the "Nightsea Chil-liren"

ZISATTA

section). Tattoos of ancient Djaynaian symbols peak out from beneath her flowing robes—signs of her fervent desire to prove her connection and dedication to Djaynai.

Personality Trait. "I have more important matters to attend to than you."

Ideal. "Tradition must be preserved at all costs."

Bond. "While Janya and Djaynai are separate nations, we must defend our Djaynaian kin."

Flaw. "I'm enraged by any suggestion that I am not Djaynaian."

WHAT ZISATTA KNOWS

Zisatta rises without introducing herself and is initially indifferent to the characters. She acknowledges Xoese-Addae and imperiously asks why he and his surface-world friends have interrupted her enjoyment of the performance.

Use the following points to guide the initial conversation, but see "Unexpected Interruption" below if the characters get into the details of their mission:

- As soon as a character speaks, Zisatta interrupts and orders all the characters to introduce themselves rather than first sharing her own name.
- If the characters speak about the ghost ship, Zisatta tensely reports that sightings of a ghostly vessel above Janya began several days ago.
- Zisatta remembers the name *Girscamen* and says the Billowing Patrol knows the location of its wreckage.

UNEXPECTED INTERRUPTION

Before the characters can share all the details of their mission with Zisatta, the door to her suite bursts open, and a figure swims in: Brother Broumane, another member of the High Court.

Brother Broumane announces he learned of a group of surface-world heroes coming to Janya through "friends among the Night Revelers." He saw the characters arrive while he was watching the performance and wants to learn if they have come to Janya on "mercenary business from the surface."

BROTHER BROUMANE

Brother Broumane is one of the charismatic leaders of the New Janyan movement, a political group focused on Janya's self-reliance and future greatness. He secretly also heads the Untethered, a cult dedicated to chaotic philosophies. He's chaotic neutral and one of the Nightsea chil-liren (see the "Nightsea Chil-liren" section). He wears robes made from a patchwork of rough-spun and fine white fabrics.

Personality Trait. "I want our culture to swim free from irrelevant traditions."

Ideal. "Janya is its own realm."

Bond. "We serve Janya by defining the future instead of dwelling on the past."

Flaw. "Cross me and you'll regret it more than you can imagine."

CAUGHT IN THE MIDDLE

Both Zisatta and Brother Broumane want to learn the scope of the characters' mission. They largely ignore each other as they each attempt to win the characters to their side. During the conversation, Zisatta focuses on the following points:

- Zisatta tries to discern whether the characters are working for the People's Stewards and is pleased if they are.
- She tries to get the characters to admit their mission is connected to lost lore essential to the future of both Djaynai and Janya.

At the same time, Brother Broumane focuses on the following points:

- Brother Broumane tries to find out if the characters are working for the Night Revelers and is pleased if they are.
- He tries to get the characters to admit they're seeking the outdated lore of a foreign land.
- He claims his faction has ways of learning everything the Billowing Patrol knows, and if there's information the characters need, he can provide it.

The two High Court members eventually insist the characters choose who they—and, by extension, Djaynai—will align with. Xoese-Addae, a consummate politician, keeps his opinions to himself.

A FRAUGHT DEBATE

It should be clear that the characters' mission puts them in the middle of a political and philosophical debate that stretches back generations. Zisatta's group, the Djaynaists, believe in cultivating the Janyan people's connection to their original homeland, Djaynai. Brother Broumane's group, the New Janyans, want Janyans to forge their own identity.

BROTHER BROUMANE

ANDREW MAR

The characters are unlikely to have strong opinions one way or the other but need to get information from one of the High Court members.

Choosing Sides. The easiest route to gaining the information the characters need is to declare support for one High Court member's philosophy. This earns the chosen person's favor, but the other leaves, insulted. While the insulted politician won't oppose the characters' mission, they take the characters' choice as indicative of all surface dwellers' stances, which might fray the relationship between the two civilizations.

Diplomacy. If the characters don't want to publicly align themselves with either faction, a character brings the debate to an end civilly by succeeding on a DC 16 Charisma (Deception or Persuasion) check. The characters can then reconvene with either High Court member in private. Alternatively, if a character succeeds on a DC 20 Charisma (Persuasion) check, they present a point that both court members agree to, winning the support of both.

Ending the Debate

Whichever High Council member the characters align with can get them directions to the *Girscamen*'s wreck with only a few hours of work. But they pass on their information only if the characters agree to a request.

What Zisatta Wants. In return for directions to the wreck of the *Girscamen*, Zisatta wants the characters to bring her whatever lore they find so her people can learn more about their lost heritage. She asserts that it is her duty to share this cultural wisdom with the People's Stewards (and believes that doing so will validate the viewpoint of her faction). Through compelling roleplaying or by succeeding on a DC 14 Charisma (Persuasion) check, a character can convince her to settle for making a copy of whatever they find before they return to Djaynai—a process that takes a week.

What Brother Broumane Wants. Brother Broumane tells the characters the location of the *Girscamen*'s wreck if they swear to return any lore they find to him so he can destroy it. When the party returns, a character can fool Brother Broumane by claiming they found nothing and succeeding on a DC 18 Charisma (Deception) check. If the characters return and give him something that looks like an ancient relic but isn't the lost Djaynaian lore, they can convince him it was all they found with a successful DC 14 Charisma (Deception) check.

Destination in the Depths. Once the characters have reached an agreement with a High Court member, that person provides a map of the region around Janya with a location 15 miles from the city marked.

This spot, known as the Trench of Love Lost, is where members of the Billowing Patrol found the wreck of the *Girscamen*.

Xoese-Addae is familiar with the region around Janya and is willing to escort the characters to the top of the trench. If the characters please, they can spend some time in Janya before seeking the *Girscamen*.

Trench of Love Lost

The region around Janya is well guarded, but dangers still occasionally slip past the Billowing Patrol. Following Xoese-Addae, the trip to the Trench of Love Lost takes 2½ hours for characters who have a swimming speed (or 10 hours otherwise). Along the way, the characters might encounter a variety of deep-sea creatures, such as three **giant sharks** feeding on the remains of deep sea whales. No spirits or ghost ships make an appearance, though.

As the characters near the trench, read or paraphrase the following description:

> Meadows of feathery, pale-pink sea lilies move slowly to and fro in the gentle current. The view is idyllic up to the trench's edge, which crumbles away to deeper depths.

Xoese-Addae assures the characters that the shipwreck should be below. He agrees to wait for the characters at the top of the trench for a few hours but is eager to get back to the safety of Janya as soon as possible.

Trench of Lost Love Features

The following features are common throughout the trench and the surrounding areas:

Ceilings. The ceilings of both the ship and ruins are 10 feet high.

Darkness. All areas are cast in complete darkness.

Underwater. All areas are fully submerged and airless.

MAP 12.2: TRENCH OF LOVE LOST

TRENCH OF LOVE LOST LOCATIONS

The following locations are keyed to map 12.2.

T1: TRENCH

The trench is 200 feet deep. At the bottom is the wreck of the *Girscamen*. Read the following description as the characters come within sight of the wreck:

> Midnight-colored coral covers the trench's sheer walls. As the bottom of the trench comes into view, you see the wreckage of an ancient, familiar-looking longship gripped by the spreading coral. Silt and debris cover the deck, but the name *Girscamen* is still visible on the hull.

Characters within 10 feet of the *Girscamen* feel a harmless supernatural chill—an effect of the unquiet spirits haunting the ship. If characters succeed on a DC 14 Intelligence (Arcana or Religion) check, they can tell restless spirits dwell nearby.

T2: WRECK

> The *Girscamen* evidently broke in two when it sank. Half the ship is embedded in the trench wall and the coral around it; the rest was lost to the tides. A sizable hole pierces the deck and the hull below.

The first time a creature that isn't a Construct or Undead comes within 5 feet of the ship's wreckage, the creature must make a DC 16 Wisdom saving throw. On a failed save, the creature takes 21 (6d6) psychic damage and telepathically hears dozens of drowning cries.

Characters who inspect the hole in the ship determine it continues through the bottom of the vessel, and beyond that a hole punched through the bottom of the trench leads into area T3 20 feet below.

Any other search of the ship reveals nothing except for ancient, rusted chain mail and scraps of decaying armor not of Djaynaian design.

T3: BROKEN ENTRY

The hole below the ship extends through the ceiling of an ancient, hidden structure. Characters who have the Stonecunning trait can tell falling rocks punched through into the structure. The chambers below are made of interlocking, dark gray stones carved into puzzle-piece-like shapes.

T4: OBSIDIAN THRONE

> The walls of this chamber are inscribed with images of sea creatures and geometric patterns. At its center, a short platform bears a high-backed, obsidian throne sculpted with stylized images similar to those on the walls. Behind and to the sides of the platform are four deep, rounded alcoves.
>
> A spectral, armored figure with blazing emerald eyes appears from behind the throne and advances. "More fools of Djaynai? I'm the captain of the *Girscamen*, and you will meet the same fate as all who set foot upon my vessel!"

This hostile **wraith** wears armor similar to that of the wraiths the characters battled previously. It fights to the death.

Ancient Art. A character who succeeds on a DC 14 Intelligence (History) check can tell the carved walls and throne are ancient and were perhaps made by the very first Janyans as a way to preserve sacred knowledge in a secure place. A *detect magic* spell reveals an aura of abjuration magic around the throne.

MIKE SCHLEY

Lurking Aboleth. In the shadows of the southwest alcove lurks the **aboleth** Ylch. It doesn't interfere with the wraith's attack and won't initially threaten the characters. Once it is revealed, it telepathically invites the characters to talk. Use the following information to guide the conversation.

- Ylch recently discovered this ruin, created by ancient Janyan stewards of knowledge.
- Ylch was attracted here by the aura of the Undead still suffering from the legacy of the Passage of Vultures.
- In investigating the site, Ylch disrupted the unquiet spirits of the *Girscamen*. It has been using its magic to control the wraiths that arose from that terrible ship.
- It wants to know what brought the characters here so it can better understand the value of the site and the magical relics it has discovered.

If the characters reveal what they seek, Ylch realizes the value of the tomes in area T5. After this, or if the characters are hostile toward it, Ylch telepathically calls upon the lingering crew of the *Girscamen* to aid it and then attacks.

Sunken Souls. At the aboleth's call, three **flameskulls**—the remains of the hateful crew of the *Girscamen*—come to the aboleth's defense via the passage to area T2. As the flameskulls enter the area, a familiar **haint**, Violette, appears in her incorporeal form and intercepts one of the flameskulls. Violette, now free from the crew of the *Girscamen*, is friendly toward the characters and keeps the flameskull she intercepted at bay. After 2 rounds she defeats that flameskull, then aids the characters against any remaining foes.

Once the aboleth is defeated, the remaining flameskulls flee to area T1 and then out of the trench. Violette offers a sincere nod to the characters, then joins Derek in area T5.

T5: FORGOTTEN LIBRARY

> The ceiling is covered with a mosaic of wide-eyed figures swimming through a sea teeming with life. Below, the walls are lined with strange, rusted weapons and the stone shelves of a library.

Soon after the characters enter the room, the friendly **haint** Derek appears—he's joined by Violette if the battle in area T4 occurred. Derek and Violette have been protecting the books hidden in this chamber. Upon recognizing the characters, Derek thanks them for coming to recover the tomes he and Violette have been guarding for so long. Derek then directs the characters' attention to a shadowy shelf where rest two elegant tomes made from iron-bound

pages of carved slate. These books bear the symbols the characters saw after the haunting at Anadoua's Rest House and are the *Book of the Blackthrone's Aegis* and the *Book of the Blackmist*.

Treasure. The weapons along the walls are rusted and made for creatures with non-Humanoid anatomies. However, two magic items inscribed with Djaynaian symbols are usable and remain intact: a *sun blade* and a *staff of frost*.

LEGACY OF THE LOST

Once the aboleth is defeated and the writings in area T5 are recovered, the spirits of Derek and Violette appear before the characters in their lifelike forms. They thank the group for defeating the aboleth and ask the characters to return the tomes to their rightful owners, the people of Djaynai. They don't elaborate on what group that might mean and know nothing of Janya. If the characters agree to return the tomes, the two haints invite the characters to bow deeply to the throne in area T4 to honor the ancestors who once sat upon it. If the characters do so, the lingering spirits reward the party (see "Gifts of the Deep" below). Should one or more of the characters refuse, Derek and Violette quietly fade away.

GIFT OF THE DEEPS

After the characters agree to return the tomes, the throne in area T5 starts shedding dim light. Each character who bows before the obsidian throne for the first time gains the charm below (a type of supernatural gift detailed in the *Dungeon Master's Guide*). Once all the characters bow before the throne or 10 minutes pass, the light fades and the throne loses its magical properties.

Seasoul Touched. Inspired by teachings in the Blackmist Way and Blackthrone Arts that ease the distinction between body and soul, this charm allows you to cast the *gaseous form* spell as an action, with no spell components required. Once used three times, the charm goes away.

CONCLUSION

Once the characters finish exploring, where they go next is up to them. Xoese-Addae is eager to take them back to Janya or can be convinced to escort them to the surface where they left the *Beden-Moon*. The journey back to Djaynai is uneventful.

How the adventure concludes depends on who the characters return the tomes to.

- If the characters bring the tomes to Atiba-Pa, he is overjoyed, declaring the Blackmist Way and the Blackthrone Arts will be a boon to Djaynai's people and help protect its shores. The People's Stewards hold a solemn ceremony of honor in Castle Djaynai followed by festivities that spill onto the streets.

- If the characters bring the books to Djeneba, the Night Reveler leader speaks ecstatically of how they will remake the old ways into new arts, and how any foes will be awed and want to emulate the people of Djaynai and their revels.
- If the characters take the books to Zisatta, she holds onto the books for further study, seeking to understand them comprehensively before returning them to Djaynai.
- If the characters deliver the books to Brother Broumane, he scans the books for knowledge he believes the Untethered can improve upon before he destroys them.
- If the characters admit to leaving the tomes in Janya or, worse, destroying them at the behest of Brother Broumane, Atiba-Pa is mournful while Djeneba is philosophical.

No matter the fate of the books of lore, the characters are celebrated by some and vilified by others, but they have an opportunity to serve in the future of Djaynai. They might be offered permanent positions of service to the People's Stewards or ritually inducted as members of the Night Revelers. Additionally, friction between Djaynai and Janya might arise if the characters followed the will of one city at the expense of the other.

In any case, many in both Djaynai and Janya come to wonder what other powerful Djaynaian wisdom might rest in the deep, waiting to be rediscovered.

DJAYNAI AND JANYA GAZETTEER

Modern Djaynai is a coastal realm descended from a grand civilization. Though the nation has never been defeated by external forces, its fortunes were greatly diminished hundreds of years ago after raiders perpetrated atrocities upon the land and its people in a series of attacks known as the Passage of Vultures. Djaynai's defenders drove the raiders off, albeit at a high cost. Even in its diminished state, the nation serves as an exemplar of self-sovereignty and dignity, defended by scouts known as the Lightsea Lancers, who watch for bandit groups and marauders aiming to raid Djaynai and its neighbors.

During the Passage of Vultures, countless captured Djaynaians leaped from the ships of the marauders, like raindrops falling into the sea. "Freedom now!" they shouted as they sought the ocean's embrace. In the midnight depths, those ancient Djaynaians called upon their magic and that of the Nightsea, and they were transformed into beings dubbed Nightsea chil-liren, gifted with the ability to live in the deep. Over centuries, they became the civilization known as Janya.

Modern Janya is a majestic, deep-sea city protected by magical wards that resemble an opalescent aurora with the sheen of a blue-black pearl. Its buildings are castle-like structures resembling those of Djaynai above, but made from magically hardened, obsidian-hued silt and studded by crystalline support beams jutting from the smooth walls.

DJAYNAI AND JANYA FEATURES

Those familiar with Djaynai and Janya typically know the following details:

Hallmarks. These lands are known for their ancestral legacies, political schisms, and transformed cultures.

Djaynai's People. Djaynai's folk are mostly human and have tightly curled hair, which is worn in a variety of natural and ornate styles. Their lustrous skin tones range from warm ebony and mahogany to the coppery glow of the setting sun. Gnomes, dragonborn, and other Humanoid folk are common and accepted in Djaynai.

Djaynai's Languages. The people of Djaynai speak Djaynaian, Common, and occasionally Aquan.

Janya's People. Janyans are an amphibious people of Djaynaian descent called Nightsea chil-liren (see the "Nightsea Chil-liren" section earlier in this adventure). They typically resemble lithe humans with sharp teeth and ribbon-like fins along their appendages. Their skin tones are usually desaturated shades of gray-brown.

Janya's Languages. The people of Janya speak an archaic form of Djaynaian that allows easy if slow communication with people who speak the modern tongue, as well as Common and Aquan.

NOTEWORTHY SITES

Djaynai is a peaceful land dominated by mangrove forests along the southern coast and jagged cliffs to the north. Its calm coastal waters are known as the Lightsea, but beyond a continental shelf the waters grow suddenly deeper. This is the Nightsea, the shadowy depths that hold the vibrant city of Janya.

CASTLE DJAYNAI

Castle Djaynai is made from onyx-colored mud brick studded with wooden pilasters and features a roof of sharp pinnacles. It is home to the rotating representative government called the People's Stewards, and its chambers hold ornate rugs and tapestries, the fragrance of essential oils, and performances of hypnotic music, which combine to create a warm welcome for invited guests. To deter intruders, the castle is lined with magical traps that polymorph victims into the saltwater salamanders (use the **lizard** stat block) common among Djaynai's mangroves.

Ancestors' Danse House

Home to the spiritual faction known as the Night Revelers, the Ancestors' Danse House in Djaynai is a mausoleum with smooth, chalky-white, mud-brick walls. Its library contains numerous scrolls of magical lore, and thousands of ancestors' bones in ossuaries throughout the site are enchanted to magically rise as **skeletons** and defend against would-be-thieves.

Trench of Love Lost

This great undersea trench near Janya resonates with mystery and foreboding. It is named in memory of the countless Djaynaians who vanished into its depths during the earliest days of the Passage of Vultures, before the first Nightsea chil-liren came to be. The trench is defined by the pale-pink meadows of feathery creatures known as sea lilies that grow along its edges. Scouts of Janya's Billowing Patrol have explored only a small fraction of the trench, which contains the wrecks of numerous ships and mysterious sites.

Cerulean Lyceum

A center of culture in Janya, the Cerulean Lyceum is a great bardic college with a connected series of vaulted halls set around a broad quadrangle. Icicle-like spikes surround the Cerulean Lyceum's main conservatory, which resembles a massive blue crystal. Djaynju, opera from Djaynai, is just one of the many musical forms practiced and perfected here.

Life in Djaynai and Janya

The following truths are known to people who dwell in Djaynai or Janya, and to travelers who spend time in those realms. Those above and below the sea share similar cultures and values, though Janya's aquatic environment drives some differences.

Education and Religion

Both realms' culture is tightly tied to Djaynai's historical roots as an advanced, influential civilization. Education and creativity are the foundations of the culture, and its people embrace philosophy, magic, mathematics, and the study of underwater societies. In keeping with these traditions, spirituality isn't focused on gods, but on revering and emulating forces such as liberation, fluidity, and change. As such, most people are open to the spiritual views of others, as long as those views don't embrace evil.

Food and Clothing

Meals are considered sacred in Djaynai, and wasting food is a major breach of etiquette. Key ingredients of Djaynai's cuisine include banana, groundnut, milk from several types of animals, red and black beans, and chili peppers. In Janya, edible undersea plants form the bulk of people's diet, supplemented by ingredients imported from Djaynai. As a rule, both peoples eschew eating meat.

Djaynaian clothing combines rough-spun and delicate materials, and it is common to see linen with lace or damask with crocheted fabrics in the same outfit. Most Djaynaians wear a form of shawl or cloak at all times, and their fashion favors muted colors. Headwear is typically worn in public, most commonly cowls with pointed caps, wide-brimmed hats, or tagelmusts and tasuwarts that can function as headgear and veil. Clothing in Janya parallels Djaynaian style but features materials like eel skin and elegantly woven sea grasses.

Government in Djaynai

The government of Djaynai is called the People's Stewards, whose leadership ranks change whenever a significant number of citizens publicly call for new elections. All citizens of Djaynai are simultaneously seen as nobles, workers, and potential Stewards. The anarchic spiritual group called the Night Revelers poses a challenge to the Stewards' authority, arguing that Djaynai must abandon all government to truly be free.

The security forces that protect Djaynai—including the scouts known as Lightsea Lancers—are highly effective in their roles, but Djaynaian law emphasizes redemption over punishment. In the direst criminal cases, controversial rituals are performed to prevent the offender from acting on their wicked impulses. The offender is then banished for life.

Government in Janya

Janya is an oligarchy ruled by a group called the High Court, some members of which are able to contact key leaders in Djaynai on rare occasions through magical means. Members of the High Court—and the many agents and liaisons who serve it—work in the city's magnificent Council Chamber, which is housed within the shell of a gigantic whelk. However, friction between the Djaynaist and New Janyan factions of the High Court can turn meetings into fraught debates.

The security forces of Janya are called the Billowing Patrol, named for their flowing, dark robes. Their headquarters is a looming silvery fortress guarded by imposing sentries in armor bristling with spikes.

Music

Traditional music in both realms functions to spiritually transfigure listeners. It emphasizes low tones and syncopated rhythms, utilizing stringed instruments such as the lute-like guembri, akoting, and xalam; the musical bow known as the berimbau; and the sonorous atabaque drum.

Names

Djaynaians and Janyans use only single names publicly, reserving family names for close loved ones. In both realms, those family names combine Djaynaian words focused on nature, such as Pineshadow or Misthare. The following are common public names:

Feminine. Chainay, Fantou, Imané, Kadidia, Khonjit, Lashall

Masculine. Adesola, Alphiadou, Bacar, D'arael, Darweshi, Mayn

Gender-Neutral. Akkia, Evlyn, Jayvyn, Kellar, Kioné, Lakarai

Legends of Djaynai and Janya

Djaynai has been a beacon of independence and knowledge for millennia. Indeed, Djaynai has ultimately prevailed over all invaders, with a key role played by the mystical practices known as the Blackmist Way and Blackthrone Arts. Unfortunately, Djaynai's friendly neighboring realms are more often threatened. For instance, inscrutable lizardfolk in the wetlands periodically congregate and cause havoc in the nearby ocean. The Lightsea Lancers—who take their name from the shallow coastal waters Djaynaians call the Lightsea—was formed to monitor such threats before they impact Djaynai. Travelers occasionally come to Djaynai to learn the Lightsea Lancers' ways, as their heroics, dance-like martial arts, and knowledge of transmutation magic are renowned throughout Djaynai and beyond.

Beneath the Nightsea, the realm of Janya has its own tales. Many tell of how early Janyans were focused not only on rebuilding their lives but on preserving what they treasured from the land above. To keep such lore safe, ancestral Janyans built structures in hidden reaches, like the Trench of Love Lost, to archive sacred wisdom before it was lost. Eventually, though, such archives faded from memory. Profound Djaynaian secrets remain hidden in the deep, awaiting rekindling.

Adventures in Djaynai and Janya

Consider the plots on the Djaynai and Janya Adventures table when planning adventures in these realms.

Djaynai and Janya Adventures

d6	Adventure
1	The People's Stewards hope to raise the regent Atiba-Pa's stormy mood by having the characters recover his famed magical cutlass, stolen by seafaring **assassins**.
2	A Lightsea Lancer seeks the characters' aid in stopping twin **sahuagin barons** and their band from raiding kelp farms between Djaynai and Janya.
3	Night Revelers invite the characters to join their seaside festivities, but they unknowingly disturb a coven of **sea hags**.
4	**Lizardfolk** marauders raid farms in lands adjacent to Djaynai, and the Lightsea Lancers seek adventurers to help repel them.
5	A botched memorial ritual at the Ancestors' Danse House transports the characters into the Djaynai of the past, bringing them face-to-face with a band of foul invaders.
6	While visiting Janya, the characters encounter a shipwreck laden with treasure—and **ghosts**. The spirits wish to be put to rest, but the **adult bronze dragon** that sank the ship considers them part of its hoard.

Characters from Djaynai

If players create characters from Djaynai or with ties to Janya, consider asking them the following questions during character creation:

How do you feel about the Will of the Insurgent Tides? Do you support the quest to recover the lore of the Blackmist Way and the Blackthrone Arts, or are they relics of an unrecoverable past?

Do you or anyone in your family have a connection to the Night Revelers? Do you embrace that faction's call to anarchy, or do you seek to undermine that call before it spreads further?

Whether you come from Djaynai or Janya, how much do you know of the other realm? Do you consider yourself a person of two worlds? Or do you yearn for a greater understanding of your kin on the other side of the water's surface?

HAINT

Rising from the sorrowful dead, haints are spirits that change their shape in tragic imitation of what they once were. A haint can shift from its spectral form to appear as the corporeal Humanoid it was in life, passing as a living creature. These spirits might mistakenly view innocents as those who killed them or entreat mortals to exact revenge on their behalf.

HAINT

Medium Undead, Typically Neutral

Armor Class 12
Hit Points 75 (10d8 + 30)
Speed 30 ft., fly 30 ft. (hover)

STR	DEX	CON	INT	WIS	CHA
7 (−2)	15 (+2)	17 (+3)	10 (+0)	13 (+1)	17 (+3)

Skills Deception +6, Stealth +8
Damage Resistances acid, fire, lightning, thunder; bludgeoning, piercing, and slashing damage from nonmagical attacks
Damage Immunities cold, necrotic, poison
Condition Immunities charmed, exhaustion, frightened, grappled, paralyzed, petrified, poisoned, prone, restrained
Senses darkvision 60 ft., passive Perception 11
Languages any languages it knew in life
Challenge 7 (2,900 XP)　　　　**Proficiency Bonus** +3

Incorporeal Movement. The haint can move through other creatures and objects as if they were difficult terrain. It takes 5 (1d10) force damage if it ends its turn inside an object.

Unusual Nature. The haint doesn't require air, food, drink, or sleep.

ACTIONS

Multiattack. The haint makes two Sorrowful Touch attacks.

Sorrowful Touch. *Melee Spell Attack:* +6 to hit, reach 5 ft., one creature. *Hit:* 21 (4d8 + 3) psychic damage.

Change Shape. The haint magically assumes the appearance of the Humanoid it was in life, while retaining its game statistics. The assumed appearance ends if the haint is reduced to 0 hit points or uses an action to end it.

BONUS ACTIONS

Shared Sorrow. The haint targets one creature it can see within 60 feet of itself that is missing any hit points, sharing its own torment with this pained soul. The target must succeed on a DC 14 Wisdom saving throw or be incapacitated.

　A creature can repeat the saving throw at the end of each of its turns, ending the effect on itself on a success. If a creature's saving throw is successful or the effect ends for it, the creature is immune to the haint's Shared Sorrow for the next 24 hours.

BURIED DYNASTY

AN ADVENTURE FOR 13TH-LEVEL CHARACTERS

FOR THOUSANDS OF YEARS, ANCIENT MAGIC and *potions of longevity* sustained imperial rule over the land of Great Xing. Each emperor's supernaturally long life span ensured the peace and stability of the realm. But now the imperial secrets of longevity have been lost, and if the long rule of the White Jade Emperor draws to a close, control of the empire will pass to another in a disruptive transition the likes of which have been unknown for generations.

BACKGROUND

Grand Secretary Wei Feng Ying governs at the emperor's command. For years, she has known that imperial alchemists sustain the emperor's life using *potions of longevity* enhanced with an ingredient that makes them more potent. But now the source of that ingredient has been depleted. The secretary fears that this additive—powdered shards from the eggshell of the legendary Dragon of Heavenly Blessings—might be irreplaceable.

Secretary Wei has sent agents to scour the land for imperial troves containing *potions of longevity*, hoping to find more of the lost ingredient. Recently, this search unearthed ancient court documents mentioning a secret cache belonging to the Mountain Cloud Empress, a mysterious figure of the long-fallen Yun dynasty. Secretary Wei gave orders to begin excavating the Old City buried beneath Yongjing, the capital of Great Xing, and she now seeks adventurers to investigate the ruins under the guise of historical scholarship—not sharing with them that they are actually hunting for a specific secret.

PRONUNCIATIONS

The Yongjing Pronunciations table shows how to pronounce names that appear in this adventure.

YONGJING PRONUNCIATIONS

Name	Pronunciation
Deng Bo Huan	dung boh hwan
Lio Gong	lyo gong

Name	Pronunciation
Lu Zhong Yin	loo jong yin
Tulao	too-lao
Wei Feng Ying	way fung ying
Xing	shing
Yongjing	yong-jing

SETTING THE ADVENTURE

Use the following suggestions to help locate Yongjing in a wider world:

Through the Radiant Citadel. Characters traveling from the Radiant Citadel arrive less than a mile from the southern gate of Yongjing in a plaza staffed by helpful attendants. If you want to add further detail to the lands around Yongjing, use the "Yongjing Gazetteer" section at this adventure's end as a starting point.

Forgotten Realms. Yongjing could be the capital of any nation east of the Sunrise Mountains or of a new island realm in the Trackless Sea. Alternatively, lands such as Chessenta, Impiltur, or another place along the southern Sword Coast could be recast as parts of Great Xing.

Mystara. Yongjing might lie west of the Republic of Darokin and unite multiple lands under the banner of its empire.

CHARACTER HOOKS

Consider the following ways to involve characters in this adventure:

Bargaining for Life. The characters need life-extending magic. Secretary Wei hears of their plight and offers to provide the characters with a *potion of longevity* if they complete a mission for her.

Bureaucratic Invitation. Secretary Wei invites the characters to Yongjing for a meeting about investigating the ruins of the Old City beneath Yongjing.

Political Pawns. An agent of the emperor or his family asks the characters to meet with Secretary Wei and aid her in any way they can—thereby drawing the characters into the city's politics.

ANY WHO WOULD SPEAK WITH THE WHITE JADE EMPEROR MUST PETITION FOR AN AUDIENCE AT THE HALL OF DIVINE WISDOM.

JULIAN KOK

SECRETS OF IMMORTALITY

This adventure embroils characters in a conspiracy involving the highest levels of Yongjing's government. Before running the adventure, familiarize yourself with the "Yongjing Gazetteer" section. Keep the following details of the conspiracy secret, revealing them only when the adventure text instructs you to do so.

DRAGON'S BLESSING

When the rulers of Yongjing reach an advanced age, they use *potions of longevity* to increase their life span. These potions are supplemented with a rare reagent called Dragon's Blessing. The primary ingredient of this reagent is powdered eggshell from a legendary being known as the Dragon of Heavenly Blessings.

Normally, a creature can benefit from only a limited number of *potions of longevity* before continued consumption is likely to age the drinker rather than reduce their age. When a pinch of Dragon's Blessing is added to a *potion of longevity*, however, the draught has no chance of aging its drinker no matter how many *potions of longevity* that individual has consumed. With enough of this reagent and enough *potions of longevity*, Yongjing's rulers could conceivably live forever. But this immortality is not

protection against a violent death: murder, revolution, or some other dire fate has ended each past emperor's rule.

END OF AN EMPEROR

The emperor of Great Xing is dying—he just doesn't know it yet. In a few months, when he next uses a *potion of longevity* to extend his life, he'll learn that the imperial supply of Dragon's Blessing has been depleted—and this potion might age him rather than adding years to his life.

Currently, only the imperial alchemists and their overseer, Grand Secretary Wei, are aware of this fact. The alchemists have not made this information known, at the grand secretary's command.

END OF AN ERA

Grand Secretary Wei, the leader of the emperor's government, knows that the secret of the emperor's long life has been depleted. A lifelong servant of the empire, Wei fears the upheaval that historically occurs after the death of a ruler, as several claimants to the throne vie for power in the political vacuum. In response, Wei has set her considerable network of agents to covertly work toward two goals:

Preserving the Emperor. Assuring the emperor's continued rule is the easiest way to maintain the nation's peace and political continuity. Secretary Wei's most trusted agents have been quietly scouring the land for more Dragon's Blessing, seeking it in the ruins and crypts of dynasties past.

Preserving the Empire. Fearing the emperor's death might be inevitable, Secretary Wei cements her political power and firms up her alliances behind the scenes. She hopes to make her political position unassailable so she can ease the transition of power from the old emperor to a worthy successor of her choice.

The Grand Secretary hides the truth of the emperor's condition from her liege and all but her most trusted agents, believing herself the only person fit to steer the empire through the challenges to come. Maintaining this secret is of the utmost importance, because general knowledge of the emperor's looming demise would precipitate a host of political schemes throughout Yongjing's vast bureaucracy.

STARTING THE ADVENTURE

When the characters are ready to attend their audience with Secretary Wei, they must meet her at the Hall of Divine Wisdom in Yongjing (see the "Yongjing Gazetteer" section). Read or paraphrase the following description when they arrive at the hall:

> Sunlight glints on the plaza in front of the grand palace known as the Hall of Divine Wisdom. Hundreds of petitioners mill about—dwarves and humans dressed in farm clothes, merchant's robes, or scholar's coats—all hoping to speak to the emperor. Ministers circulate among them, easily distinguished by their winged black caps. A minister speaks briefly with each petitioner. Most of these exchanges end with the minister dismissively directing the petitioner to turn around and leave through the main gates. Soon enough, a minister approaches you.

The minister who meets the characters greets them and indifferently asks what their business is at the hall. If a character politely explains they're expected by Secretary Wei, the minister ushers them forward with a bow. If the characters aren't civil or they waste the magistrate's time, a character must succeed on a DC 12 Charisma (Persuasion) check or they are made to wait for an hour while the indignant magistrate takes his time confirming the party's story.

Once it's clear the characters are here to see Secretary Wei, the minister directs the crowd to part, opening a path through the onlookers.

GRAND SECRETARY
WEI FENG YING

MEETING THE SECRETARY

Two guards meet the characters at the entrance to the Hall of Divine Wisdom and escort them to an elegant meeting room:

> The walls of this room are paneled with delicate latticework, and beautifully carved rosewood chairs surround a matching table. One wall bears a sumptuous silk hanging that depicts a gold dragon soaring through the clouds.

After a short wait, a middle-aged human woman enters, wearing fine red robes embroidered with stylized ki-rins. She introduces herself with amiable professionalism as Grand Secretary Wei. The characters already know that Wei holds a lofty political position and has influence exceeded only by Yongjing's emperor.

GRAND SECRETARY WEI

Wei Feng Ying (lawful neutral, human **archmage**) commands respect from all as Grand Secretary, the leader of the government of Yongjing. Since the nation's rulers' source of extreme longevity has vanished, Secretary Wei is determined to hold the country together (as detailed in the "End of an Era" section). The secretary has an array of *spell scrolls* and other magic items at her disposal, and she often makes use of her *crystal ball of telepathy* and spells like *project image* when dealing with her agents.

Personality Trait. "Others need to know only what's necessary to accomplish my goals."

Ideal. "Peace, efficiency, and the smooth running of the imperial machine must be upheld whatever the cost."

Bond. "My life and my service to the empire are one."

Flaw. "I know what's best for the empire."

ARCHAEOLOGICAL ASSIGNMENT

Secretary Wei thanks the characters for answering her call and for their interest in investigating the historic ruins of old Yongjing. As attendants enter to serve tea, she ask the characters about their training, their education, and what skills they bring to an underground expedition into a potentially dangerous area. She's eager to hear about their most spectacular deeds and is quick to flatter those who indulge her with such tales.

After hearing about the characters' exploits, Secretary Wei explains the assignment, highlighting the following points:

- This archaeological expedition seeks to collect accounts and relics from past rulers for the benefit of future ones.
- Historians believe that the palace of the last ruler of the Yun dynasty—known as the Mountain Cloud Empress—lies in the Old City beneath present-day Yongjing.
- Wei wishes the characters to guard her hand-picked scholar as they delve into the Old City.
- Of particular interest to Wei are the diaries of the Mountain Cloud Empress, which would have been kept along with her greatest treasures.

As the conversation concludes, a friendly young human arrives and bows to Secretary Wei. The secretary introduces this newcomer as Lu Zhong Yin, the expedition's lead historian.

Secretary Wei also presents a scroll bearing a contract for the characters to sign. The contract calls for an initial payment of 1,000 gp per character, plus an additional 1,000 gp per character when Lu Zhong Yin is brought safely back from the Old City and the scholar deems the investigation complete.

Finally, the secretary provides the characters with a *spell scroll* of *sending*, which they can use to contact her if the need arises. Wei intends for the expedition to set out as soon as possible after the characters collect their initial payment, but they can take a few hours to rest and prepare if necessary.

WHAT'S LEFT UNSAID

Secretary Wei's true goal is to search the buried Yun dynasty ruins for any sign of Dragon's Blessing—a magical reagent of particular importance to the emperor. She has no interest in the Mountain Cloud Empress's diaries, but she suspects that such secret writings would be held alongside other state secrets, like any stashed trove of Dragon's Blessing. Wei does not reveal her true agenda to the characters, but she has briefed Lu Zhong Yin on her goals, the need for secrecy, and the necessity of recovering this reagent (though not why it's important).

Secretary Wei also plans to monitor the group's investigation by using her *crystal ball of telepathy* to regularly cast *scrying* on Zhong Yin. During the investigation, Zhong Yin purposely fails the saving throws to resist the spell.

THE SHY SCHOLAR

Once the contract is signed, Secretary Wei directs the characters to take the scroll to the Ministry of Finance to collect their first payment. With the shy excitement of someone who can't believe they're in the presence of heroes, Zhong Yin escorts the characters to the ministry offices in the domain of the Octadic Council (see the "Yongjing Gazetteer" section for more information).

LU ZHONG YIN

Lu Zhong Yin (lawful neutral, human **spy**) is an unremarkable human, about twenty years old and exuding an eager-to-please air. To the characters, Zhong Yin claims to be a scholar of ancient Xing history. In truth, the scholar is an Imperial Ghost, a spy of the court. Zhong Yin serves Secretary Wei and is currently helping with the search for Dragon's Blessing.

Personality Trait. "There's nothing interesting about me. Tell me about yourself instead."

Ideal. "My work might go unseen, but it contributes to a greater whole."

Bond. "Secretary Wei saw the hidden potential in me, and I am forever grateful."

Flaw. "I'll follow any order from my commanders if it serves the greater good."

THE OLD CITY EXPEDITION

Zhong Yin is bright and eager to hear about the characters' past adventures. During conversation with the characters, the following topics might come up:

- The city of Yongjing has existed on this site for thousands of years, enduring numerous dynasties and countless disasters. Ruins known as the Old City lie beneath the modern city.
- Expeditions into these scattered, unconnected ruins can be dangerous. Beyond collapsing

Lu Zhong Yin in Their Imperial Ghost Uniform

architecture, ancient traps and monsters sometimes lurk within.

- Traces of ancient magical protections linger within the ruins. The most common bar the use of magical methods of travel, such as teleportation.
- The part of the Old City the group is meant to explore has only recently been discovered beneath the Hall of Merit. This first foray will pave the way for further investigation into the Yun dynasty ruins.
- The Mountain Cloud Empress is a controversial figure in Yongjing history, both romanticized and reviled. The Yun dynasty ended when the starving common folk stormed the palace and removed the empress from power.

The Ministry of Finance

When the party arrives at the ministry offices, Zhong Yin departs to make other preparations. The scholar will meet the characters at the Hall of Merit at the center of the city when the characters are ready to depart.

The Minister of Finance, Deng Bo Huan, is straightforward but friendly. He verifies the characters' contract and pays them each their initial 1,000 gp. Deng Bo Huan is also an opportunistic schemer, and he offers the characters an additional 100 gp each if they share with him details of why the Grand Secretary hired them and what they expect to find in the Old City. If the characters refuse his proposal, the minister smiles, tells them he understands, and wishes them good luck.

The Old City

When the characters are ready to begin their expedition, they can go to the Hall of Merit, where Zhong Yin is waiting for them. Zhong Yin leads them to an empty basement where a pair of guards flank a section of crumbled wall leading into darkness. The guards nod as they see Zhong Yin and stand out of the group's way.

Beyond the crumbled wall, a short, cramped hall leads to a stone stairway that descends to area Y1 in the Yun Dynasty Ruins. Characters who succeed on a DC 14 Wisdom (Perception) check can tell the stonework beyond the basement wall is many hundreds of years older than the modern Hall of Merit. Characters who have the Stonecunning trait have advantage on this check.

General Features

The Yun dynasty ruins of the Old City have the following features:

Illumination. The Old City is not illuminated, and the current occupants rely on darkvision to see. Area descriptions assume the characters have a light source or some other means of seeing in the dark.

Ceilings. The chambers in the ruins have 20-foot-high ceilings, with 10-foot-high ceilings in the tunnels that connect them.

Failing Magic. Ancient magical defenses still ward the ruins. Creatures in the ruins can't use teleportation or any type of planar travel to leave the Old City; magic that creates such an effect automatically fails. Spells that enable travel to other sections of the Old City still function, though.

Yun Dynasty Ruins Locations

The following locations are keyed to map 13.1.

Y1: Servants' Quarters

> Crumbling plaster walls, rotted bedding, and broken clay pots suggest this long chamber was once a series of sleeping quarters and storage spaces. Stray yellowed bones litter the dirt floor.

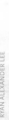

A character who examines the rodent-gnawed bones and succeeds on a DC 14 Wisdom (Medicine) check can tell they are hundreds of years old and belonged to humans and dwarves who met violent ends.

Ropers. Three **ropers** cling to the ceiling in the southeast part of the chamber. They shoot their tendrils at any creature that comes within 50 feet. Any spell used against the ropers that affects an area could jeopardize the box that rests on the floor beneath them.

Fragile Box. A wooden box in the southeast corner of the room holds a collection of well-written but worthless Yun dynasty romance novels. The box has AC 10, 3 hit points, immunity to poison and psychic damage, and vulnerability to fire damage. If the box is destroyed, the books within it are thoroughly scorched and rendered unreadable.

If Zhong Yin sees the burned books, the scholar momentarily fears the books are the Mountain Cloud Empress's diaries but then realizes their true nature. Nevertheless, Zhong Yin encourages the party to prioritize preserving any other historical artifacts the characters come across.

Treasure. Cracked hair combs, earthenware teacups, and other worthless items are scattered throughout this area. A character who spends 5 minutes searching the area and succeeds on a DC 16 Intelligence (Investigation) check discovers a single pearl hairpin worth 300 gp.

Y2: DESTROYED ENTRY

> Huge shards of wood showing traces of paint litter this area, along with rusted farm tools and ancient bones. The hard dirt floor is gouged in several places.

Upon seeing the wreckage, Zhong Yin says this area must have been the former main entryway to the Yun Dynasty palace. The scholar notes that the bones likely belong to common folk who rose up in revolt and ended the Yun dynasty.

Hungry Ghosts. An **otyugh** hides among the debris in the northwest corner of the room. When it notices the characters, it's excited at the prospect of a meal other than the rats that infest the ruins. The creature extends several dirty rags on its outstretched tentacles, gives a moan, and telepathically says, "We are the hungry dead. Honor us with lunch, or suffer our curse." Characters who hear the otyugh can make a DC 12 Wisdom (Insight) check. On a successful check, they realize something is pretending—poorly—to be a ghost. If given food or garbage, the otyugh continues to pretend to be three rag-ghosts, but it can telepathically warn the characters about the ropers in area Y1 and mentions having seen vicious spirits amid the ruins (a reference

to the wraiths in area Y5). The otyugh attacks if any creature tries to enter area Y3 before the otyugh has been fed.

Treasure. A character who searches the debris and succeeds on a DC 16 Intelligence (Investigation) check finds a rotting courier's pack containing a *spell scroll* of *scrying* and three packets of *dust of disappearance*.

Y3: THRONE ROOM

> Images of coiled blue dragons decorate the cracked floor tiles of this chamber, and dragon statues—some missing their heads or limbs—stand along the walls. In the middle of the room, a raised platform bears a bronze throne decorated with carved dragons holding bronze orbs.

Portions of this audience chamber have crumbled, but hints of its former splendor remain.

Dragon Throne. The throne is fixed to the platform and can't be moved. It radiates an aura of transmutation magic to a *detect magic* spell. A character who searches the throne and succeeds on a DC 20 Intelligence (Investigation) check notices that one of its bronze orbs is missing. This portion of the throne is in area Y6. If it is returned to the throne, the platform holding the throne slides aside, revealing a 10-foot-square opening that leads down into area Y3a.

Y3A: BENEATH THE THRONE

A hidden chamber lies beneath the throne in area Y3. When the platform slides aside, four **revenants** emerge from the chamber and attack. These Undead, dressed like Yun Dynasty magistrates, were buried alive under the throne to ensure that they would protect the ruler's treasures even after death.

Additionally, Secretary Wei uses her *crystal ball of telepathy* to scry on Zhong Yin soon after this area is revealed. See "Wei's Betrayal" for details.

Treasure. The chamber holds five cabinets carved with symbols that represent luck and long life. Four of them have the following contents: rotted documents, a suit of *adamantine splint mail*, *slippers of spider climbing*, and ancient coins worth 5,000 gp.

The fifth cabinet radiates an aura of abjuration magic if *detect magic* is cast on it. Among the carved symbols on the cabinet is a glyph created by the *symbol* (pain) spell. A character who searches the cabinets for traps finds and identifies the glyph with a successful DC 18 Intelligence (Arcana) check. A creature that opens the cabinet without negating the symbol must succeed on a DC 18 Constitution saving throw or be incapacitated with excruciating pain for 1 minute. Within the trapped cabinet are the diaries of the Mountain Cloud Empress, shattered flasks, and three *potions of longevity*.

Development. Zhong Yin shows strangely little interest in the diaries before collecting them but eagerly seeks to examine the potions and the shattered flasks. A character who succeeds on a DC 14 Wisdom (Insight) check realizes the scholar is clearly focused on recovering something other than the diaries. If none of the characters notice Zhong Yin's strange behavior, the scholar curses upon inspecting the potions and flasks, then mutters, "Nothing. There's no Dragon's Blessing here."

If the characters press the scholar on this, Zhong Yin brushes off their questions, encouraging the party to complete its investigation and then return to the surface. If the characters insist that Zhong Yin explain themself, either through roleplaying or by succeeding on a DC 16 Charisma (Intimidation) check, the scholar admits that they were actually searching for a magical substance called Dragon's Blessing, which is of great importance to Secretary Wei. Zhong Yin doesn't know more than that and urges the characters to question the Grand Secretary about it when they return to her.

Y4: Receiving Hall

> An altar and a decaying tapestry on the north wall are all that remains in this chamber.

The wooden altar here is bare and retains no hint of its former use. A character who looks behind the tapestry or who succeeds on a DC 14 Wisdom (Perception) check while investigating it discovers a mirror on the wall.

Hidden Mirror. Behind the tapestry is a damaged but functional *mirror of life trapping*. Eleven of the mirror's extradimensional cells have been destroyed, and only one remains intact. Any creature that pulls back the tapestry and can see the mirror must succeed on a DC 15 Charisma saving throw or become trapped in the mirror.

If a creature becomes trapped, the mirror frees its only other prisoner: Lio Gong, the Mountain Cloud Empress's favorite spouse.

Lio Gong. Lio Gong (neutral good **veteran**) is a youthful-looking, athletic dwarf wearing coarse silk robes. When she emerges from the mirror, she's in a state of shock, but she is friendly toward those who try to communicate with her. Lio Gong speaks only an ancient dialect of Xingyu (the language of Yongjing). Zhong Yin can understand what the dwarf says if none of the characters speak Xingyu. Once she is given a moment to take everything in, Lio Gong shares the following information:

- The ruined palace was once Lio Gong's home.
- She was the favorite spouse of the Mountain Cloud Empress, the last ruler of the Yun dynasty, whose painted portrait she carries and can show the characters.
- The empress was obsessed with attaining immortality, eternal life beyond even the longevity granted by magic potions.
- Not wanting Lio Gong to grow old while she sought the key to everlasting life, the empress forced her lover to enter the mirror to await her eventual triumph.
- Before Lio Gong entered the mirror, the empress's focus on magical research had begun to consume much of the imperial treasury and was leading to unrest among the common folk.

Lio Gong knows the command word for the *mirror of life trapping*, "lanhua," and offers to share it immediately if the characters promise to escort her to whatever remains of the palace gardens (area Y6).

If asked about Dragon's Blessing, Lio Gong knows about it from her life alongside the Mountain Cloud Empress. She can share the information from the "Dragon's Blessing" section at the start of the adventure.

Y5: Bedchamber

> The lacquered iron frame of a huge bed stands on the north side of this room. All its other furnishings, including red curtains that once enclosed the bed on three sides, are rotted away to almost nothing.

Four **wraiths**, spawned from royal courtiers who died when the palace was overrun, linger in and around the ruined bed. They bide their time until more than one creature enters this area, then attack.

Y6: Underground Garden

> This sanctuary might once have been a garden, but the only color here now comes from three green limestone rocks shaped like tall, wispy spirits. A dried-up fountain carved in the shape of three intertwined dragons stands at the center of the room.

This private garden has fallen to ruin and been buried along with the rest of the Yun dynasty palace.

Fountain. The fountain and the three limestone sculptures give off an aura of conjuration magic discernible by a *detect magic* spell. A search of the fountain reveals a mallet made of green limestone that radiates the same aura as the fountain and the

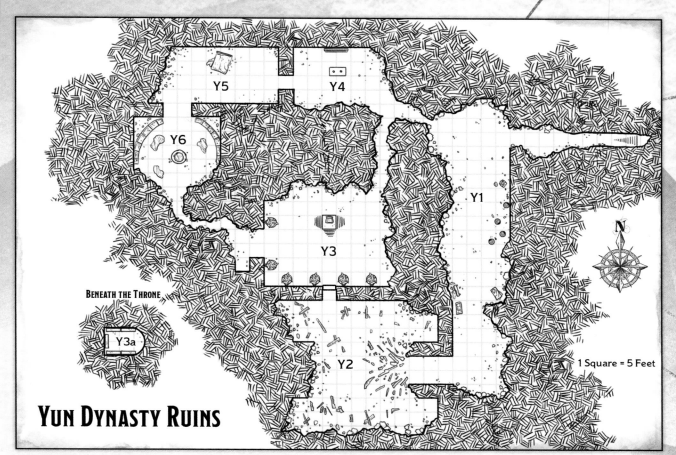

artwork. Striking the sculptures with the mallet produces a sound like the ringing of a bell. If each of the three rocks is struck, water erupts from the dragon-fountain's mouths along with a fist-sized bronze orb (see "Treasure"). The water that fills the basin of the fountain is safe and refreshing. The first creature to drink from the fountain in a 24-hour period regains 7 (2d6) hit points.

Lio Gong's Vision. If the characters haven't already activated the fountain, Lio Gong does so when she comes here. When the fountain's basin is full, she touches the water. Every creature in the room witnesses a silent, smiling reflection of the Mountain Cloud Empress appear in the water as the garden springs to life. Trees and flowers erupt from the stony ground, and the air is filled with the scent of plum blossoms. For a moment, the garden is magically restored to its ancient splendor, but after 1 minute this vibrancy vanishes and the area returns to normal. Upon witnessing this, an emotional Lio Gong thanks the characters for freeing her, and—if the characters haven't already noticed it—she retrieves the bronze orb from the basin and gives it to them. If the characters haven't discovered the magical features of the throne in area Y3, she also shows them how to access the hidden chamber below. Lio Gong requests the characters escort her out of the ruins after they complete their investigation, seeking only to enjoy her remaining days.

Treasure. The bronze orb is the missing part of the throne in area Y3.

WEI'S BETRAYAL

Soon after the characters find area Y3a, Secretary Wei uses her *crystal ball of telepathy* to scry on Zhong Yin. Unless the characters can see the spell's invisible sensor and dispel it, she witnesses the discovery of the *potions of longevity*, the lack of Dragon's Blessing, and any slips Zhong Yin makes when talking about the reason for the investigation.

After this, whenever the characters decide to head for area Y1 to leave the ruins, read the following:

> Rumbling fills the tunnels, and a tremor disturbs the nearby rubble. All goes quiet again, but now a haze of dust hangs in the air.

Secretary Wei has ordered a court mage to magically collapse the stairwell leading from area Y1 to the surface. When the characters enter area Y1 again, read the following description:

> The result of the tremor is now clear—a great pile of rubble fills the space where the stairway once stood.

A character who searches the rubble and succeeds on a DC 16 Wisdom (Survival) check sees no reason for the collapse and suspects that tons of rock lie between the ruins and the surface. Characters who have the Stonecunning trait have advantage on this check.

A New Way Out

Give the characters time to discuss ways to escape. Keep in mind the Old City's wards against teleportation and planar travel beyond the ruins. If the idea of contacting Secretary Wei for assistance using the *spell scroll* of *sending* she gave the group doesn't come up, Zhong Yin makes that suggestion if the scroll hasn't already been used. If it has, Secretary Wei uses her *crystal ball of telepathy* to contact a character after they start concocting ways to escape.

Secretary Wei informs the characters that she has been made aware of the collapse and that they shouldn't be worried—cave-ins are a known hazard of investigating the Old City. She says she's already working with court mages to create a gateway to another section of the ruins through which the characters can escape.

A few minutes later, a shimmering portal forms in front of the party. A character who makes a successful DC 14 Intelligence (Arcana) check knows this is a one-way portal, but the destination can't be seen through the magical passage.

Secret Grotto

Characters who step through the portal are transported to another portion of the Old City in the northeast section of Yongjing.

General Features

The areas in this underground grotto have the following features:

Illumination. The glowing jade in area S1 fills that area with dim light. Lanterns holding *continual flame* spells line the walls of the other areas.

Ceilings. Ceilings throughout the grotto are 15 feet high except in area S1, where they're 30 feet high.

Failing Magic. Creatures in the ruins can't use teleportation or any type of planar travel to leave the Old City; magic that creates such an effect automatically fails. Spells that enable travel to other sections of Old City (whether elsewhere in the secret grotto or back to the Yun dynasty ruins) still function, though.

Secret Grotto Locations

The following locations are keyed to map 13.2.

S1: Jade Golem Tomb

Characters who pass through the portal appear in the center of this area. When all the characters have arrived, read the following:

> The walls of this hexagonal stone chamber are shot through with pale white veins of faintly glowing jade. A bronze double door bearing a design of two ki-rins stands in one wall. Dozens of alcoves holding jade statues of soldiers line the rest of the chamber's perimeter. Bodies are scattered around the room—some clothed in finery, some in rags, all in states of decay.

Secretary Wei uses this ancient trap to dispose of those she considers a threat to the empire. She now considers the characters such threats, no matter how little they know about her plans or Dragon's Blessing.

Any investigation of the bodies in the room reveals them to be humans and dwarves, some only a few months deceased. A character who succeeds on a DC 12 Wisdom (Medicine) check determines that most of the victims were killed by giant blades.

A Final Courtesy. As the characters get their bearings, read or paraphrase the following:

> A shimmering, illusory image of Secretary Wei appears in the center of the chamber. "Your service is much appreciated, adventurers," the image says grimly. "But you've learned just enough to be dangerous. I won't allow our great nation to succumb to the same chaos as the Yun dynasty. If you have last wishes, please write them down. We will retrieve them and do our best to honor them after your demise."
>
> The Grand Secretary then hesitates, and the image wavers. "Zhong Yin, I will not be retrieving you as planned," she says. "I am sorry."
>
> The image flickers, then vanishes.

Any attempt to respond to Secretary Wei fails, as she ignores the characters.

Zhong Yin. Zhong Yin is shocked at Secretary Wei's betrayal. From this point on, the spy is willing to aid the characters and will share any information in the "What's Left Unsaid" section earlier in the adventure.

Stone Defenders. After the image of Secretary Wei fades, a sculpted soldier detaches from its alcove, then steps forward to attack. The soldier uses

JULIAN KOK

the **stone golem** stat block, except that its Slam action deals slashing damage because it wields a giant glaive.

At the start of the soldier's next turn, a second stone soldier animates and attacks. This soldier is identical, except that the designs on its armor are slightly different. Each time one of the stone soldiers is destroyed, another activates in its alcove and attacks at the start of the next turn. No more than two soldiers are ever active at once.

The soldiers continue to animate and attack until the bronze gate is opened (see below). Characters who have a passive Wisdom (Perception) score of 14 or higher notice that different animal designs decorate each of the statues.

Bronze Gate. Magic seals this bronze double door. It opens only if the ki-rin symbol on one of the statues in the room—the only statue that doesn't animate—is pressed. A character who succeeds on a DC 14 Wisdom (Perception) notices that all the jade statues have distinct designs suggestive of different animals on their armor and that these designs are rendered in a style similar to the ki-rin symbol on the doors. A character who takes an action to further scrutinize these designs or looks for a ki-rin symbol on the statues can make a DC 18 Wisdom (Perception) check. On a failed check, the character investigates a few statues and doesn't see anything

remarkable. On a successful check, the character notices that the decorations on the statue ten alcoves south of the door matches the ki-rin symbol on the gate. If a creature touches the symbol on that statue, the gate opens, and all currently animate statues return to their alcoves and deactivate.

S2: HALLWAY ALCOVES

> A long hallway is roughly carved out of the surrounding rock. Lanterns embedded in the walls cast light into a number of irregularly shaped alcoves.

Secretary Wei uses this area as a storage place for valuables that might be useful in the future. A character who spends 5 minutes searching the alcoves finds numerous files detailing years-old court proceedings and one of the following objects at random:

- An empty carrying case with a dozen compartments. A tag reads "Potion of Longevity × 12."
- A *wind fan* painted with an image of flat-bottomed ships. A tag identifies it as a gift for one of the emperor's children.
- Three fragile porcelain vases worth 800 gp each. A receipt identifies them as gifts for the emperor.

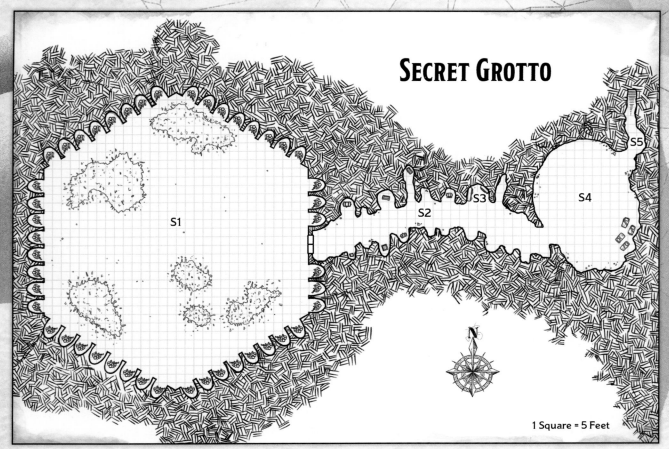

SECRET GROTTO

S5

S3

S2

S4

S1

N

1 Square = 5 Feet

MAP 13.2: SECRET GROTTO

S3: DOCUMENTS ALCOVE

This alcove has shelves cut out of the sandstone, each one stacked high with scrolls. Characters who search the shelves and succeed on a DC 12 Intelligence (Investigation) check find a series of scrolls with orders from Secretary Wei and reports back from her agents. These documents capture the following information:

- Secretary Wei believes the emperor is dying.
- She has secretly been sending agents to ancient imperial sites across the land to search for something called Dragon's Blessing (the document doesn't note what this is).
- Finding Dragon's Blessing will save the emperor.
- Maintaining secrecy is of the utmost importance, lest the imperial court be thrown into chaos.

Any resident of Yongjing or a character who succeeds on a DC 12 Intelligence (History) check knows that the nation's rulers use magic to give themselves long life and ensure the stability of the land. If the imperial line has lost the ability to do this, upheaval is sure to follow.

S4: DRAGON GROTTO

As the characters approach this area, they hear the ragged breathing of a large creature.

An enormous gold dragon lies coiled against the near wall of this gloomy chamber, its four legs shackled to the ground. Claw marks score the walls and floor.

Several workstations are carved into the eastern wall, each covered in alchemical devices. Muttering figures cluster around these stations. Four simple cots stand nearby.

Imperial alchemists work in secret here, trying to recreate the lost secrets of Dragon's Blessing. Passages lead to the west and northeast.

Gold Dragon. An **adult gold dragon** named Tulao has been a captive of a secret cabal of imperial alchemists for over a year. He has 5 levels of exhaustion and 20 hit points remaining. Magic shackles on his legs prevent him from using any of his actions. The dragon is hostile to his captors but friendly toward anyone who removes his shackles. The shackles can be removed either by using one of the mages' keys or by picking the lock with a successful DC 18 Dexterity check using thieves' tools. Freeing Tulao reduces his exhaustion by 1 level. If freed, Tulao thanks the characters and shares the information in the "Secrets of Longevity" section below before transforming into a canary and flying out of the chamber through area S5.

Mages. Three **mages** work here. They are lawful evil and serve Secretary Wei as the dragon's handlers. They're hostile toward any creature that's not another agent of Secretary Wei. Each of them carries a jade key that opens the dragon's shackles and will do anything to prevent the dragon from being released.

Secret of Longevity. If Tulao is freed or if any of the mages are captured and coerced, they explain what's happening here, highlighting the following points:

- They can share all of the information in the "Dragon's Blessing" and "End of the Emperor" sections at the start of the adventure.
- Secretary Wei had the imperial mages magically capture and bind the gold dragon, hoping that her alchemists could use it to create Dragon's Blessing. Their efforts have met with no success.

Treasure. The workstations here hold two *potions of healing* (supreme), an *elixir of health*, several gold dragon scales, and three sets of alchemist's supplies.

S5: Exit Tunnel

A cobweb-filled passageway leads out and up from the grotto, quickly becoming a steep slope with metal rungs bolted to the sandstone walls. The passageway ends in an iron grate that requires a successful DC 12 Strength check to push open. If Tulao escaped using this route, he has already slipped through the grate and out of the crawlspace beyond by the time the characters arrive.

Surprise Audience

When the characters emerge from the hatch, read or paraphrase the following:

> The space beyond is a windowless room with a wooden ceiling only four feet off the floor and a trapdoor at its center. A smiling mask with peeling paint lies on the floor. From above comes the sound of someone singing an operatic aria.

The characters are in the crawlspace beneath the stage of the Pear Garden Imperial Opera. The room has no doors, but the trapdoor in the ceiling can be pulled down to provide access to the stage above.

An Unexpected Cameo

Read the following if the characters open the door and climb up onto the stage, or if they unexpectedly emerge in some other manner:

> Two singers wearing heavy makeup freeze in mid-embrace as you make your presence known. At the back of the stage, musicians stare in shock but continue playing.
>
> The audience area beyond is a profusion of colorful parasols held by people wearing expensive clothes, all watching the performance with rapt attention.
>
> Sitting on a raised dais in the center of the crowd is the White Jade Emperor, dressed in magnificent yellow and gold robes. Several guards stand nearby.

The emperor's dais is 30 feet from the front of the stage. The emperor's guards notice any disturbance immediately, and two **mages** and five **veterans** move to surround the emperor. They order the characters to lay down their weapons and submit themselves for arrest.

If a character addresses the emperor, the ruler raises his hand and the guards pause. If no character does so, Zhong Yin calls to the emperor, and he prevents the guards from arresting the group.

Characters should be encouraged not to attack the emperor or his guards, but if they do, more **mages** and **veterans** join the fight until the characters are taken into custody, soon to be exiled from the city.

Conversing with the Emperor

With a few imperious words, the White Jade Emperor (lawful neutral, hill dwarf **noble**) dismisses everyone except his guards. As the crowd disperses, Secretary Wei remains on the scene. As soon as the area is empty of opera-goers, he orders the characters to explain themselves.

Presenting Evidence

The emperor listens patiently to the characters' story. He believes their tale if they can support it with any three of the following pieces of evidence:

- The documents to and from Secretary Wei found in area S3
- The confession of one of the alchemists from area S4
- The *potions of longevity* the characters found in the Old City
- A gold dragon scale from area S4

Zhong Yin's confession also counts as a piece of evidence, but the spy is reluctant to betray the Grand Secretary. A character who succeeds on a DC 18 Charisma (Intimidation or Persuasion) check can compel Zhong Yin to fully confess.

Additionally, a character who succeeds on a DC 20 Charisma (Persuasion) check can convince the emperor to believe them even if they present only two pieces of evidence.

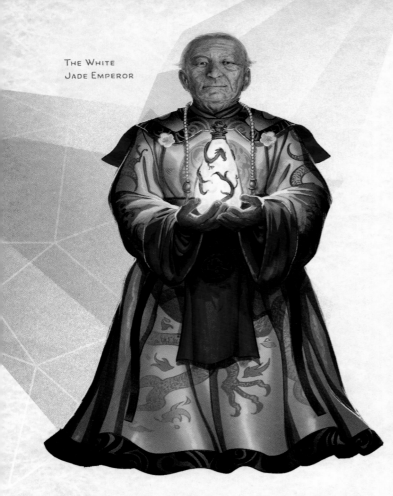

The emperor will not allow the characters to reenter the Old City to search for additional evidence.

THE EMPEROR IS NOT CONVINCED

If the characters aren't able to convince the emperor of the truth of their story through presenting evidence, he asks Secretary Wei what she has to say about the situation. The secretary flatly denies the accusation, claiming that Zhong Yin and the characters were sent on a scholarly investigation into the Old City, but stole relics from the site and eluded her attempts to capture and punish them.

The emperor accepts her answer as the truth of the matter. Unless the characters come up with a compelling way to convince the emperor that Secretary Wei is lying, he gives them and Zhong Yin one hour to exile themselves from the city before his guards compel them to do so. Continue with "Conclusion" below.

THE EMPEROR IS CONVINCED

If the emperor believes the characters' story, he finds the evidence against Secretary Wei irrefutable. Nevertheless, in her defense, the secretary shares the information from the "End of an Era" section at the start of the adventure, claiming that she sought to protect not only the emperor but the stability of the empire. She'll go on to calmly answer any

questions the characters have, revealing any details from the "Secrets of Immortality" section. She clearly believes what she says and considers her actions to be in the best interests of the empire.

After Secretary Wei has spoken on her own behalf, the emperor dismisses the characters and those with them, but he tells the secretary to stay for a private audience. This session ends with the Grand Secretary being taken into custody by the imperial guard.

CONCLUSION

If the characters are exiled, they are never welcomed back in Yongjing while the White Jade Emperor rules. Zhong Yin leaves the party's company as soon as possible.

If the characters convinced the emperor of Secretary Wei's schemes, they—along with Zhong Yin—are invited to a private audience with the emperor a day later. The emperor rewards each character with 1,000 gp, plus another 1,000 gp if they promise not to speak of what they have learned about Dragon's Blessing and his eventual death. If the characters break their promise, rumors spread quickly, but the emperor does not seek to punish the characters.

Before dismissing the characters, the emperor goes on to ask what they think he should do with Secretary Wei, who has served the nation well for decades and whose schemes seemed driven by a desire to keep the empire safe—even if she did keep his impending death a secret. He favors exiling her but will consider whatever the characters propose.

A RARE SIGHTING

As the party leaves their audience with the emperor, characters who have a passive Wisdom (Perception) score of 12 or higher catch a glimpse of a rare, fortuitous omen: the shadow of a serpentine dragon—like the mythical Dragon of Heavenly Blessings—soaring through the clouds. All the characters, whether they saw this omen or not, gain the following charm (a type of supernatural gift detailed in the *Dungeon Master's Guide*).

Way of the Dragon. You are as elusive and free as the Dragon of Heavenly Blessings. This charm has 6 charges. As an action, you can expend 1 charge and gain one of the following benefits:

- Difficult terrain doesn't cost you extra movement until the end of your next long rest.
- The next time you end your turn paralyzed or restrained, that condition ends on you. This benefit then ends.

After you expend a charge, you can't do so again until you finish a long rest. Once all its charges have been expended, the charm vanishes from you.

Yongjing Gazetteer

For centuries, the nation of Great Xing has been synonymous with power and prestige, with no finer example than the country's glorious capital: Yongjing. The city teems with scholars, bureaucrats, artisans, and performers. But Yongjing was not always so vibrant. Beneath the fine floor tiles and immaculate garden paths lie the remains of prior dynasties and their long-dead citizens—concealing a turbulent past marked by war, subjugation, and famine.

The rule of the Xing dynasty has brought wealth, stability, and peace to Great Xing. But now the imperial secret of longevity has been exhausted, which means the White Jade Emperor's long reign will end soon. The Grand Secretary who governs Great Xing according to the emperor's command knows that it's only a matter of time before word of the emperor's impending death gets out and the stability of the empire is put to the test.

Yongjing Features

Those familiar with Yongjing know the following details:

Hallmarks. Yongjing is known for its courtly drama and labyrinthine bureaucracy. Its rulers enjoy exceptionally long lifespans.

People. Humans and dwarves make up most of the population of Yongjing, with humans outnumbering dwarves three to one. Almost all residents have black hair, warm skin tones, and rounded faces.

Languages. Xingyu is the primary language of Yongjing, and most residents are also fluent in Common. Xingyu is written in the Dwarvish script, though scholars and upper-class citizens often also learn the language's older and more complicated pictograph representations.

Noteworthy Sites

The city of Yongjing is a bustling network of tightly packed buildings and narrow alleys. A wide central avenue bisects the city and connects the grand palaces of the emperor's court through a series of plazas.

Hall of Divine Wisdom

Each morning, the Gate of Ascendance is thrown open, and petitioners seeking the ear of the emperor crowd onto the plaza in front of the palace known as the Hall of Divine Wisdom. Ministers interview each petitioner—and swiftly reject requests too trivial to warrant the emperor's involvement. The plaza is also a prime location for pickpockets and spies. Most days, wealthy petitioners are turned away and must seek other means to solve their problems.

Inner Butterfly Court

The north side of the city is taken up by the palaces of the royal court, which make up their own district—the Inner Butterfly Court. Only the emperor's family and their attendants are permitted in this area, and most residents rarely leave the district except for opera performances and holiday festivals.

Spousal palaces line the east and west sides of the Inner Butterfly Court, each building the residence of a royal spouse and their children. Two larger central palaces are occupied by the emperor, who resides in the Palace of Heavenly Command and reserves the Palace of Favored Unity for visits with his expansive family.

Kiln District

The southwest part of Yongjing houses hundreds of earthen kilns, where the famed white-and-blue porcelain of Great Xing is painted and fired. Potters work in assembly lines to meet a quota of hundreds of pieces a day, with twenty percent of those pieces going to the emperor. Xing porcelain fetches exorbitant prices in foreign markets, so armed guards accompany every shipment that leaves the city. At the Office of Authenticity, imperial artificers apply intricate identifying marks to each piece. Despite this, counterfeiting is a constant problem.

The Old City

Over the centuries, the rulers of Yongjing have expanded and updated the city, building on top of existing architecture. As a result, many structures conceal forgotten chambers, hidden passages, dusty traps, and ancient artifacts beneath their floors. Expeditions into the subterranean Old City are common, whether staged officially on behalf of the emperor or undertaken in secret by criminals and treasure hunters.

Life in Yongjing

Residents of Yongjing take great pride in their city and frequently boast about everything from its venerable age and historic architecture to its lack of unsavory elements—such as the rats and diseases that are so common in other, lesser cities.

Chasing Longevity

The importance of a long life is drilled into children from an early age. The folk of the empire and Yongjing proudly consider their society a meritocracy, where anyone can work hard and rise above their current station—provided they live long enough. Therefore, citizens maintain healthy lifestyles, drink medicinal teas, and carry symbols of longevity such as long-lived animals or plants.

COURT INTRIGUE AND SUCCESSION

In the imperial court, tradition dictates that the social standing of each member of the emperor's family is determined by the preferences of the emperor. If the emperor publicly favors one spouse over another, the pecking order is reset accordingly, and everyone must quickly adjust their behavior to recognize this new hierarchy.

At no time is an emperor's favor in greater question than when they die. Rarely do Yongjing's long-lived rulers have to consider the prospect of death, and they put even less consideration into designating a particular heir from among their shorter-lived family members. When an emperor dies unexpectedly, a period of squabbling follows, as imperial family members, secret offspring, and pretenders produce evidence of being the past emperor's favorite. These squabbles ultimately devolve into secret wars, as the Inner Butterfly Court becomes beset by intrigue, assassinations, and disappearances until a single heir claims and holds the throne for a year's time. Only then is that individual universally accepted as the new emperor.

DELICIOUS BOUNTY

A typical meal in Yongjing might include sweet or savory buns, salty pork, and stir-fried dandelion leaves. Wintertime stews are flavored with bone marrow and laden with sliced lotus root, mushrooms, and bamboo shoots. In summer, Yongjing's courtyard gardens are filled to bursting with oranges, lychees, plums, and peaches.

FASHION AND SOCIETY

Clothing in Yongjing favors loose and flowing styles—and the wealthier the wearer, the more elaborate the embroidery. Ministers are identifiable by their black winged caps, while members of the royal family wear elaborate headdresses.

The households of city residents are built around the clan, made up of several generations of family members and multiple spouses of any gender, typically joined through arranged marriages. A clear hierarchy within each of these complex familial structures helps to facilitate social harmony. Members of a clan keep close eyes on one another, because the deeds of an individual affect the social standing of the clan as a whole.

GRAND DYNASTY

Yongjing is the governmental center of the flourishing Xing dynasty. At the top sits the White Jade Emperor, the third since the rise of the Xing dynasty. Like nearly all the previous monarchs, the emperor is a dwarf, with a life span long enough to have experienced the cyclical nature of history firsthand—a trait considered necessary to rule.

IMPERIAL SERVICE

Most of Yongjing's bureaucrats are humans. A Grand Secretary appointed by the emperor leads the Octadic Council, a group made up of the leaders of the city's eight Ministries: Agriculture, Arcana, Bureaucracy, Culture, Diplomacy, Finance, Imperial Lineage, and Public Works. A position in one of the bustling ministry offices is the most prestigious employment in Great Xing, promising lifelong access to luxury and elevated status for an entire family. Children from all backgrounds study for the annual Imperial Exams, hoping to score high enough to be selected to fill a vacancy. Those who show aptitude for more clandestine work might be selected to join the ranks of the Imperial Ghosts, versatile soldiers who serve as spies for the empire.

NAMES

Names in Great Xing are ungendered and place an individual's family name before their personal name. Personal names are formed of two words; the first is usually determined by birth order, social status, or rank, and the second is an aspirational or lucky name representing the parents' hopes for their child. The following names are common in Xing:

Family Names. Jia, Ke, Li, Song, Sun, Tai, Tian, Xing (royal family only)

Status. Bo (firstborn), Meng (firstborn), Xia (second-born), Zhong (second-born), Shu (third-born), Ji (fourth-born or more), Jun (noble), Si (heir), Wen (scholar)

Aspirational. Jie (heroic), Mei (charming), Ming (bright), Qian (rising), Tong (leader), Yi (virtuous), Zi (gentle)

LEGENDS OF YONGJING

Countless stories recount the country's illustrious beginnings, when a great dragon, one of three majestic siblings, descended from the heavens to establish the culture that would become Great Xing. The area in which the city of Yongjing would one day rise was originally populated by nomadic dwarf shepherds. As humans immigrated to the region, conflict between the races broke out. Legends say that the violence persisted for a century, until the Dragon of Heavenly Blessings who had founded Great Xing returned. Descending from the clouds, the great dragon bowed before a young dwarf leader, bestowing on him the ability to inspire and unify folk of both human and dwarven ancestries. This dwarf became the Yellow Dragon Emperor, founder of the nation's first ruling dynasty.

Numerous dwarven dynasties have ruled Great Xing, with the human population generally content to be so governed. One fable, however, tells of the

YONGJING

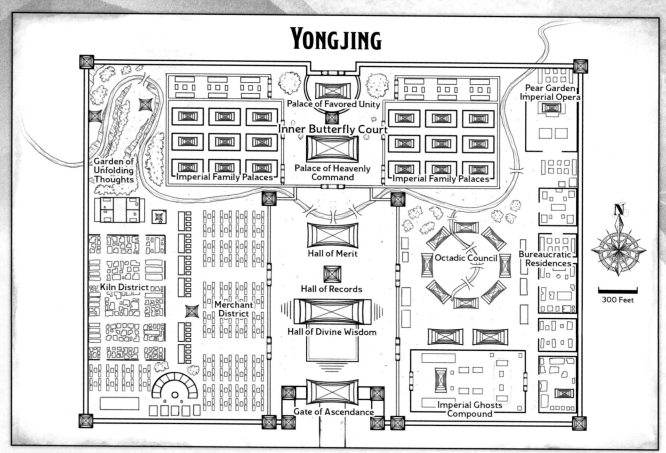

MAP 13.3: YONGJING

Winter Crane Empress, who was dethroned by a human. As the story goes, three of her advisors came forward with three different plans for war, but the exiled dwarf empress instead called for a sumptuous bed to be made for her. She then took a nap until the usurper died of old age, reclaiming her throne without violence and swiftly undoing the little he could accomplish in his brief human life span.

ADVENTURES IN YONGJING

Consider the plots on the Yongjing Adventures table when planning adventures in Yongjing.

YONGJING ADVENTURES

d4	Adventure
1	The characters are hired to investigate strange behavior by a notoriously aloof minister who has shut himself in his offices and communicates only through his door. No one yet knows the minister has been replaced by an opportunistic **kenku**.
2	After saving the emperor from a **reef shark** placed in his bath, the emperor's primary spouse, Lord Meng Shan, hires the characters to disprove accusations that he planted the creature himself.

d4	Adventure
3	Agents in the Ministry of Arcana hire the characters to kill four treasonous **mages**, not realizing two of the traitors are the emperor's own children.
4	The **ghost** of Wang Ji Miao, a potter executed for blowing up kilns, begs the characters to clear her family's name by finding out who framed her.

CHARACTERS FROM YONGJING

If players want to create characters from Yongjing, consider asking them the following questions during character creation:

Do you have family connections to the emperor?
Do you use those connections to make your life easier, or do you conceal them to reduce the threat of assassinations or intrigue?

What personal symbol of longevity do you carry?
Is it an elephant, a turtle, or another long-lived animal, or perhaps ever-growing bamboo or some other ageless plant? If you don't carry a symbol, why is that?

Do you serve the empire in some official means?
Do you serve as a bureaucrat, having passed the Imperial Exams? Are you one of the emperor's defenders? Or have you left such service behind?

ORCHIDS OF THE INVISIBLE MOUNTAIN

AN ADVENTURE FOR 14TH-LEVEL CHARACTERS

T HE LAND OF ATAGUA EXISTS AT A WEAK point between several planes of existence. Feywild influences work upon the land, but in recent years, corruption from the Far Realm has begun leaking into the savanna. The characters must journey to the Feywild and beyond to quell the alien forces spreading across the increasingly surreal plains.

BACKGROUND

The land of Atagua shares a connection to the Ghost Orchid Tepui, a mysterious region of the Feywild. That realm's serpentine protector, the spirit Chimagua, was fond of mortals and would bestow visions upon the folk of Atagua. However, when Atagua fell to invaders from a distant land, visions from Chimagua ended. The sages known as the Green Doctors sought to reconnect the land to the Feywild, but their attempts failed and weakened the planar fabric around Atagua. Soon, the region's people began experiencing terrible nightmares that gradually began manifesting in the form of terrifying creatures connected to an inscrutable Far Realm entity known as the Drought Elder. Horrified by their mistake, the Green Doctors scrambled to push back the eldritch creatures with a hastily woven magical ward.

Today, though Atagua is independent again, its magical ward has finally collapsed. The influence of the Drought Elder seeps in to Atagua once more. For years, this corruption has manifested only as dreams or the rare otherworldly predator, but recently more beings from the Far Realm have begun to slip into Atagua. Only the return of the spirit Chimagua might save the land, but all is not as it should be at the Ghost Orchid Tepui. Unless Atagua's ancient connection to the Feywild is restored, creatures from the Far Realm will overrun the land.

PRONUNCIATION GUIDE

The Atagua Pronunciations table shows how to pronounce key names in this adventure.

ATAGUA PRONUNCIATIONS

Name	Pronunciation
Alfonz Rubinaz-Zumdi	AL-fonz ru-BIN-ahz ZUM-dee
Atagua	ah-TAH-gwah
Camino Rojo	kah-MEE-no RO-ho
Chimagua	chee-MAH-gwah
Cht-Chak	chit-CHAK
El Caparazón	ehl kah-pah-rah-ZONE
Llanos	YAH-nose
Melecio	may-LAY-see-o
Nene	NAY-nay
Phik-Pik	fik-PIK
Sarire	sah-REE-ray
Tepui	teh-PUH-wee
Yarana	yah-RAH-nah

SETTING THE ADVENTURE

When preparing to run this adventure, use the following suggestions to help contextualize Atagua in a wider world:

Through the Radiant Citadel. Characters who visit Atagua from the Radiant Citadel arrive not far from the Sarire sugar mill.

Forgotten Realms. The Plains of Purple Dust in Mulhorand or the Shining Plains along the Vilhon Reach could host the grasslands of Atagua.

Greyhawk. Atagua could occupy a region of the Plains of the Paynims east of Ket and the Barrier Peaks. Alternatively, the plains of the Great Kingdom might include or border Atagua, with the land's culture holding connections to the sky-worshiping Aerdi people.

CHARACTER HOOKS

Consider the following ways to involve characters in this adventure:

Dream Message. A character suffers nightmares of a radiant snake fighting a massive, crumbling centipede. They awake with one word in their mind:

The Grassroads span the vast savannas and forests of Atagua, a boon to both travelers and predators.

"Sarire." If they investigate, they learn the word is a location in the land of Atagua, where a spirit called Chimagua speaks through dreams.

Planar Instability. According to a sage, a planar conjunction is affecting Atagua. She hires the characters to travel there, visit a site near the Sarire Sugar Mill, and record any planar anomalies.

Sugar Man's Summons. Alfonz Rubinaz-Zumdi, a powerful landowner, has agents reach out to the characters with an offer of employment, but he requests they discuss it at his place of business, the Sarire sugar mill in Atagua.

DREAMS AND PORTENTS

Strange dreams are common in Atagua, the result of psychic energies from the Feywild and Far Realm. Whenever a character sleeps or meditates while in Atagua, roll on the Dreams in Atagua table to determine if they have a strange vision.

DREAMS IN ATAGUA

d10	Dream
1–4	No dream
5	You are swimming up a sky-high waterfall.
6	Orchids speak to you in the voices of fallen friends.
7	A thri-kreen entrusts you with a crown of feathers.

d10	Dream
8	While you watch, one thousand weavers stitch together a massive hammock.
9	A friend you haven't seen in years walks backward alongside you on a bridge of leaves.
10	A snake twists around a massive centipede, the two struggling for dominance.

UNREALITY

Atagua is influenced by dreams from the Feywild and nightmares from the Far Realm. Throughout the adventure, highlight how the Feywild has influenced the land, with vegetation and animals demonstrating friendly or capricious behavior, the sun rising amid a psychedelic dawn, or characters experiencing random instances of good luck. Meanwhile, Far Realm energies manifest as eyes staring from the dark, insidious insects, or misshapen silhouettes looming in the distance. The land's fraying planar boundaries might also allow glimpses into other planes or ghostly appearances of strange figures. Let Atagua's place between the real and surreal inspire your descriptions.

Starting the Adventure

As the adventure begins, the characters are traveling to the Sarire sugar mill, most likely coming from Port Panela. If the characters seek to learn more about the region there, consult the "Atagua Gazetteer" section at the end of this adventure. From the port, the route called the Camino Rojo stretches between flamingo-filled wetlands and grassy plains covered with sugarcane fields. The surrounding flatland is hot, and few clouds provide respite from the relentless sun. The road is safe, and traders frequently pass by.

Burning Sugar

As the Sarire sugar mill comes into view, the smell of cooking sugarcane rises on the breeze. Read or paraphrase the following text when the characters are about a quarter mile from the mill:

> Ahead stands a sugar mill, a massive wooden shed with a pointed thatched roof. Smoke rises from its many chimneys, and the area is busy with workers sorting through piles of sugarcane.
>
> An otherworldly shimmer warps the air around the mill, like a haze of silver rain that vanishes as quickly as it appears. A moment later, a scream rings out, followed by a crash. A column of smoke rises through the structure's roof.

Workers race toward the building as smoke billows through the roof and doors. A character who succeeds on a DC 16 Intelligence (Arcana or Religion) check suspects that the shimmer in the air could have been some manner of planar disturbance.

Fire at the Mill

When the characters reach the mill, they see the full scope of the disturbance:

> Through the broad, open doors of the mill, you see that the interior has collapsed into a great sinkhole. Large, overturned kettles spill boiling sugarcane juice across the broken floor, and the fires that once heated those kettles leap up nearby columns and race along the thatched reed roof. A half dozen workers have fallen into the sinkhole and struggle to clamber out.

The mill is in chaos as a dozen workers make disorganized attempts to douse the fires. Over the noise, a character who has a passive Wisdom (Perception) score of 18 or higher notices an eerie, whistling emanating from no place in particular.

Sinkhole. The opening of the sinkhole is 20 feet wide and descends into a 20-foot-deep pit. Six workers (neutral, human **commoners**) are at the bottom of the pit, frantically trying to climb out. Climbing the sinkhole's crumbling walls requires a successful DC 14 Strength (Athletics) check, but the panicked workers repeatedly fail to escape. A character who investigates the sinkhole and succeeds on a DC 16 Intelligence (Nature) check sees that the earth of its walls is dry and dead, like it's from somewhere else entirely.

Whistlers. A moment after a character looks in the hole, two large, gaunt, bipedal figures appear within. These are creatures from the Far Realm called **whistlers** (detailed at the end of this adventure). They've teleported into the sinkhole and seek to feed on the trapped workers. If unimpeded, the hostile whistlers slay one worker per round, taking their time to savor the confused mortals' fear. If attacked, they teleport near their attacker and ignore the workers. The alien beings fight to the death.

Mysterious Manifestations

Once the whistlers are defeated, the threat isn't past. The mill's burning roof threatens to collapse. The characters have time to escape with the workers, but the structure gives way moments after they leave. The mill's workers can only watch as the building is consumed by flames.

After the characters escape, another strange event occurs. Read the following description once all the characters are out of danger:

> A tearing sound precedes the appearance of a silvery ripple hovering in the air nearby. From the anomaly, a frantic-looking scarlet macaw shoots forth, trailing silvery motes. A figure appears behind the bird, pushing as though trying to pass through, but held fast by the portal's flickering magic.
>
> "Is anyone there?" a woman in a beaded vest shouts. "I can see you, but I can't get through!"

The figure is Yarana, an Ataguan warrior lost to time. She stands on the far side of an unstable planar rift between the Material Plane and the Ghost Orchid Tepui in the Feywild. A character who succeeds on a DC 16 Intelligence (Arcana) check recognizes the planar rift, a temporary and potentially dangerous portal created by multiplanar energies, not deliberate magic. While Yarana's macaw was able to slip through, the rift is fading, preventing further passage in either direction.

After a moment, Yarana continues:

> "Listen, please!" the woman calls. "I'm Yarana. The Ghost Orchid Tepui is under siege by alien creatures. Chimagua, our guardian, has fallen into a deathly slumber. If the great spirit dies, all is lost. If you are brave souls, seek the tepui. Find the portal in the Llanos. Nene knows the way. But be—"
>
> With a sound like breaking glass, the rift collapses and is gone.

Characters who succeed on a DC 16 Intelligence (Arcana or History) check recognize references to the Ghost Orchid Tepui, along with any of the stories from the "Legends of Atagua" section at the end of this adventure.

The macaw that passed through the rift squawks as he circles frantically. This is Yarana's companion, Nene. He lands on the shoulder of any character who beckons to him.

Nene

Nene is a macaw from the Feywild. He uses the **hawk** stat block but has the Fey type, has Intelligence 7, and can speak and understand simple phrases and concepts in Common. Nene has a boisterous personality but is easily distracted. He can mime straightforward responses to questions, tap objects to get his point across, scratch simple images in the dirt, and so forth. The macaw is confused by the process of passing through the rift but is eager to get back to the Feywild and can lead the characters to a portal to the Ghost Orchid Tepui (see the "Across the Llanos" section).

The Sugar Man

Though the mill can't be saved, the workers prevent the fire from spreading, and they are happy to accept the aid of any characters who want to help. As they work, several laborers whisper fearfully, claiming they saw whistlers. If asked, a worker tells the characters that whistlers are beings that emerge from the shadows, whistling a creepy tune as they steal away the unwary. They're a well-known local legend, but few have ever seen one—until now.

Soon after the mill collapses, its owner, Alfonz "Sugar Man" Rubinaz-Zumdi, arrives on the scene, escorted by several bodyguards.

Alfonz "Sugar Man" Rubinaz-Zumdi

The venerable Alfonz (neutral, human **noble**) reminds everyone he meets that he is the patriarch of a great estate and the landlord of every sugarcane field surrounding the city of El Caparazón. In just three generations, the razor-tongued Sugar Man has transformed his clan, the Zumdi, from farm laborers into the closest thing to nobility that Ataguan society has yet seen. From the stately old hacienda he calls the Sugar Alcázar, the Sugar Man hosts dazzling galas and subtly manipulates local farm owners and bosses from across Atagua to his service.

Assessing the Situation

Workers quickly describe to Alfonz what happened. The Sugar Man asks the characters to join in the conversation, forgoing introductions to get to the heart of the situation. Use the following to guide the discussion:

- The Sugar Man is astonished to hear of the sinkhole. He's thoughtful if the characters suggest a planar disturbance was responsible for it.
- He pays particular attention to any report of Yarana's words. A worker mentions this to the Sugar Man if the characters don't.
- In response to any description of the whistlers, the Sugar Man scoffs openly. He is taken aback if a character shows him evidence of a whistler.

Once he has a grasp of the situation, the Sugar Man orders his bodyguards to help the survivors, assess the damage to the mill, and leave him to speak with the characters alone.

YARANA AND NENE

The Sugar Man's Offer

Alfonz leads the characters into the privacy of a storehouse and thanks them for their aid. He focuses in on what Yarana told them and asks what they know about the Ghost Orchid Tepui. He can reveal any information from the "Legends of Atagua" section, but he insists that whistlers are folk tales to frighten children.

He shares the following as he sets out an offer for the characters:

- This Yarana person seems to think the macaw can lead the characters to the legendary Ghost Orchid Tepui. The Sugar Man wants the characters to undertake a mission for him if they find a way to that mysterious mountain.
- Legends say that mythical plants called ghost orchids grow on the tepui. The white seed pod of a ghost orchid is said to have the power to bring the dead back to life. The Sugar Man wants the characters to bring him one of these white seed pods.

The Sugar Man's excitement is obvious. If pressed as to why he wants the seed pod, he says only that someone dear to him was once lost, and he wishes to see that person live again. He doesn't share the details, but the Sugar Man plans to use the power of the seed pod to resurrect his son, Endis, who died a year ago. In exchange for procuring a white seed pod for him, the Sugar Man promises to pay the characters 1,250 gp each. Whether or not the characters take the Sugar Man up on his offer, Nene the macaw is anxious to return to Yarana. He begins repeating what the characters and the Sugar Man say in mocking tones until they move on.

Across the Llanos

Long ago, Nene traveled across the grasslands of Atagua, known as the Llanos, with Yarana. He knows the location of the secret gateway that leads from Atagua to the Ghost Orchid Tepui, but much has changed in the years since the fey-touched bird explored the region. His directions are general and often as simple as "this way" or "that way." Regardless, Nene's directions are accurate and eventually lead to the Feywild portal.

Provided the characters follow Nene's directions, the journey from the sugar mill to the Ghost Orchid Tepui portal passes through El Caparazón, over the Grassroads, and along Zula's Trail before venturing into the grasslands. The entire trek is about 48 miles long and takes 2 days to complete at a normal pace.

Alternatively, characters who have access to the *plane shift* spell can forgo the journey and travel directly to the Ghost Orchid Tepui. If they use this spell to do so, proceed with the "Ghost Orchid Tepui" section.

Visiting El Caparazón

The largest settlement in the region, El Caparazón is partially shaded by a gigantic, half-dome lattice structure created in the distant past. This shelter cools the city's homes and its vast markets, which are largely peopled by Humanoids and visiting thri-kreen traders. The characters can find ample places to rest and resupply here. They can also purchase a map of the region, similar to the one that appears as map 15.4 at the end of this adventure, for 1 gp. El Caparazón is further detailed in the "Atagua Gazetteer" section at the end of this adventure.

The Grassroads

The Grassroads is a network of cleverly constructed wood-and-reed bridges standing 15 to 40 feet above the ground. Approximately every 5 miles along the walkways, collections of 10-foot-wide lean-tos offer travelers protection from the unrelenting sun and a comfortable spot to hitch hammocks. Charitable travelers leave items they can afford to share in the lean-tos. Each time the characters stop at such a lean-to waypoint, roll on or choose from the Lean-To Items table to see what they find.

Lean-To Items

d10	Item
1–4	Nothing
5	1d4 cones of panela
6	A guitar with one broken string
7	A pouch of coffee or cacao beans
8	A fine straw hat and a lightly used pair of sandals
9	A thri-kreen weapon called a chatkcha (detailed in the "Thri-kreen" section of the *Monster Manual*)
10	A sleeping rooster (use the statistics for a **hawk**, but with no flying speed)

Ambushed Thri-Kreen

After the characters have traveled the Grassroads for about a day, the following encounter occurs:

> The Grassroads appear infinite and disappear into the haze. Ahead, an insectile traveler trudges toward you. Suddenly, there's a shriek overhead, and a vulture-headed griffon dives toward the traveler.

The **thri-kreen** is 100 feet ahead of the characters and has little defense against the **griffon**. Roll initiative. The characters can drive off the griffin by dealing damage to it or by succeeding on a DC 18 Charisma (Intimidation) check. If they don't drive it off, the griffin grapples the thri-kreen and carries its panicking prey 20 feet into the air. The griffon tries to fly away, moving at half speed as it carries the thri-kreen back to its lair.

If rescued, the thri-kreen introduces himself as Phik-Pik, a trader headed to El Caparazón with a fine selection of salted meats—likely what attracted the griffon's attention. Aside from offering the characters a great deal on capybara jerky (only 1 gp per pound), he gifts them his gythka (detailed in the "Thri-kreen" section of the *Monster Manual*) and a *bag of beans* with three beans remaining.

Termite Mounds

Nene guides the characters across the eastern extent of the Llanos, growing more excited as he recognizes familiar terrain. Read the following description when the characters reach the plains near the bend of the Holroro river:

> A wide stretch of tombstone-sized termite mounds is dominated by a tall mound with an unusually flat top. Giant anteaters mill around the mounds but pay little attention to anything except their search for a meal.

The termite mounds here are natural and aren't dangerous; the giant anteaters (use the **giant badger** stat block) ignore the characters unless disturbed.

Characters who can communicate with the anteaters find them to be lazy, well-fed beasts. If asked about the tall termite mound, the anteaters explain that they live in that mound but the eating's better among the smaller mounds. The anteaters don't explain further and might doze off if characters persistently ask boring, non-food-related questions.

The Giant Mound

Nene's excited squawking confirms that the giant mound is where the portal to the Ghost Orchid Tepui stands, and the macaw flies straight for it. Characters who investigate the 18-foot-tall mound find it crawling with termites but also discover a sizable crack in one side. This supernaturally dark gap is wide enough for a Large creature to squeeze into. A character who casts *detect magic* finds the gap radiates an aura of conjuration magic. A creature who passes through the gap enters a planar portal that transports them to the Ghost Orchid Tepui.

THE MYSTERIOUS GHOST ORCHID TEPUI IS A FAMILIAR SIGHT IN THE DREAMS OF ATAGUA'S PEOPLE.

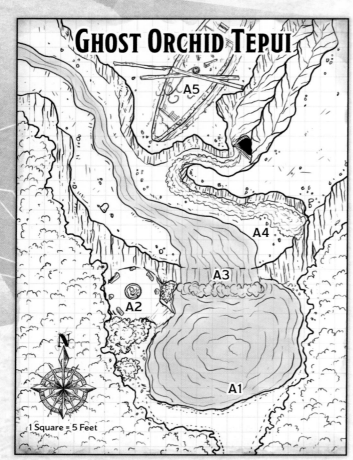

MAP 15.1: GHOST ORCHID TEPUI

GHOST ORCHID TEPUI

When a character enters the giant termite mound in the Llanos, read the following description:

> The Llanos vanishes, replaced by the earthy scent of jungle. As you emerge through a hollow in a large tree, thick rain forest vegetation surrounds you. Heavy mist hangs in the air, obscuring the top of a spire rising hundreds of feet into the sky, no more than a hundred feet away. A roaring waterfall cascades down the tepui, and a well-trodden path twists toward it through the trees.

Upon passing through the portal, the characters arrive at the Ghost Orchid Tepui, a mysterious corner of the Feywild. This tiny realm stretches about a mile in all directions around the tepui—a steep, pale, flat-topped mountain. Around and atop the mountain is a lush rain forest full of mist, colorful flora, and curious insects. Creatures that wander into the rain forest find it increasingly dense and difficult to traverse. After an hour of travel, creatures emerge near the Ghost Orchid Tepui no matter which direction they were headed.

With a shriek, Nene encourages the characters to proceed down the path toward the tepui. He then flies up the side of the tepui and over the top.

TEPUI LOCATIONS

The following locations are keyed to map 15.1.

A1: WATERFALL POOL

As the characters approach the base of the tepui, read or paraphrase the following:

> The path ends at a clearing before an immense waterfall. It cascades down the tepui's cliffs into a pool coated with oily, gray slime. Dense mist hangs above the pool.

The water of the pool, the waterfall, and the stream that feeds them in area A4 has been magically tainted, causing creatures that touch it to rapidly decay. Any creature that enters the water for the first time on a turn or that starts its turn in the water takes 44 (8d10) necrotic damage. A character who investigates the water and succeeds on a DC 16 Intelligence (Nature) check, or who tests the water by submerging any sort of organic material, recognizes the water's magical corruption. The *detect magic* spell reveals that the water has an aura of necromantic magic.

A2: ANCIENT STATUE

> A small stone platform rises from the edge of the pool, supporting a larger-than-life quartz statue of an elf priest with outstretched arms.

The ruins here belong to an elven tribe that once dwelled in this region. They moved on long ago but left behind a statue of a forgotten healer.

Cloaker. Two pale **cloakers** that can speak Common and Elvish cling to the statue's back, disguising themselves as leathery wings. When a creature nears the statue, the cloakers take turns posing as the spirit of the statue. They offer to bless any character who shows their purity by bathing in the pool. A character who succeeds on a Wisdom (Insight) check contested by the cloakers' Charisma (Deception) check recognizes that the "spirit" is a little too eager with its request. Additionally, a character who succeeds on a DC 18 Wisdom (Perception) check realizes the voices are coming from behind the statue. The cloakers attack when a creature comes within 5 feet of the statue or it's clear no one's buying their lies.

Statue. A spirit actually does linger in the statue. Once the cloakers are defeated, the statue glows faintly. The first injured creature to touch the statue regains 45 (10d8) hit points. Once the statue heals a creature, its glow fades and the spirit departs.

A3: Waterfall Ascent

The walls of the tepui rise 1,000 feet but boast plentiful handholds, making the tepui easy to climb without an ability check. The waterfall's water is deadly, as described in area A1.

Tainted Mist. A character who succeeds on a DC 14 Wisdom (Perception) check notes that the mist surrounding the tepui grows thicker 100 feet up and has a faint green tinge. This mist is 50 feet thick and extends 100 feet from the cliff wall. Creatures that enter the mist must succeed on a DC 15 Constitution saving throw or become infected with sight rot (detailed in the *Dungeon Master's Guide*). Strong wind disperses the mist for 1 minute, while removing its source in the Crystal Caves causes the mist to vanish.

Through the Falls. Characters who have a passive Wisdom (Perception) score of 20 or higher, or who pass through the waterfall to see what's behind it, find a ledge about 100 feet from the ground. Upon the ledge rests an elf skeleton. In the skeleton's moldy backpack is a shard of white crystal (worth 300 gp), a *dagger of venom*, and a *potion of invulnerability*.

A4: Tepui Plateau

The top of the mountain is covered by brilliant green rain forest vegetation. A deep stream cuts through the foliage, running alongside a ridge before cascading off the tepui's edge. A trail vanishes through a cleft in the ridge, with low, green vapor billowing along the path. Above, a shattered ship teeters atop a higher ledge.

The stream's waters are deadly, as detailed in area A1.

The cleft in the ridge is the opening to a short, narrow canyon. Within lies a cave with green-tinged vapor flowing from it. This passage leads to area C1 of the Crystal Caves (see below) and the source of the gas. A creature that enters this trail of gas or the cave into the Crystal Caves suffers the effects of the mist, as detailed in area A3.

As soon as the characters arrive, Nene flutters excitedly toward the cleft in the ridge, leading them toward the entrance to the Crystal Caves while avoiding the toxic vapor.

A5: Crashed Airship

A crashed airship rests precariously atop the tepui. Those who ascend an additional 30 feet up the mountainside reach the deck of the shattered vessel.

Vines cover the ship's shattered hull. Little more than a moldy deck and toppled masts remains. Bits of frayed rope and broad scraps of patchwork fabric litter the deck.

This airship found its way to the Ghost Orchid Tepui decades ago and became stranded. There is no evidence of its former owner. A character who succeeds on a DC 18 Intelligence (Investigation) check surmises that the scraps of fabric and rope are all that remains of a blimp-like balloon the ship was once suspended from.

Below Decks. The ship's lower decks are crushed, creating a narrow, crumbling space between the surviving upper deck and the stone below. A drowsy **displacer beast** makes its den in this tight space, accessing it via a gap in the northern part of the hull. The creature is indifferent to the characters and attempts to hide from them if they remain on deck. It tries to flee if cornered within its den.

Treasure. Bones and scraps of hide litter the displacer beast's den. Characters who search through the debris find an electrum septum piercing worth 150 gp and a set of *dimensional shackles*.

Crystal Caves

Nene leads the characters to the mouth of a cave but refuses to enter the noxious mist that flows from within. This is the entrance to the Crystal Caves, the dwelling place of the spirit Chimagua, whom Yarana entreated the characters to save.

Crystal Caves Features

Locations throughout the Crystal Caves have the following features.

Ceilings. Most cavern ceilings are 20 feet high and are hung with crystalline stalactites.

Lighting. Crystals embedded in the walls and ceilings radiate dim light for 30 feet. Once a crystal is removed, it stops glowing.

Crystal Caves Locations

The following locations are keyed to map 15.2.

C1: Pool of Skins

A tunnel filled with noxious gas runs 100 feet from area A4 on the Ghost Orchid Tepui before opening into a larger chamber. Read the following description when the characters enter the cavern:

> Glowing crystals speckle this cavern's walls like stars in the night sky. At the chamber's center, a thick, foul-smelling mist billows from a shallow pool of brackish liquid. Something large and scaly lies within. Beyond it stands a sculpted pillar and a broad stone table.

The pool in this room once served as a reflecting pool for a pillar sculpted with images of serene, intertwined snakes with glowing crystalline eyes. The waters have since been despoiled by rotting skin shed by the spirit snake Chimagua.

The stone table bears two empty stone candle holders.

Tainted Mist. The same tainted mist from area A3 fills this chamber and the tunnel leading back to the Ghost Orchid Tepui.

Pool. The pool is the source of the tainted mist. Air from deeper in the cavern blows the mist rising from the pool outside. Any creature that enters the pool must succeed on a DC 18 Constitution saving throw or become infected with sight rot (detailed in the *Dungeon Master's Guide*). If the pool is drained (perhaps using spells like *stone shape*) or the skin within is destroyed or removed, the poison mist ceases rising from the water.

Snake's Skin. Partially submerged in the pool is a 100-foot-long, opalescent skin shed by the gigantic anaconda Chimagua. The skin has AC 15, hp 40, immunity to poison and psychic damage, and vulnerability to fire if it is removed from the water. Creatures that touch the skin without protective gear must succeed on a DC 18 Constitution saving throw or become infected with sight rot (detailed in the *Dungeon Master's Guide*). A character who examines the skin and succeeds on a DC 14 Intelligence (Nature) check can tell it comes from a Feywild creature, not a natural snake, and that the skin has become riddled with disease as it rotted.

C2: Meditation Nook

> Several sleeping mats circle an empty firepit in this small side cave. Upon a modest altar sits a stone censer and several sticks of incense.

Students and guests of Chimagua once rested and meditated here.

Incense. The incense sticks are broken and useless, with the exception of one. If the intact incense stick is burned, the area within 10 feet of the incense fills with acrid smoke for 5 minutes or until the incense is extinguished. A creature that enters the smoke or starts its turn there must succeed on a DC 16 Constitution saving throw or become poisoned for 1 hour. A creature poisoned by the incense is unconscious and experiences what feels like years' worth of dreams about infinitely long, psychedelic serpents. When the creature awakes, it gains inspiration.

Secret Path. A character who searches this cavern and succeeds on a DC 18 Wisdom (Perception) check discovers a segment of the stone wall behind the altar easily shifts aside, revealing a passage leading to area C4. Characters who have the Stonecunning trait have advantage on this check. This door is obvious to any creature in the passage beyond.

C3: Whistling Hall

Two **whistlers** (detailed at the end of this adventure) lurk in this hall. If creatures make considerable noise in area C2, the whistlers attempt to teleport behind the intruders, following them into area C4 to ambush them with the other whistler in that area. Otherwise, they attack when the characters enter this passage.

C4: Orchid Cavern

> Ledges within this cavern overlook a pool of black liquid twenty feet below. At the center of the cave, an island supports an ancient, bare tree. Rope bridges connect this island to the ledge at the cavern's entrance and another along the back wall.

A **whistler** (detailed at the end of this adventure) lurks at the western edge of the northern platform. It waits to attack until intruders appear vulnerable—such as when they're crossing the rope bridges.

Rope Bridge. The rope bridge to area C5 looks ancient and fragile. It has AC 10, hp 14, and immunity to poison and psychic damage.

Secret Door. A character who searches the southwest ledge and succeeds on a DC 18 Wisdom (Perception) check discovers a segment of the stone wall moves, revealing a passage leading to area C2. Characters who have the Stonecunning trait have advantage on this check. This door is obvious to any creature in the passage beyond.

C5: Ghost Orchid Tree

> The roots of a great, bare-limbed tree wind through the flat-topped rock at the cavern's center. Orchids bearing large white flowers wrap around the tree.

The ancient tree is a sacred plant that Chimagua cultivated. It rises 20 feet to the cavern ceiling.

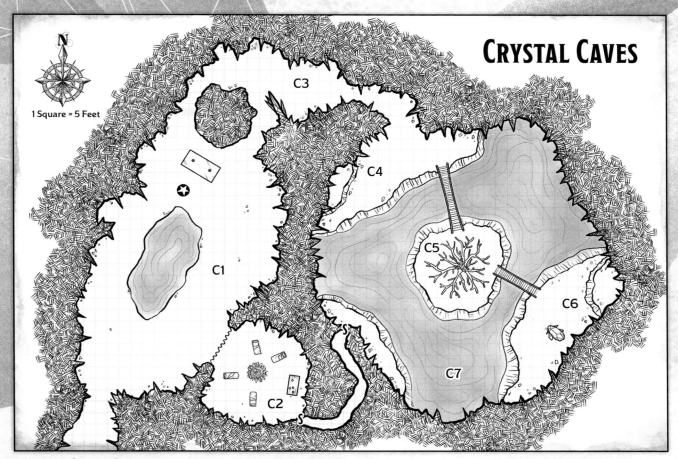

MAP 15.2: CRYSTAL CAVES

Night Hags. Three **night hags**—Lola la Lúgubre, Tia Tóxica, and Ofilia la Odiosa—claim this cavern and the ghost orchids that grow here. The crones are invisible and lurk at the base of the tree. As soon as a character reaches the island, all three appear, disguised as elf priests in white robes. They claim to be magically bound to the island by the creature that lies on the ledge beyond—pointing to area C6. They try to convince intruders to free them by slaying the monster there. In truth, they want to trick the characters onto the rope bridge so they can destroy it, dropping the characters into the water of area C7 and then disposing of them via magic.

Ghost Orchids. The pale flowers growing on the tree are ghost orchids. A character who succeeds on a DC 18 Intelligence (Nature) check identifies the ghost orchids and their properties (see the "Ghost Orchids" sidebar). Additionally, a character who succeeds on a DC 16 Wisdom (Perception) check notices the orchids bear one black seed pod and one white seed pod, both of which can be removed.

Treasure. The hags have left their treasure in a hollow at the base of the tree. Inside are three black opals (worth 1,000 gp each), a *bag of devouring*, a *potion of flying*, and a toucan skull with a wax plug that is a container filled with *sovereign glue*.

C6: The Sleeping Stone

> A ten-foot-tall, chipped gray crystal rises from this ledge, pulsing with pale light. On the rock shelf behind it, a familiar woman stands near an enormous anaconda that's coiled and motionless.

Chimagua, the guardian spirit of the Ghost Orchid Tepui, lies here. Tainted by foul Far Realm energies, the coiled, 40-foot-long anaconda is unconscious. A character who has a passive Wisdom (Perception) score of 14 or higher sees that Chimagua is incorporeal, fading in and out of existence with each slow breath.

Yarana. Since contacting to the characters, Chimagua's ally Yarana (**scout**) has been enthralled by the aboleths lurking beneath the water in area C7. When a character approaches this area, Yarana urges them to come quickly, saying that Chimagua is dying and needs assistance. As soon as the first character reaches this area, she attacks. Any time Yarana takes damage, she can make a DC 14 Wisdom saving throw to escape the aboleths' control. If freed, Yarana points to the water and warns that the true threat is there, prompting the aboleth Glol to emerge and attack if the characters haven't already encountered that aboleth. If Yarana is incapacitated, the aboleths from area C7 emerge and attack.

The Sleeping Stone. The crystal is the Sleeping Stone, a magical device Chimagua once used to influence the dreams of Atagua's people. The power of the Drought Elder has corrupted the stone, forcing Chimagua into a deathly slumber and accelerating the planar instability in Atagua.

Any creature that touches the Sleeping Stone must make a DC 20 Wisdom saving throw, taking 42 (12d6) psychic damage on a failed save, or half as much damage on a successful one. Regardless of the saving throw result, the creature also receives the following grim vision:

Within an expanse of broken worlds drifts a gargantuan alien form—one that is far from a centipede yet closer to that shape than any other. The shape is shattered and crawling with convulsing, bipedal parasites. Despite the shape's ruin, the darkness within one of its hollow eyes deepens and fixates. It sees you.

C7: Polluted Pool

Two **aboleths**, Glol and Kilzilg, lurk in the brackish but mundane waters of this pool. These servants of the Drought Elder infiltrated the tepui and used their master's magic to corrupt Chimagua and the Sleeping Stone. When Yarana arrived, they took control of her. They are using the warrior to watch Chimagua's final days.

The aboleths prefer to stay in the cavern's foul water, which heavily obscures them while they're below the surface. If the aboleths are revealed or the characters enter the water, the aboleths attack. Both use their telepathy to threaten foes, promising eternities of desiccated doom within the Drought Elder's immortal corpse.

Ghost Orchids

Manifestations of Chimagua's magic, these magical plants are unique to the tepui named after them. Every few years, a ghost orchid colony grows a black pod as thick as a human fist that holds three soft, black seeds. A creature that consumes one of these black seeds is affected by the spell *feign death*. If the creature is unaware of the pod's effects or does not wish to be affected, it can resist the effect by succeeding on a DC 16 Constitution saving throw. Otherwise, it is considered to be a willing recipient of the spell.

More rarely, the orchids produce a smaller pod holding a single white seed. Among its various magical properties, if a white seed is ground and scattered over a dead body, the body is affected by the *resurrection* spell. A white ghost orchid seed has no effect if consumed.

The Tepui's Fate

When the Drought Elder's minions in the Crystal Caves have been dealt with, the characters have a chance to talk to Yarana. If Yarana died during the encounter with the aboleths, Chimagua's spirit can telepathically reach out to the characters and convey the information Yarana would have—see "Yarana's Hope" below.

Once the characters are out of danger, they might try to heal Chimagua. The great anaconda can't be revived by any ability or magic available to the characters. A character who succeeds on a DC 16 Intelligence (Arcana) or Wisdom (Medicine) check determines that a magical affliction affects Chimagua, and the guardian will die in the coming weeks if the affliction is allowed to run its course. Yarana knows how to heal the great spirit, though.

Yarana

Born nearly one thousand years ago in Atagua, Yarana (neutral good, human **scout**) was the most talented of the elite Cababa warriors of ancient times. Days before becoming her people's chief, Yarana and her faithful companion Nene were murdered by an envious rival. Their remains floated down the river Holroro and slipped into the realm of the Ghost Orchid Tepui. There, Chimagua found Yarana and Nene and restored them to be protectors of the spirit's mountain. Over ages, Yarana has protected Chimagua and learned the ways of the Feywild. But everything changed in recent days when beings from the Far Realm attacked the Ghost Orchid Tepui.

Yarana would like to take a more active role in combating the threats to her original home, but her immortality is tied to the Feywild. If she leaves that plane, she will rapidly age and die after 24 hours. She risked this when she contacted the characters earlier only because of the dire circumstances to Chimagua.

Yarana's Hope

Yarana thanks the characters for undertaking her mission. She shares the rest of the story she began when she first contacted the characters, along with any information in the "Background" section:

- The Sleeping Stone, a focus of Chimagua's power, has sent the spirit visions of a Far Realm terror known as the Drought Elder that's trying to exert control over Atagua.
- Recently, creatures from the Far Realm slipped from Atagua into the Ghost Orchid Tepui and attacked Chimagua.
- The invaders broke the Sleeping Stone and spirited a piece of it away. This put Chimagua into a deathlike slumber.

- Yarana believes they returned the fragment to the Drought Elder, which is using it as a way to draw power from the nightmares of Atagua's people.
- Only by recovering the missing piece of the Sleeping Stone might Chimagua be saved.
- Yarana believes the Drought Elder is vulnerable to Chimagua's magic, such as that of white ghost orchid seeds.

Yarana beseeches the characters to help by stealing into the Drought Elder's domain and recovering the stolen Sleeping Stone fragment. She has little to offer them except for two *potions of healing* (supreme) and a pouch of Feywild herbs that functions as *Keoghtom's ointment*, but she suspects Chimagua will reward them handsomely if they aid the spirit.

If pressed about the Drought Elder itself, Yarana knows only that it is a terrible being of desiccation and ruin. She doesn't know how to combat it, but she suggests the characters takes the white seed pod from the Ghost Orchid in area C5. Since the white seed pods hold the power of rebirth, perhaps it can be used against an entity of decay.

Opening a Path

Reaching the Drought Elder in the Far Realm is no easy task. While spells like *plane shift* can convey characters to the Far Realm, reaching the unfathomable entity requires a more precise method of travel. But Yarana has a plan:

> "A relic of Atagua's past holds the key to reaching the Drought Elder," Yarana says. "The *Hammock of Worlds* once allowed people to visit Chimagua, using the Ghost Orchid Tepui's connection to Atagua. But with the Far Realm's influence affecting the land, the hammock could likely follow those corrupted planar connections as well, creating a path to the Drought Elder. But if it's to work, we must move quickly."

Yarana shares the following information, explaining how to recover the *Hammock of Worlds*:

- The *Hammock of Worlds* is held by one of the most ancient beings in Atagua, the Dawn Mother.
- The Dawn Mother is an ageless giant that wanders the Llanos and is said to call forth the sun every morning. She frequents an oasis called the Basket. Although she's aloof, she loves the land and is sure to help.
- Once the characters have the hammock, they must take it to the mystics known as the Green Doctors at the Silver Tapir Monastery.
- Yarana can't come with the characters because her immortality is tied to the Feywild (see the "Yarana" section).

Back across the Llanos

Once the characters are ready to return to Atagua, Yarana escorts them back to the portal they used to reach the tepui. Nene travels with them through the portal, carrying with him a message to the Green Doctors. Upon returning through the portal, the characters find themselves back in the field of termite mounds in eastern Atagua. The macaw swiftly departs to deliver his message to the Silver Tapir Monastery.

The Basket is 30 miles from the portal, a journey that takes one full day and a quarter of the next at a normal pace. The fastest route by land is via the Grassroads. During this journey, the characters might encounter any of the sights mentioned in the "Journey across the Llanos" section from earlier in the adventure.

Sugar Bug

As the characters near the Basket, they encounter an iridescent-hued **thri-kreen** hurrying along the Grassroads in the opposite direction. The thri-kreen hails the characters and explains that her people need help. If the characters agree to listen, she rapidly shares the following information:

- The thri-kreen's name is Cht-Chak, and she's a leader of a nomadic band of thri-kreen traders who deal in panela.
- Her people were camped at the Basket when a terrible storm appeared out of nowhere.
- Soon after, a terrifying, root-covered giant—the Dawn Mother—appeared and attacked her people without provocation.
- Cht-Chak is desperately trying to find help.

If pressed for details, Cht-Chak explains she's never seen the Dawn Mother act like this. She's willing to pay the characters to help her band, though she can offer only a load of panela worth 200 gp. She can, however, lead the characters directly to the Dawn Mother.

The Dawn Mother

It takes Cht-Chak and the characters only a few hours to reach the Basket and, from there, to follow a trail of lightning scorches to where the Dawn Mother still pursues a group of thri-kreen. Read the following as the characters approach:

> Numerous thri-kreen dash through the tall grass, attempting to avoid the steps of a massive figure. A gigantic, ancient woman dressed in thick tree roots and vines stomps after the mantis-folk. Amid her roaring, she occasionally plucks a sizable seed pod from her garb and chucks it after her quarry.

THE HAMMOCK OF WORLDS

The *Hammock of Worlds* is a colorful hammock woven with traditional Ataguan designs. It functions as a *well of many worlds* with two exceptions:

- It can be used only by a member of the order known as the Green Doctors.
- The portal it creates can connect only to the Ghost Orchid Tepui in the Feywild or to the Drought Elder in the Far Realm (the user's choice)—the two planes linked to Atagua.

Any member of the Green Doctors at the Silver Tapir Monastery can use the *Hammock of Worlds*.

SILVER TAPIR MONASTERY

The Silver Tapir Monastery is approximately 15 miles from the Basket, a journey that takes 5 hours at a normal pace. As the characters approach, read the following description:

> A large, oxidized silver statue of a tapir stands before a broad stone structure covered in carvings of stylized local animals—tapirs, capybaras, hawks, and more. Dozens of people stand outside the building, many wearing distinctive green sashes.

The hostile **storm giant** chasing the thri-kreen is the Dawn Mother. Although the giant has long been a stoic guardian of the Llanos, her recent dreams of otherworldly insects have confused and enraged her. Fearing the thri-kreen are to blame, she has attacked Cht-Chak's innocent band.

If attacked, the Dawn Mother turns her rage on whoever harmed her. Her rage continues until she is reduced 50 hit points or fewer, after which she comes to her senses and stops attacking. Characters can also use an action to talk her down, then make a DC 22 Charisma (Persuasion) check. Succeeding on this check once dulls her fury, while two successful checks cause the Dawn Mother to stop attacking.

CONSULTING WITH THE DAWN MOTHER

Once the Dawn Mother comes to her senses, she apologizes for her rage and explains that she's been suffering terrible dreams. If asked for the *Hammock of Worlds*, she rummages amid the vines covering her and produces it. If the characters explain why they need it, she's eager to help them and not only gives them the hammock but also leads them to the Silver Tapir Monastery.

If the Dawn Mother is calmed or defeated, Cht-Chak thanks the characters and rewards them. If the characters kill the giant, Cht-Chak helps them retrieve the *Hammock of Worlds* from the giant's body and directs them to the Silver Taper Monastery.

An elder Green Doctor named Melecio (neutral good, elf **archmage**) steps from the crowd, with Nene perched on her shoulder. Melecio explains that the Green Doctors have been expecting them and shares the following information:

- Melecio understands the characters have been sent to fetch the *Hammock of Worlds* and seek to use it to travel to the Far Realm. She believes this can be done—though it hasn't been tried before.
- The *Hammock of Worlds* is traditionally employed only at dusk during a ritual dance, one the Green Doctors are prepared to host this coming dusk.
- At Melecio's invitation, leaders from across Atagua are gathering to represent their people during this rare, important ritual.
- Melecio can also share details on the Green Doctors and legends from the "Atagua Gazetteer" section.

Until the ritual, the characters are welcome to rest and prepare for their journey. Green Doctors (neutral good, human **priests**) can use their magic to heal the characters during this time.

The Sugar Man is among the leaders who arrive to participate in the dance. He asks if the characters retrieved a white seed pod for him. If the characters did not, or choose not to give it to him, he is disappointed but understanding. Otherwise, he pays them the agreed-upon price.

The Portal Ritual

At sunset, the ritual for travel through the *Hammock of Worlds* begins:

> Two wizened trees stand before the Silver Tapir Monastery, their ancient boughs lit by dusk light. Between them stretches the *Hammock of Worlds*, its patterned fabric loose and empty. Soon the Green Doctors and other visitors who have come to participate in the ritual begin a rhythmic drumming. All around the monastery, the dance begins, with the sound of drums, flutes, harps, and chants rising. Mystics, people from nearby villages, thri-kreen travelers, and even enthusiastic capybaras shuffle and gyrate in time to the music. As they do, the hammock sags and an otherworldly glow emanates from within it.

At the height of the ritual, Melecio uses the hammock to open a portal to the Far Realm. When the characters are ready, they can pass through the portal, arriving inside the Drought Elder (area D1).

The Drought Elder

The Drought Elder rots within a region of the Far Realm filled with shadows and dead stars. Characters who pass through the *Hammock of Worlds* emerge within the gigantic, lifeless, yet still malicious being. The Drought Elder cannot move, but it is aware of creatures within itself and uses its powerful telepathy to read their thoughts. However, as an immortal being that embodies unfathomable forces of apathy, desiccation, and planar dissolution, it doesn't actively impede the characters or attempt to communicate with them. It can feed information to any of the various aberrations infesting its body, though.

Drought Elder Features

Areas within the Drought Elder have the following features:

Carapace Exterior. Characters can access the exterior of the Drought Elder's carapace from areas D3 and D5. It can be climbed by any creature that succeeds on a DC 16 Strength (Athletics) check. However, traveling outside the carapace beyond area D3 or D5 attracts the attention of 1d3 **whistlers** every minute. These whistlers are hostile.

The dessicated husk of the Drought Elder endlessly drifts through a lifeless void in the Far Realm.

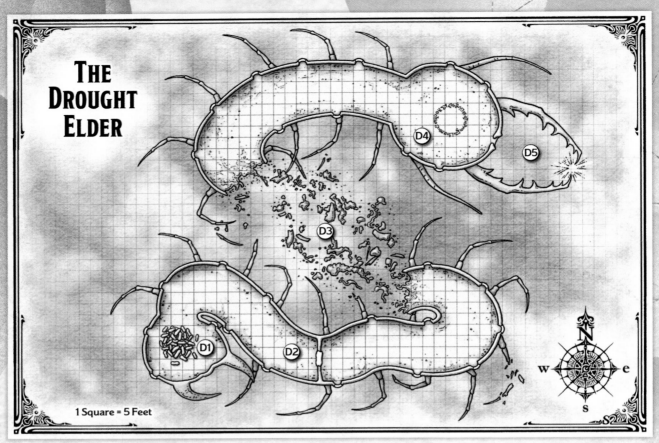

THE DROUGHT ELDER

1 Square = 5 Feet

15.3: THE DROUGHT ELDER

Ceiling. The ceilings within the Drought Elder are 20 feet high.

Darkness. The interior of the Drought Elder is not illuminated; its occupants rely on darkvision to see. Area descriptions assume that the characters have a light source or some other means of seeing in the dark.

Floor and Walls. The floor and walls are made of moist, russet chitin. Any 5-foot-square, 1-foot-thick segment of chitin has AC 12, 60 hit points, and immunity to poison and psychic damage. If damaged, a section of chitin unleashes a wave of psychic pain. Each creature within 15 feet of the damaged chitin must succeed on a DC 18 Intelligence saving throw or take 17 (5d6) psychic damage.

Spiracles. Holes in the walls allow fetid air to cycle through the Drought Elder's interior. Peering through these spiracles reveals the Drought Elder's body and an endless alien void beyond.

NAVIGATING THE DROUGHT ELDER

The following areas are keyed to map 15.3.

D1: EGG CHAMBER

Characters who pass through the *Hammock of Worlds* have the feeling of jolting awake from a dream, then emerge into the Drought Elder standing up. Read the following description:

> The air is dense and humid. Slick, chitinous walls rise around you, forming a space that feels like the interior of some vast, insectile organ. Dozens of pale, oblong masses lie piled at the room's center, and a curved passage leads out of the space. Nearby, a glowing, oval portal leads back to Atagua.

A character who investigates the walls and succeeds on a DC 16 Intelligence (Investigation or Nature) check realizes they're inside some gigantic creature, though it doesn't seem to be alive.

Eggs. A heap of oblong insect eggs filled with swirling, psychedelic colors fills the center of the room. These eggs are a manifestation of the dream energy the Drought Elder is stealing from Atagua. The eggs are easily broken; each has AC 10, 5 hit points, and immunity to poison damage. If they're destroyed, the energy within dissipates, leaving the closest creature with a fleeting impression of a dream belonging to someone from Atagua.

Egg Sucker. A moment after the characters arrive, a **whistler** (detailed at the end of this adventure) enters the chamber from area D2, moves to the pile of eggs, cracks one open, and feeds on the energy within. It ignores the characters unless attacked.

Portal. A creature that enters the portal emerges back at the Silver Tapir Monastery through the *Hammock of Worlds*.

D2: Dead End

> This short tunnel ends in a wall of pallid meat, devoid of the thick chitin covering the other walls.

If a creature approaches what appears to be the tunnel's end, hundreds of saucer-sized eyes with fanged pupils open and begin repeating a random character's name. The wall is a **gibbering mouther** controlled by the Drought Elder. It moves out of the way for any Aberration, revealing a 5-foot-diameter gap in the wall, but it attacks any other creature. Destroying the gibbering mouther leaves the gap in the wall unguarded.

D3: Void Striders

> The structure falls away, opening into a void filled with floating chunks of insectile parts. Hundreds of feet away, a similar opening gapes in the other half of the massive body. That segment ends at a wide, cave-like mouth.

Part of the Drought Elder's body has been shattered, reduced to a mass of broken chitin islands floating between the two halves of its body.

Shattered Path. Five-foot-square chunks of chitin drift in this area of low gravity between the two halves of the Drought Elder. The pieces stay 10 feet apart. Any creature that can't fly through the area must leap between these platforms. The low gravity doubles the distance creatures can jump. However, any creature that jumps must make a DC 14 Strength (Athletics) check. On a successful check, the creature lands in the intended spot. On a failed check, the creature lands 5 feet away from its intended spot and is suspended in the area's strange gravity. Suspended creatures are restrained until they use an action to pull themselves onto a nearby platform or until an adjacent creature uses an action to help them to stable ground.

Servants of Dissolution. Drifting amid the shattered body is an old and withered **beholder** called Ozk. It blends in well amid the floating meat and has advantage on its Dexterity (Stealth) checks. If Ozk notices any non-Aberration, it stops meditating on its own decay and attacks, shouting in Deep Speech that the characters should "welcome the endless" and "escape the tyranny of breath."

D4: Vestige of Consciousness

> The chitinous tunnel widens into a domed, circular area. At its center, a ring of strange runes is etched into the ground. The symbols move, crawling in a circle. Above them hovers a mass of insectile limbs encompassing an alien light. Beyond it, a narrow passage opens into the vast void outside.

A vestige of the Drought Elder's obscene consciousness lingers here. Beyond, its maw opens into the void.

Runes. The runes are manifestations of the Drought Elder's obsessive thoughts. They're written in Deep Speech and change constantly. A creature who reads them realizes they recount terrifying ends for Atagua and Chimagua, and that creature must make a DC 20 Wisdom saving throw. On a success, the creature shakes off the horror. On a failure, the creature is stunned, and the words change to name that creature. The stunned target can repeat the saving throw at the end of each of its turns, ending the effect on itself on a success.

Nexus of Dissolution. A sphere the size of a human head and composed of oversized centipede limbs encompasses a foul light. This sphere is a fraction of the Drought Elder's alien consciousness. It uses the **demilich** stat block but is an Aberration rather than Undead. It ignores the characters unless they try to harm it or try to enter area D5—either through this area or via another route. This nexus of the Drought Elder's being is vulnerable to Chimagua's power. If it comes into contact with a seed from a ghost orchid's white seed pod, it and the pod are destroyed instantly.

Maw. A gap lined with dull mandibles opens into area D5. The tiny mouth-parts twitch occasionally but are harmless.

D5: Mandible Walk

> Massive mandibles extend from the dead mass of the alien husk. Between their tips hovers a starlike crystal.

Approximately 40 feet from the Drought Elder's maw hangs the Sleeping Stone shard, twinkling between the being's two gigantic mandibles. The Drought Elder's servants avoid this area, fearing that their master might awake and consume them.

Void Walk. Creatures that can fly can easily reach and recover the fist-sized crystal. Alternatively, a creature that succeeds on a DC 16 Strength (Athletics) check can climb the Drought Elder's exterior and mandibles. Any creature that falls from the mandibles or is knocked into the void begins slowly drifting away from the Drought Elder at a rate of 10 feet per round. Unless the creature has a tether thrown to it or is recovered by another flying creature, it gradually drifts out of sight and is lost.

Sleeping Stone Shard. The fragment of the Sleeping Stone is weightless and contains a portion of the dreams of Chimagua. The first creature to touch the crystal must succeed on a DC 20 Wisdom saving throw or fall unconscious for 1d4 minutes as the creature's mind is overwhelmed by visions. An unconscious creature begins drifting away from the Drought Elder. Once the stone has been touched, though, the psychic energy stored within is expelled, and the stone can be touched safely.

ESCAPING THE DROUGHT ELDER

Once the characters have claimed the shard of the Sleeping Stone, they must still return to Atagua. The Drought Elder does nothing to physically impede the characters, but it telepathically urges the creatures inhabiting its massive corpse to attack the intruders. At your discretion, additional pairs of **whistlers** (detailed at the end of this adventure) and groups of 2d4 **gibbering mouthers** menace the characters as they return to the portal.

CONCLUSION

When the characters return to Atagua, Melecio greets them and can use the *Hammock of Worlds* to speed them back to the Ghost Orchid Tepui. There, they find Yarana attending the weakening Chimagua. If the fragment of the Sleeping Stone is restored to the whole, the crystal glows in a rainbow of colors. Chimagua awakens with full awareness of what the characters have done, having dreamed the characters' adventures. The spirit thanks the characters and awards them a lesser version of the *Hammock of Worlds*. This magic item functions as a *well of many worlds*, but the user can cause it to always reliably connect to the Ghost Orchid Tepui.

With the tepui's magic and guardian restored, the nightmares and Far Realm incursions plaguing Atagua cease. If the characters return to Atagua later, people across the land know of their heroics, and they're celebrated wherever they go. Some may seek out the heroes, hoping they can solve other threats facing the land.

ATAGUA GAZETTEER

Much of Atagua consists of grasslands, wetlands, and narrow stretches of tropical forests bordering the Holroro River. Two extreme seasons each year of intense rain and dusty drought have shaped this land and blessed its people with resilience. They live, work, and tell stories in villages built on platforms or in sprawling hacienda estates surrounded by sugarcane fields or cacao orchards. Though their villages might be separated by many miles, Ataguans meet each other in their dreams due to the connections between this land and a mystical mountain in the Feywild.

For nearly two hundred years, the people of Atagua have thrived, peacefully trading among diverse outposts connected by the Grassroads—a system of walkways elevated to protect from floods, fires, and other threats and engineered by the ancient Flood People who first settled these lands. Yet danger remains. In some years, the rains that end the dry season are late, increasing the risk of wildfires. Bulettes and other predators shadow travelers on the Grassroads or stalk the thri-kreen folk who wander the Llanos. And among the Green Doctors, a guild of healers and scholars, old tales warn of strange whistling creatures that sometimes pass into Atagua from dark realms—and that might someday emerge in unstoppable numbers to consume this land.

ATAGUA FEATURES

Those familiar with Atagua know the following details:

Hallmarks. This land is known for the chocolate and sugar produced there and for the elevated walkways that traverse its forests and tropical savannas. Folk there experience vivid dreams, often of an invisible, flat-topped mountain .

People. Ataguans are predominantly humans with tan to dark-brown complexions, along with smaller numbers of dark-skinned forest gnomes and tieflings, the latter of whom typically bear three horns. Nomadic clans of thri-kreen with iridescent carapaces also wander the Llanos; they're rarely encountered in towns and cities.

Languages. Quirapu is the language of Atagua, a melded derivative of the original languages of the Flood People who first settled these lands and the colonizers who came after them. All folk of Atagua also speak Common.

NOTEWORTHY SITES

Atagua is a rugged country of tropical grassland plains and gallery forests—a great savanna known locally as the Llanos. Spread across the basin of the twisting Holroro River, the peoples of this land dwell in scattered outposts connected by walkways called the Grassroads.

THE GRASSROADS

The Grassroads are a system of elevated, 15-foot-wide roads ranging from 5 to 20 feet in height and punctuated by lean-to shelters; the roads and shelters alike are constructed from wood, reeds, and

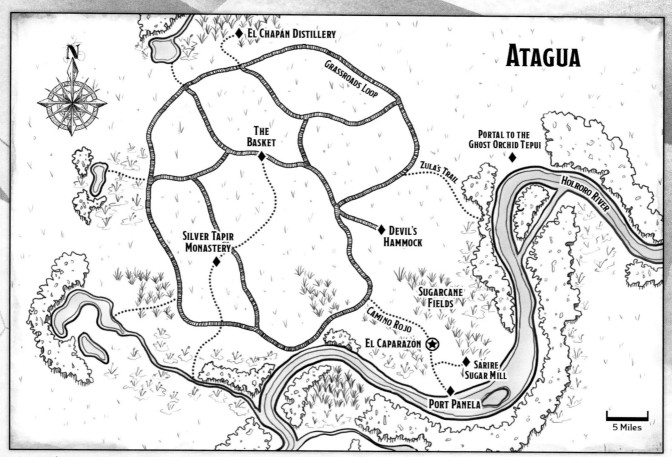

Map 15.4: Atagua

stone. The folk of Atagua use these roads to ensure safe passage above the many hazards of the Llanos. Traders and farmers walk the roads day and night, protected by the elite fighter-scouts known as Cababa warriors, who patrol constantly for poachers and bandits. Thri-kreen can often be found scavenging the ground beneath the pathways for items dropped from above. They then trade these items for panela—cones of brown sugar cooked in mills across Atagua.

El Caparazón

Hundreds of farming villages dot the Llanos, bordered by sugarcane fields and orchards of cacao trees. El Caparazón ("The Shell") is the largest of these settlements and the capital of Atagua. It was named for a latticework partial dome built by the Flood People hundreds of years ago. The dome provides precious shade to the central square known as the Mercado Sucre and to a grand hacienda roofed with amber-hued tiles. Called the Sugar Alcázar, this hacienda is home to Alfonz Rubinaz-Zumdi, the powerful landowner known as the Sugar Man.

About 5 miles outside the city, Port Panela serves as Atagua's port. It boasts dozens of wooden docks as well as thatched huts on stilted platforms, and the harbor teems with sleek trade boats returning or departing with sugar, cacao, goods, and travelers.

The Outposts

Three remote settlements, collectively known as "the outposts," are home to the most notable factions of Atagua. One is a busy encampment that serves as a base for the Tribe of Builders, the engineers and workers who repair and extend the Grassroads. Every six years they rebuild this encampment, which they affectionately call the Devil's Hammock. The second outpost was once the El Chapán rum distillery; after it closed down long ago, it became a trading post for the thri-kreen of the Llanos. The third outpost is the Silver Tapir Monastery, which serves as the sanctuary and school of the Green Doctors.

Life in Atagua

Those who live in Atagua or travel through the Llanos are shaped by the following truths.

Hard-Won Independence

Nearly five hundred years ago, an invading force rolled across the Llanos of Atagua, thereafter invading the neighboring region of San Citlán. But after three centuries of occupation, the mixed descendants of the Flood People who first settled Atagua and former invaders who made peace with them decisively expelled their would-be rulers after a thirteen-year war of independence. Atagua's people are the result of the multigenerational intermingling between the native Flood People, the descendants of invaders who rebelled against their leaders and settled here, and a steady stream of new immigrants and adventurers drawn to the freedom and challenges of life on the Llanos.

The aftermath of war was marked by a vibrant rebuilding period. Large settlements such as El Caparazón retained some of the cultural aspects of the long colonial occupation, while rural villages primarily drew on the legacy of the Flood People.

Even after two centuries of peace, tensions sometimes arise between clans and factions due to feuds and the revival of ancient grudges. These conflicts flare but are resolved through hard work, patient negotiations, and compromises by all sides. Overall, the people of Atagua embrace the idea that they form a complicated, diverse culture—and that together, they will shape a hopeful future.

LIVES OF THE PEOPLE

Sugar and chocolate are abundant in the cuisine of Atagua, especially in the favored beverages: drinking chocolate, strong coffee, and even stronger rum sweetened with panela—the cooked-down juice of sugarcane. Corn, black beans, and plantains are the cornerstones of every meal, and arepas—grilled buns made from ground corn—are eaten by the wealthy and the poor alike.

The folk of this land work hard by day, but they mark each noon as the start of the siesta, which offers a much-needed respite from the midday heat. People retire to the shade of haciendas or huts, to rest or quietly gather with their closest kin, for it is said that only the untrustworthy conduct their \ affairs under the blistering midday sun. And when work is done, evenings explode with social activity and music.

Cropped cotton trousers, long-sleeve tunics, long and loose sleeveless jackets known as gilets, full skirts, and straw hats are everyday dress for people of all genders in Atagua. Geometric tattoos or angular designs painted with butterfly-based pigments are commonplace on faces and hands. And the Cababa warriors and the workers of the Tribe of Builders bear accessories made from feathers and flowers, paired with snakeskin kilts.

FAITH AND FORTUNE

Religion in Atagua revolves around the Suwa, a shifting pantheon of hundreds of folk heroes. Small, colorful statues of Suwa heroes are found everywhere in Atagua and are honored with offerings of rum or sweets. Ataguans are tolerant of different beliefs and often adopt legendary figures from other cultures into the Suwa.

THE GREEN DOCTORS

The collective of mystics known as the Green Doctors weaves together knowledge of magic and herbal medicine to heal the people and creatures of Atagua. The leader of their order is an elf named Melecio. Green Doctors are recognized by the green sash they wear around their waists, but any healer, mage, or storyteller can study medicine at the order's home, the Silver Tapir Monastery.

NAMES

Some Ataguan names honor the ancestral heroes of the Flood People, while others are derived by mixing those names with ones from the colonial past. In addition to given names, insightful nicknames from a person's childhood often linger into adulthood. The following are examples of such names:

Feminine. Cruz, Tibísay, Yamaira, Zulibeth
Masculine. Estwaldo, Jecson, Oru, Payaro
Gender-Neutral. Ara, Riaguey, Tamí, Zamiri
Nicknames. Arrow, Little Toucan, Orchid, Quipper
Surnames. Periro, Secuentes, Táreru, Zárates

LEGENDS OF ATAGUA

Ataguans dream vividly of a great tepui—a tabletop mountain surrounded by jungle. Though the site is unseen and unreachable, many claim the shared experience of having explored the mesa in their dreams, seeing others like themselves in passing, and meeting otherworldly beings.

The secret behind these dreams is found in the oldest legends, which speak of the Ghost Orchid Tepui existing simultaneously in the Llanos and in the Feywild, parallel to Atagua. The source of the dreams is a powerful crystal called the Sleeping Stone, which many who dream have seen, alongside magical white orchids growing in the crystalline caverns below the tepui's summit.

As counterpoint to these bright dreams, sinister creatures haunt the history of Atagua. During the war of independence, rattling whistles rose from the Llanos at night. As the fighting increased, the whistling manifested near villages and haciendas, inspiring nightmares or incurable despair for those who survived hearing it. Some reported seeing hunched giants from the corner of the eye—a new threat to terrorize a war-weary people.

When the fighting ended and Atagua was free once more, the nightmares ended. The menacing whistlers were largely forgotten as the peoples of Atagua embraced peace and reconstruction. But even today, whistlers occasionally appear in the Llanos, evidence that the Far Realm still influences the land. And some among the Green Doctors whisper that Atagua might yet face an invasion by those terrors.

Adventures in Atagua

Consider the plots on the Atagua Adventures table when planning adventures there.

Atagua Adventures

d4	Adventure
1	The characters stumble across the plans of a expansionist cacao farmer, who has hired mercenaries with trained **behirs** to tear down a section of the Grassroads near his farm.
2	Several Green Doctors require an escort for a mission to tame **shambling mounds** rampaging across the Llanos.
3	A planar traveler is found dead in the Llanos, with a magical device that supposedly can trap a **whistler**. The characters must determine how the device works.
4	A disgraced Green Doctor seeks adventurers who will help him infiltrate the Ghost Orchid Tepui and steal a ghost orchid seed pod.

Characters from Atagua

If players want to create characters from Atagua, ask them the following questions:

Have you traveled far in Atagua? Are you familiar with the Grassroads? Do you have contacts among thri-kreen traders?

Are your dreams remarkable? Have you had visions of serpentine dream spirits or strange flowers? Do you have nightmares of terrible insects? Do you not dream at all?

Have you interacted with the Green Doctors? Did they heal you, or a dear friend or family member? Have you learned about traditional magic from them?

Whistler

Whistlers are inscrutable stalkers hailing from airy, screeching reaches of the Far Realm. They are difficult to see as they're not tethered to one point in space, blurring in a state of perpetual physical uncertainty. A dead whistler appears as a gray, featureless, humanlike biped with long limbs and thin fingers. Those stalked by a whistler can't shut out its soundless, seven-note tune, an otherworldly melody that invades and scourges the mind. Few creatures that encounter a whistler escape; those that do are forever haunted by the stalker's frightful tune.

Whistler
Large Aberration, Typically Neutral Evil

Armor Class 15 (natural armor)
Hit Points 180 (24d10 + 48)
Speed 40 ft.

STR	DEX	CON	INT	WIS	CHA
13 (+1)	16 (+3)	14 (+2)	15 (+2)	16 (+3)	18 (+4)

Saving Throws Dex +7, Cha +8
Skills Stealth +11
Damage Resistances psychic
Condition Immunities charmed, exhaustion, frightened
Senses blindsight 60 ft., passive Perception 13
Languages Deep Speech, telepathy 120 ft.
Challenge 9 (5,000 XP)   **Proficiency Bonus** +4

Blurred Form. Attack rolls against the whistler are made with disadvantage unless the whistler is incapacitated.

Unusual Nature. The whistler doesn't require air, food, drink, or sleep.

Actions

Multiattack. The whistler makes three Psychic Swipe attacks.

Psychic Swipe. *Melee Spell Attack:* +8 to hit, reach 10 ft., one creature. *Hit:* 15 (2d10 + 4) psychic damage.

Otherworldly Melody (Recharge 5–6). The whistler telepathically whistles an otherworldly melody into the minds of up to two creatures it can see within range of its telepathy. Each target must succeed on a DC 16 Wisdom saving throw or take 33 (6d10) psychic damage and become frightened of the whistler for 1 minute. A frightened creature can repeat this saving throw at the end of each of its turns, ending the effect on itself on a success.

Bonus Actions

Surreal Step. The whistler teleports up to 20 feet to an unoccupied space it can see.

BEYOND THE RADIANT CITADEL

HEN THE RADIANT CITADEL WAS rediscovered, the Dawn Incarnates lay dormant in the Preserve of the Ancestors. Thirteen were reawakened, but no one could revive the Pearl Carp, Sard Elephant, or the Dawn Avatars associated with the Radiant Citadel's other missing founding civilizations. Recently, agents of the Court of Whispers rediscovered paths to the lands known as the Tayyib Empire and Umizu. When peoples from those realms arrived at the Radiant Citadel, the Pearl Carp and the Sard Elephant awakened, and representatives have since joined the Speakers for the Ancestors. This gives the people of the Radiant Citadel hope that other lost civilizations might also be found.

This section provides overviews of two additional lands connected to the Radiant Citadel. Detail and incorporate them into adventures as you please.

TAYYIB EMPIRE

The Tayyib Empire recently emerged from a brutal civil war, but its peace is fragile. Monsters roam the hinterland, and people vie for power to stave off desperation during the recovery.

The war began in response to the death of Emperor Tasneem, whose older heirs turned to sinister magic in their attempts to rule. These heirs burned the former capital and unleashed legions of unliving horrors. Chaos ruled the land until the emperor's youngest daughter, Firuzeh, defeated her siblings and ascended the throne.

She inherited a nation stretched to the limit. But across war-torn territories, people rebuild marble domes and sparkling minarets to raise a new empire that serves its citizens as past rulers failed to do. It is a precarious time, but also one of great opportunity.

NOTEWORTHY SITES

The Tayyib Empire spans a region called Suristhanam. Its geography includes a great central flood plain, fertile hills, and tropical swamps.

QARAGARH

A metropolis filled with breathtaking plazas and public reflecting pools, the empire's new capital teems with people who see the city as the promise of the empress made manifest. Adventurers come to Qaragarh seeking employment from the empress, who needs support to stabilize her empire. Travelers arrive and depart through the Hall of Doors, which houses teleportation circles linked to locations across the empire.

BIJABAD

Bijabad and the surrounding region were the breadbasket of the empire until war took its toll. Now bulettes and griffons terrorize the countryside, and work crews periodically unearth Undead left behind by the conflict. The city's struggling reconstruction efforts are chronically understaffed, so a grassroots network of veterans and influential townsfolk called the Old Sickles has taken efforts into its own hands.

CHURAPOOR

A natural harbor shelters the port of Churapoor from seasonal monsoons. Despite the devastation of war, the city boasts a healthy economy, but it always needs adventurers to guard its shipments of alchemical concoctions, spices, and rich textiles.

LIFE IN THE TAYYIB EMPIRE

The Tayyib Empire is a cosmopolitan mix of the native peoples of Suristhanam, immigrants, and various invading groups. Nearly half the population are brown-skinned humans, with significant elf, hobgoblin, lizardfolk, and yuan-ti populations making up most of the remainder.

FAITH AND RELIGION

The dominant faith is Iwahhid, a philosophy that rejects idols and promotes worshiping the source of divinity rather than its fallible manifestations. Its adherents are called Muwahhid. Some erudite worshipers join the Imperial Ulema, an order of Muwahhid scholars sponsored by the throne. The Ulema provides spellcasting services to the populace and maintains the empire's infrastructure of magical street lights and teleportation circles.

FASHION AND FOOD

Clothing in the empire tends to be long and billowing. Men's fashion includes jamas and sherwanis, or loose kurtas secured with a shawl. Women's fashion includes saris and salwars. Clothing is colorful and patterned, with some wealthy citizens sporting garments bearing magic that perfumes the wearer on command or changes color.

SECRETS AND DANGERS FROM PREVIOUS DYNASTIES LURK WITHIN THE STEPWELLS OF THE TAYYIB EMPIRE.

Tayyib dishes are creamy and mildly spiced, cooked with yogurt, and served with rice or flatbreads. Dried lentils are soaked and made into various dal dishes, while slow-cooked rice, spices, and vegetables are transformed into fragrant biryani. Faithful Muwahhid avoid alcohol and predator meat, and many are vegetarians.

MONARCHY AND ORDER

Authority in the Tayyib Empire stems from Empress Firuzeh. Nobles who hold prewar titles are respected, while state-appointed judges enforce the law across the empire. This system is prone to corruption, but the empress's agents vigilantly ferret out dishonest officials, delegating that task to trustworthy adventurers when necessary.

ADVENTURES IN THE TAYYIB EMPIRE

Consider the plots on the Tayyib Empire Adventures table when planning forays through the empire.

TAYYIB EMPIRE ADVENTURES

d4	Adventure
1	An alliance of nobles and pre-empire royalty pays the adventurers to seek their families' lost treasures within Churapoor's **nothic**-infested ruins.
2	**Jackalweres** are spotted outside a town before an Iwahhid holiday. The local emir asks the characters to drive them off, but the town priest believes the jackalweres merely want to join the celebrations.
d4	Adventure
3	Emir Nur, Master Architect of Bijabad, accidentally unearths a trapped **efreeti** during a building project. Nur hires the characters to convince it to leave quietly.
4	The empress hosts a wyvern hunt, promising fabulous rewards to whoever tames the largest **wyvern**.

UMIZU

Residents of the city-state of Umizu enjoy their fair share of luck, but good fortune comes at a cost: a season of bad luck that arrives with the yearly monsoon. During this time, locals pray at shrines for protection against misfortune, and attendants keep a watchful eye for grim portents in the rains.

Set amid glittering turquoise waters, Umizu has long enjoyed prosperity that masks ever-simmering tension. Daimyo Hogishi Takemi does his best to rein in crime, but the city's lackluster bureaucracy is run by complacent samurai administrators and riddled with corruption. Crime syndicates control the city's underground trade and administer their own brand of justice. Meanwhile, the Southwest Whaling Concern, an influential merchant organization, builds a private navy and clashes with the Rurapo, an indigenous clan of tritons who monitor fishing and whaling activity. In the wake of the whalers' blatant overfishing, the Rurapo are divided on whether to renegotiate their treaty with Umizu or declare war.

ROBSON MICHEL

Noteworthy Sites

Each city district features its own architectural aesthetics. The districts cling to volcanic islands connected by sturdy stone bridges, ferries, and steam-powered funiculars.

Bright Moon Pier

This collection of massive piers hosts a marketplace and is the haven of Umizu's premier criminal syndicate, the Safe Oceans Society. Most merchants here deal with the Safe Oceans Society eventually, whether to smuggle goods, avoid taxes, or quietly resolve conflicts. Society lieutenants run gambling dens disguised as tea rooms along the pier, while samurai and scoundrels test their mettle beneath the waves in underwater fighting rings. To avoid scrutiny, the Safe Oceans Society employs adventurers as independent operatives—while virtuous samurai-class bureaucrats hire them to investigate the syndicate's crimes.

Rurapo sometimes visit the pier to trade or sample crunchy Umizu pickles. Some have forged uneasy alliances with the Safe Oceans Society, providing illegal relics from sunken temples and shipwrecks.

Governor's Palace

A massive villa serves as the central administrative offices of Umizu and the residence of its mayor, Daimyo Hogishi Takemi. The palace is famous for Hogishi's elegant parties and for an annual poetry competition that draws nobles to Umizu—along with their bitter rivalries and personal guards.

Shrine of Storms

The Shrine of Storms is an ancient place of spiritual power. Cut deep into its island alongside residencies for the shrine's warrior-priests and libraries holding relics from around the world, the shrine is central to Umizu's many celebrations. Each winter, citizens gather for the Thunder Festival and honor the Turtle Sage—the guardian spirit of the islands—with three days of drumming, dancing, and prayer.

Life in Umizu

Umizu is a welcoming city, and many citizens hail from far-flung lands. Humans are the most numerous, with skin tones ranging from pale to medium brown, and with hair and eyes ranging from dark brown to black.

Social Mores

Umizu is a matrilineal culture with a preference for succession by women. Most families live in multigenerational homes, and the wealthiest favor polyamorous marriages, typically with a clan matriarch and several spouses of any gender. Powerful clans compete for prestige through formal dueling matches every few months.

Umizu has few taboos around sexuality and gender. Titles such as "daimyo" are gender-neutral, as are most names. Clothing varies by class status rather than gender—instead, people express their gender through perfumes. Bright citrus scents are feminine coded, musky wood tones are gender-neutral, and floral scents are masculine. Umizu has rigid sumptuary laws that reinforce the social hierarchy, restricting colors, fabrics, and styles of dress based on class.

Ancestor Spirits

Respect for the spirits infuses daily life. Native residents keep shrines to their ancestors in their homes and leave out offerings at dawn and dusk. They consult ancestral spirits before making life-changing decisions, but the perspectives of the dead can be just as flawed as those of the living. Disagreements in large family clans sometimes result in battles involving hundreds of ancestor spirits, with tumultuous consequences for their living descendants.

Seasonal Misfortune

The Demon Festival kicks off the summer monsoon season, marking a city-wide period of misfortune. Citizens visit the Shrine of Storms to purchase talismans of protection and beseech the Turtle Sage for good luck. At sundown, the shrine's attendants ride barges through Umizu's waterways, shouting taunts to draw out fell spirits while people dressed as demons dance on bridges and walkways.

Adventures in Umizu

Consider the plots on the Umizu Adventures table when planning explorations in Umizu.

Umizu Adventures

d4	Adventure
1	A scholar in the Radiant Citadel believes the Shrine of Storms holds secrets to understanding the Keening Gloom, the cyclone threatening the Radiant Citadel. She sends the characters to gather information as pirates (**bandits**) prepare to plunder the temple.
2	Daimyo Hogishi recruits the characters to help defend the city from theft during the Demon Festival, but this year, the priests' taunts provoke **shadow demons** intent on taking lives, not property.
3	Rurapo and the fishers of Umizu blame each other for a dying reef, leaving the characters to uncover the real culprits: a trio of **oni**.
4	The Southwest Whaling Concern begins operating near the lair of a slumbering **dragon turtle**. A carp that benefits from a druid's *awaken* spell warns the characters that the dragon turtle could cause a tsunami if disturbed.